the
Meanderers

a novel

by

DHAWAL TRIVEDI

www.dhawaltrivedi.com
Enquiries: info@dhawaltrivedi.com

ISBN-13: 978-0-6483622-1-0 (Paperback)
ISBN-13: 978-0-6483622-0-3 (ebook)

First Edition, 2018

Editing: V.P. Allasander

Cover Designed by: Rob Allen

Book Layout & eBook Conversion by manuscript2ebook.com

TABLE OF CONTENTS

PART 1

PART 2

PART 3

PREFACE

I REMEMBER BEING five years old, sitting by the porch of the verandah of my maternal grandma's house. I used to call her 'Naani'. The day was sunny, there wasn't any noise around. One ice-cream vendor stood by the end of the road. A few children played in the garden across the road. I remember feeling profoundly peaceful.

As years went along, I saw how the equation between different emotions and feelings evolved over time. The nuances were subtle, of course, but quite palpable. For example – how I interacted with people around me, how I looked at love, friendship, fear, etcetera, evolved over time. Broadly, I felt that I could categorise my 'boyhood' into three different phases based on the broad category of emotion(s) I felt during those times.

When I was five years old, the emotions that defined my life were amazement, wonder and innocence. I grew up being very close to my Naani. I was the only child in the house, between two old people; and they gave me all the space in the world to be myself. From that space, emanated my deep comfort with my own self. Unlike most other children, I would feel no urge to play with other children all day, or make mess. I enjoyed lone walks in the garden, accompanying my grandparents to the shopping market, or just being by myself sitting by the window.

I saw the next big shift in my life when I turned fourteen and hit puberty. I suddenly started perceiving the female form and my feeling towards it, in a different way. I could sense the subtle but sudden shift in perception. There was a different energy, a certain current that would flow within my being when I was close to the female form. As a result of my quiet childhood, I also found it hard to adjust with the certain loudness that adolescence comes with. I didn't feel like I belonged, or I felt like there was something wrong with myself and I needed to do something about it. This resulted in experiencing a gamut of emotions, particularly characteristic of adolescence, such as peer-pressure, bullying, status-quo and self-confidence.

As time rolled along, another pivotal moment in my life was when I was around twenty years old. Time had come to step out into the "real" world and stand on my own feet. That age marked the age of aspiration, ambition, dreams and drive. Around that time, I experienced the first soul-stirring love of my life; something that warped my outlook towards my aspirations and ambitions.

'The Meanderers' is an ode to those days of growing up, those days of my 'boyhood'. It is a tribute to every character, every situation, every conflict, every resolution and every unfinished chapter, in all its glory.

Through the story, I wish to explore the subtleties of emotions such as innocence, love, loss, lust, fear, courage, friendship and impermanence.

One of the important facets while doing that was being totally honest to myself and my expression. Very often, in almost all creative endeavours, it becomes hard to be completely sincere with your voice. Thoughts of how it might be perceived, the kind of image it will portray and how to make it successful start, playing in the head.

'The Meanderers', since day one, has been a meditation in sincerity. I have stayed absolutely wholehearted to my expression. At times during the story, it makes it very raw, perhaps even crude. However, I've kept it that way rather than creating a carefully manufactured product for the market. I have been asked by many professionals in the industry, who are my great well-wishers, to alter certain parts of the story, but I have stuck to what I feel is the story that I want to tell, the way I want to tell it. It is one of the reasons I bypassed the traditional publishing route – to have complete control over the creative process.

'The Meanderers' will at times offend, switch moods abruptly and even not make sense – pretty much how life is. And I have made no effort to alter that. While I understand that it might come across as being indulgent at times, that's how this story has come into being; this was its journey. I've tried to keep the process of creation as unadulterated as possible.

I hope the story challenges the readers, makes one think about something one might not have thought about or might not have thought from a particular perspective. Above all, I hope it inspires the reader to look at life from a bigger-picture perspective, because it's in the bigger-picture that the beauty and the poetry of life lies.

Before I end, I want to equivocally thank all the people who have been a part of my life – the lovers, the friends, the bullies, the strangers. Ultimately, perhaps we're all one, just meandering through life in our own ways.

P.S.: While I wrote the novel in English (UK), my editor convinced me to convert it into English (US). So, if you find any discrepancy somewhere (though it has been very carefully edited many, many times), please excuse.

P.P.S.: Yes, I know 'Meanderers' is not a word in the Oxford English Dictionary. I've taken a little bit of poetic leeway here ☺

Happy Meandering,
Dhawal Trivedi

PROLOGUE

Let me tell you a story,
Of a fallen dandelion by the funeral pyre,
Of a sucker punch by the departing beachside,
Of a poem buried by the tree where a small sun disrupted the first kiss.

I want you to know,
That I never wanted to find you.
The rusty metal boots were too heavy for the mountains of water.

You lured me.
With red, ripe tomatoes,
Growing from the touchable roof,
Of the house you said would be ours forever.
The cinnamon muffins the doors were made out of,
Bloomed in the shadow of the setting sun.
They ate me,
As soon as I walked in.

You weren't who I thought you were.
You never stripped naked in front of me.
But in your defence,
I never showed you the rape mark on my back either.

I thought we were the lovers who build a garden together.
The Meanderers who circle the rumpled pillows.

I painted you in the shades of a mind in me.
I assumed you.
I created you out of my own dream.
And then…

I lured you.
With the red, ripe tomatoes that I hankered for,
Growing from the untouchable roof,
Of the house I dreamt would be ours forever.
The cinnamon muffins ate the doors you were made out of,
While the sun was still burning,
While I was still not ready to leave.

PART 1

CHAPTER 1

"I NEED TO jump over this fence," Om told himself as he ran with the last vestiges of energy that he had within himself. He was running away, chased by five dogs. Yes, five – same as his age.

He hadn't meant any harm. Not long ago, his Naani, which was how he addressed his maternal grandmother, had given him fifty paise or half a rupee. That was his daily afternoon ritual. He would get the money from his Naani, upon which he would go to the local convenience store to buy his favourite snack. It was called 'Natkhat'. In the Hindi dictionary, the word literally meant mischievous. Natkhats were crispy, tangy corn puffs, which would make a strange satisfying noise when someone took a bite. He would chew on them like a rabbit would at a carrot, gnawing at its end, until the morsel dissolved in his mouth.

There were times when Naani would just look into his eyes and instead of the customary fifty paise, she would hand him more. Some other time, she would give him what he used to call 'aato halwa', which was a trip to heaven made out of wholemeal flour, along with the money. Then, there were times when she would ask him to lie down on her lap. For every minute he did, she gave him fifty paise. Four rupees was the maximum he could manage. After, he got so restless that he would jump out. Perhaps money was never a priority for him.

That afternoon, Naani had given him a full one rupee. He usually walked to the convenience store. However, he was feeling really hungry that afternoon, enough to make him run to the store to buy his favourite "Natkhats". The backside of the store was but a left turn and an alley away from Naani's house. The alley was usually deserted, especially during the scorching afternoon heat that the state of Rajasthan witnessed.

That day, however, Om met five strangers at the end of the alley behind the shop. All of them were stray dogs, around the same height as he was.

For a moment there, time froze. He had stopped running as soon as he saw them. He stood motionless at the end of the desolate alley with his left foot on the ground and the right one in the air. Three of the five dogs were already up on their feet. The other two were almost there. Then, the clock started to tick again. He turned around and started running in the opposite direction.

Certain quantitative strategies for co-existence with our ecosystem are taught to us as children while we learn some with experience; the latter not being the smarter way. That day, he learned that running up to stray dogs and turning around to run away wasn't a smart move. Before he could feel the ebbs of time flowing, he heard loud barks from behind him in the alley. Om ran and five angry – perhaps even hungry – canines followed him.

There are moments in ordinary life where we are totally absorbed in the moment. Sometimes, those remarkable moments arise out of deep love as Naani would explain when she told him stories about Rumi, a revered Sufi saint; sometimes out intense devotion such as that possessed by Meera towards Krishna; and sometimes out of deep prayer like that of Jesus. That day, though, he found out that such moments could also rise out of fear. All semblance of ego, of identity, and of surroundings just vanished at that point, leaving the only feeling left: death, or rather, the fear of it. His energy was tremendously concentrated and he ran at a speed even he couldn't have anticipated. Om wasn't running for a medal or fun or glory. Not even reputation, fame or money. He was – literally – running for survival. There wasn't a doubt in his mind.

He could see a metallic fence leading into the community park at the end of the lane, which the alley merged into. He didn't know the exact distance.

"I need to jump over this fence," he told himself and kept running. He could hear the barks getting louder, its tone more ferocious. In that fearful and desperate moment, all he could see was the fence in front of him and his mind preoccupied with the thought that he needed to get over it if he had to survive.

With about five paces to go, he leaped. Midway, he came to a realization that he wasn't going to make it to the other side. In that incredibly condensed state of mind, his mind somehow signalled his body to use his hands to propel itself and scrape through the fence. If it wasn't for the sheer intensity of the situation, he might never have pulled it off. It was astounding how clearly his mind was able to think when the time froze and all the incessant chatter in the mind came to a grinding halt. There was just one thought enveloping his entire being. His mind was unflinchingly devoted to that one thing on which his survival depended – getting over that fence.

All of this must have lasted about fifty seconds in ordinary time. To him, however, it felt like a fleeting moment and a lifetime at the same time, giving him his first experience of a paradox.

He was on the other side of the fence in shock of what had just happened. That's when his mind began to process what it had done on pure instincts alone. As the immediate danger and fear subsided, he felt a rush of blood to the head and blacked out.

❖

Om started hearing voices as he regained consciousness. "Om, Om, Om..."

He was in the living room of Naani's rented house, - 'Sapra House', as it was called, named after the surname of the owner. His grandmother sat with a glass of water by his side with Aunt Nargis standing quietly in the background. Lord Krishna stared at him from a poster on the wall.

"What happened?" asked Naani, who looked perplexed.

"Who got me here?" he asked, dazed and confused.

"Nargis Aunty," answered Naani, turning her head towards Nargis, who was standing behind her, covered in a black burka, though recognizable by the texture of her eyes. "She saw you lying unconscious in the park," added Naani.

Naani thanked Nargis with her hands folded in a 'Namaste', a traditional way of expressing gratitude that meant "I bow to thee".

"I was being chased by five dogs," he said as he saw Nargis move towards the sofa near the exit. "I was running towards the convenience shop", he said, "when I ran into five stray dogs right behind it."

I thought I was going to die," he continued, after a brief pause, looking at Naani.

"These stray dogs have become an utter nuisance," said Nargis, moving her lips from behind the veil of her burkha. "Just the other day, there was a news report of stray dogs eating an infant. Horrifying! Why doesn't the municipality do something about it?" she continued.

"There are over three hundred thousand stray dogs in the city. What can the municipality do?" said a gravelly voice in the background.

Babu, as everyone in the family called Om's maternal grandfather, had just woken up from his afternoon nap on a dry summer afternoon in the city of Jaipur, wearing nothing but a lungi (a piece of cloth wrapped around the waist like a full-length skirt, but for men). It was something that never went down well with the fashion police, but it did with a hot summer day.

"Shukran Allah, Lalla is safe", said Nargis as she made her way out. It was time for her to do her afternoon prayer.

Nargis was Naani's neighbour, married to a man named Tariq Ahmed. She often called Om 'lalla' out of affection, as did the others. 'Lalla' meant a child.

"My lalla," said Naani, placing Om's head on her lap, well aware that the boy still needed comforting. She knew what he liked and needed, almost always. She would call him 'Lalla' whenever she wanted to lift him up. It always worked.

"I don't know how I managed to outrun those dogs, Naani," Om voiced his thoughts out loud. "If you tell me to do it now, I won't be able to do it."

"That happened because you were in deep fear," said Naani in a quaint, reassuring voice. "A thought so overpowering took over your mind that it did not leave space for anything else. Your whole survival was at stake. The fear was so powerful that it completely condensed your consciousness. You experienced a profound moment. Keep it with you, lalla," she responded. "But I want you to experience this with love as well. Let your journey in life be the pilgrimage from fear to love," she said in a way only she could.

There was a tenderness in her voice that never came across as preaching. It sounded like love itself.

"This evening, we will find those dogs and say hello to them," she continued as she patted his back.

"Hold my hand. Nothing will happen to you," Naani asserted as she took Om to the same place where he had run into the stray dogs. He could see the five dogs still there. It was strange because he had expected them to leave. Perhaps they brooded over a missed prey. Or, as Naani would have suggested, a lost friend. She always inspired Om to see the rose in the mud, and not vice-versa.

Even as he hid behind Naani's sari, he could see the dogs in the background. She pulled him, albeit gently, from behind her and handed him the biscuits to feed the dogs. They began to bark, each louder than the one before. They were probably anxious. Maybe even angry.

He had an indecisive look on his face, like he couldn't figure out what the dogs were feeling. He could see one of them rise up to a stance, growling.

Naani held his hand tight. She knew he was looking at her. That was her indication to him to face the fear, to watch the fear; and not suppress it, not bog down to it.

He dropped the first biscuit on the ground. He did not stop at that. He let the others fall down too, one after the other. Before he knew it, the barking stopped and a chaotic race ensued to get hold of the biscuits. Once all the biscuits had been snapped and chewed on, the barking stopped. Only now, the dogs had long tongues sticking out. Om wondered if that was how he looked like when he craved for a packet of Natkhat.

"Pat their head one by one," said Naani. "And give names to your five new friends," she added.

He was fresh from watching an episode of 'The Mahabharata', the great Indian epic where five pious brothers, called the 'Pandavas', with the help of an enlightened saint called Krishna, won back an empire from their hundred evil cousins in the epic battle at Kurukshetra.

He named his new friends after the five Pandava brothers – Yudhishtir, Bhima, Arjun, Nakul and Sahadev.

"Mahesh ji, I don't know where Koshi and Om are," said Babu as he placed himself in front of the water cooler that ran at full speed, blowing away the few strands of hair Babu had on his head. Mahesh used to visit Naani's place in the evening, quite frequently. Usually, after work if he had a job, or as was the case in those days, after searching for one. Sometimes, he would take Om home, despite the fact that Om preferred to stay at Naani's place and would often refuse to leave. Mahesh used to love the chai Naani made. Perhaps that was the main reason, than to actually take Om home, or rather, take Om to his home.

Naani and Om walked into the living room just then.

"Enough now. I've come to take you home," said Mahesh. "You haven't been home in over a week," he added.

"I'll go tomorrow, promise," Om said.

"No way, you have been saying this for three days now. You are getting on my motorcycle right now," Mahesh spoke with a raised voice.

"Let me get you some chai, Mahesh ji," Naani intervened and made her way towards the kitchen, taking Om with her. It was just Babu and Mahesh in the living room.

"How was the job interview, Mahesh ji?" asked Babu.

"It went well. They said they will get back with a response," responded Mahesh as he opened the top two buttons of his shirt. It was a hot, summer day.

"Any timeline within which they would respond?" asked Babu, interrogating further.

Mahesh avoided Babu's question with a sheepish look on his face. What answer could he give? It was his seventh interview in the past two months. He had gotten similar responses from everywhere, not counting the three rejections. Just that the number of days to get back with a 'response' would differ from company to company. In the initial days, one saw both hope and helplessness in his eyes at the same time, although, recently, the latter seemed to have overshadowed the former.

"There you go, Mahesh ji," said Naani as she placed the cup of chai on the table.

That's how Naani and Babu would call Mahesh, whose full name was Mahesh Vats. They added a 'ji' at the end of his name because it was customary to do so. It symbolized respect, usually reserved for elders, high-ranked officials, and a son-in-law.

"Mummy, I don't care what anyone says. Om is coming with me this evening," said Mahesh. "Kiran hasn't seen him in over a week and she isn't feeling well today. I am sure she will appreciate," he justified.

Naani gave Om a stare. That moment, he realized that he needed to go home that evening – to his parents' home, that was.

"Om, my lalla!" remarked Kiran, Om's mother, as she drowned him in a sea of kisses and hugs. She was seeing Om after a few days, though they both were in the same city.

"You never come home," she said, "but I am happy you are with me today."

"What happened to you, Mummy?" asked Om.

"Nothing. I'm fine, now that I've seen you," replied Kiran.

"When are we getting dinner?" Mahesh interrupted the mother-son interaction.

Kiran gave a sly look on her face before she proceeded to the kitchen.

❖

"How was the interview today?" Kiran asked Mahesh at the dinner table.

"They'll respond as soon as possible," replied a visibly frustrated Mahesh.

"Why do these people need so many days to say yes or no?" complained Kiran. "Do they realize the kind of impact they have on other people's lives, huh?" she lamented further.

Mahesh made a subtle gesture to Kiran, suggesting her not to talk about such matters in front of their young son, which Om noticed.

Mahesh worked as a salesman. Now, there were many kinds of salesmen. What kind was Mahesh, one might ask? He was just a general one who worked in the lowest rung. The ones that were usually the ones easiest to hire...or fire. Until a few months ago, he sold razors door-to-door before he was fired from his job. In a fit towards his boss he wasn't fond of, he denied shaving his own beard – a rather reasonable requirement of a razor salesman.

Kiran lived her life as a homemaker. She never finished school but did possess a penchant for ceramics and pottery. She was a fairly decent painter too, given the few artworks that adorned the walls of their rented one-bedroom apartment. Despite her talents, she could never make money out of them. She couldn't do anything for money. To make money, especially the first money of one's life, one needed courage. She could never gather that courage.

Naani often motivated Kiran to pursue her interest in arts, at least for self-evolution if not for monetary pursuits. Kiran, though, was just not built for it.

"Come, Om, it's time for you to sleep," said Kiran as she lifted her son up in her arms, tickling his belly at the same time. It was pure joy and agony, at the same time, for the little boy.

"What is happening in five days? Tell me, tell me…," asked Kiran as she placed Om in the bed and continued tickling his belly.

Om's birthday was due in five days. A spurt of joy glowed on his face, happy that he was going to be six soon – one number more than the count of dogs that had chased him the other day.

He continued to frolic around with his legs folded up to his chest and his hands pushing his mother's away from his belly. A few seconds later, Kiran stopped. Perhaps she glimpsed some tears that streamed down his cheeks.

"What does my lalla want to distribute in school for his birthday?" Kiran asked Om with a tone that reflected a love only a mother could have.

Distributing gifts to the whole class at school was a pop culture – an undocumented ritual. Whosever's birthday it was, they had to distribute something of their choice to the entire class. Some distributed sweets, some stationeries. The kids of richer parents would distribute chocolates. The poorer ones' – well, they would just take a leave on their birthday. It was quite the nightmare for their parents.

"Natkhat! You know that," Om replied to Kiran with an excitement he found hard containing.

She looked at him and smiled. It didn't matter what the financial situation was. It didn't matter whether she was even in a position to deliver what he had requested. She had the confidence that came married with pure love. It believes, truly believes, that love alone has the power to make things happen, which to a rational mind, seems totally implausible.

She turned the lights off and kissed his cheeks good night.

CHAPTER 2

ANOTHER HOT AND dry summer morning dawned on the streets of Jaipur – popularly known as the pink city. The city seemed to have a love affair with the colour 'pink'.

In perhaps an ode to the city's signature color, a pink cycle-rickshaw pulled by a man named Ahmed usually picked Om up from Naani's place in Jawahar Nagar. But Mahesh alerted Ahmed to pick his son up from Raja Park the next morning instead. Raja Park was the suburb where Mahesh and Kiran lived.

Cycle-rickshaw was an ingenious result of an Indian version of "jugaad", which meant "a hack". It had two padded wooden boards fitted atop an adult-sized tricycle, separated by a small back support in between. It's meant to seat two adults on the front side with their feet resting on a makeshift footrest and two kids sitting at the back with their legs hanging. It could be called the ultimate family taxi. It was eco-friendly and cheap. However, for the purpose of cheap school transportation, some pullers in the city managed to fit in as many as eight kids with a few innovative extensions to both sides of the rickshaw.

School was a terrifying experienced for Om to get used to. Just going in and sitting among so many people, most of whom were strangers, and adhering to a set curriculum wasn't something he enjoyed.

He always grabbed a seat right next to the window and often gazed outside, looking at the road without any thought. He would sometimes watch the specks of dust sparkle in the sunlight, try to catch the sound of the wind pass through the window panes, or just ogle at the security guard, who wore a pink turban and sat next to the pink-coloured gate. At some other times, much to his chagrin, he was made to stand in a corner of the classroom as a punishment for not being attentive.

"Om, do you hear me?" he heard a voice in the background, disrupting his intimate exchange with the sun.

"Present, Ma'am!" he exclaimed, rather perturbed, assuming that he was meant to answer an attendance call.

"Om, come here with your diary please," said Ratna Devi with a stern look in her eyes. Ratna Devi was the class teacher, a middle-aged woman who hailed from the state of Bengal.

This phrase was something everyone in the class dreaded to hear. He would rather be chased by dogs than go with the diary towards the class teacher. When she summoned anyone with the diary, it meant trouble, humiliation, and shame in front of the whole class.

"I want to see your father day after tomorrow at 9 A.M.," she said as she wrote the note in his school diary. The school diary was the official mode of communication between the parents of a student and the teachers at school. The parents were meant to check

21

their child's diary each day and sign if a remark or a meeting request was put in.

Once his diary was handed back, Om returned to his seat, his head bent down, creases on his forehead.

———— ❦ ————

One of Om's favourite parts of the day was when the final bell rang at school. It wasn't because it meant freedom and being out in the open. It was more so because it meant he got to see Farheen.

Farheen was the daughter of Naani's neighbour, Nargis and Tariq. For Om, she was his best friend. As soon as the school bell rang, he would just run and take a seat on the backside of the rickshaw. That's where she would always sit.

He never quite knew what he felt when she saw her, but he did know that he wanted to be close to her. It felt like the rays of sunlight beamed down on his face in the middle of the class, like his mother's thousand kisses, like Naani's lullaby. Afternoons were the only time Om got to be close to her since in the morning, Tariq used to drop Farheen off to school.

Om and Farheen never spoke much, but they always enjoyed each other's company. Every day, he would give her lemon pickle with two small roti breads that Naani used to pack for him. Sometimes, she would show him the drawings she made during her class. There were times when she would ask him whether her ponytail ribbon was in place or not and some other time, she would tell him what her Ammi and Abbu fought over the previous night.

Om, however, would just look at her like it was the only thing that was important in that moment, listen to her like there was no other sound around. He would just sit there, next to her, and hoped that this ride back home would never reach home.

—◆—

"What do we have for lunch today?" asked a visibly hungry Babu.

Sometimes, Om thought that Babu wasn't married to Naani but to a clock. He had joined the British administration in a small town called Boondi in the state of Rajasthan as a junior clerk in the Sales Tax department. He retired as a senior clerk in the state capital of Jaipur. One would guess that his biggest promotion was actually moving from a village to the state capital. In all fairness to him, his morals always took priority over his hunger for position, the latter being a quality essential to advancing in a bureaucratic career during the license Raj in India.

"Om's favourite lentil soup," answered Naani. That's how she described a rich preparation of split green gram seasoned with onion, cumin seeds, and some secret she never revealed. There were occasions when Mahesh or Kiran would prepare it using the same recipe, in a bid to lure Om to spend more time at home. But that soup never turned out to be the way Naani made it. She added something of her own being, something that only belonged to her. Or, perhaps she never really told Mahesh and Kiran what exactly the recipe was.

Babu was at his favourite spot – right in front of the water cooler running at full speed.

"Many times, I feel Om is much more mature than other children his age," Babu said. His voice echoed a little, inside the water cooler.

Naani was listening. "I feel so too. His consciousness is way beyond his years. He is an old soul, I've felt," responded Naani, from the cot on the other end of the living room. "I feel he sees and perceives his surroundings deeper than not just children of his age, but even most adults," continued Naani. There was a noise from outside, as if someone had pushed open the metallic gate.

"There's Om", said Naani, looking at him as he entered the house after getting his daily dose of Natkhat. "Come lalla, look what I have made for lunch," said Naani as she enticed him with a bowl of his favourite soup in her hands.

❦

"Om, are you ready?" asked Babu.

Twice or thrice a week, Babu would take Om to the fruit and vegetable market nearby to buy food supplies after lunch. He would pull out his pink Bajaj Chetak scooter. When Om would ask how old it was, Babu almost always shut his mouth. Looking at it, anyone would guess it would be at least twice Om's age.

The Chetak scooter was the symbol of the Indian middle class. Whoever didn't have a Chetak wanted one, and whoever had one rode it with great pride.

Om would often ask Babu to let him kickstart the scooter. Most of the times, the latter would let him do it, although with a bit of hesitation. Kick-starting the scooter was a fun activity for the little

Om. He used to literally jump on the kick again and again until the engine would go vroom, a sound he enjoyed with immense pleasure.

Babu, one could say, was a reluctant scooter driver. Balance was definitely not his forte. Whenever a turn was to be made, he would stop the scooter well before the turn and ask Om to get down and meet him by the kerbside after the turn. Om would do as he said and watch him slowly make the turn with his feet. The passers-by and other travellers would look at them, with both amused and heckled expressions on their faces, wondering about the stranger rider-pillion relationship. There were six turns on the way to the market and six on the way back. That was Om's regular source of amusement.

"I want ladyfingers. Please, please, please," said Om as he tugged at Babu's shirt. His tone was rather one of pleading.

"What rate are the ladyfingers?" Babu asked the vegetable vendor.

"Seven rupees a kilo," replied the vendor.

Babu looked hesitant, but then he looked at Om, who kept tugging at his shirt.

"Pack a quarter kilo, please," said Babu to the vendor, who sat with a pile of vegetables on one side and a dodgy weighing machine with pink plastic bags on the other.

"Ladyfingers were seven rupees a kilo today," said a frustrated Babu. The news on the Doordarshan channel ran in the background.

"I've got a quarter kilo, just for Om. We'll have potatoes instead," he lamented.

Naani didn't respond.

"These politicians just don't care about the plight of the common man. What is V. P. Singh doing about inflation? First, it was the UPA government under Rajiv Gandhi scamming the common man, and now it is V. P. Singh along with Lalu Yadav. Bofors Scam is just the tip of the iceberg. There will be many more to follow, I'm telling you now," Babu continued.

Naani, as usual, kept quiet in such situations. She might have liked Rajiv Gandhi, the tenth Prime Minister of India. He did have a quaint yet powerful charm about him.

"I'm going off to sleep," said a tired Babu as he flicked the remote towards Naani. It was 10 P. M. – time for Naani's favorite show on television, 'Amanat'. It was a story about a man named Lahori Ram, who moved to India from Pakistan during the 1947 partition with his seven daughters.

The serial sometimes reminded Naani of her desire to have more children. She had wanted more, but when she was pregnant with Kiran, complications arose because of which she was not able to conceive again. It was heart-breaking for her since she had always wanted a son along with a daughter. Perhaps that was one of the reasons Kiran let Om stay with Naani so often.

CHAPTER 3

MAHESH WAS ON time for his meeting with Om's class teacher. For all the challenges he was facing in his life, this was a formality he couldn't wait to get over with. On top of that, he knew Om's calibre as a student. Om was not like everyone else who could adjust to a certain behavioural structure or be educated using a pre-set curriculum.

Ratna walked into the meeting room at the school.

Mahesh stood up and greeted her politely.

"Mr. Mahesh, Om is totally lost during the class," Ratna began saying, without bothering to initiate the conversation with niceties. "It looks like he doesn't even make an attempt to focus. He is constantly looking outside the window, or when I make him sit at the back, he is drawing something on the notebook instead of participating in the class. He is aloof from everyone else. Something needs to be done about it," added a staunch Ratna while Mahesh looked on, rather clueless.

"But he gets good grades at the ...." Mahesh had just begun when Ratna cut him off.

"That is not enough. And I think he somehow cheats his way to the grades. I am going to personally monitor him in the next examination," retorted Ratna.

"What do you think we should do?" asked a responsible but rather delirious Mahesh. He had his own woes to take care of, which occupied most of the space in his mind.

"I'm going to give him special homework each day, separate from the rest of the class, and you need to ensure that he gets it done before he reaches school the next day," replied Ratna.

"All right," gasped Mahesh.

He just wanted to get out of there as soon as possible. Not a rare feeling with Ratna around.

"Oh, and Mr. Mahesh, before you leave..., this month's fees are yet to be deposited. I didn't want to send this message through Om. I just wanted to let you know that this is the second time in a row and the school management has flagged Om's name," said Ratna.

"I will get it deposited by the twenty-fourth of this month," said Mahesh with no idea of how he was going to achieve that.

"That's two days from now?" Ratna wanted to confirm.

"Yes," answered Mahesh.

"You will hurt yourself. What are you doing?" asked a doting Kiran as she noticed Mahesh trying to get something out of the storage compartment right below the ceiling of their bedroom. He was standing on one leg on a rickety stool.

Kiran saw Mahesh taking his Hawaiian guitar out. Hawaiian guitar is a form of classical guitar. A Hawaiian guitar is to an acoustic guitar what Subhash Chandra Bose was to Gandhi – almost as important and effective, but not nearly as famous.

"You haven't played the guitar in ages," remarked Kiran.

"I'm going to sell it," responded Mahesh.

"What? Why?" Kiran was surprised.

"I need to pay Om's school fees and I only have ten thousand rupees left in the bank account. That is barely one month of bare minimum survival," he answered. Anxiety was evident on his face.

"On top of that, Om's term at primary school will be coming to an end next month. We need to get him admitted to a good private school before the summer vacations end," added Mahesh.

"Time is running out," he babbled in an undertone, almost as if he was talking to himself.

Kiran went silent for a few moments. She couldn't quite figure out what to say.

"Do you think you can get your job at the razor company back if you shaved?" asked Kiran, hesitating a bit.

It was a sensitive topic for Mahesh. His eyes opened wide and he gave Kiran an unpleasant stare.

"I think I should look for some work," suggested Kiran, trying to divert the topic.

Mahesh was surprised. He had never expected that out of her. She was never the kind of person who would do something for earning money.

"What are you going to do?" asked Mahesh, still surprised.

"Just the other day, Seema was telling me that her previous landlady, Monica, was looking for a cook. I think I should ask Seema to recommend my name," said Kiran, though with a certain reluctance.

"Monica, the wife of the guy who runs leather factories?" asked Mahesh.

"Yes, his name is Ranjit," she replied.

"How much does it pay?" he asked further.

"I don't know, yet. Seema just casually mentioned it to me during our morning walk. I'll speak with her about it tomorrow," she replied.

"Maybe I can get a job at Ranjit's leather company as well," Mahesh thought out loud.

"Also, can you speak with your parents and ensure that Om does his homework every day?" asked Mahesh as he bid good night.

Om was once again gazing outside the classroom through the window. There was another big window in a room right across the road. Each morning at 10 A.M, a man, with a cup of tea in his hands, would sit by the window and stare at the world that passed him by. Sometimes, he had a paper and a pen in his hands. Om would often see him scribble something down. At other times, Om would see him close his eyes and sit there in silence, without moving. Many a time, they would both look at each other for a few moments. It had developed into a peculiar bond.

"In total, there are twenty questions in the assignment and everyone has thirty minutes to complete it." announced Ratna Devi.

"Answer all the questions truthfully. Anyone caught cheating will be made to stand in the corner for the rest of the day", added Ratna, in a firm voice.

Many students were looking at each other. Ratna distributed the assignment paper to the whole class and ordered a pin-drop silence.

Om buried himself in the assignment sheet as he began answering it. He wasn't concerned about anybody around. He loved solving problems. Ratna was closely observing the whole class, especially Om. She had been suspicious about Om's stellar grades, given how inattentive he was in the class.

Om felt a sharp poke on his back from behind. He ignored it at first. But, he felt it again a few moments later. His concentration was disturbed.

He turned around, perturbed. It was Gopal, who bore a helpless look on his face.

Gopal's face pleaded Om to help him.

Om shook his head slightly before turning around. He then moved himself as left as he could on his chair and shifted his assignment paper to the right, so that Gopal could copy his answers easily. With this arrangement, Om started writing the assignment again.

After a few minutes, Gopal seemed to have lost Om. He couldn't keep pace with him. He poked Om with his pencil, which hurt Om. Om sprung up and impulsively turned around. Gopal began murmuring something to Om. Ratna took notice.

"Om, stand up!" exclaimed Ratna, in a loud voice. The whole classroom was looking at Om.

"Stand up and come over here with your answer sheet," repeated Ratna. Om was embarrassed and scared.

"But ma'am, I was ..." Om had just started saying before Ratna shut him down.

"Don't argue with me. Do as I say," said Ratna, cutting Om in between. Om picked up his assignment paper and walked up to Ratna.

"Now I know how you've been getting the exceptional grades in the past," Ratna taunted Om.

Om didn't respond. Ratna took the answer sheet from Om and asked him to stand in the corner. He was to do that for the rest of the day.

He didn't bother arguing further. He just stood there quietly, thinking about the rickshaw ride back home and Farheen.

———— ❖ ————

"Ahmed, why have you kept this at the spot on which I sit?" Om asked Ahmed, the puller for the rickshaw ride back home.

Om was perplexed and pointed at a bag he saw on the spot at which he used to sit every day.

"Oh, ummm, it has some important stuff of mine. You sit here in the front today with me. I'll tell you a story about Alibaba and the forty thieves," replied Ahmed.

"No, I am not interested in any story. I am going to sit where I sit every day," asserted Om and moved the bag from the seat and took his usual position.

That's what Om would do every afternoon. He would sit on that spot he preferred so much with his hands wrapped around the bag on his lap, his legs hanging from the seat in the air, and his eyes fixed on the pink gate from which Farheen would come out.

Farheen was in a different class than Om's. The school used to release each batch of students a few minutes apart in order to avoid a stampede. It was a small school, built in a home on a small plot of land in Bapu Nagar, a suburb close to Jawahar Nagar where his Naani lived. The school board above the gate read its name: 'Alpha-Beta'.

Om's first tryst with poetry began at the 'Alpha-Beta' – watching Farheen walk out of that small gate, in her uniform with a pink bag that was bigger than her back, A water bottle hung around her neck like a grand necklace. She wasn't fast as he was, when he came out of that gate. She walked slowly as if she was doing so for the first time. Perhaps because she didn't have a purpose like he did.

Every day he would see her thus, sitting on the back seat of the rickshaw, waiting to greet her. She would give him her water bottle while Ahmed would lift her up and place her on the spot next to Om.

"Why don't you eat the pickle and roti your Naani gives you?" Farheen asked Om as the latter performed his daily ritual of offering her the lemon pickle with roti bread.

"I just don't like it," he replied.

33

"Then, why don't you ask Naani to stop giving it to you?" Farheen countered.

Before Om could say something, he heard a voice from behind him.

"Get down and come with me, Farheen," said a firm voice in the background as the rickshaw approached Farheen's house.

It was Tariq, Farheen's father. He was there outside the school the pick Farheen up. Farheen bore a look of surprise on her face. So did Ahmed, the rickshaw puller. Tariq had a stern look on his face. Om used to see Tariq in the neighbourhood at times and used to wonder why he always had a dour appearance on his face. He wondered if Tariq had ever experienced Natkhat, which according to Om, was the ultimate road to happiness.

"Naani, do you know who I am going to marry?" Om asked Naani as she placed him on top of the bed and took his tie off. Naani couldn't control her smirk but tried her best to hide it as possible.

"No, I don't. Tell me who the lucky girl is," she replied.

"Farheen," he said with remarkable confidence.

Naani was amused. "Why Farheen?" she asked with a smile on her face.

"She is the most beautiful girl in the world," he said.

"Even more beautiful than me?" Naani asked.

"No, not more beautiful than you. But equal to you. The two most beautiful girls in the world," he said.

Naani smiled and gave him a pat on the back of his head. It was almost like she murmured, 'silly boy.'

This was one of the hallmarks of Naani's character. She was born in a very small village in the 1930s, could barely read or write; but she was strikingly aware, surprisingly progressive, and remarkably intelligent. Her intelligence wasn't intellectual or bookish or cultivated, but one that was inherent to humans. One only needed to be aware of it to unearth its true potential.

She never saw Farheen as someone from a different religion, more specifically Islam. Neither did she make light of the fact that Om was just a five-year-old boy and was talking about marrying someone. Her open mind was as vast as the sky.

"Namaste, Seema," said Kiran as she greeted her.

Seema returned her gesture with folded hands of her own.

"I spoke with Mahesh last evening about the cooking job at Monica's. He wasn't too keen, but I have been able to convince him to allow me to give it a try," said Kiran.

Mahesh had never stopped her from doing anything or pursuing whatever she wanted, but she wanted to show Seema some reluctance in joining the job. According to Mahesh, this would give her some power over the negotiation if she was offered the job.

"How much does it pay?" Kiran asked further.

"Three thousand rupees a month. You need to visit once each morning and cook for the entire day," replied Seema.

That was good money compared to the market standard. The usual pay was around fifteen hundred per month.

"When can I begin?" asked Kiran.

"You will have to give a trial first. I will speak with Monica and set you up for a trial Saturday morning, if that's all right," replied Seema.

Saturday was two days away.

"That's fine. Please let me know," said Kiran. She was trying hard to control her desperation.

CHAPTER 4

A WEEKDAY MORNING was the time when the men of the household would usually be out working, and women would be out in the market, shopping fruits and vegetables.

Mahesh, however, was at home, wearing a torn-out pyjama, which was perhaps older than Om. He wore no top except for a thin piece of thread around his chest, commonly known as 'janeu'. 'Janeu' is a sacred thread worn around the chest by the highest class in the Indian society called 'Brahmins'.

He hadn't taken a sip out of his morning tea when Kiran asked, "You look tense."

Mahesh shook his head, indicating nothing, which Kiran knew, in most cases, was a cry for attention.

"Tell me what happened," she insisted, placing her hands upon his.

"I received two rejections yesterday. One from a detergent company and another from a razor company," Mahesh said, hesitating at first. "I had even shaved for the second interview," he continued. "I performed all the sales drills so confidently. I don't know what's happening. What am I doing wrong? How do I correct it?" Frustration had gotten to him and hope was dying fast.

Kiran had no answer to his conundrum.

"I just don't know what I am going to do. How am I going to pay next month's rent? How am I going to get Om into first grade at a good private school? I don't even know how much donation I need to arrange for that. These are his last few days before kindergarten gets over and he needs to be admitted into first grade in a full-fledged school. How is it going to happen?" Mahesh sounded miserable.

"Can we get Om admitted to a government school in the interim till we sort our finances out? I have managed to get a trial at Monica's. The pay is three thousand per month," said Kiran in a bid to calm him down.

"No way! You know the quality of education and students at government schools. No one from our immediate family has been admitted to a government school. Do we want Om to have a life like ours where there is a struggle each day to figure out how the rent and food is going to be covered? I want Om to be an engineer from IIT and go to America one day. I want him to have a life we couldn't have," Mahesh ranted.

He looked clueless on how that was going to happen. Kiran just remained silent and took the unconsumed cup of tea from the rickety coffee table into the kitchen.

"I'm going to meet Ravi today," said Mahesh in a voice loud enough for Kiran to hear. "Apparently, he has started a new business and believes he can change my life," he added.

Ravi was Mahesh's friend from his college days at the Polytechnic Institute of India.

"Oh, and it's Om's birthday tomorrow. He wants to distribute whatever his favourite snack is at school," replied Kiran from the kitchen.

———◆———

"What does my lalla want for his birthday?" asked Naani as she placed Om on the bed and started changing his clothes.

"I'm going to distribute Natkhat to the whole class. One for everyone, even though I don't want to give Ms. Devi one," he answered.

"That's not fair, Om, you should distribute it with love to everyone," Naani responded as he raised his arms up in the air to wear the vest Naani held in her hands.

"She hates me and insults me in the class in front of everyone. Is that fair?" he retorted.

"What did I teach you the other day when you made five new canine friends?" Naani questioned Om.

He immediately recollected the lesson and mentally cursed himself for not remembering it.

"Always remember to imbibe the lessons you learn in life into your daily behavior," Naani added as she picked him up from the bed and placed him down on the floor.

"What is the biggest lesson you have learnt in your life, Naani?" Om asked with great curiosity as he followed Naani into the kitchen to help her put lunch together.

"Love," Naani replied. "It is all encompassing. All of life's great qualities fall under the one umbrella of love. The qualities of compassion, of acceptance, of prayer, of patience, of perseverance -- they all stem from the larger spectrum of love. If you are to remember one thing, let that be the quality of love. Always make your decisions from the stand-point of love, okay, lalla?"

He stood there in utter silence, though aware and attentive. He might not have intellectually understood the depth of what Naani had just said but felt the expression as it was meant to be felt.

⸻ ❖ ⸻

The day had been witness to really hot weather and Babu had spent more than an hour bargaining with the vegetable vendors in the afternoon. On top of that, Om had to run with two large bags of vegetables at each turn Babu made on his scooter. Om deserved a late afternoon nap in front of the cooler, dislodging Babu from his usual spot. As he took a seat there, he had begun to wonder where Babu got his energy to bargain from, on such a hot afternoon. Little did he know that scarcity of money was a great source of energy, capable of making mankind do many things.

"Om, look who's here?" Om heard a voice as his sleep broke and his eyes saw a hazy figure walk into the living room at Naani's house. It was his father.

Mahesh sat on the weary, two-seater sofa on the other side of the living room. Naani brought him a glass of water. Babu tightened his lungi and accompanied Mahesh on the sofa.

"I have great news," Mahesh said with incredible excitement as he looked at both Babu and Naani. Om was still on the bed with his eyes closed, pretending to be asleep, not wanting to be disturbed.

Babu and Naani must have thought Mahesh had got a new job. Their eyes lit up.

"I just met Ravi and he has a great business proposition for me. He has recently signed up as a distributor for a new company that makes machines which count cash. So, there is no need for people at banks, shops, restaurants, etcetera to count cash. You just put the money in the machine and the machine counts the cash for you," continued Mahesh.

"You only need to buy the first machine from the company and the rest of the machines are on credit. Let me explain to you with a paper and pen," added Mahesh and took out a pen and paper from his pocket. It looked like he was prepared for this.

"Each machine costs me only fifteen thousand rupees and retails for twenty-five thousand each. That is more than sixty-five per cent margin on each, or ten thousand rupees on each machine. There are thousands of banks, restaurants, jewellers, shops in Jaipur itself; even if I sell two units a month out of those thousands, I will make twenty-thousand rupees a month, which is more than any job out there for me." Mahesh sounded exuberant. This business plan had given him a new hope...a new light.

"What if the machine you buy initially doesn't sell?" Babu asked, his tone pessimistic.

"Oh, Babu, you are always thinking negatively. Out of thousands of prospective clients, you think I wouldn't even be able to sell five. Ravi has already sold three machines so far in less than two weeks." Mahesh tried to laugh it off.

"How are you going to buy the machine?" Babu's interrogation continued.

"Now this is what I wanted to talk to you about," said Mahesh. "I have six thousand rupees left after the rent and bills this month, plus I can sell the TV at our house for another one thousand. I just need another eight thousand," added Mahesh.

Babu understood what Mahesh was trying to suggest in his subtle manner.

There was a bit of awkwardness in the air between Mahesh and Babu. Naani looked at Babu, who knew what she was suggesting.

"I only have two thousand rupees spare at the moment, given the rent and the medicine expenses of myself and your mother-in-law," Babu said, his tone carrying his hesitation.

"I have a small gold chain. I can give it to you, which should fetch you another three thousand," Naani interrupted in between.

This got an immediate stare from Babu.

"Thank you, Mummy, you are so kind. I will pay you back within three months, I promise. Now, I only need to arrange another three thousand," said Mahesh with the biggest smile any of them had seen on his face in a long time.

"Om! Come, we need to go shopping for your birthday. Your mother told me you want to distribute Natkhat in the class," said Mahesh loudly as he walked towards the cot Om was sleeping on, to wake him up.

"You look quite in the mood today," said a surprised Kiran as Mahesh started massaging her neck and kissing her while she watched her favourite daily soap on the television, 'Buniyaad' -- a story that told tales around the partition of India in 1947 and its repercussions.

"What do you want to get out of me today?" Kiran pushed Mahesh away and asked, with a smirk on her face.

"I've got great news. I just met Ravi and he has a great business plan for me. He has recently signed up as a distributor for a new company of cash counting machines. So, there is no need for people at banks, shops, restaurants to count cash. You just put the money in the machine and the machine counts the cash for you. You only need to buy the first machine from the company and the rest of the machines are on credit. Each machine costs me only fifteen thousand rupees and retails for twenty-five thousand each. That is more than a sixty-five per cent margin on each. Or ten thousand rupees on each machine. There are thousands on banks, restaurants, jewellers, shops in Jaipur itself; even if I sell two units a month, I will make twenty thousand a month. Imagine life if I made that kind of money." Mahesh had already memorized his sales pitch.

"What if you are not able to sell even a single machine?" asked Kiran, confirming she had the same gene pool as Babu.

"Oh, come on, even Babu asked the same question. You two should believe in me. Ravi has sold three machines already inside two weeks," responded Mahesh as he tried to kiss Kiran again.

"And how are you going to arrange the fifteen thousand rupees for starting this business?" asked Kiran, pushing Mahesh, who was clearly trying to seduce his way into something.

"I have already arranged eleven thousand. We just need to sell this TV for about thousand and then arrange another three thousand only," replied Mahesh.

"TV! NO WAY!" snapped Kiran. "Now I know why you're being so sweet," she said in a loud voice.

"I'll get you another one, a bigger one, within three months I promise," Mahesh continued to try and kiss Kiran in a bid to seduce her into his demand.

Kiran relented eventually, allowing him to kiss her. His hands grasped the back of her neck.

"Just have faith in me," said Mahesh as he continued kissing Kiran.

"How are you going to arrange another three thousand after the TV is sold?" moaned Kiran.

"I am going to pledge my wedding ring to Sharma Ji, the jeweller on M.I. Road," said Mahesh.

"What!" exclaimed Kiran, pushing him away. "You are going to give your wedding ring away?" Kiran couldn't believe it.

"I'm not giving it away. I'm just giving it as a guarantee for a small loan. I will get it back within three months," answered Mahesh as he made a move towards her again.

"Stay away," she warned as she tied the knot of her salwar and headed towards the bathroom.

"I got Om his favourite snack for his birthday tomorrow," shouted Mahesh as Kiran shut the bathroom door with a bang.

CHAPTER 5

OM'S SIXTH BIRTHDAY had arrived. Mahesh dropped Om to school on his motorcycle – the iconic Yezdi. It was the same Yezdi which Mahesh used to drive Kiran around after their marriage was fixed. Kiran would sometimes recollect those memories with a smirk on her face. How Mahesh would steal a kiss right before he dropped her off at her after a date. That was the quite the brave act then – in the India of 1980s.

The Yezdi had been witness to many such stories. Om wondered whether machines in their own subtle ways owed any allegiance to their owners, like accelerate differently for different owners, break down if not treated well, or feel abandoned if they were sold to a new owner. The machine was a hundred twenty thousand kilometres old and twice divorced. It looked like the Yezdi really liked Mahesh, given the mediocre care he was giving it because of the lack of funds.

Om sat on the backseat with two bags of Natkhats in each hand and leaned forward into Mahesh's back so that he wouldn't fall off when his father accelerated.

The packets of Natkhat were carefully counted. One for each student in the class, which meant he had forty-six of them for his fellow students, one for Ratna Devi, one for Om himself, and two for Farheen. Om reached the class, nervous, excited and late.

"As if being inattentive wasn't enough, now you are late to the class as well," Ratna taunted Om, but soon realised that it was his birthday.

"Come in, Om," she continued.

He entered the class and remembered Naani's words - "love has to be the way". He went straight to Ratna, shifted both the bags on to one hand, and with the other hand, offered her a packet of Natkhat. The look on her face suggested she didn't fancy one but took it nevertheless.

He continued surfing through every student in the class, offering them a packet. He teased Arun, the serial front-bencher and Ratna's favourite, by not offering him a packet and walking past him, but then he backtracked and threw one at him with a smile. That was the first laugh both of them shared.

All but three packets were distributed. One was left for Om himself and two for Farheen.

Om stood right next to the rickshaw, his eyes focused on the exit gate, waiting for the girl in pink to walk out as only she did – slowly, with the sun shining on her face. There was an enchanting rhythm in each step she took – slow and soft. Sometimes, she sipped from her bottle, sometimes she stopped in the middle of her walk to adjust the heavy bag on her tiny shoulders. Those were the moments that made the torture with Ratna bearable.

He extended the bag with the three packets of Natkhat to Farheen who now stood right in front of him. She looked at them and then at him. "Is it your birthday?" she asked.

He nodded.

She picked up a packet from the bag. He picked up another and gave her another one.

"Why two?" she asked.

"I got two for you," he replied, a smile on his face.

"Why two for me?" she questioned further even as she tried to rip the packet open with her tiny hands.

Om kept quiet. Words refused to come out of his mouth.

"What does Uncle Tariq do?" Om asked Farheen, who was busy making up her mind as to whether she liked his birthday snack or not.

"He works at a shop," she answered, more concerned about the snack in her hands than his irrelevant question.

"Does his shop sell Natkhat?" he asked further, curious.

She shrugged her shoulders indicating what he could construe as two options. Either she didn't know, or she was just not concerned.

"You don't eat it that way," he said and took the packet away from Farheen. "You gnaw away at it like a rabbit does at a carrot and then you let the finely cut pieces soak in your mouth till they get really soggy. This is when you swallow them in," he explained.

To him, eating Natkhat the wrong way was criminal.

Farheen tried to snatch the packet back from him. He took it way over to his other side, so she couldn't reach it. Her left hand touched his right arm. Her skin was supple, silken smooth. He had goose bumps all over his arms.

The rickshaw stopped. They had reached Farheen's house. Om gave in and handed Farheen's packet back to her. He saw Tariq, in a white kurta and a white taqiyah -- a circular cap with mesh that covers half the head -- looking at him. His gaze was stern and his eyes smeared with kohl.

<hr />

"NMCC Enterprises! That's what the new company is going to be called," announced an excited Mahesh as Naani and Babu looked on.

"NMCC? How did you come up with that?" asked Naani, curious.

"No More Cash Counting," said Mahesh with a cheeky smile.

Everyone had a bellyful of laughter. Perhaps they thought that he needed to be given credit for thinking out of the box.

"So, I've arranged for the first machine to be delivered here within three days. I've registered your address as the office. Can I use the small room on the outside facing the gate of the house as my office?" added Mahesh, not giving much of a choice to the other party.

"Also, Babu, I'm sure you can setup some meetings for me, please?" Mahesh kept continuing with Naani and Babu just listening. "Your friend, Mr. Sharma, the jeweller, will benefit tremendously from the machines. Please set up a meeting with him tomorrow."

Babu looked on.

"He is just someone I know. We haven't spoken for a few years now. Don't know how it might seem, if I called him up after all this time only to sell something," replied Babu.

Naani felt relieved that Babu had never got into sales. That field wasn't for the socially conscious, inept or the ones who didn't adjust well to situations and surroundings.

"Don't think about all this. Just call him up and fix up a meeting for me tomorrow at his place. You and I will go together. In the meanwhile, I'm going to go to the tax office now," Mahesh said to Babu as he picked up his helmet and started to make a move.

Om was aware that Farheen used to go the terrace every afternoon after coming from school to offer namaaz along with Nargis and Tariq. Naani's terrace was usually locked by the landlady, who was named Jyoti. She kept the keys in a pouch and the pouch in her blouse. She would only open the lock to the terrace when she had some work there. Sometimes, she needed to leave freshly prepared pickles to dry in the sun, sometimes the television antenna on the terrace needed adjustment, some other time she needed to dry manchester in the sun. One had to walk through Naani's living room to access the stairs to the terrace. Whenever Om found Jyoti going to the terrace, he followed her. It was his golden opportunity at catching a glimpse of Farheen after school hours. He offered to help Jyoti with whatever she had to do. Being an elderly woman, she always welcomed the help. Om, however, only cared about one thing

– to catch the surreal glimpse of Farheen surrendered in prayer, two terraces away.

Farheen and Nargis in prayer, was one of Om's first trysts with sheer innocence and simplicity. Their eyes closed, heads bowed to the almighty, arms up in the air, begging the universe for grace and benediction.

Tariq, unlike the other two, would often keep his eyes open and look around. Om never understood that because he used to think that prayer meant a deep communion with God – a surrender to the universal energy, as Naani used to tell him. Tariq was often quite distracted. Many times, Om found Tariq with his eyes open and gaze fixed on him.

But all such thoughts would fade away at the mere sight of Farheen bowing her head in prayer, her eyes closed, her hands facing her face, and the fingers pointing upward. She would turn her face in both the directions a few times during the prayer. Every time, Om hoped that she would open her eyes and look at him. That never happened; her prayer was always sincere. However, sometimes, after the prayer ended, Farheen would turn around and catch a glimpse of him before she climbed down the stairs, hand-in-hand with Nargis.

It was half past seven in the morning. With the dawn, came Kiran's first day at Monica's house. For that matter, it was her first day ever at any kind of work that involved monetary exchange. For someone like her, it was a brave effort because she had stepped way out of her comfort zone. She found it difficult to sleep the entire night. She tossed and turned in worry, making up one scenario after another in her head. When such thoughts went over the line, she would tell herself how foolish all this was, only to begin again a few moments later.

Dressed in a pink sari, her hair braided into a pony tail, Kiran rang the doorbell outside Monica's house. For over a couple of minutes, which seemed like a long time to Kiran, no one answered the bell. Just as she was about to ring it a second time, the door opened. A bare-chested man with bloodshot eyes had answered the doorbell.

Kiran's nervousness only increased.

The man stood there at the door, eyeing her from top to toe. She assumed him to be Ranjit, Monica's husband and owner of the leather factories Mahesh was thinking of landing a job in.

"Are you the new maid?" asked the man.

"Ummm, yes, the new cook," answered Kiran.

He took a step to his left, indicating her to come inside.

"Is Monica ji at home?" asked a hesitant and nervous Kiran.

"I will inform her. The kitchen is that way," said the man, pointing in the direction of the kitchen.

Kiran stepped into the big and lush kitchen. The kitchen slab was all granite and there was room for two people to stand and cook in comfort, something luxurious in her perspective.

"Come out and get me some breakfast. I need to leave for work. That new maid is in the kitchen." Kiran heard a voice from across the hall. She pretended to not have heard anything, but her nervousness was only building up, also in part because she had no idea what to cook.

Within a few minutes, Monica came out, adjusting her night gown. Her hair was messy and she had dirt all over her gown.

"Look what Ranjit got me today," said a beaming Monica, exhibiting her supposedly new earrings. They were golden, big, and beautiful.

"What do you want me to cook, madam?" asked Kiran.

"Ranjit loves ladyfingers. So, cook that and along with it, prepare a vegetable korma," replied Monica. "Vegetables sit in the lower compartment of the fridge and all the spices are here," continued Monica, pointing towards the cabinet containing spices.

"And... How many roti breads?" asked Kiran, still hesitating.

"Ten for Ranjit and four for me", answered Monica.

Kiran folded her hands and gave a subtle nod using her head, indicating gratitude and subservience.

CHAPTER 6

THE DAYS AT Alpha-Beta were coming to an end. All the young kids were supposed to move into the first grade at a full-fledged school where they ran classes all the way till the twelfth grade. After that, the studies had to be pursued at a university.

Most of the kids imagined they would be adults, now that they were about to move into a full-fledged school. Big men and women who ought to be respected! Some would take admission into the bigger branch of the same school across the road. Some would join a different one, all depending on how much their parents could afford to spend. Each school had its own quota and system of 'donation' needed for admission.

Om was going to miss Alpha-Beta. In spite of Ratna Devi and the daily dose of her putting him down, the school was his excuse for meeting Farheen, five days every week.

None of them had an idea where they would go. Friendships were going to be dissolved, making way for new ones. For most of them, perhaps everyone, it was their first tryst with impermanence.

Ratna walked into the class wearing a bright pink sari and a big, red bindi – a round, velvety decorative -- pasted where the mystical third eye was said to be located. She had a stack of paper in her hands. Whenever that would happen, it usually meant that there was a circular from the school office that was meant to be distributed to the class.

She went to her seat, hung her tote bag on the back of the chair, and handed over the pile of paper to Arun, her favourite student, who always sat on the front seat. Arun went to each desk, which seated two children, distributing the circular. After distributing one circular each to a student, Arun handed the rest to the class teacher. She then stood up and began reading the circular aloud, wearing her trademark golden reading glasses.

"This is to notify that the current session of school is going to end on the 10th of April. Enrolments to Alpha Major, the main school wing, for admission into Class 1 will commence 15th April onward. Parents are requested to book their appointments for admissions by contacting the front office between 9 A.M to 5 P.M. In case a current student is not registered with Alpha Major by the 30th of May, he/she will be deemed out of the school rolls. New session begins after the summer vacations, on the 1st of July," she announced with a sigh at the end, as she finished reading the circular in her typical Bengali baritone.

Om guessed she was going to miss Arun. Or, perhaps she was petrified at the thought of another Om in her class in the next session.

As for the rest of them, there was a complete silence, along with a few tears.

A strange sense of loss caught hold of Om that afternoon. He was there in the rickshaw as usual, waiting for Farheen to come. She came out of the school gate with that white piece of paper in her hand. None of them said a word to each other and took their seats. The rickshaw started moving and they had their stares fixed on the school gate until it faded away from their sight. He didn't even remember reaching home.

———◆———

"Guess what I have made for you today?" said Naani as she welcomed Om with a bowl of aato halwa. Like always, she had had a feeling that her young grandson might be in need of some comfort.

He kept his bag on the floor and sat right in front of the cooler. That was Babu's spot – he knew. Babu would curse him if he saw him sitting there.

Naani saw the circular he had in his hands and took it from him. She was feeling nervous. She woke Babu up and asked him to read it for her.

"In less than a week, Om's session at school will end and we only have another six weeks after that to finalize his admission," Naani murmured as Babu finished reading out the circular to her.

Reality had struck at that precise moment. Although they were aware of the circumstances, that moment though, reality announced itself emphatically.

"How are we going to get the money to get Om admitted to a private school?" Naani continued to murmur.

Naani could sense the stress on her face. She had been worried about this for a few days now without telling anyone; although by now, it had become obvious to Babu.

"Don't worry, Koshi. Mahesh ji has started a new business and Kiran has also started working. Everything will fall into place," said Babu with as little conviction as possible.

Needless to say, it didn't have any impact on Naani. It is indeed a mystery that despite knowing that consolation doesn't work in the moments of true despair, we are almost always compelled to offer it to the other person. One could say that objectivity gives a certain perspective, creates a distance from the issue at hand, which makes giving advice easier than following it.

"Mahesh ji has just started the business and Kiran has also only just started working. How much time do we have?" Naani snapped, which was rare.

Babu came up to her and placed his calm hands on her shoulders. Though, on the inside, he felt as worried as Naani. But he had to put up a hard front. "Do not worry. Everything will be all right," he said and turned to face the young kid he had grown so fond of. Om was sitting with his face buried in the water cooler, enjoying the tiny sprinkles of water kissing his face every now and then.

Mahesh took a seat on the couch. On the table in front of him was the school circular and a fresh cup of ginger chai Naani had made for him. Tension in the air was easily palpable.

"Don't worry. We still have almost two months at our disposal. The school has set a cut-off date of 31st May for enrolments. I am going to work something out. It will be fine," said Mahesh, with what felt like confidence.

"But how is it going to work out?" Naani started questioning. Even her interrogation had a sense of tenderness, a touch of softness. "You have just started working. I have already sold my chain. Kiran was telling me you have pledged your wedding ring as well. We have exhausted many of our resources and assets. Kiran has also just started working. How much will she earn? Three thousand a month. How much time do we have? Six weeks. Eight weeks at most. How much money do we need? At least fifty thousand," Naani continued as the tenderness in her voice turned into one of anxiety. All her points were valid. Both Babu and Mahesh knew it.

"No, Mummy, I don't think we need fifty thousand. New private school enrolments should happen within twenty thousand," said Mahesh, as if it was easy to arrange even twenty thousand. He was on the verge of bankruptcy. Naani was not convinced.

"Babu, can you please start approaching all the private schools within a ten-kilometre radius from tomorrow?" Mahesh requested Babu. Babu nodded.

"I've managed to take a small loan from Ravi to run an advertisement in the daily newspaper. The advertisement will go out by the end of the week and I am expecting the first machine to be delivered by tomorrow morning," said Mahesh. One could easily feel the sense of urgency in his demeanour. "Did you set up a meeting with Mr. Sharma, the jeweller?" Mahesh asked Babu.

"He is okay with a 3 P.M. meeting any time this week in his office. He has just asked to give him a call an hour before on the day we want to meet him. I didn't tell him the agenda. I just said that it had been long and I wished to see him," replied Babu.

"That's great. Thank you, Babu. In all probability, machine should arrive by tomorrow. As soon as it arrives, let's go and meet Mr. Sharma," said Mahesh with a hint of excitement in his voice, though it was the nervous kind.

CHAPTER 7

A RATHER COOL and overcast morning dawned upon the pink city. A loud thump on the door disturbed Naani during her morning meditation. She opened the door and saw a delivery man with one big carton. She assumed it to be Mahesh's cash counting machine. Babu was sitting on the sofa in the living room, reading the newspaper. He called Mahesh and informed him.

"You should make pakoras today with chai for breakfast," said Mahesh as he lay on the bed with Kiran on a grey, overcast morning in the pink city.

"I have to get to work within half an hour. I have no time to make you pakoras," Kiran retorted.

"I know what we can do within half an hour," he remarked as he reached out to kiss Kiran's neck, caressing her breasts at the same time.

"Not today," said Kiran, despite enjoying his advances. "Did I tell you how weird Ranjit was on my first day at Monica's house?

He opened the door bare-chested and then went inside and shouted at Monica, who was equally weird. She had dirt all over her night gown, which was strange," she continued.

Mahesh seemed least interested. "Maybe she was up to some cleaning in her room," he murmured as he kissed Kiran's right breast and caressed the other with his left hand.

"I need to get ready now," said Kiran, strengthening her resolve and pushing him away. Mahesh looked disappointed with her refusal to engage. The phone in the house started ringing. Kiran answered the call.

"Mahesh, it's Babu. He is saying there is a parcel delivery for you at your office," she said from the living room.

"Tell him I'll be there in fifteen minutes," responded Mahesh in an instant. Within a minute, he put on his trousers and grabbed the keys to his motorcycle.

"Why are you in such a hurry?" asked Kiran.

"The first machine has arrived!" remarked Mahesh, excited, as he rushed out of the house. Kiran got excited too before she realized she needed to be at work within the next twenty minutes.

Kiran wore a salwar kameez this time instead of a sari. Ranjit's bare chest was enough to make Kiran's midriff uncomfortable.

Within minutes, Mahesh was in his new office with the cash counting machine which had just arrived. There was a glow in his eyes that spoke of an excitement he used to have when he was a small boy who had just gotten his favourite toy.

"Let's go and meet Mr. Sharma today," said Mahesh.

"Do you even know how to operate the machine?" Babu questioned.

"Oh, I already took lessons from Ravi. I also accompanied him to a few sales meetings," replied Mahesh. Babu seemed surprised.

"What about some cash for demonstration?" Babu questioned further.

"We will use Sharma ji's money itself. That's what the machine is for – to count his own money!" joked Mahesh.

Babu was amused.

"I'll set this machine up in the office and contact a few inquiries I have got. There's a lot of work to be done; my advertisement in the newspaper goes out tomorrow as well. Also, Babu, although I have setup a phone line in the office, I have used your phone number as the secondary contact number everywhere. Whenever you receive a call, please answer as Naresh, assistant of Mr Mahesh at NMCC Enterprises," said Mahesh with a smirk on his face.

Naani gave a laugh.

Babu was just happy that things were happening. Maybe this was a sign of the times changing for the better. Om was still at school, oblivious of how big of an issue his enrolment in a new school was.

Kiran rang the doorbell like she had done the first time. She expected Ranjit to open the door, like before. However, this time, more than a couple of minutes had passed. No one had answered. Kiran rang the bell again and waited. There was still no answer.

She had been waiting at the door for more than ten minutes. Hesitating a bit, Kiran decided to twist the door knob and see whether the door was open. It was.

She opened the door, knocking it twice again. She even called Monica by her name in hope that someone would show up. She closed the door behind her and proceeded towards the room Ranjit had entered yesterday to speak with Monica.

She knocked on the door and waited. There was no response. She repeated the knock again, yet there was no response. She began to feel anxious. She twisted the knob again and started to push the door open.

Little beams of sunlight made its presence felt in the room, coming in from a narrow gap in the curtains at the other end. Kiran couldn't find anyone inside, though she did see a bouquet of jasmine flowers and red, lacy lingerie set on the bed. Suddenly, as Kiran turned her eyes around, she saw a hand from underneath the bed making a move. Kiran freaked out, closed the door, and went towards the kitchen. She paced around, opening and closing the refrigerator, pretending to work.

"Did you just walk into the room?" asked Monica as she came out of the room with messy hair and dirty night gown.

"Umm, no Monica ji, I just knocked on the door a few times...," replied Kiran nervously.

"Who let you in?" interrogated Monica further.

"Err, em, I rang the doorbell many times, but when no one answered, I checked if the door was open. It was. I came in and knocked on your door once before coming to the kitchen to start working," answered Kiran. "Did Ranjit sir leave without eating?" Kiran tried to change the subject.

"He must have eaten some leftover from last night. He comes home late and often brings something from a restaurant," said Monica.

Kiran felt a little relieved.

"Make Aloo Gobhi today with raita. Eight rotis for Ranjit and six for me," said Monica as she moved towards her room.

Kiran bobbled her head fast, a movement that indicated a convincing yes. A slow bobble meant an unconvincing or a hesitant yes.

Kiran took a sigh of relief and started cooking the cauliflower.

It was an insipid morning; Naani had a duster in her hands. For her, like most women, cleaning was therapeutic. She loved to pick each of the family photo frames from a showcase and dust them. She adored them – they were the memories she had etched over the years and held dear to her heart. She would then place them back in their place – in the small showcase with sliding glass doors right above the sofa in the living room.

"As-salaam alaikum." Naani heard a voice in the background. She turned and saw Nargis enter the room and remove her veil. She usually wasn't allowed to do that in front of the infidels, but she shared a bond with Naani too strong for her to pay heed to that superficial ideology.

"Wa-alaikum Salaam," Naani greeted in return. "I was thinking about you some time ago, Nargis. Thank you for coming. It's been a few days and I haven't seen you. Have you been taking your daily walk regularly?" asked Naani as she made her way to the kitchen to fetch a glass of water for Nargis.

"It's been very hectic," started Nargis. She took a deep sigh. "Tariq has been talking about moving back to Malda," added Nargis.

"What!" came a voice from the kitchen. Malda is a remote district in the state of West Bengal in India.

"What are you saying? What about Farheen and her education?" Naani sounded shocked.

"Tariq has also been talking about admitting Farheen in a madrasa. He knows a Maulana at Malda and is talking about working there in one of the madrasas," replied Nargis.

"But it will be disastrous for Farheen. After so much difficulty, you were able to get Farheen admitted to a school and get her the education she deserves," lamented Naani.

Nargis leaned against the sofa, tilted her head backward against the wall and stared at the ceiling fan, which went round and round, without a purpose of its own except to be an instrument of comfort used by others.

Naani could feel her numbness from a distance.

"I had so many dreams when Tariq got a job in a big city. Dreams about Farheen -- her future, my own future. I thought this move would change Tariq and our whole lives," muttered Nargis. Her eyes moistened; so did Naani's.

"He couldn't even last three months in the job. The only reason Farheen and I have managed to stay this long is because of her school's session. I was somehow able to convince Tariq to stay. I thought in the meantime he would find some work. I kept pushing him, but it just never happened. Now the time has come," Nargis continued as tears rolled down her cheeks. Naani just listened.

"I was about to ask you what you were going to do about Farheen's enrolment in a private school. I am tensed about Om's," said Naani in a soft, delicate voice.

"I hope you are able to find a way," responded Nargis as she moved her gaze away from the ceiling fan to Naani, who stood at a complete loss for words.

"Let me know if you need any help from me," said Nargis. She didn't even realise that she had said something out of courtesy, which she wasn't in any position to fulfil.

Naani walked across and held Nargis' hand. The latter hugged Naani and started sobbing. It took a few minutes for Nargis to regain her composure.

"I haven't seen Kiran in a while," remarked Nargis.

Nargis and Kiran were the same age. Perhaps that was one of the reasons Naani treated Nargis as a daughter.

"She has started working as a cook in Raja Park in order to make some extra money for Om's school admission," answered Naani.

"I've worked there as a cleaner too when I had just come into this city. But left within a week," said Nargis.

"Did Tariq allow you to work? Why did you leave within a week?" asked Naani as she got up to resume her dusting routine.

"Tariq wasn't aware, I just made an excuse of going to the dargah for a ladies' daily prayer. It was just an hour's worth of work each day, so I thought he wouldn't find out," said Nargis and added, "I left because it was a very weird household. I found out that the husband used to come home drunk each night and beat up his wife, who would sleep under the bed to save herself from the beating. In the morning after, he would get her expensive gifts to make up for his behavior. I left because it touched upon a lot of wounds I had myself."

"Why didn't the woman just leave that man or complain about him?" Naani was perplexed.

"I never confronted her about the same thing, but I guess she enjoyed how alive the pain made her feel. I thought it was best to just leave the house," responded Nargis.

Naani shook her head in disbelief.

CHAPTER 8

MAHESH HAD SET up his office in a small room outside Naani's house, which could have passed off for a spooky outhouse. He had, with much care, set up the cash counting machine on one side of the room. On the opposite side, he had pasted a selection of motivational posters. One of them, by Voltaire, read: 'Life is a shipwreck, but we must not forget to sing in the lifeboats'.

His office desk was a wooden ply board nailed atop four thin steel legs. None of them were aligned well, which was why one of the legs needed a paper to be placed under it to prevent the table from being rickety.

Mahesh had borrowed one of the chairs from Babu. That one had a wooden frame that had synthetic strings woven together in a tight manner to make the seat. Two plastic Neelkamal chairs were placed on the other side of the table for guests or prospective clients.

Though he didn't have the money to set up his office the way he wanted, Mahesh had the spirit to put every bit of his soul into his new venture. A large reason behind that was to be able to help Om get the best possible education.

Babu walked into the office and took a seat while Mahesh packed the machine with the utmost care. It was time to leave for Mahesh's first meeting with Mr. Sharma, a jeweller Babu had set up the meeting with.

"I have set up appointments with a few private schools for Om's enrolment. I'll start visiting them tomorrow onward. When is your advertisement going out in the newspaper?" asked Babu.

"Tomorrow. Anyway, it's time for us to go," said Mahesh. He was too preoccupied with his first sales pitch to think about anything else.

Mahesh and Babu went outside the house where Mahesh's motorcycle was parked. Mahesh kept the carefully packed machine on the ground.

"Okay, Babu, so you take the back seat first and I'll then hand over the machine to you. Finally, I will sit in whatever space I have available," said Mahesh.

Babu took his position on the back of Mahesh's Yezdi. Mahesh handed the machine to Babu, which the latter held like he would have held the first woman in his life. Mahesh finally lifted his leg and crossed it over the motorcycle to sit with half his body on the seat and the other half crossing over to the fuel tank behind the steering handle. It was a sight that amused Naani, who looked from the window of the living room.

Mahesh kick-started the motorcycle and left the office towards their destination.

Mahesh and Babu reached Mr. Sharma's jewellery showroom, which was a lavish setup on M.I. Road. That place was home to many renowned jewellers, some dating back to pre-British era.

Mr. Sharma walked in with a cordless landline phone in one hand while the other scratched the left side of his pot-sized belly. The shirt he wore barely held his belly together. It looked like the buttons on the shirt were strongly sewn together. The top three buttons were loose and thick grey hair popped out with an even thicker gold chain. The gold chain alone could have funded Om's entire education, Mahesh thought.

"What is it called? Com-poo-ter? No, com-peu-ter? Okay, Com-peu-ter," said Sharma on the phone. "So, you're saying that with this new machine, I can send a letter to my designer in Dubai within minutes?" asked a very surprised Sharma. There was a brief pause as Sharma listened to someone at the other end of the phone.

"What int-net? Inter... Internet, are you saying? So, you're saying that first I need to get a com-peu-ter and then I need to get something else called internet to be able to send a letter to someone? Do you have an idea how much money this is going to cost?" Sharma continued his interrogation with pauses in between. Then, moments later, he shook his head and disconnected the call. Mahesh and Babu were looking on. "Frauds everywhere, I tell you," said Sharma after hanging up the phone. "Naresh, long time no see. Come give me a hug, brother!" he added as he kept the phone on his office desk and got up to hug Babu.

"I'm good, Sharma. Just busy these days trying to get my grandson enrolled into a private school in Class 1. Have you met my son-in-law, Mahesh?" said Babu, introducing Mahesh to his friend.

Mahesh stood up and shook Sharma's hands.

"These conversations can continue as they will. First tell me. What would you like to have?" asked Sharma as he grabbed for himself a mouthful of Paan -- a stimulant made out of betel leaves, areca nut, and sometimes tobacco as well. It could be swallowed or spit out. Though, looking at the public walls of Indian toilets, it could be safely assumed that people preferred to spit it out rather than swallow it.

Mahesh and Babu sat there perplexed, looking at each other.

"I'm getting you some Samosa and Jalebi," said Sharma as he signaled his assistant sitting at the other end of his cabin. Sharma's cabin was bigger than Babu's and Mahesh's house combined.

"So, tell me. How can I serve you?" asked Sharma. It is a culture in India to not ask someone what brought them to you but to ask a guest how they may be served.

Mahesh mustered up all he courage he had, remembered all the sales drills he had practiced, and said, "When I walked in to your showroom, I saw that there are two people sitting at the cash counter. What do they do?"

"Both of them are cashiers, but one of them also acts as a sales rep from time to time, if needed. But, essentially, cashiers, since we have a large influx of cash transactions daily," answered Sharma.

"So, they count and maintain cash for your company. I'm assuming they must be getting their salaries paid each month, bonuses at least once a year. They must be getting sick on a few days each year and then must also be asking for a raise!" said Mahesh as he got up from his chair and started taking a walk around the room with Sharma and Babu listening.

Babu looked impressed with the confident start by which Mahesh had begun the sales pitch. He hadn't seen it coming.

"Yes, you're right," responded Sharma.

"What if I told you that I have a person from another planet who can do all that work for you, never ask for a monthly salary, no bonus, no sick leaves, and never asks for a raise? Would you like to meet that person?" continued Mahesh.

"Absolutely," said Sharma.

Mahesh went outside the room where he had placed the machine and brought it in.

"Meet your new best friend. 'Cash Counter' by NMCC enterprises!" said Mahesh with enthusiasm as he unwrapped the machine in front of Sharma. "This will do all that you want from your cashiers with no tantrums whatsoever," Mahesh continued his sales pitch.

Sharma was listening with keen interest. Meanwhile, the samosas and jalebi also arrived.

"Let me show it to you how it works. I can prove it all by using my own money, but what good will that be? Let's get your own money and let me demonstrate using a real-life situation," said Mahesh. Sharma looked at Mahesh for a few moments before turning his gaze towards his assistant at the other end of his cabin.

"Bunty, get all the cash collected in Register 1," said Sharma to his assistant. Bunty went and got the cash. The notes were a thick bundle of multiple denominations - one, five, ten, fifty, hundred.

"All right, let's get this started," said Mahesh as he looked at the bundle of notes. "We now need to separate the fifty and the hundred-rupee notes," murmured Mahesh as he started sorting the cash out.

"Why do you need only fifty and hundred-rupee notes?" asked Sharma.

"Because the machine currently only counts fifty and hundred-rupee notes," answered Mahesh.

"Fifty and hundred-rupee notes is where the big money is. You can store more value in less space using the fifty and hundred-rupee notes," added Mahesh.

Sharma didn't look convinced.

"All right, so I have all your fifty and hundred notes here with me! That's a lot of money," said Mahesh as he pointed to a thick bundle of notes.

"Let's get them counted within seconds," said Mahesh.

Mahesh plugged the machine in the electrical socket. Both Sharma and Babu stood up from their seats and were looking at the machine which Mahesh had placed on Sharma's desk.

"All right, let's go," said Mahesh, as he placed the stack of notes in the machine and pressed the start button.

The machine ingested the notes one by one from the input tray and threw them out on the output tray. Within seconds, there was a number on the screen. 7,550 said the machine, meaning that the machine counted INR 7,550.

"Let's now tally that with the cash," said Sharma as he picked up the notes from the output tray and began counting, in front of Babu and Mahesh.

"These notes amount to 7,650 rupees," said Sharma as he finished counting the notes to verify. Babu and Mahesh had both mentally counted while Sharma was physically counting the cash. They knew Sharma was right. Mahesh still wanted to double check. Mahesh took the cash in his hands and started counting. It was 7,650 indeed.

"Let's try this again. It's a brand-new machine. Even a baby takes a few tries to start walking in a proper manner", said Mahesh, embarrassed, requesting the bundle of notes from Sharma.

"Here we go," said Mahesh as he placed the stack of notes in the input tray. He prayed to all Gods that ever existed before he pressed the start button. The machine started counting again.

About halfway through the stack, an error warning appeared on the machine saying the following words on a small digital screen - 'Jam'. It meant that one of the notes had stuck in the machine. Mahesh was cringing. Babu almost had a heart attack. It was obvious that Sharma wasn't impressed.

"Looks like there is a jam. Just give me one moment," said Mahesh as he nervously took a tool kit out of his bag and opened the machine. A hundred rupee note, quite old, lay crumpled within. Mahesh took it out and said, "It rarely happens, but if it does, it's super easy to open the machine using the tool kit that comes complimentary with the machine."

Mahesh closed the machine, prepared the notes to be counted again, placed them on the input tray, and pressed the start button again. The machine started counting.

"7,650!" exclaimed Mahesh. "The machine has counted it perfectly within seconds, what would take a man at least five minutes," said Mahesh, ignoring all the time that had gone into the machine reaching that correct figure.

"But why didn't it calculate correctly the first time?", asked Sharma.

"One of the notes might have stuck together since most of these are pretty old notes," answered Mahesh.

Sharma took a seat, followed by Babu and Mahesh. "How much do you pay your cashiers?" asked Mahesh.

"Six thousand each per month plus bonus," answered Sharma while biting into his samosa.

"Six thousand per month for two people, leaving the bonuses aside for now, equals seventy-two thousand per annum for each. This is too much money you're spending, Mr. Sharma," asserted Mahesh.

"This machine sells in the market for twenty-five thousand, but I am going to sell it to you for twenty. Within two months, you are going to recover the cost and after that, it's only profit," added Mahesh.

Sharma continued to gorge on his samosa and jalebi. Babu looked on. He hadn't said a word over the last twenty minutes or so. Mahesh looked at Babu, who knew what Mahesh wanted him to do.

"What do you think, Sharma?" asked Babu.

"I think it is a useful technology and a good idea. I'll think about it. Right now, I have to visit the temple," said Sharma. He then drank a full glass of water. Fried snacks and sweets make one thirsty.

"Still haven't let go of your habit of appeasing Goddess Lakshmi three times a day? How much more money do you need?" Babu said to Sharma.

Both of them chuckled. Sharma reciprocated the banter. "Need to keep the Goddess of wealth and prosperity happy," said Sharma.

"Sure, Mr Sharma," said Mahesh, "Just see how much money you can save and the impression it creates on your customers. People like going to a state-of-the-art store. I'll call you tomorrow," continued Mahesh.

Sharma didn't respond enthusiastically. To make the moment less awkward, Mahesh extended his arm for a handshake, which he regretted when he noticed the empty plate that had six samosas twenty minutes ago.

Babu and Sharma shared a hug while Mahesh carefully re-packed the machine. After Babu and Mahesh left the shop, they repeated their seating plan on the motorcycle.

"How did you think it went?" asked Mahesh as Babu held on to the machine and himself on the motorcycle.

"You started off well, but the machine was such a let-down in between. Also, I didn't know that the machine only counts fifty and hundred-rupee notes," replied Babu.

"I am going to call Ravi as soon as I reach office and tell him about what happened. It was so annoying," lamented Mahesh as he rode the Yezdi.

That morning, Kiran woke up a little late. Mahesh had had a big meeting with Sharma yesterday and Kiran had listened to his stories with apt attention. However, as soon as she was up, she rushed to get ready, reached Monica's house, and rang the doorbell. She made a point to herself that if no one answered the bell, she would go back. But the door opened within seconds. Kiran was greeted once again by Ranjit's bare-chested body and bloodshot eyes. He took a step aside and an uncomfortable Kiran stepped in.

"Why are you late today?" asked Monica as she was walked down the living room towards Kiran, wearing what looked like a new necklace. A box of Swiss chocolates sat in her one of her hands.

"My husband is not well, so I had to take him to the doctor in the morning," answered Kiran, surprised at her speed of making up an excuse.

Ranjit, dressed only in his towel, stepped towards Monica, took the box of chocolates from her hand, and started feeding her. Kiran pretended to look elsewhere.

"Go in the kitchen and make a sandwich for Ranjit. I will have a potato curry with rice for lunch and dinner, " Monica instructed Kiran.

Kiran could see one of Ranjit's hands grabbing Monica's buttocks. She made her way into the kitchen. She heard faint sounds of moaning in the background followed by a loud thump. Nonetheless, she carried on with her business – which was to cook and leave.

CHAPTER 9

THE FINAL DAY at Alpha-Beta was getting closer. With each passing day, the realization of not knowing where Farheen – or he himself – would go from here got stronger in Om's mind.

Farheen's walk became slower and the rickshaw ride home quicker. It felt like time was slipping away and there was nothing Om could do about it.

That afternoon, Farheen came and sat beside him in the rickshaw. Ahmed was arguing with a car driver who had parked his car right in front of the rickshaw, rendering it difficult to move.

Om opened his lunchbox and offered Farheen pickle and roti bread as usual. She opened her bag, took out a box, and opened it for Om. "You always offer me something, but I have never offered you anything. Today, I got this for you. Ammi made it for me, but I saved it to share with you," said Farheen. Om was taken aback.

"I share whatever I wish to share with you, out of my own accord." responded Om. "I like it, hence I do it. Not out of any compulsion." he added.

"Is that sevai?" he asked a few moments later, looking at the lunch box Farheen had opened. She nodded. Sevai is a kind of vermicelli, which when cooked with milk makes a popular dessert in India. It is usually reserved for festivals or special occasions.

They exchanged each other's boxes even as Ahmed was finally able to get the rickshaw moving.

"What do you like about me the most?" Om asked Farheen.

"I like your nose," replied Farheen as she tried to break the lemon pickle's thick base with her tiny teeth.

"My nose!" Om remarked, bursting into laughter. She smiled as well. "What do you like about me?" she asked.

He paused and thought about it. "I like the way you walk," he said.

She turned her face towards him. It was so enchanting that it almost made him drop out of the rickshaw. She was surprised.

He just looked at her as she turned her gaze towards the sevai in his hands and snatched some back from him.

"I thought you said it was for me", he said as he tried to snatch it back from Farheen's hands.

"Farheen, get down." They heard the voice as Ahmed rang a bell on his rickshaw, reminding Farheen that her stop had arrived. The rickshaw turned around. Tariq was standing again in the balcony, staring at Om.

Mahesh had been anxiously waiting for Sharma's call. After all, Sharma had told Mahesh that he would think about it. Only a day had passed since the meeting, but Mahesh's urgency was understandable given what was at stake and how quickly his life needed an overhaul.

He knew that Sharma paid a visit to the temple every afternoon. So, he parked his motorcycle behind a tree close to the Lakshmi temple near M. I. Road. Then, he stationed himself in a perfect position to catch hold of Sharma as soon as he arrived at the temple.

The clock read 4:30 P. M. There was still no sign of Sharma. Yesterday, Sharma had left for the temple well before four. It was a short ten-minute walk from the showroom. Nevertheless, Mahesh decided to wait for an opportunity and sat there.

About 4:45 P.M, Mahesh saw a big pot-bellied man from a distance. He looked like Sharma. In a few seconds, it was clear that it indeed was Sharma. Mahesh took a deep breath and began to make his way towards the entrance of the temple.

The entrance to the temple began with a long flight of stairs, which most devotees bowed down to before ascending. Mahesh covered his head with a white handkerchief to avoid being recognised and stood at the footsteps. He got down on his knees and pretended to offer his salutations to the Goddess with his eyes closed. He, however, kept opening his eyes every now and then to trace Sharma's location. As soon as Mahesh saw that Sharma was within ten meters, he opened his eyes and turned around.

"Sharma ji, such a pleasant surprise," said Mahesh. The Gods must have been amused.

Sharma's first instinct was to turn around and run. But, he was stuck. He took a second or two to process what was happening before eventually saying, "Oh, Mahesh ji, how come you are here?"

"I just had a successful meeting with another jeweller on M.I. Road. Got an order for two machines. Was passing by and thought I'd offer my salutations to Goddess Lakshmi," responded Mahesh. Sharma didn't say anything apart from giving an awkward smile.

"How was your day?" asked Mahesh, a bit later, as they both started walking up the flight of stairs.

"Very busy." Sharma didn't seem to be in the mood for much conversation. Perhaps he could anticipate what was coming his way.

"I have just got confirmation from the company that I can sell the machine for 18,000 instead of 20,000. Such great news, yes?" asked Mahesh in a suggestive manner.

Sharma pretended to be lost in prayer as he closed his eyes and started singing the aarti for Goddess Lakshmi loudly.

Mahesh was adamant as well. He wasn't going to let Sharma go without answering. He started singing the aarti even louder. The passers-by thought that two of the fiercest devotees of Goddess Lakshmi had descended upon the pink city.

As the aarti finished, Sharma started walking down the stairs with a pace quicker than what Mahesh believed possible of such a man. The latter followed suit.

Sharma took notice and snapped, "See, Mahesh ji, currently, I don't need the machine. The machine only counts fifty and hundred-rupee notes. My cashiers double down as my sales representatives as well. On top of that, the machine failed to perform yesterday. So, right now, I do not want to invest there. I am already investing heavily in getting a com-peu-ter and something called as internet with it, using which I can send a letter anywhere in the world within minutes. That is my bigger priority. Please contact me again after a year. Situation might change. And please convey my regards to Naresh," said Sharma in one long breath with folded hands. Then, he turned around and started walking back towards his office.

Mahesh stood there for a few moments with his head bowed down after bidding Sharma goodbye. He turned around and started walking back to his motorcycle. It was time to go home.

"What happened, Mahesh ji?" asked Naani as Mahesh entered the living room of Naani's house. "You look tired."

Babu sat in front of the cooler while Om was fast asleep on the cot across the sofa.

Of all the things so far about his new office, Mahesh enjoyed the facility of being able to enjoy a nice cup of chai right across from the office.

"Just been a long day," said Mahesh as he crashed into the sofa.

"Did you hear anything from Sharma?" asked Babu, worried.

"He isn't interested. Asked me to get in touch again after a year," replied Mahesh after a long pause.

"And Ravi -- did Ravi mention anything about why the machine malfunctioned the other day?" Babu question him further.

"He said that the notes must ideally be crisp and not old or crumpled," answered Mahesh.

"But, in day to day life, not many people carry crisp notes," Naani remarked.

Everyone went silent. They were aware that all these things should have been thought of beforehand.

"Anyway, the good news is that I got two calls today from the advertisement that had gone out in the paper. One is a stockbroker and the other is a restaurant owner. I've invited both to my office day after tomorrow, for demonstration. One in the morning at ten and the other one in the afternoon at three. Hopefully something will work out," said Mahesh.

"I have set up another meeting for you with Chaubey, the manager at the State Bank of Jaipur. The bank has twelve branches in Jaipur alone. Each branch has a minimum three to four people just counting cash. If this turns out well, it could be very big business for you," said Babu.

Mahesh's eyes lit up. "Thank you, Babu, thank you so much. When is the meeting?" asked Mahesh, getting back his enthusiastic tone.

"I can call Chaubey and find out if a meeting can take place tomorrow in his office," replied Babu.

Mahesh seemed to see a ray of hope. That was the best thing he had heard all day.

"Also, I went to two private schools today regarding Om's admission. One asked for forty-five thousand rupees as donation and the other one asked fifty-five thousand. It is a mad race out there. The school offices were jam packed with parents. I had to wait two hours at one school and three at the other, just to get a meeting with the admission officers. It is not going to be easy," warned Babu.

Naani listened to it all along while Mahesh remained silent.

CHAPTER 10

TARIQ SAT AT the small dining table in the corner of the living room, right next to the kitchen. It could barely seat three, leaving just enough space for one person to walk in and out of the kitchen. There was a pin drop silence all around. He stared at the kitchen door. His kohl-lined eyes that bore an intense look while he caressed his freshly-dyed beard, at the same time.

Nargis came with a biryani and mutton korma and placed it on the table. The three began eating, ignoring the eerie silence that followed.

"I see that boy very often around Farheen, even on the terrace when we are offering namaaz," said Tariq with his mouth full of biryani and hands drenched in the mutton korma gravy.

Nargis didn't answer him. She didn't want to create a scene which may adversely affect Farheen. She just did what so many other women did – she kept quiet. Farheen had just come out of her room, which was nothing but a small storage area converted to fit her bed and other things.

"I am moving Farheen to Karimuddin Madrasa in Malda after her pre-school gets over. Majid's daughter is going to the same and she already knows two hadiths by heart, fasts during Ramadan, and has embraced the niqab. I can't believe how I gave into your demand of sending Farheen to a non-Islamic school with boys. Shukran Allah, the end is near, " continued Tariq as he ate his biryani with a hurry.

Nargis gave a careful, side-glance to Tariq, asking him not to talk about this in front of Farheen.

"Why shouldn't she hear?" asked Tariq. He banged his fist on the table in a fit of rage. His action sent Nargis into a panic attack and stunned Farheen, who sat motionless with a spoon full of rice in her hand dangling in front of her small mouth.

"She should know what is expected of a good Muslim girl. Unlike you, who doesn't even know how to cover herself properly. Against all my wishes, you dared to get her admitted to a co-ed school. At least, have the shame to teach her how a girl must conduct herself with dignity," said Tariq as his voice grew louder.

Nargis, with moist eyes and trembling hands, quickly got up and picked Farheen in her arms. "Come, sweetheart, let's put you to sleep," said Nargis as she took Farheen into her room, wiping her tears away.

"I've told you so many times not to behave like this in front of Farheen", said Nargis as she came out of Farheen's room after a few minutes. She was sobbing inconsolable tears. "Do you have no respect for me?" cried Nargis.

"Why don't you cover your eyes and hands when you go out? I've asked you so many times," said Tariq as he took a few steps and grabbed Nargis by her hair.

"Cover your eyes and hands when you go out. Do you hear me? Cover your eyes and hands when you go out. Cover your eyes and…"

Tariq kept repeating loudly while he bent Nargis over and lifted her gown.

"I'm still sore from last night, please sto...," begged Nargis.

Tariq's voice kept getting louder and louder. He pinned Nargis' head to the half-eaten plate of Biryani on the congested dining table.

Within a minute, Tariq was finished and threw Nargis on the floor.

"I don't want to see that boy around Farheen again," he said and made his way towards the bedroom while tying the knot of his pyjama.

Nargis entered Farheen's room after she wiped the tears from her face, taking a deep breath. Only a mother could enter the space of her child with such softness and silence. She silently switched the study lamp on to check on Farheen. The child's eyes were open.

"Will my <u>beta</u> listen to a story?" asked Nargis, referring to Farheen as 'beta', which meant son. Farheen, like most girls her age, loved talking like a boy, being addressed like a boy, and being treated like a boy.

Farheen held mother's hands and nodded.

"When I was your age, I used to have a friend – Rizwan. Rizwan and I studied, played, laughed, and cried together. Rizwan would give me a toffee every day and I would do his homework for him. We used to play a game every evening. I would close my eyes and count till one hundred while Rizwan would find a place to hide. After I finished my counting, I would open my eyes to find Rizwan.

If I found him before he could touch me, I won; but if he touched me first, then he won. You know, I always won. Each time, I would find him. But, one evening, I didn't. He was nowhere to be seen. I searched all over, kept shouting his name until there was no voice left in me. That night Allah appeared in my dream and asked me if I wanted to see Rizwan again. I begged him. Allah warned me that Rizwan had been captured by Shaitan. I was mortified. I thought that was cruel, abhorrent, and sinister. But Allah was merciful, as he always is. He offered me two keys – one key led to an empty room. If I entered that one, Rizwan would be freed from Shaitan's hold, but I would never be allowed to talk to Rizwan again. The second key led to Rizwan, but it meant that I would be separated from Ammi and Abbu, and Rizwan would never be freed from the grip of Shaitan. I felt like my whole life was about to come to an end. I was confronted by a puzzle I had no solution for. Spring, summer, autumn and winter went by, but I couldn't decide. Then one day, Allah held my hand and said, "Just let it go". And that was it. I could not be selfish anymore and had to go away from Rizwan, for Rizwan's sake. That was the only path to save Rizwan from the gallows of the Shaitan," finished Nargis. Farheen was tearful.

"I don' think Abbu loves you as much as Rizwan did," said Farheen as she wept.

Nargis didn't know what to say. A few moments of silence passed during which Nargis caressed Farheen's forehead.

"It's very heart-breaking to know, but Om has been kidnapped by Shaitan. I have prayed and begged Allah for mercy. He has offered two keys again, which you have to pick. You know which one to pick, Farheen," said Nargis with moist eyes, holding Farheen in her arms.

The child's sobbing had turned into loud wails.

"Is Om okay right now?" asked Farheen after a few minutes, breaking down again at the end of her question.

"He is in great pain and suffering," remarked Nargis. "But you can save him by picking the first key. This will mean that you will never speak with him again," she continued.

"I will do anything," said an inconsolable Farheen.

"I will relay your choice to Allah. By tomorrow morning, Om will be free from Shaitan," said Nargis as she kissed Farheen good night.

She gently got up and switched the table lamp off.

"We haven't caught up properly in a while," said Kiran, hugging Mahesh as he came into the house. Either Kiran needed some comforting, or, perhaps she saw that Mahesh needed some.

"How is work going on for you?" asked Mahesh. There was sadness in his voice.

"It's fine, but really weird. This man, Ranjit, is a creep and Monica's behavior seems odd. The other day I caught her sleeping under the bed. Unbelievable! And she gets new gifts from Ranjit every day," answered Kiran. "How has your day been? Has Sharma ji given an answer? Any other developments?" Kiran asked questions of her own as she ran her fingers through Mahesh's hair, massaging his head.

"Sharma isn't interested right now. He asked me to get back in touch after a year. I have two meetings lined up tomorrow through the advertisement that went out in the paper today. Babu has also set up a meeting with Chaubey, the manager of the State Bank of Jaipur in Jawahar Nagar," said Mahesh as he leaned on Kiran's shoulders. A few moments of silence ensued.

"Babu also visited two private schools today. One of them is asking forty-five thousand as donation and the other one fifty-five thousand," added Mahesh, moving his head back and looking into Kiran's eyes.

"Fifty-five thousand! How are we ever going to manage it? You barely have any money left. I haven't even got my first salary yet. We have already mortgaged mummy's gold chain, your wedding ring, sold our TV off. What else is left? And how much time do we have? Just about a month!" said Kiran. Her anxiety hit the roof.

Mahesh kept mum.

"We need to talk to Babu and Mummy about this. It is the question of Om's future, the future of our only son," said Kiran. Her eyes were moist. It was getting too much – all this struggle which did not seem to have any resolution at all.

Mahesh kept silent, but hugged Kiran.

"Don't worry, something will work out. State Bank of Jaipur has twelve branches in Jaipur alone and hundreds across the country. Something will fall into place. Also, I'll get Om for you tomorrow. You haven't seen him in days," said Mahesh as Kiran's tears wet her skin.

"Come quickly, Babu," shouted Mahesh as he waited outside his office by the side of his motorcycle. He wore black-pleated trousers and a blue-checked shirt. The carefully packaged machine was lying wrapped on the floor. This time, Mahesh had borrowed a brand-new set of crisp fifty and hundred-rupee notes from Ravi to use at the demonstration.

Babu arrived within seconds, almost running. Fathers-in-law have this sense of indebtedness and submissiveness towards the sons-in-law in India, just for the act of marrying their daughter.

Both Babu and Mahesh sat on the motorcycle. Babu knew the drill this time and Mahesh went about his business as usual.

At the State Bank of Jaipur, it was just another day. A regular affair of middle-aged to old people occupied majority of clerical positions. Mahesh and Babu were seated right outside Chaubey's cabin. Chaubey, the bank manager, was busy in a meeting.

"I have been observing for the last ten minutes. Those three cashiers at the cash counters are so slow. This queue at the cash counter is building up, instead of shortening," said Mahesh to Babu with a beam of hope in his eyes.

This was his big chance. A bank was where a large amount of cash was collected and counted each day. They also asked customers to separate smaller notes from the bigger denominations of fifty and hundred, which Mahesh's machine counted. There were hundreds of bank branches within Jaipur itself. Slowly, he could expand into the state of Rajasthan or the whole of India.

Mahesh and Babu saw a couple of gentlemen walk out of Chaubey's cabin. The meeting was over. Mahesh and Babu were then invited inside to start their meeting with Chaubey.

Chaubey was a really busy executive, so Babu had done a good job in being able to secure a meeting in a matter of a few days. Everybody, including Babu, understood the urgency.

The manager's cabin was quite modern for its time. In an age where polished wooden cabins were quite popular, his cabin was all glass – floor to ceiling, and right in the middle of the bank. Whatever was spoken in there did not reach the ears of outsiders, but all the proceedings were visible to the naked eye. The State Bank of Jaipur had 'Total Transparency' as their tagline. The glass cabin was testament to it.

Mahesh commenced the meeting as soon as Babu and Chaubey took their seats after exchanging the normal pleasantries.

As Mahesh kept the machine on the table and started giving the demonstration, a few curious eyes started gathering around the cabin, trying to get a sneak peek into what was happening inside. Word started going around that a man was pitching a machine which was able to count cash. Thus, if he succeeded, the machine would have the potential to take away many jobs from within the bank. The curiosity started building up. Two of the three cashiers began to take frequent water and toilet breaks to walk around the cabin to see what was happening inside.

Forty minutes later, the curious employees saw Mahesh and Babu shaking Chaubey's hands before leaving the cabin.

❖

"Mahesh ji, congratulations! Finally, all your hard work has paid off. The sales pitch was perfect this time. Chaubey was seriously impressed," said Babu as both walked towards Mahesh's motorcycle with a spring in their step.

Mahesh had just secured his first order for the machine which would be trialled in the bank for a week, and if found successful, Chaubey would order another two for the bank and set up a sales presentation for Mahesh to the Head Office of the State bank of Jaipur. This had the potential to be huge.

"Imagine, Babu, State Bank of Jaipur itself has twenty-four branches across Jaipur, three-hundred-and-twelve branches across Rajasthan, and six-hundred-and-twenty-five across all of India. At an average of two machines per branch, that is one-thousand-two-hundred-and-fifty machines for State Bank of Jaipur alone. And then, there are hundreds of banks in India," said Mahesh.

Babu's eyes lit up at this. He wished that Mahesh's venture would succeed. It had to. Everything depended on it.

CHAPTER 11

IT WAS ONE of the hottest afternoons of the summer. Naani had drawn all the curtains to a close in the living room to prevent sunlight from entering. The water cooler was on full blast and Om stood in front of it, drying his sweat away. Naani approached him from behind and wiped his face with a hand-towel.

"How does my lalla feel?" asked Naani as she ran the towel through Om's face. "It's the last day of school tomorrow, no?"

He kept silent.

"I'll fetch lunch for you." said Naani as she made her way towards the kitchen. A few minutes later, she served him his lunch.

"Where am I going to go after the school ends, Naani?" Om asked innocently as he grabbed a spoon of the dal Naani prepared. The spoon was as big as his mouth, perhaps even bigger.

"We are going to get you admitted to a new and better school," said Naani, looking away from him.

"Will that school be far away from here?" he asked again.

"No, lalla, very close. You will be able to come to me anytime you want," replied Naani.

"And Farheen? Will I be able to meet her whenever I want?" he asked again.

Naani paused and looked at him. She stayed silent but ran her soft fingers through Om's hair, massaging his head.

"What happened, Naani?" asked Om as he saw her grimace.

"Just a little discomfort in my chest," said Naani. "Can you bring me some water please?"

Om rushed to the kitchen to get her some water. She took a couple of sips and lay down on the cot in the living room. Whenever she lay down on the cot, Om was reminded of how tiny she was; not more than a hundred and fifty centimetres.

"Are you all right, Naani?" asked Om.

She nodded and held his hand. "Take a nap, Naani. I'll sit here by your side," he said as he sat down on a stool, holding her left hand in his. She closed her eyes and lay there motionless. There was such peace and serenity in her presence.

Mahesh and Babu entered the house with bags full of vegetables. Om sat beside Naani, munching on some Natkhat he had been saving since his birthday. Naani had given him twenty of those on his precious day so that he wouldn't need to go out in the afternoon's scorching heat.

"I rarely see Mummy sleeping at this time," murmured Mahesh to Babu.

Babu kept the bags of vegetables on the floor and stood in front of the water cooler; an unconscious ritual both Om and Babu followed.

Naani woke up, disturbed by the rambling going around.

"I'll make you chai in a minute," said Naani, as she forced herself out of the bed.

"No no, Mummy, you take rest. Today I'm going to make chai for you and Babu," said Mahesh.

Both he and Babu smiled at each other. Naani was curious.

"Mahesh ji has got his first order for the cash counting machines from Chaubey, the manager at SBJ," said Babu.

Naani looked thrilled.

Om, however, didn't quite understand what the fuss was about. Nevertheless, he had Natkhat with him, so he did not bother himself.

"Congratulations, Mahesh ji!" greeted Naani.

A few minutes later, Mahesh returned to the living room with three cups of chai. Om had seen all three of them smiling at the same time after a long time.

"Om, you are coming with me tonight. Your mother hasn't seen you in days. She needs you now," said Mahesh as he dipped his favourite biscuit 'Marie Gold' in his chai.

Om looked at Naani and immediately knew what she was suggesting. He had to go home to Kiran that evening.

A few minutes later, Mahesh held him in his arms, tickled his belly, and took him outside.

As soon as they moved out, Mahesh was in shock. His motorcycle lay on the road, its lights smashed into pieces, seats torn apart, and tyres stabbed with what looked like a powerful and sharp tool.

Mahesh and Om couldn't believe their eyes. The former ran towards his motorcycle and picked it up. He was shaking with nervousness as he couldn't process what had just happened. A few onlookers gathered nearby but didn't help at all.

Om saw Babu in the background.

"Mahesh ji, there's a call for you," said Babu. He was shocked to see what had happened to Mahesh's motorcycle. Mahesh picked the motorcycle up and parked it on its stand before he proceeded inside to take the call. Babu stared at the Yezdi and gestured at Om, who shook his head with raised eyebrows. Babu and Om walked back into the living room. A few moments later, Mahesh arrived.

"What happened to the motorcycle?" asked Babu as both Naani and Om looked on with worry writ on their faces.

Mahesh subtly suggested Naani to take Om away, which she did.

"Someone from the bank did it. I just got a call saying that if I supply even one machine to the bank, Om will meet the same fate as that of the motorcycle," said a very nervous Mahesh.

"That is barbarism, that is illegal. How can somebody do something like that?" said Babu, angrily. "Let's go to the police station right now," he added.

Mahesh was sweating. Naani and Om heard everything from the other room, nevertheless. Nothing could be hidden in such a small house.

"You know police very well, Babu. They need money to even file a complaint. I don't know. I'm going to wait till tomorrow. I'll call Chaubey tomorrow after my first meeting in the morning and discuss it with him discreetly first. I think I'll leave Om with you tonight," said Mahesh with a sigh as he stood up again to leave.

Given what had happened last evening, Mahesh was on time to work the next morning. Much to everyone's surprise. That day was a crucial day. He had two meetings lined up from the newspaper advertisement he had run after borrowing money from Ravi. He also was to speak with Chaubey about what had happened to him yesterday.

Mahesh had only just opened the door to his office when he saw the landlady, Jyoti, and her only daughter, Seema, step into the house. He raised his hands in the air and waved at them, without getting his gesture reciprocated. Jyoti had been widowed eleven years ago with her husband leaving her with two properties and their daughter. She lived next door on the second one, having rented the first to Babu and Naani.

Soon after they had arrived, six other people gathered along with them in the verandah. Mahesh was confused about what was going on. Nevertheless, he waved at each of them.

"Namaste, Mahesh ji," said Jyoti as she walked towards Mahesh. Her congregation followed her.

"Namaste Jyoti ji," Mahesh greeted her back.

"We need to speak with you and Naresh ji about something important. My relatives and I have been concerned about something; and it's urgent we talk about it," said Jyoti.

Mahesh was flummoxed. However, he said, "Sure. Can we do that in an hour because I have a meeting starting in ten minutes?" he asked in a very polite and courteous tone.

"Sorry Mahesh ji, that is what our concern is about. We need to have a discussion right now," Jyoti retorted as her congregation continued to look intently at Mahesh and his office.

Mahesh couldn't understand what their urgency was about and was getting nervous about his own meeting, which was due to start in a few minutes. Nevertheless, he knocked on the door leading to Babu's living room, just on the opposite side of Mahesh's office. Babu was quick to answer.

"Namaste, Mahesh ji," said Babu, a look of surprise crossing his face as he looked over to Jyoti and her relatives in the background.

"Babu, Jyoti ji and her relatives want to have an urgent discussion with us," said Mahesh.

Babu looked at Jyoti, Seema, and the rest of the people behind them.

"Please come in," said Babu as he looked around the living room, wondering how he would seat so many people. Om was off to his last day at the Alpha-Beta school. Naani was in the kitchen.

Babu guided Jyoti and Seema to the sofa while Mahesh and Babu took a seat on the cot. Jyoti's relatives preferred to stand.

"Namaste, Naresh ji," Jyoti addressed Babu. "See, you have been a great tenant for us. The rent has always reached me on time and the house is taken care of. We are thankful to you and Koshi ji for that. But as you know, I am old and I do not have much energy now. My relatives here, who are my well-wishers, have brought to my notice that Mahesh ji has been carrying commercial activities in the house, which is against the lease agreement, and I am not okay with it. I had been seeing some activity over the last few days but didn't question. However, my brother-in-law informed me that there was recently an advertisement in the newspaper with the address of our house on it. I am here today to ask you to stop any commercial activity at this address with immediate effect," asserted Jyoti.

Mahesh and Babu looked at each other.

"But, Jyoti ji, I have merely setup a small office with nothing more than a desk and two chairs. Most of my business work happens at client locations. I don't understand how it causes you any concern," responded Mahesh.

Jyoti looked at her relatives.

"Mr. Mahesh, we simply do not want any commercial activity in the house. Recently, there was a case where a tenant ran a business in the house for a few years and then when he was asked to vacate the house, he filed a legal petition. The courts granted him a stay order since it was his only source of income and his family was dependent on it," retorted one of Jyoti's relatives and looked back at Jyoti.

"See, Mahesh ji, I have no energy anymore for these things. I want to lead a simple life where I am not bothered with these things. I rented out this place to your in-laws to live since I saw they were an old couple and I wanted an easy, secure monthly income. If any complications arise, I am going to have to ask them to vacate the house," said Jyoti.

Babu and Mahesh had no idea what to say. Naani was listening to all this from the kitchen.

Just then, a doorbell rang. Mahesh's first prospective client of the day, the stockbroker had arrived. Mahesh realized that and became even more nervous than he already was.

"All right, I understand your concerns. Can I please, however, at least conduct my meetings today since they are already scheduled? Please?" Mahesh begged as he looked helplessly at Jyoti and her relatives.

They looked at each other and nodded. "Today is the last day," said Jyoti's relative.

Mahesh lowered his head and went out to receive the guest.

"How was the pitch to the stockbroker?" asked Babu as Mahesh walked into the living room. Babu, Naani, and Kiran were already sitting there.

"It was fine. He seemed impressed. He asked me to send him a formal quotation upon which he will get back to me. Need to continuously follow-up now," replied Mahesh. "When did Kiran come here?"

"Babu brought me here literally five minutes ago. He told me about the episode with Jyoti ji this morning," Kiran said and looked nervously at Mahesh.

Mahesh took a seat next to Naani on the cot with Kiran and Babu seated on the sofa.

"It's Om's last day at school today. He was asking me about where he will be going after this, yesterday," Naani mentioned, reluctantly.

Everybody in the room knew it. That's why they were there.

"Wherever I've been to, the donation is nowhere less than forty thousand rupees. We're not even close to it having that amount," said Babu with a restraint in his tone.

"Can you sell your scooter?" Naani asked Babu.

Babu stared back at her for a moment before saying, "How much will that fetch, no more than six or seven thousand. It's a bloody old scooter."

Mahesh was still running his ransacked Yezdi as it was left by the hooligans.

There was a brief, awkward silence in the room before Mahesh took a deep breath and said, "Babu, can you get the admission form for the government school tomorrow?"

There was a stunned silence for a moment, which Naani broke by saying, "Mahesh ji, never. I want the best education for my Om. Even if I have to die for it I will ensure it happens," said Naani, her lips shivering.

"I know, Mummy, so do I. But we just do not have any other option. All doors are closed right now," said Mahesh with a sigh.

Both Naani and Kiran had tears in their eyes. Everybody felt like a failure. Naani got up and left for the kitchen. Kiran followed soon after.

"Chaubey called me when you were in the meeting," Babu began saying, in a sombre tone that reflected reluctance. It immediately caught Mahesh's attention.

"He said that the employees have signed a petition and sent it to the head office regarding their concerns about cash counting machines. The head office has asked to pause any order until the bank management looks into the matter," added Babu.

Mahesh heard it, shook his head and looked out of the window. It was a major blow to his plans.

Another meeting he had lined up for the day was soon scheduled to begin.

CHAPTER 12

IT WAS THE last day at the Alpha-Beta for Om. That day the sun hadn't come out. It had rained heavily last night, and the hangover was still visible. The streets were waterlogged. The window panes were soddening. The skies still sported a grayish hue.

Everyone around him seemed to love it. The weather was such a respite from the scorching heat. To him, however, it just didn't feel right.

He had gotten used to the innuendos with Ratna Devi, the brief but profoundly enchanting moments with Farheen - her walk, her pink dress, the two pony tails and the water across her neck.

Ratna walked into the room in her favorite bright red sari. The mood was nonchalant, albeit emotional at the same time. It was the last day and everyone had been allowed to wear casuals instead of the usual school uniform.

"We are going to play a game today - Sunshine Sonata!" exclaimed Ratna as she kept a bag on the first desk, right in front of her favorite student, Arun. "Each of you will write your best memory during your days at Alpha-Beta and drop it in this box without your name on it. So, nobody knows who wrote what. Thereafter, each of you will come to the stage, pick a chit randomly and read out the memories for all of us to cherish and relive," added Ratna.

It was a beautiful and heart-warming exercise. Some expressions were funny, some emotional, some grateful. Each student was called out one by one on the stage in the classroom, asked to take a chit out from the box and read it aloud for the whole class to hear. Om's favorite was: "My most memorable moment was when Ms. Devi slipped and landed on her face while entering the class". It sent everybody into a fit of laughter except Ratna. She immediately looked at Om.

The final bell of the day rang. Almost everyone had tears in their eyes. Some hugged each other for what seemed like eternity while a few others gave gifts to one another. Om didn't really have a friend, but he went up to Arun and shook his hand. In spite of Ratna's love for Arun and her aversion for Om, the two always shared a friendly banter between themselves. There was an unsaid camaraderie between them, though they never spoke much. Arun returned Om's hug with an equally tight embrace.

Once the pleasantries were done with, Om moved towards the exit gate for the moment he had long anticipated and dreaded – the last rickshaw ride with Farheen. He had picked a flower for her – a lily. It was the closest to the color pink he could find in the garden opposite Naani's house. It was a color he associated with her; also, with Alpha-Beta and Jaipur.

But on that day, as he walked outside the school's gate, he saw Farheen already sitting in the rickshaw, next to Neha on the front seat. The rickshaw wasn't far away from him, but the steps he took seemed weighed down. It was the slowest he had ever walked. As he reached the rickshaw, he took the bag off his shoulders. There was a look of sadness on his face as he took his usual spot. Eventually, everyone else too, took their seats. Instead of Farheen, it was now Bobby who took the spot next to him. As the rickshaw started rolling, it hit Om that he hadn't brought the roti and the pickle that day.

Throughout the ride, he kept his neck turned backward, hoping to catch a glimpse of Farheen. She didn't look at him even a single time. A couple of times in between, he poked her shoulder with his index finger as well, but she didn't bother.

As they reached Farheen's house, it began to rain. Om was drenched. He saw Nargis at a distance, waiting to pick her daughter up. Tariq stood in the balcony with his eyes fixed on Om. That was the first time during that ride that he had turned his face away from Farheen.

"What happened, lalla?" asked Naani as Om ran into the house, sobbing and drenched. He didn't answer, but just continued to cry.

Naani got a glass of water and sat beside him, waiting with a kind of patience the devotees had for the object of their devotion.

He gradually stopped his tears and drank a glass of water.

"Farheen didn't sit with me today, didn't even look at...," Om had just started saying before he began crying again.

Naani poured him another glass of water.

"I'll get your favorite soup for you and then we'll go for a walk in the garden outside. Will you do this for Naani?" she asked politely.

He nodded as she wiped the tears off his face with her supple fingers. Her hands were remarkably delicate and soft, in spite of having worked decades in the kitchen, cooking, doing dishes for the entire household with bare hands. Or maybe, it just felt soft to Om; the hearts of lovers beat in their own rhythm.

Naani understood Om's love for flowers, for nature, and for the walks in the park. Even as a young kid of his age, he relished that. This appreciation of solace, of natural beauty, of silence was perhaps a result of a child growing up with two old grandparents around. There had been no other child in the house to play around with. No cousins, either. He seldom visited his parents.

"Naani, don't pluck the petals please. Why are you doing that?" he said, perturbed as Naani removed petals out of a rose flower in the community garden.

"Since you love them so much, I am going to keep them in our house, so you can enjoy them anytime. I'm doing it for you, and you are reprimanding me?" retorted Naani.

"But they will die if you pluck the petals like that. What am I going to do with a dead flower?" he asked Naani, concerned.

"Then why did you pluck a flower for Farheen in the morning?" responded Naani as soon as Om had ended his question.

Om had no answer. In that moment, he realized the hypocrisy.

"Friendships are exactly like that. They have a beauty, a fragrance, a magic, but only till the time they are alive; and they are alive only till the time we leave them free and nurture them with kindness. When we try to own them, monopolize them, control them, they die. The food for friendship is freedom. Remember that," said Naani in a tender yet assertive voice.

Om looked at her in awe. He hadn't thought about it when he plucked the flower for Farheen in the morning. In that moment, he found a new perspective.

Naani had such openness to teach him the subtle nuances of life – the profound truth that truly mattered. It wasn't a bookish knowledge. Neither were they from the scriptures or the religious doctrines. They were the truly significant things of life that added value to it. She never was aware of commerce or business or politics or religion, but she was aware of love, friendship, openness, kindness, and compassion. Her teachings shaped Om into setting the latter as benchmarks of intelligence, rather than the former.

"When I go to IIT to be an engineer, you will be old and I will not be in Jaipur. How will we meet then, Naani?" Om asked Naani as she held his hand. They started walking back towards the house.

"You will catch a train and come see me whenever you have holidays," said Naani, assertiveness seeping through her voice.

"But I will have other important things to do when I get older," he said casually.

Naani paused for a few moments before slapping the back of his head.

"Where's Om?" asked Babu as he entered the house with his pale blue kurta drenched in sweat. It was scorching hot outside.

"I just put him to sleep in our bed room. He needed some comforting," replied Naani as Babu took his kurta out and stood bare-chested in front of the water cooler. A minute or two later, he went and sat on the sofa, pulling the centre table in the living room towards himself and began filling out a form.

"What is it that you're doing?" asked Naani.

Babu paused for a bit before saying, "Filling out the admission form for Om".

"Which school is it?" Naani asked, nervously.

"Sarvodaya Vidyalaya in Jawahar Nagar," said Babu.

Naani's heart sank in her chest. Sarvodaya Vidyalaya was the government school in Jawahar Nagar, the suburb where Babu and Naani lived.

"There's no scope of education in that school. Our Om deserves much better. This is just not fair," said Naani with her eyes tearing up. She started towards the bathroom and slammed its door shut.

Naani only grew angry in the rarest of times. Babu could feel her anguish, but there was nothing he could do about it.

Om woke up feeling heavy that day. He felt as if a stone had been tied to his chest and he was carrying that burden wherever he went. He had no answer to why it was that he felt that way. It was like this invisible yet ubiquitous feeling of emptiness and void. There were times he felt like that. He used to think of it being a part of human existence. Whatever happened with Farheen had been causing turmoil within him. He kept pondering about it.

"Naani, give me some money," Om said to Naani as if he was ordering her.

"You already have so many packets of Natkhat left from what I gave you on your birthday," snapped Naani.

"I don't need Natkhat. I want to buy an ice-cream. Please Naani, please..." He kept nagging her and pulling at the drape of her sari, making her even more irritated and ruffled.

"I said, Om, not today. You've had a good sleep. Please go to the living room and read one of your books. I'll bring you tomato soup," Naani snapped back at Om.

He staggered. It was the first time his Naani had treated him like that. It was the first time in his life she had denied him and snapped back at him. She still couldn't come to terms that Om was being admitted into a government school. But he wasn't aware of that. He couldn't understand why Naani was being rude to him. He felt heavy as well; he was upset too. That wasn't a reason sufficient enough to be rude. He started tearing up and said with much disdain, "I am going to my home today. I will not stay with you."

His words hurt Naani. It hurt him deep to say that too, but then again, he had never meant to say it. The words had just come out of him.

Om stormed into the living room and then went outside the house, crying. He could hear Naani calling out his name from behind, but he ran outside and into the community park across the road. He spent the next couple of hours crying and sitting alone in the park, waiting for Mahesh to arrive and go back with him to his home – rather, Om's actual home.

———◆———

"You were very rude to Naani today, Om," said Mahesh as Om sat on Kiran's lap.

Kiran would always give Om so much love whenever she saw him, which was infrequent to say the least. Perhaps he should be more considerate towards her and spend more time with her, Om thought to himself.

"He didn't even come inside when I was having chai with Babu and Mummy. He just stood outside by my motorcycle," said Mahesh, looking at Kiran.

"Why, Om?" asked Kiran.

Om wanted to tell her how heavy he felt, about what had happened with Farheen, about how hurt he was when Naani had denied and snapped back at him. As Kiran asked him those questions, he realised that he didn't have the bond with her to open up and express himself freely; the kind of bond he had only with Naani, nobody else.

"She was rude to me first," Om told Kiran.

The landline phone rang just then. Mahesh answered the call.

"Om, it's Naani calling to speak with you," said Mahesh as he looked at Om from across the living room.

Om shook his head, sulking on Kiran's lap on the sofa.

Mahesh raised his eyebrows and said that Om should come over and speak with Naani.

But Om was adamant as well.

"No, I don't want to speak with her," shouted Om.

"Om, don't be discourteous," said Kiran as she put him away from her lap, indicating that he should get up and speak with Naani.

Seeing that Om was not moving, Kiran got up. Om understood that his mother would force him towards the phone. He immediately lay down the floor, grabbed the foot of the sofa, determined not to be moved.

Mahesh said something to Naani on the phone and hung up.

CHAPTER 13

WHENEVER OM USED to stay over with Kiran, she would make Mahesh sleep outside on the sofa and Om would sleep inside with her in the bedroom. Perhaps that is why most husbands avoid having kids for as long as they can. Perhaps that was why Mahesh wasn't keen on getting Om home unless she pestered him.

Om couldn't sleep at all. All he did was toss around and think about Naani. It had been some time since the anger had subsided. He was thinking whether the thing he did was right. What had made him behave that way? She had only snapped at him once. Couldn't he have repaid her love with more patience? Couldn't he have given her the freedom to be herself – the kind she had given him all along? Such thoughts crossed his mind the entire time and sleep eluded him.

Suddenly, in the middle of the night, around 2 A.M, the phone rang. It sounded louder than it did during the day. Om saw his mother's sleep breaking. He heard a few noises from the living room and the phone stopped ringing.

Within a few seconds, Mahesh came running into the room and spoke in a loud voice, "Mummy has suffered a heart attack. Babu just called. The ambulance is on its way. Rush, quickly."

Om didn't understand what Mahesh meant by a heart attack and what the consequences were. He had been feeling heavy the whole day. Perhaps Naani was feeling it too. But as Kiran rocked herself out of the bed, he sensed that it was something important and consequential. He got up as well.

In no more than a few minutes, the three of them were on Mahesh's motorcycle with Om quashed between his parents. All he could think about was Naani and what he could do to cure the heaviness in her heart.

⋘❖⋙

As soon as they reached Naani's house, Kiran jumped out of the motorcycle and ran inside. Om followed her.

Naani lay unconscious in Babu's arms on the ground. He looked quite helpless.

Kiran ran to the kitchen, brought a glass of water, and sprinkled it on her mother.

"I've already done that," said Babu. He was shivering.

"Babu, make her sit instead of lying down," said Mahesh loudly as he entered the house. "Kiran, go and get aspirin quickly."

Kiran did as said. Mahesh opened Naani's mouth as she lay half upright in Babu's arms and crushed a tablet of aspirin on her tongue. A few seconds passed by; there was no reaction from Naani.

All of a sudden, they heard the siren of an ambulance in the vicinity and looked at each other. The sound was approaching them. Mahesh rushed outside. The ambulance had arrived. A few neighbors had also lined up outside, curious to know what was going on. Paramedics rushed out of the ambulance, and within seconds, Naani was on the stretcher. Within a minute, all of them were with her inside the ambulance on their way to the nearest public hospital.

"What has happened to Naani?" Om asked Kiran as she couldn't stop her tears.

"It is a heart attack. It happens when the heart doesn't function properly," answered Mahesh, putting his hand around Om's shoulders.

"What happens now?" Om asked again, anxiously, since it all felt discomforting.

"We are taking Naani to the doctors now. They will be able to cure her," answered Mahesh.

Om was in shock. He couldn't comprehend what had happened. He still didn't understand what Mahesh meant by a heart attack, but it didn't feel like the appropriate time to be asking a lot of questions.

In about ten minutes, they arrived at the nearest public hospital. Naani was rushed into the emergency intensive care unit while the three of them waited outside in the waiting area. For the next half an hour, no one spoke. Suddenly, the door to the intensive care unit opened and one of the doctors came out.

All of them stood up from their seats that instant and greeted the doctor with an immeasurable anxiety that flooded their being. The doctor looked at them for a few moments, then lowered his eyes, and said, "I'm sorry to inform, but Mrs. Koshi Atri is no more with us."

There was a stunned silence. Om looked at Mahesh first, who was staring at the doctor; then he looked at his mother who took a deep breath, and then at Babu, who crashed on the seat just behind him. Within seconds, Kiran's tears turned into loud sobs. Mahesh and Babu had moist eyes as well.

Om figured out something was not right. He didn't say anything for the next few minutes, but tears started rolling down his cheeks.

After a few minutes, Om tugged Mahesh's shirt and asked, "What happened, Papa?"

Mahesh paused for a bit and said in a timid voice, "Naani has died."

Om was confused and maybe Mahesh could see it. "Naani has passed away to heaven and is no longer in her body," added Mahesh.

"What does that mean? Can I go and at least talk to her?" asked Om as tears started flowing down his cheeks.

"It means that there is no life in the body now. The heart has stopped beating. You will not be able to speak with her anymore." answered Mahesh, wiping some tears of Om's and then his own face.

Om was shattered. He stood frozen for a few moments and then started crying. "Why can't I speak with her anymore? You just said that she has passed away to heaven. It means she can come back as well," he cried out.

"No, son, that's not how it works. Once someone leaves the body, they cannot come back," replied Mahesh as he tried to take Om in his arms.

Om avoided him and headed over to the ICU where Naani's body was covered from head to toe under a white sheet.

The doctor instructed Mahesh to keep Om in check and not go near Naani's body until the doctors had completed certain formalities.

Shortly after, the hospital staff came with a stretcher and carried the body away, which was to be handed over to the family after some paperwork.

❖

The family brought Naani's body back to the house and placed it on a white bed sheet in her bedroom, with its head facing south. In a short time, a few neighbors had gathered to enquire about her well-being. Mahesh and Babu catered to the guests while Kiran went to the room and locked the door.

Om sat in one corner, feeling numb, still processing what had happened.

Kiran washed Naani's naked body with sponge and water, reciting a mantra. Once the cleaning was done, she tied the big toes together, which is supposed to keep the limbs in place. Pieces of cotton were placed in both the nostrils and both the ears. Finally, the body was wrapped in a white sheet, covering all the parts except the head. When Kiran was done with the ritual, she opened the door and asked for help from a few of the females who had gathered in the house. Together, they transported Naani's body from the bedroom to a small mattress placed on the floor inside the living room.

By that time, about thirty people had gathered in the house to offer their condolences. They were mostly neighbors.

Sheets were spread on the floor to seat the guests. There were sad faces and tears all around. The landlady, Jyoti, and her daughter walked in shortly after and took a seat on the futons. Mahesh and Babu greeted them with folded hands.

The local priest arrived soon after. Mahesh started the funeral arrangements for the cremation. 3 P.M was the time finalized for cremation in the Adarsh Nagar crematorium. It was the nearest one.

Babu had begun calling friends and relatives to inform them of Naani's demise and extended an invitation to attend the cremation and say their final goodbyes to the deceased.

Om stood right next to Naani's body, which lay right next to the wall, covered in a pristine white sheet. He walked up to her and took a deep and long look at her face. There was no tension in the face. Flowers were all over her body and eyes closed as if she was dreaming a nice dream. She looked beautiful, serene and loving, even in death; exactly as she looked like in life. Om couldn't stop tears from flowing down his cheeks.

The next couple of hours saw hordes of family friends and relatives arrive. He had never met most of them and wondered whether they even cared for what had happened. Or was it just a formality that they were conforming to because it was rude not to. He realized that Babu and Naani knew many people in their lives, yet, to him, they had always seemed lonely.

It was 2 P.M. and time to walk the body towards the crematorium. A few logs of wood were tied together to form a bier and the females placed Naani's body on it. Naani was tiny, after all.

116

Four males hoisted the body on their shoulders. That was done usually by the ones closest to the deceased. Females weren't allowed inside the cremation ground as per the ritual, so they bid their final farewell at the house from where the men took the dead body to the cremation grounds for burning.

Mahesh and Babu took the two front ends of the bier while two of Babu's cousins took the rear ends. Naani didn't have a big family of her own. Whatever little she had stayed in a small town called Boondi, which was five hours by road.

Om stood right next to his father, clutching on his shirt, as they walked out of the house, beginning the deceased's final journey from its home to the burning grounds. The sobs and the cries grew louder as the men departed.

Everyone began to chant, 'Ram Naam Satya Hai', which meant that the name of Ram was the absolute truth. The continuous repetition of that phrase meant that the dead body was no longer the truth since it had no life and hence, no 'Rama'. Anything without 'Rama' had no value whatsoever.

As the men walked out of the house further into the street on their way to the cremation ground, some of the lesser known neighbors came out of their houses and chanted the mantra with them. Others stayed in their balconies and paid their obeisance to the departed soul.

At the corner of the park, hidden behind the banyan tree at its corner, were Farheen and Nargis. Nargis had tears in her eyes as she saw Naani's body leave by her side for the final time. Om, however, had his eyes fixed on Farheen, who stood with her head bowed and hands locked together. He kept looking at her.

By the time they reached the crematorium, all the women in the vicinity had disappeared. The body of the woman who was most important in Om's life was bound to, soon. The bier was placed on the funeral pyre, its feet facing the north. All the strings and the bamboos of the bier were untied and placed on the pyre. The tied toes were also undone. Clarified butter drops were poured on the nostrils, ears, and eyes using holy basil leaf. Babu lit the fire to the funeral pyre as Om stared at his grandmother's face all along, right till the time there was no difference between the face and the flames.

What couldn't Om have done in that moment, to be able to speak with Naani just once before she left? If only he could go back in time and answer the phone when she had called to speak with him! He had turned her down with a scorn, with such disdain, when she had given him nothing but love with infinite patience. He couldn't stop thinking if her death was his fault.

There was a dandelion seed right by the side of the funeral pyre, which shone majestically as sunlight fell on it through an opening in the roof of the crematorium. He walked up to it, bent down to pick it up as his tears kissed his feet, and gave a final farewell gift to Naani.

PART 2

CHAPTER 14

OM WONDERED WHETHER his Mohawk looked like the one David Beckham had. He paced across the two-hundred-meter long corridor to reach his class. His hands grazed his hair to see whether the hair gel worked well. It was the first day of the new session at his school – Shah International. He was to join the 'A' Section of Class-IX.

In the last year – which was Class -VIII, the school had around three-hundred-and-forty-two students divided across nine sections. Each section had its own 'class teacher'. Most of the subject teachers, however, were common for all of them and would teach the different sections at different times of the day, divided into 'periods'.

As it happened at the end of each year, the students were distributed across different sections. That was an exciting and nervous time for most of them. The mischievous ones were sent into those sections whose class teachers were the most feared, the students who were rumoured to be in an affair were set apart, and the school toppers were put in Ritu Verma's class.

Om tucked his shirt in a hurry and adjusted his cross-body bag as he stood just behind the classroom door to his left. After he had tidied himself up, he took a step forward and turned left. Soon, he stood just outside the classroom door, facing the entire class.

"May I come in, Ma'am?" His voice was loud yet nervous.

"So, the class topper is late on the first day of new session," said Ritu as she looked at him while the rest of the class laughed. It was embarrassing, but he enjoyed the attention. She allowed him to come in.

Ritu was the darling of the school. Whether it was the Principal Mrs. Singh to the school chairman, Mr. Anand Shah; whether it was the Class I students or Class XII students; everyone loved her. Well, except other teachers in the school – both young and old – who envied her.

She had risen through the ranks quickly. Joining as a primary school teacher, she had made her way to leading the best group of Class -IX. Soon, if things progressed as they had been, it would not be long before she climbed up the ranks and represented Class XII.

She was young, not more than twenty-five. Some thought she looked like Kareena Kapoor while others thought Monica Bellucci. Om did not bother much about who she resembled. He just loved her voice – the way she spoke, that gentle and sensual tone of her voice.

He had just been moved to Class -IX-A, which meant Section A of Class -IX. Last year, he was in Class -VIII-D. He was the only one to be moved to the 'A' Section this year. He thought it was partly because the management put all the bright students under Ritu and partly because of his association with Karan and his sidekicks in Class -VIII-D. They were known for being the most mischievous lot.

"Om, before you take a seat, can you please show the whole class your innovative hairstyle?" taunted Ritu Verma, the class teacher, in her sweet but shrill voice.

Om couldn't help but snicker. He felt embarrassed yet was enjoying the attention. A few laughs rippled throughout the classroom. He could feel a few girls staring at him, which gave him a high.

"You know this hairstyle is not allowed in the school. Next time I see you with it, I'm going to call Viru. You know how he takes good care of people with fancy hairstyles," said Ritu with a sarcastic tone.

Viru Pandey was the physical education teacher as well as a discipline professor. At one-hundred-and-ninety-centimeters tall and over three-hundred pounds, he could have easily made a lucrative living as a nightclub bouncer. Instead, he decided to help the students live a 'disciplined' life. He wasn't fond of long hair or fancy hairstyles. He had become quite famous for organizing surprise barber visits to the school, which was a nightmare for many students.

Om proceeded to the back of the classroom with a coy smile on his face and took a vacant seat.

"Today, we also welcome the new admissions to Shah International School," announced Ritu as she referred to a piece of paper in her hand. It had the names of new students who had joined the school for the new academic session.

"Mohit Mehra, Manik Pasi, and Varsha Sen," said Ritu.

They stood up one by one except the last one. Nobody stood up when Varsha Sen's name was called out. The last one was a girl. The boys were excited to find out who the new girl in the class was.

"Seems like Varsha is not with us today. We'll welcome her when she joins," said Ritu. She then turned to the other two boys.

"Mohit and Manik, welcome to the greatest school in Jaipur and the coolest class in the school. Please introduce yourselves to the class," said Ritu, looking at Mohit and Manik. They gave a boring and nervous introduction about themselves, which most of them didn't even bother hearing. If Varsha were here and had given her introduction, Om gathered that the entire class would have paid a lot more attention.

The bell rang, disturbing his thoughts. Ritu's lecture was over.

The fourth lecture – period as it was called – had come to an end. The recess period arrived, which lasted for forty-five minutes every day. Students went out to have lunch or catch up with friends in other sections. The boys tried to chat up the girls. The girls would wait, most of them in groups, for the boys they liked to hit them up.

"Very cool hairstyle, eh!" Om heard a voice from behind him.

He felt a hand run through his perfectly styled mohawk. He could sense it was Sahil Garg, but he didn't want to react and create a scene. Perhaps, he was afraid it might get worse if he reacted. Within seconds, another hand made a run through his hair. It felt different. Om assumed it to be one of Sahil's friends who decided to imitate him. He didn't react.

Sahil was one of the most notorious boys in the school. He was always surrounded by three boys – Suraj, Danny, and Nimit. Om called them Sahil's side-kicks. Any one of them could have done the deed. Om didn't look back, though. The four of them weren't the most academically brilliant students. It was rumoured, though, that Sahil's father was one of the unnamed trustees to the school. Sahil would come to school driving a car of his own. He used to park it at the back of the school. It had become routine for boys and girls to watch him perform dangerous stunts after the school finished for the day.

Most of the students in Class -IX had touched 14; some of them were about to. Everyone used to wonder how he was able to drive a car to school at that age when the minimum legal age for driving was eighteen years.

Om continued pretending to ignore. He quickly hurried out of the class on the pretext of drinking water. He could hear people laugh behind his back, but he never once looked in their direction.

The school got over at 2 P.M every day. Om had just received his pocket money for the month. It was the same as usual. He used to get two hundred rupees a month – just enough to buy five or six pies from a nice bakery.

He took the public bus number 437, which dropped him straight in front of the 'Master Pool Academy' in the suburb of Sodala. He had off late developed an obsession with the game of '8-ball Pool'. Many of the 'cool' seniors in the school played the table game at that hip joint, ten minutes from the school. Some of them were accompanied by the most popular girls in the school. Their shirts were tucked out, sleeves folded, socks pulled down, and skirts rolled up.

The seniors played what was called as 'table money'. The one who lost the game paid the table's rent.

Om didn't have that kind of money. He was still learning. He always looked out for other novices to partner with and split the cost. However, he was a regular there. Some of the seniors and most of the staff at the Pool lounge had come to know Om by face, if not by name.

With a disturbed mind thinking about Sahil and his sidekicks, he began to play his usual game.

He lived with his parents, Mahesh and Kiran. They had recently moved to a one-bedroom house in Shyam Nagar, a silent suburb near his new school. His parents had taken the bedroom. Much to his dismay, he had to be content with a single bed and a study table set up in the living room. Mahesh worked as a life insurance salesman and Kiran took up her favourite job – being a mother and a homemaker.

Om had excused himself from reaching home directly after school, saying that he needed to go to Varun's place after school to study in a group and complete the school homework there. He used to do that often to avoid being pestered by his mother whenever he returned home late from school. Kiran was especially finicky about it. This behaviour of his mother used to remind him of Naani. He vividly remembered how easy-going and relaxed she was, even when Om was just a small child. Om learned an interesting fact as he grew older. Faith in the universe was a remarkable quality that not many possessed.

"You're very late today, lalla. Why do you do that? You know I get worried," said Kiran as Om entered the house.

The clock read 8 P.M. It wasn't too late. Darkness had not completely settled yet.

"We have started quadratic equations at school. There was a lot of homework I had to complete," Om responded.

"You always have something or the other each day. You're not the only one who has started Class Nine. Anita's son, Rahul, is home each day, straight after school," Kiran began her lecture.

Rahul was Om's arch-nemesis. He was the one his parents compared Om with. He was to Om at Shah International what Arun was to him at Alpha-Beta.

"I'm not Rahul," Om replied and threw his school bag on the couch.

Without looking at his mother, he went towards the washroom to cleanse his limbs of the dirt.

Kiran served Om dinner. It was bottle-gourd curry with three roti breads.

Om hated bottle-gourd curry. He thought of it as a bland, lifeless dish that deserved to be served only at the hospitals.

"We had this just two days ago", he said, frustrated.

"Be thankful you at least have food on your plate," retorted Kiran.

Om wasn't in the mood for another of his mother's lectures. He got up and moved to leave.

"Where are you going?" asked Kiran.

"I'm going out to have some real food," he replied.

He wanted to go out and eat Kachori at the new joint, 'Shankar Namkeen Bhandar' that had opened near the house. After all, he had just received his pocket money and it was still the beginning of the month.

Kiran gave in. She didn't have any option but to go with her son's desires. "Just don't be too late, lalla. You know there is Naani's death anniversary tomorrow," said Kiran. It was the death anniversary of Naani as per the lunar calendar.

Om nodded.

Just as he walked out of the house, he saw his father coming back home. He turned left even though the joint was to the right.

Kachori was a delicious, spicy, fried puff pastry round ball made of flour and dough filled with a stuffing of yellow moong dal, black pepper, red chili powder, and ginger paste. If done well, not many things in the world matched up to the joy it brought.

Just as Om had finished his plate, he heard a voice. It belonged to Ankit, one of his neighbors who studied in Class XII. He was just walking by to a game of badminton some of the other guys from the locality played at night in the community park. It was just a couple of blocks away from Om's house. Ankit invited Om to the game.

Om thought about his mother's request to come home early and Naani's death anniversary the next day. He wanted to decline the offer, but just couldn't. Ankit was an assertive fellow and Om had not yet learned the art of saying 'no'.

Om reached home at 1 A.M. He softly inserted the key into its designated hole and turned it around to open the lock. Then, with the precision of a professional burglar, he opened the door as slowly as he could, trying hard not to make any noise. Unfortunately for him, rust had accumulated on the hinges and no matter how precise one was, it was impossible not to make any noise.

He walked in with a sheepish face and got into the bed as quick as he could. The bedroom door opened and Kiran came out of it to grab a glass of water from the kitchen. She had been awake, waiting for Om to come back home.

CHAPTER 15

THE NEXT MORNING, Om reached school earlier than most. He wanted to take a seat at the other corner, opposite from where Sahil and his sidekicks had sat the day before. He placed himself at the second desk from the back.

There were usually four rows of desks in each class. Each desk had the capacity of seating two students. The first row, which students saw as soon as they entered the class, was next to a white-washed wall. The last one was right next to a line of square windows.

He could see only a handful of bags in the class. They were placed on seats to reserve them. It was said that a wolf marked its territory by peeing around it. Here, the other children marked theirs by placing their bags on the seats. One could remove a bag and seat himself on it, but then, it would be bad form. It was, to a large extent, an unsaid understanding that the seat belonged to whoever kept their bag on it. However, a new session had just begun and this was still an open market.

Om leaned by the side of the window, taking the sunshine on his face, which was an old habit of his.

A boy named Garv entered the class. The first thing Om noticed about him was the length of his hair, which he knew would be of particular interest to Viru. He had seen Garv around the school but had never been in the same section as him. On the last seat of the row, next to Om's, was a bag. Garv removed the bag and kept his instead.

The action amused Om. He was just thinking how bad of a form it would be to remove a bag from a claimed seat and sit there like a conqueror. He wondered if there would be a fight between this Garv and whosoever's bag that was.

Shortly after, another boy entered the class. Om had never seen him around the school, but he wasn't one of the new students who Ritu had introduced to the class. It meant that he was not a fresh joiner.

The unknown boy looked surprised to find his bag replaced by Garv's. The latter had just gone out to grab a glass of water. He picked up Garv's bag and kept it aside.

Garv came soon after. An intense exchange followed.

"I had kept my bag here," said the unknown boy, aggressive yet with a tone of respect.

"Yes, but I was sitting here the day before. It's my seat," replied Garv.

Om finally understood what was happening. He rolled his eyes at the exchange. He wished nothing violent would happen.

But, as luck would have it, it did get confrontational. Garv held the other boy's collar.

Om was the only other person present in the class at that time and felt the urge to intervene. He stepped in and pushed both of them away from each other. He picked up both their bags and placed them on two vacant seats. They both looked at Om for a second but relented a moment later. Considering Om was a school prefect, they didn't really have an option.

Within the next five minutes, the class began to fill up fast. Om saw Sahil walk in and instinctively turned his face in the opposite direction.

Sahil, though, had spotted him. Om felt it and it made him anxious. He saw Sahil throw a wry smile. Sahil's sidekicks followed soon.

The clock struck 8 A.M. Ritu, wearing a purple sari and her hair still wet from the bath she must have taken not too long ago, walked in. The boys in the class had barely taken a gasp when Garv decided to walk up to Ritu.

"That boy took my seat," said Garv.

"Ma'am, I was the one who kept my bag here first. He moved my bag and snatched the seat from me," the boy replied the next instant.

Ritu looked at the boy. "What's your name?" asked Ritu politely.

"Rohit Sahu, Ma'am," replied the boy.

"Rohit, pick up your bag and sit there." Ritu pointed to the vacant seat next to Om and continued, "Garv, you pick up your bag and sit there." She pointed to the vacant seat right in front of her on the front desk.

Garv wasn't happy. Perhaps he thought it would have been better if he had let the matter be how Om had sorted it.

"Hi, Rohit," said Om as he extended his hand for a handshake.

Rohit accepted the handshake and said, "You are Om. I have seen you around. You made me pay a fine last year when I wasn't wearing a tie to the school assembly," said Rohit with a smile on his face.

Om couldn't figure out whether it was a sarcastic smile or a smile that welcomed a friendship despite a turbulent past. Om smiled back. "Do you mind if I took the seat by the wall next to the window? I feel like soaking in some sun," Rohit asked in a polite tone.

Om heard that and thought whether a friendship could exist between the sun's two lovers.

"Sorry, Ma'am, may I come in?" asked someone at the class door within minutes of Ritu starting the first lecture of the day. It was a female voice.

No one in the class had ever seen her, but she did wear the school uniform. Her hair was all over the place, shirt half-tucked as if she had worn it in a hurry, and the bow that held the tie just below the collar button hung so loose as if she had forgotten it altogether.

Ritu turned to her left and observed the girl from head to toe for a second before she gave a nod of her head, indicating to her that she was allowed to come in.

"You must be Varsha," said Ritu even as everyone sported thoughtful faces, each trying to figure out who the girl was.

"Good morning, Ma'am. Sorry, I am late. I was out for a spring break vacation and just came back this morning," said the girl.

"Everyone, meet Varsha Tandon, new joinee to Class -IX-A. Please welcome her into the class and say hello to her during the break," said Ritu. "Varsha, if you need any assistance, please feel free to reach out to me. Also, you must be aware – your hair must be tied in a ponytail, shirt tucked in, and tie fastened right up to the collar button. Today is your first day, so you will be pardoned, but tomorrow onward, this will not sit well with Viru sir, the discipline-in-charge," she warned Ritu, though she had her usual sweet smile on her face.

Varsha returned her smile with one of her own. Her look was condiment. She was tall – taller than most girls her age. She was well-rounded too – physically, for sure. Her shirt seemed tighter around the chest than elsewhere. Her skirt appeared shorter on the back side because of it rolling around her buttocks. She had lush, spotless pink lips. Her hair was brown, ending just a tad below her shoulder. Her skin had a dusky complexion – exotic, some thought, while her legs were like a freshly draped chocolate-colored silk sari as some passed a comment in whispers.

She looked around for a vacant seat and took one in the row next to Sahil's.

Everyone looked at her. Most girls had a look, which anyone could tell was a mix of envy and curiosity. Most of the boys had a smirk on their faces. Sahil and his sidekicks looked at each other, so did Om and Rohit.

Varsha didn't look at anyone. She just opened the knot of her thick hair, ran her fingers through them a couple of times, and tied them high up.

Om took the public bus number 122, which ran straight from school to home. He knew that Kiran would be waiting for him. It was Naani's eighth death anniversary according to the lunar calendar. As he rode the bus, he could not help but reminisce about how he had picked up a dandelion seed from the ground and placed on Naani's body, which laid peacefully on the funeral pyre. That action had been etched into his mind like a photograph, fresh as the morning dew, although it had been eight years.

Her love, her life, her lessons, her conduct, her demeanor – everything she had stood for, in one way or the other, inspired Om's outlook and approach to life. It was because of her that he was studying in a good, private school, getting the quality of education he deserved. It was because of the money from the life insurance company after her death that Om was able to get admission in a private school. She had not only lived for him; she had died for him too. Perhaps it was on purpose, as if she had summoned her own death so he could have a bright future. Naani would have thought of it to be a small price to pay for her lalla's prosperity.

Om always carried her picture in his wallet. Not that he believed that she was only the body, or that face, or that form; she often told him not to believe that. But he wanted to keep her close to himself, in some kind of a tangible way.

Babu had passed away soon after Naani did. Perhaps he had lost any will to live without her and the existence was kind to him.

The death anniversary of an ancestor involved a few rituals meant to pay homage to them. Om wouldn't usually participate since he was against dogmas, especially a ritual he didn't resonate with. But since it was Naani, none of that mattered. He did as Kiran asked him to, for Naani's sake.

The local priest was already at the house. He started the ceremony with 'pindadaan' – an offering of rice, cow's milk, ghee, sugar, and honey in the form of 'Pinda', a rounded heap of the offering, to the ancestors. He insisted that this 'pindadaan' be done with whole-heartedness, devotion, and respect to the deceased soul to fulfil it. It was then followed by 'Tarpan' – an offering of water mixed with black sesame, barley, Kusha grass, and white flour. It was believed that ancestors were appeased by the offering of Tarpan. The final stage involved feeding the 'Brahmins'. The word 'Brahmin' literally meant someone who was one with the 'Brahman'. The Sanskrit word for 'Brahman' was cosmos but was eventually reduced by the society to a social class. Om and his family belonged to that class as well. Mahesh would, with pride, assert it every now and then during a family get-together or whenever some conversation brought the topic up. Om, though, never bothered.

The local Brahmins were at the house and had a plate full of freshly prepared food placed in front of them. As Om looked at that, for a brief moment, he considered being a Brahmin that Mahesh always used to say he was.

The next day, Om arrived early at the school as usual, but to his surprise, so had Sahil. For a moment, they were the only two people in the class before Om sheepishly escaped. He didn't want to be alone in the class with him, so he just stepped out and waited for the class to fill.

He saw Varsha from across the corridor. He couldn't help but observe her tightly-tucked in shirt kissing her breasts as she pulled up her skirt. There was a moment where everyone in the corridor looked at one person – Varsha. Not far behind her, Rohit came in. Rohit and Om spotted each other from a distance and saw Varsha get in the classroom. They both exchanged glances.

"Why aren't you inside the class?" asked Rohit, walking up to Om.

"I was trying to strike up a conversation with Varsha," said Om, too embarrassed about telling him the real reason why he was out of the class.

"Well, come into the class then! That's where she is" Rohit said, gesturing.

Om nodded and followed his friend into the classroom.

As they entered the classroom, most of the students had arrived. To Om's surprise, Sahil had placed his bag right next to the seat where Varsha sat the day before and was already chatting her up. It looked like they were having a good time. She looked entertained.

Sahil then suggested her to look Om's way. Both of them looked at Om and began to laugh. Om immediately became self-conscious. He started looking elsewhere and went straight to his desk. Rohit followed.

"Bro, during the recess, go and talk to her," said Rohit.

"I can't do that. What do I say?" Om responded.

"Just go and introduce yourself. Say your name and ask hers," replied Rohit.

136

"I already know her name," said Om.

Rohit looked at him like he was an idiot, which Om probably thought he was.

⬥

The recess had started. Om expected Sahil to be around Varsha, but he was out with his sidekicks. Varsha, on the other hand, had four girls around her, who had been friendly to her since the day before. They followed her wherever she went, often laughing at her jokes and complimenting her.

Rohit and Om had both just had lunch. The former egged him to go and introduce himself to her. The latter, however, just couldn't muster up the courage. But he told Rohit that he would do that when Varsha was alone. He knew that she wasn't going to be alone at any point in time. Perhaps it was a good excuse to shy away.

The chat between Varsha and the girls soon ended and Varsha went back to her seat, sitting alone with legs crossed. Her skirt was more than half-way up her thighs. She had opened her hair during the recess and applied some balm to her lips. As soon as she was alone, Om felt a push on his back.

He stared at Rohit who gazed at him and bobbled his head. Before Om could respond, Rohit got up and shouted out to Varsha, "Hey, Varsha, this is my friend Om. And I'm Rohit. Welcome to Shah International."

Om was stunned and stood there frozen.

Varsha smiled at the two of them and said, "Hey guys! Thanks for the welcome. Why don't you come over here and have a chat?"

Om's nervousness hit the roof. His friend got up and gave him a pat on his back. He followed him, still wondering why Rohit had done that. Was Rohit not confident that he could have done it himself? He totally would have, so thought Om. Perhaps Rohit knew better.

"Hi, Om, I've heard about you. You were the batch topper last year, if I'm not wrong" said Varsha. Her voice was incredibly soft and sensual. Her head tilted slightly towards her left. Her open hair fell all over the right side of her face. She ran her fingers through them and gave them a flick. Om gave her a nervous smile.

"He is one of the most intelligent people you are ever going to meet," said Rohit.

Om laughed it off.

"And what about you, Rohit? What is your talent?" asked Varsha, winking at Rohit.

"I play good cricket. I'm fairly good at mathematics, but I'd say, my biggest talent is friendship. I make friends and I will do anything for them," said Rohit.

In whatever little time Om had spent with him, he could testify that.

Varsha seemed impressed before they were all startled by the ringing bell. The recess was over. Mrs. Kaur, the history teacher, walked in immediately as if she had been waiting outside the classroom the whole time. Couldn't even give them a breather, thought the three of them.

Sahil and his side-kicks immediately followed her in. They saw Om and Rohit with Varsha. Sahil and Om locked eyes for a second before Om looked elsewhere and made his way back to the seat.

CHAPTER 16

"SO, THIS IS where you usually go out after school. I saw you a few times walking in this direction as I was in the school bus back home," said Rohit.

Om had taken him to the Pool lounge. It was the first time Rohit had bunked his school bus. The school buses were pretty expensive and only some of the students opted for it. Rohit was one of them.

To Om's surprise, it was Rohit's first time playing Pool. Considering he belonged to an affluent family, Om assumed he would have some fancy past-times. Playing Pool, he thought, was one of them. They had a good half-hour for which they were supposed to pay twenty rupees.

They had a few good games before their allotted time was over. Rohit took the money out first to pay for both of them, but Om insisted on pitching in with his share. Rohit wouldn't budge, so Om put ten rupees back in the front pocket of his bag without his friend knowing.

"Do you want to taste the greatest Kachori on earth?" Om asked Rohit, as they both walked out of the Pool lounge.

"I love Kachori," replied Rohit.

Om took him to Shankar's Kachori joint, which was just across the road from the Pool lounge. Om looked at Rohit taking his first bite of the Kachori. Being a frequent visitor to Shankar's eatery, he had seen many people take their first bite. The expression on their faces was priceless and similar, irrespective of gender, caste, color, creed or religion.

Om paid for the Kachori, insisting that since Rohit had paid for the Pool table, he should pay for the Kachori.

"I don't know why you have that roti bread and lemon pickle every day for lunch. This is what you should be having," remarked Rohit.

"I love that, equally," replied Om with a smile as they started walking again. None of them realized they were walking in the same direction even though their houses were in the opposite direction.

"Let's go this way. I'll show you the house of the girl in my locality that I really like," said Rohit, pointing towards a lane.

They started walking in the direction Rohit pointed.

"You never told me about this girl you like. What's her name?" Om asked, taunting Rohit in a way.

"Her name is Sara. She recently moved to the locality, maybe about six months ago," replied Rohit. "We used to see each other every evening when I would go out in the streets to play cricket, and she was out with her friends playing their evening games."

Rohit paused for a breather.

"We would exchange looks every now and then, and then one day, I told her my name and asked her to meet me in the park after school. She was very nervous as someone from her family might find out. They are very strict, she tells me. But, she met me anyway.

We meet every Friday in the park after school. She makes the excuse of staying back at school on the pretext of practicing for the school choir," added Rohit with a twinkle in his eyes. Om was listening with intent.

"That's her house." Rohit pointed towards a three-storey house with a Mercedes parked in front of the house.

"Wow, looks like a rich family," said Om.

"Yes, rich but regressive! Sara isn't allowed to receive phone calls from boys after school and cannot step out of the house after her father gets home," responded Rohit.

"Do you want to come to my place? You can stay over as well if you want to," said Rohit. "I've got a computer and Dad just got an internet connection the day before. I've been browsing these things called websites and chatting on Yahoo. I also have this really cool game on the computer. It's called Zelda Classic." added Rohit, trying his best to lure Om.

"That sounds incredible, bro. I have heard about the internet, websites and Yahoo, but haven't experienced it yet. Thanks. I'll do that some other time, but not this evening. It was Naani's death anniversary the day before and my mother has been a bit emotional. I think I should be spending some time with her and not be late," replied Om.

Rohit blinked his eyes, expressing his understanding.

"No problem, bro. See you tomorrow. It was a great day today. We will do this often," said Rohit as they hugged. "Oh, and I was wondering if we should enter the school together every day. Will look cool and will get Sahil and his side-kicks burning," said Rohit as he winked at Om.

Om felt a little nervous as he heard Sahil's name.

"Meet me outside the school gate at 7:45 A.M tomorrow," added Rohit, before Om could say something.

They hugged and bid each other a good night.

———◆———

At 7:40 A.M, Om stood in front of the school gate. He was nervous as he didn't want to bump into Sahil. He hid behind some of the small trees near the gate and looked out for any sign of Rohit.

Rohit arrived ten minutes later than scheduled.

"Sorry, I'm late, bro. Come, let's go in," said Rohit.

Both of them began their walk towards the classroom through the corridor.

Rohit wasn't a popular student in the school, but he had an aura of self-confidence around himself. The way he walked and carried himself spoke volumes about him. That aura told Om that his friend didn't give two hoots about what the others thought of him. It didn't matter to Rohit whether he had fifty people around him or five or none. He didn't need people's approval either; neither did he seek attention. That was a remarkable quality. In their short friendship so far, Om had already begun to look up to him, inspired by his personality. Om found that attractive and profoundly liberating.

They walked into the classroom with Rohit entering first. Varsha waved at them.

Sahil stared at Rohit the whole time, which Om couldn't help but notice. They took their seats. With that, Ritu walked in for the first lecture.

"All right, students, the school management has appointed a class monitor. For Class -IX-A, it is Om," announced Ritu.

Everyone looked at Om. He was surprised and nervous, but also happy. Rohit patted his back.

Om got up and went to collect the badge for the Class Monitor, put it on his sleeve, and returned to his seat. A small round of applause followed soon. But what made his day was seeing Varsha clap for him.

"Bro, I came across something incredible last evening after I got home," Rohit murmured into his ears.

Om looked at him and quickly moved his eyebrows up and down, asking what it was about.

"There was no one home and I dialled the internet. I was creating an account on Yahoo when I saw an advertisement for this website called Desibaba.com; and I went ahead and clicked on it," Rohit continued murmuring.

"Sshhhh, no talking in the class please," said Ritu, looking at both of them.

They immediately went quiet.

However, a minute or two later, Rohit murmured again, "It had naked pictures of such stunning and beautiful women."

Om started staring at Rohit, perhaps with the widest set of eyes he might have ever seen. "No way. On a computer screen? Cannot be real," Om murmured back.

Rohit tilted his head slightly and did a quick dance with his eyebrows. He meant it was the real deal.

"For the first time I saw what a breast actually looks like," Rohit whispered back. "No way!" replied Om, immediately.

"Om, what's wrong with you? You've just been made the class monitor and you can't stop yourself from being distracted during the class," exclaimed Ritu, threw a chalk towards them both.

They both immediately sat up straight and went quiet before looking at each other a few seconds later.

———◆———

Recess followed soon. Rohit went to say hello to some of his friends in the other sections. Om remained in the class by the side of the window. Varsha and her girlfriends were out of the classroom. So were Sahil and sidekicks. It felt good to be alone; just like those old days at Alpha-Beta.

The thought of Alpha-Beta brought memories of Farheen. He wondered where she was; whether she was fine and taken good care of.

"Look at this cool dude here and his shirt." Om heard a voice as he saw Sahil and his sidekicks approach him. He looked petrified seeing them.

"Look how smart this hunk looks," said Sahil as he started tugging at Om's shirt.

Om couldn't even look him in the eye. He wished Rohit was around.

"And these black shoes," said one of Sahil's friends, who went by the name of Nimit, as he crushed Om's shoes with his feet, spoiling the neat polish Kiran used to apply on his shoes each morning.

"Look at our handsome class monitor," said Danny.

All of them started laughing.

144

The school bell rang. Sahil pulled the shirt out of Om's pants and pushed him away. Om felt humiliated but couldn't manage to look Sahil in the eye. The latter left before any of the teachers walked in.

CHAPTER 17

"YOU LOOK UPSET, beta. What happened? Did anyone say something to you at school?" asked Kiran as Om walked into the house straight after school and threw his bag on the sofa. "And what did you do with your shoes?" Kiran continued to ask, looking at the state of his shoes.

"Will you let me relax for at least five minutes?" Om snapped back. "I haven't even reached home and you have started blabbering. You should look for work to keep yourself busy."

There are many times we don't realize what we end up saying in the moments of deep unconsciousness. They are usually the things which we don't mean to say, but in anger or fear or any other unconscious emotion, they tend to come out. He didn't know what had happened the last time she worked, and that she had worked only to support her son's education. In that moment of unconsciousness, he side-lined how much she had sacrificed for his upbringing. He saw his mother tear up, which immediately made him feel a pang of regret. But, it was too late. She stormed into the kitchen with moist eyes.

Mahesh walked into the house, wearing trousers, a shirt and a neck-tie. It was the perpetual uniform for any salesman. He had done fairly well for himself over the last eight years; at least to the extent that there was money to pay the rent, Om's school fees, the bills, groceries and eat out once every three to four months. But nothing more than that. However, even this felt like a heaven compared to the crisis a few years ago during Naani's last days.

"I want a new shirt, Papa. Look at this. This would be loose even for you, let alone myself," said Om.

Mahesh looked at the shirt. "It's perfectly fine. You are a young man who is still growing. You are going to outgrow this shirt in no time. We don't have money to keep buying new shirts," responded Mahesh as he finished getting into his lungi. Some habits never changed.

"But everyone makes fun of me because of this. And who knows whether I will grow anymore or not? I want a new shirt or I am not eating anymore," retorted Om.

He was adamant.

"All right, don't eat then. Kiran, don't serve food to Om," responded Mahesh in a loud voice so that Kiran, who was by then in the kitchen, could hear.

Dinner was served to Mahesh at 8 P.M. Kiran wanted to serve to Om despite being angry with him. She did not look at him in the eye or speak with him.

Mahesh forbade her from serving Om dinner.

Om was also adamant not to eat. The clock struck 9 P.M. He hadn't eaten.

The clock struck ten. He still refused to eat.

Kiran looked at him a couple of times. After all, she had the heart of a mother.

An hour passed. Om's resolve was shaking, but he didn't budge.

Mahesh was also resolute. He went to bed at midnight. Om just sat on the sofa in the living room, the same two-seater sofa Naani had in her house.

At midnight, Kiran came to Om with food served in a plate and two hundred rupees. She didn't look at him or speak with him, even then, but gave him the food and money. He hugged her.

———— ✦ ————

The next day before the class commenced, Om bought a new shirt from the school uniform shop right next to the school. Its signboard read 'Sethi Stores'. Rohit's father knew the owner and it got Om a discount of forty rupees. That made him think immediately of Pool and Kachori.

After getting his new shirt, there was a spring in Om's steps. He felt more confident and attractive. The classes went on as usual during the day. In between, Rohit kept telling Om about Sara, the girl he was fond of; Yahoo Messenger, which he kept using to chat with strangers; and the new websites he had been discovering.

Rohit and Om went out during the recess into the school ground. It was a cool, breezy day. The weather was perfect for a stroll outside even though it was a dry and hot summer. They returned to the school building with about ten minutes to spare before the recess came to an end. Varsha stood at the classroom door and smiled at both of them as if welcoming them to a chat.

"You look a little extra beautiful today," said Rohit, looking at Varsha.

Om wondered how Rohit could be this smooth without putting much of an effort.

Varsha smirked at Rohit.

"How did you go with the Maths homework the day before?" Om asked Varsha. It was obviously a nervous attempt.

"I was stuck on question number five, which I want to discuss with Ma'am in the class today," replied Varsha.

"Om can help you with that. He is the topper of the class after all," responded Rohit and looked at Om.

"Why don't we all exchange numbers? We can help each other out with assignments and maybe even study together during examinations," suggested Rohit.

Varsha seemed to like the idea. Rohit took out the pen from his pocket, took Varsha's hand, and wrote Om's and his own home landline numbers. Rohit then handed over the pen to Varsha.

She took Rohit's hand and wrote her number, and then, she took Om's hand in hers.

He felt as if his hand held a bouquet of flowers that was so soft that it felt unfair for his rough hands to come in contact with those supple fingers. She finished writing her number on his hand and grinned.

Rohit and Om gave her a smile, walked into the classroom to make their way to their seats. As they turned around, Om noticed that Sahil had been watching them all along.

"You took her number so easily, bro," Om said to Rohit as they walked towards the Pool lounge in Sodala after school had ended for the day. it was a really hot day, but Om was a rich boy after the discount he got while buying his new school shirt. He wanted to play Pool and eat Kachori. Hence, he tagged Rohit along with himself. Rohit wasn't far away from getting the Pool bug.

"I just go for it, bro," replied Rohit. "I have come to understand that with emotions that belong to the realm of heart - such as friendship or love, there is no room for intellect or thought. It's not like economics or business or history where those qualities will help. In realms of life that belong to the heart, you just go for it and express yourself honestly, and accept whatever happens of its own accord," professed Rohit.

Om never knew him to be a thinker or a philosopher, but whatever he said reminded him of Naani. He liked every word that had been said.

"For example, I am going to propose to Sara the next time I see her. I'm not going to ponder over it, brood over it; I am going to do it. I have a voice within me that wants to be with her right now and I will pursue it," he continued.

Om listened in awe and with intent.

They reached the Pool lounge and started playing before one of the seniors challenged Om to a game of 'table money'. Om's game had reached a decent level. He had always wanted to take it further and delve into that competitive zone, but money had been scaring him away.

Rohit egged him on as he always did.

The game began. Om was nervous, which reflected in his game. He missed shots that he would otherwise score easily in the usual games. Rohit looked at him, perplexed. Even he couldn't believe what was going on. The first contest was a 'race to five'. That meant whoever won five games first, was declared the winner of the contest and consequently, had to pay the rent for the table. Om lost the first contest within half an hour.

The senior then challenged him to another contest -- a best of five. That meant whoever won three games first would win the contest. Om just wasn't able to get his game right in the first contest and felt perturbed because of that. Yet, on Rohit's insistence and encouragement, he took the contest up. He lost again: three games to one. That was all his riches down the drain within an hour. His own personal riches to rags story.

Om paid sixty rupees at the end of the two contests and thought about quitting Pool altogether.

"Let's go and have Kachori. It was just an off day. Your game is way better than this. You just need more competitive practice," said Rohit as he tried to comfort Om.

"No, let it be. I just want to go home. I hardly have any money left over anyway and we're not even half way through the month," responded Om in a jaded voice.

"It's on me. Just forget about the money," said Rohit and placed his arms around Om's shoulder.

The next day, the history teacher had reported absent. So, Class -IX-A had a free period. That was one such period the students looked forward to, considering they had nothing to do except chat and play games for a whole period. However, there were a few times when a strict teacher would come to the class and spoil it for everyone.

That day was not the time. The teacher who came to the class was Preeti Kaur, the economics teacher from Class XII. Five minutes later. She said, "Do whatever you want to do as long as noise doesn't get out of this classroom."

The students became ecstatic. She got up and left, closing the door behind her. The students looked on in awe. Now they knew who they wanted their class teacher to be when they reached Class XII. It was Preeti Kaur.

As soon as Preeti left, everyone was upto something. Some played book-cricket. Some just played cards. A few of them dared to get out of the class. If caught, they were in for some serious caning from Viru, Rohit joked to Om.

Rohit and Om played pen fight, a super fun game where you placed your pens on the desk and struck them with your fingers like you would a striker on a carom board in a bid to oust the other pen from the desk. Whoever's pen was the last to remain on the desk, won.

Across the desk, Om saw Sahil, Varsha and their sidekicks play truth or dare. Om couldn't listen to what was going on, but he could see bits of it. They had created a closed circle and spun a bottle. Whoever the bottle pointed to after it stopped spinning was given a choice - truth or dare. If they selected 'truth', they needed to truthfully answer a question. And that could be anything. No restrictions. If 'dare' was selected, they would be given a task, which needed to be done, no matter how risky or grotesque.

At first, Om saw Danny get up and pull a boy's chair just as he was about to sit down. The poor boy fell on the ground. The entire group caught on a fit of laughter. Next, it was Neha, who seemed to have said something that caused everyone to open their eyes and mouth wide. She must have chosen 'truth', Om thought to himself as he continued his pretence of being interested in the pen fight. This went on for the next few minutes as Rohit continued beating him at the game of pen fight, which Om couldn't be less bothered about.

A minute or so later, Om saw everyone in that group look at Varsha. It seemed like the bottle's head pointed at her. Sahil said something to Varsha at which everyone seemed to be taken aback. It indeed was Varsha's turn. A couple of girls dropped their jaws and shook their heads while still giving coy smiles. Varsha laughed but shook her head. Sahil and his sidekicks were persistent. Within seconds, everyone in that group went quiet.

Varsha took her hands to the top of her shirt and opened the first button after looking around. She looked at Om for a split-second before he turned his gaze away. She then moved on to the second and the third button. Her hands were over her breasts. She paused for a moment and looked around, but not at Om.

Om was looking at her again, discreetly.

She then unbuttoned the fourth one. Everyone who followed their game had their eyes popped out of their sockets. She held the ends of her shirt, one with each hand, and quickly moved them apart to expose the black brassiere that held her breasts firmly together.

Within a split-second, she quickly closed the ends of her shirt, did the buttons, and looked around. Sahil had his hands to his mouth and seemed to make a gesture, but Varsha shook her head, as if denying something Sahil had suggested.

The bell rang. The free period had ended and it was time for the next lecture.

"I saw what happened during the free period," Rohit said to Om as the bell for recess went off.

"Bro, go and talk to her. Show your interest in her, let her be aware. And make an effort. That's what Sahil is doing. And you're just sitting and watching," he added.

What Rohit said did make sense to Om, who knew it but didn't know how to muster up the courage for that.

Rohit must have sensed that and walked towards Varsha who stood by the class door all by herself.

"Come, let's go to the door. Come on!" said Rohit as he got up from the seat and started moving towards the door; their lunch still half uneaten. Rohit didn't give him a choice. He was already out of his seat.

"Om thinks you look really beautiful today," Rohit told Varsha as he started to move out of the class, suggesting that they should go and drink some water.

Om was frozen; he totally hadn't seen that coming.

Varsha gave Om a coquettish smile and winked at him.

154

He was still frozen with a thousand thoughts going through his head.

She had a bottle of water in her hands. She asked Om if he wanted some water. *Am I sweating?* He asked himself and tapped his forehead gently with one of his hands.

Not getting any answer from Om, she opened the water bottle, bent her neck backwards, opened her mouth wide open and poured the water from the bottle straight into her mouth. She looked like a Roman Goddess drinking straight from the Trevi fountain. A little bit of water spilled over onto her white shirt. "Oh sorry!" she said as she wiped off the spilled water.

Om had no idea how to respond. He started looking elsewhere, conscious that she might observe him staring at her breasts like a creep.

"Ummm, how did you go with the Trigonometry homework the other day?" asked Om as he finally managed to muster up some courage to say something. It was ridiculously boring, but, at least, he had initiated a conversation. Before Om got an answer, he got a strong push from his right, throwing him on the floor.

It was Sahil.

Om had not even begun to get up from the floor when he saw Rohit shove Sahil to the ground, right beside where he was. To Rohit's left were Sahil's sidekicks.

Rohit, then, turned to his left and pushed one of them. His name was Danny. Another one of Sahil's side-kicks, Suraj, took a step towards Rohit. Rohit took two towards him and stared him in the eye. He was like a lion disturbed during his peaceful slumber. None of them did anything. Om was up on his feet, so was Sahil.

"Why are you interrupting?" Sahil began to show some aggression and walked towards Rohit. He signalled his side-kicks to join him.

Rohit didn't say anything. He took two steps forward, paused for a moment, and then suddenly, grabbed Sahil's collar and pushed him all the way back to the blackboard.

"If you touch him ever again, I'm going to break your fucking neck," shouted Rohit into Sahil's face. Om and a couple of other students in the class tried to break the scuffle apart.

A few people had gathered around the class to witness the drama. Varsha watched it from the background as well. The bad-boy of the class fighting the academic topper over herself.

The bell rang. The recess had come to its end.

Rohit let go of Sahil's collar.

Sahil broke into a cough and took a deep breath. "You don't know who my father is. If you have the guts, see me outside today, fucker," dared Sahil. He was furious but didn't have the guts to take Rohit on. His sidekicks egged him on but kept themselves on the sideline.

A student warned that one of the teachers was approaching the classroom. It was time for the next lecture. Everybody quickly went back to their respective seats.

The scuffle was over. Everybody had retreated to their seats and expected the Civic-Science teacher to walk in as per the time-table. However, to their surprise, it was Ritu who walked in with a bunch of circulars in her hands.

She handed over the circulars to a boy named Arun who was sitting on the front bench. Om wondered about the obsession the teachers had with boys named Arun; and the obsession boys named Arun had with front benches.

Arun went around the class distributing the circular. When he was done, Ritu read the circular out loud for everyone.

"The school is proud to organize a group trip to Goa. It will be a five-night trip - one night each back and forth to Goa, and three in Goa. The group will be supervised by the school teachers at all times, in addition to the tour guides. We will be staying at a four-star resort or equivalent. The detailed itinerary is printed at the back of the circular. The total cost of the trip is INR 3,250 per person, all inclusive. The last date for submitting the trip money to your class teacher is 24th April," announced Ritu.

There was a buzz in the classroom. All knew Goa to be the party capital of India. Every one of them had heard stories about it. There were tales of how gorgeous foreign women roamed its beaches in bikinis. Om had never seen a woman in one, except in pictures. It was the stuff of dreams for boys his age. Everyone looked at their friends and others around them. Om looked at Rohit, who seemed excited. It was quite a wonder how his friend could so seamlessly move from rage to excitement in a short span of time.

"You are coming," murmured Rohit into Om's ear.

"I want to. But I don't know how I am going to arrange the money," he responded.

"Leave that to me," said Rohit.

Om didn't want that. He didn't want to take any favours, especially Rohit, who had just got into a fight because of him. "We'll discuss it after school," said Om.

Ritu left, making way for the Civics teacher, who waited outside the classroom.

CHAPTER 18

"I NEED TO convince my father to give me the money," Om said to Rohit.

"Go home today and speak with them," Rohit replied as both of them walked across the corridor towards the exit gate. The school had ended for the day.

As soon as they reached the exit gate and turned left towards the bus stop, Sahil emerged right in front of them. He had been hiding behind a few small trees near the school gate. To his side were his sidekicks and seven other people, who looked like hired goons. Rohit and Om had never seen them. They seemed older, and bigger than any of them.

Rohit and Om looked at each other. Om was sure that they were both thinking the same question - how was Sahil able to get a message out of the school to arrange these people? Before they could even guess an answer, a hockey stick hit Rohit's left leg. He fell to the ground.

To Om's eyes, there was only a flicker of movement and he couldn't comprehend anything until Rohit had actually fallen down. He was never the confrontational sort until then, but that moment felt more than just a simple fight. He jumped towards the goon who had hit Rohit and landed a full-blown punch on his nose. The goon started bleeding. It took him a second or two to regain composure before he landed a big blow back to Om's face.

Rohit had gotten up in the meanwhile but was pinned down again. They were two against eleven. Considering that Om was an absolute amateur at this, one could say that it was just one against eleven. Rohit at least seemed to have the heart of a fighter.

Both of them were on the ground, curled up and secured their heads with their hands. The first few blows were hard and painful, but after a few, Om didn't even feel a lot of pain. He wondered if Rohit was all right. He was waiting for the goons to get tired and leave.

"Viru is coming out," shouted Nimit, who was standing in front of the exit gate to make sure that they did not get caught by anyone from the school staff. Within a second, the blows stopped. Sahil and his entourage ran full speed and vanished from sight.

"Who was it?" asked Viru, the discipline in-charge, as he walked in. Om and Rohit were still on the floor. That's when Om started feeling the pain again.

"Sahil, Nimit, Danny, Suraj, and seven other people," replied Om. He had copped fewer blows than Rohit. He was bleeding from his leg and the upper end of his right eyebrow. He stood up with a little help from Viru. So did Rohit. It looked like none of them had broken any bones.

"Come inside, we'll get you bandaged. And I want to listen to what you boys have been up to. Om, you are getting more and more troublesome by the day," Viru said, almost in a way that taunted Om.

❦

Om returned home. Viru had got a school car to drop them both. They were meant to appear before the principal, Mrs. Singh, the next day.

"Oh my God! What happened to you, lalla?" exclaimed Kiran as he looked at Om.

In that instant, she completely forgot that she had been upset and wasn't supposed to be speaking with him.

"Was just a small accident after school," replied Om.

"He is lying. He got into a fight. This doesn't look like an accident," remarked Mahesh. He was home early that day.

Om didn't respond.

"Since when have you been getting into fights? Just keep away from all these things. The next few years of your life are about your studies and you getting into IIT. Focus on that instead of focusing on fights and getting new clothes," Mahesh took a jibe at Om.

Kiran gave Mahesh a stare, suggesting him to stop. She opened the bandages slightly to check the extent of the damage. "It looks better than I thought it to be. You will be totally fine in a few days. Thank God," said Kiran.

Om wasn't too fussed by then; he was more concerned about the meeting in the Principal's office the next morning. Yet, he felt a strange sense of satisfaction. The fight -- his first fight -- had empowered him in a certain way. He felt lighter, happier, even though he was beaten up. He didn't know why he felt that way.

"Papa, there is a school trip going to Goa. All of my friends are going. I want to go as well," Om said to Mahesh as the latter drank his chai and ate a break-roll Kiran had prepared for him.

"You have just come home from a fight, broken and bruised. Plus, I hardly see you studying these days. Now, you want to go to Goa?" exclaimed Mahesh in a loud voice.

Om didn't say anything.

"How much is it?" asked Mahesh after a brief pause.

"Don't worry about my studies, Papa. I will top the examinations, leave that to me. I will not let you down. It is only three-thousand-two-hundred-and-fifty-rupees, all inclusive," said Om, purposefully keeping the mention of the amount to the end.

"Three-thousand...! No way. I don't have that kind of money," said Mahesh as he looked away from Om, leaving him angry, anxious, and frustrated at the same time.

"So, you have the money to buy a new watch for yourself and a new briefcase, but you don't have money for me," complained Om.

Mahesh looked taken aback by that. He seemed surprised at Om's acute observation.

"Okay, so I am now going to leave all money with you and you can take care of the rent, your books, your school fees, all the bills, and everything else. Okay? Let's do this and then you can go to Goa," Mahesh lambasted Om, clearly agitated.

"You always do this. Whether it is for a shirt or a game or a school trip." Om started to cry before rushing into the bathroom.

He felt helpless. He never had the money to do the things he wanted to do.

⬥

The next morning, Viru had asked the two of them to report outside his office. Both were then taken to the Principal, Mrs. Singh's office. As they entered it, Sahil and his sidekicks were already there with their hands behind their backs, heads hung and eyes looking down at the floor. Even the biggest troublemakers were afraid of Mrs. Singh and her office. It had doled out many tales of suspensions and rustications, over the last twenty years.

The Principal's office was twice their classroom's size. Awards, trophies, and certificates decorated her table and the walls. At the corner of the room to where the entrance door was, sat her personal assistant. At the other end, there was a lot of space. It seemed that the frequent summoning of students was taken into account as an important parameter while designing the room.

"Sahil says that you guys hit him in the class during recess the day before. Is that true?" Mrs. Singh asked Rohit and Om. Her tone was assertive, voice loud and firm.

"But that isn't a valid reason to bring goons and attack someone with hockey sticks," Om replied immediately.

Rohit stared at him for his audacity and the tone with which he had answered the Principal back.

Before Om knew it, a tight slap landed on his right cheek, the one which didn't have any bandage.

"You don't answer me back in that tone. Do you get that?" said Mrs Singh in a loud voice, enough to send shivers through Rohit.

"But, you only asked me a question, which I answered," retorted Om, after a brief pause.

It was apparent that he was still frustrated about all that happened the day before -- first inside the school during recess, then outside it, and then at home. Another tight slap came flying at Om.

"Yes, Ma'am, I was the first to hit Sahil in the class. He has been bullying Om for a very long time. He pushed Om so hard that he fell on the floor. That is when I hit Sahil," Rohit intervened. He had had enough.

Mrs Singh turned her attention towards Sahil.

"Ma'am, Om was standing at the door of the class blocking my way in. I just tried to get in the class so that I would not be late for the lecture and Om just wouldn't let me in. Then he did the drama of falling to the floor. I have nothing to do with it," said Sahil.

Rohit and Om were both staring right into Sahil's eyes by the time he finished saying that. "That is complete and utter lies, ma'am," said Rohit, before Om could say anything. His voice was shrill because of the urgency with which he said that.

Mrs. Singh looked at all of them one-by-one but didn't say anything.

"Listen, all of you. This is my last warning to each of you," she said after a long pause. "If such an incident ever happens again, you are going to be rusticated from school. Not suspended, mind you, but rusticated forever. Do not test my patience. And you, Om, you are no longer the monitor of Class-IX-A. We can't have someone so misbehaved to be the monitor of the class," added Mrs. Singh as she removed the badge from Om's sleeve and handed it over to her assistant.

All the students made their way out of the room. Om was shaking with fury and looked at Rohit. Both of them couldn't believe the confidence with which Sahil had cooked up lies.

"I am sorry to get you in this trouble. It was my fight, not yours. You shouldn't have to go through this. I'm really sorry, bro, and thank you for all you have done for me over the last few days," said Om in an emotional tone to Rohit as the school finished. They were walking towards the bus stop.

"Come on, bro! These bruises will be gone within days. We are brothers. Your fight is my fight unless you are fighting with me, in which case you are gone," joked Rohit.

Both of them smiled before they realized that their faces were still sore.

"It was not just a question about you. It was a question of standing up against what I thought was not a fair way of treating anyone. He physically attacked you. It's another thing to say something from the mouth. It's our mouth and our tongue, and all of us should have the freedom to make whatever noises we want to make using them. But a physical attack is completely different. It crosses the boundary and I will stand up for anyone whose physical freedom is violated. So, it was not just about you, it was about my own values," added Rohit on a more serious note.

Om was beginning to greatly admire the philosopher in Rohit. There were so many layers to him, which he was starting to uncover, if only bit by bit. Come to think of it, this was a boy he had never heard of until about a few days ago. Now, he was not only his best friend but also someone Om looked up to, although he never let it be known.

"You should come to my house tonight. You've never been home. Even mom and dad want to meet you," said Rohit as he jumped right in front of him.

Om was a bit hesitant, especially because he was a bit embarrassed to meet Rohit's parents. After all, it was because of him that their son had suffered injuries. "Come on, I'll create you a Yahoo account, we'll play games and surf some websites." Rohit winked at Om.

Om knew what he meant by 'websites'. He thought about it for a few seconds and then nodded his agreement.

Om couldn't board the school bus, which Rohit used, so they just caught the public bus to Rohit's home.

———◄●►———

The bus numbered 418 dropped the two boys right in front of Rohit's house. Om wondered why his parents spent so much money on the school bus when public transport was so convenient. But he then entered his house – a sprawling duplex – and figured that money wasn't much of a concern for them.

The ground floor had a living room as large as Om's house. There was a sitting space on the left with four plush sofas, each facing the other one. A Venetian glass center-table adorned the space between the sofas atop a Persian rug. Slightly in front of the sitting space was a finely-crafted computer table – home to the latest Apple Macintosh computer.

Om had never seen an Apple computer in his life. There were a few computers at school which ran Microsoft Windows. Students would get access to them once a month. The entire class had to work with just four computers.

There were three bedrooms on the ground floor. One to the corner was his, Rohit told Om. Rohit's parents had their bedroom upstairs – the master one. The other two on the ground were vacant, or so Om thought.

Right at the end of the living room was a huge poster of a bearded man with the most intense gaze Om had ever seen. It was so intense that Om felt uncomfortable. Though it did not stop him from becoming curious and inspired, all at the same time.

He asked Rohit who he was.

"Osho," replied Rohit. "My father is a big fan of him. He spent some time with him at his ashram in Oregon, United States. I have been reading him lately as well," said Rohit as they walked towards one of the seemingly vacant rooms. Both entered a room, full of books neatly arranged over many layers of shelves.

"This is my father's library," informed Rohit.

The library was almost as big as the living room and filled with so many books that one could barely see the walls through them. Om walked around and saw books from authors, most of whom he had never heard of – Fyodor Dostoevsky, Kahlil Gibran, Friedrich Nietzsche, Richard Bach, Jiddu Krishnamurti, Omar Khayyam, Franz Kafka, David Bohm, and Leo Tolstoy. The list went on.

"I've heard a lot about Tolstoy and his work, 'Anna Karenina'," said Om.

"This is possibly my favourite book," said Rohit as he handed Om a book. The title read 'The Book of Mirdad'.

"It is an extraordinary book. My father made me read it when I turned thirteen. Hardly anyone knows about it, but it is a masterpiece like no other," said Rohit. "If there is only one book you read in your life, make it this one."

Rohit's mother walked in. She must have heard noises from downstairs, Om thought. He felt a bit nervous and embarrassed to face Rohit's mother, given what Rohit had recently gone through because of him.

"So, you must be Om. Very nice to meet you, son. Rohit has great things to say about you. Maybe in your company Rohit can also start scoring some marks in examinations," joked Rohit's mother.

"Thank you, Aunty. I think Rohit has much more than grades going in his favor," Om said, feeling a bit sheepish. He was not good at taking or giving compliments.

"Come to the dining table and I'll serve you both lunch," said Rohit's mother. They both walked out.

Rohit's mother and their full-time housemaid brought two big bowls. One had 'dal makhni', a typical North-Indian dish brought to India by the Mughals. It was a preparation of black beans simmered in creamy gravy, sautéed with tomatoes, onions and mild spices. The second bowl had 'bhindi masala' – a dish made of okra cooked with spices and often other vegetables such as onions or tomatoes. Along with them came roti breads, rice, raita, salad, and pickle.

Om's mouth dripped saliva just by looking at them and smelling the aroma.

"Please take your time, feel comfortable, and if you both need anything else, just let me know. I'm going to take a nap and I'm sending Meena out to collect clothes from the laundry," said Rohit's mother and started walking up the stairs towards her bedroom. Meena was the house maid.

⟴

"Bro, the maid takes a long time to get the clothes from laundry, and Dad isn't home for another hour at least. Let's connect to the internet now. I'll show you Desibaba.com," said Rohit in an excited tone. By the time Om could respond, Rohit had already scampered away and switched the computer on.

To connect to the internet, a dial-up connection had to be established.

"Get one of the cushions from the sofa there," said Rohit.

Om was confused. "What does a cushion have to do with connecting to the internet?" Om asked Rohit.

"The modem makes a lot of noise for a few seconds when it is establishing a dial-up connection. I'll place the cushion on top of the modem to cancel out as much sound as possible so that Mummy doesn't find out," explained Rohit.

It made sense to Om then.

Rohit entered a username and password in a dialog box that had appeared on the screen. Before clicking the 'ok' button, he took the cushion from Om and placed it tightly above the modem. As soon as he clicked the 'ok' button on the computer screen, the modem dialed a number and started making weird noises. It was as if an alien civilization was sending cryptic messages. After a few seconds, the noise stopped and Rohit looked upstairs for the last time to see whether his mother had woken up or not. They had been successful in connecting to the Internet.

He opened what was called a 'web browser'. It was a software that helped access websites. He asked Om to keep an eye upstairs towards the door of his parents' bedroom. Should it start to open, Om was to immediately signal Rohit by tapping on his shoulder. Rohit was sitting on the chair, right in front of the computer screen and Om stood to his left. Rohit started typing 'Desibaba.com', letter by letter. He then looked at Om with a naughty smile on his face before hitting the enter button on the keyboard. Desibaba.com was fully loaded on the computer screen in a few seconds.

Right on the home page was a ravishing woman – blonde, fully naked, posing side-on by the corner of a swimming pool. Her firm breasts needed no support as her disrobed bathrobe hung on her arms exposing half of her derriere.

"Oh my God! So, this is how breasts look like… this is… unlike anything I've ever seen." said Om. Both of them were staring at the screen, captivated by the feminine energy in front of them.

"I wonder what they feel like when you touch them…" remarked Rohit.

Om was stiffening. So was Rohit.

"Click on that girl, bro. Enlarge the picture." Om said to Rohit. It was a thumbnail image of what looked like a stunning dark-skinned woman at a picturesque white-sand beach. Rohit clicked on the thumbnail. A new page opened up on the web browser and the image started loading.

At the same time, Om turned around and monitored the bedroom door upstairs. The picture started loading, so slow that it almost drained his patience. The face appeared first. The seemed to be at a beach. Then, her neck and the top of her chest, though her nipples weren't visible. Within a few seconds, her breasts, became visible. She had big, dark brown nipples and she was squishing her breasts between her arms covered in sand.

Both the boys were feeling heat building up within their body. It was starting to get uncomfortable around the crotch.

In the next instalment, her legs were loaded on the screen. They were spread wide and wore red stilettos. Eventually, in front of the two adolescent boys, was a full-blown picture of a vagina. It was clean-shaven, cherry blossom pink. It was the first time Om had ever seen a woman's genitalia, even in a picture. It seemed strange and felt unnatural since all his life he had been used to having something stick out of his body.

He was, however, far more fascinated by breasts. Their curvature, the way girls would hide them and yet flaunt them, in a subtle way – it all created an aura of mystery around them.

"But, Rohit, how do girls pee if they do not have something to aim with?" asked Om.

"I had the same question. I asked my cousin brother. He said that the girls sit and pee," answered Rohit.

"That sounds really weird. I can't even imagine myself sitting and peeing," said Om, still perplexed.

"Let me click on this image here," said Rohit as he hovered the mouse over the image of what looked like an exotic Latino.

Rohit had just clicked on the image when they heard a noise. A moment later, Rohit's father entered the house. They froze. Rohit had a panic attack and fumbled. Om stepped in front of the screen to give Rohit some time to close everything.

"How come you are early today, Papa?" asked Rohit, concealed behind Om.

"I had a meeting nearby and it got cancelled last minute. What are you doing on the computer?" asked Rohit's father.

Rohit got up from the chair and stood by Om's side.

Om immediately turned around. The computer was switched off.

"Nothing, Papa. I was just showing Om how to create a new e-mail account on Yahoo," replied Rohit.

"You are sweating so much. I'll turn the air-conditioner on," said Rohit's father. He turned the air conditioner on.

Om had never been in an air-conditioned room before. Within no time, it was like there was no summer in the state of Rajasthan at all.

"Rohit speaks a lot about you, Om. I'm glad to finally meet you today. Please feel at home. Hopefully in your company, this fool will also start scoring some marks," said Rohit's father as he looked at Rohit.

"Thank you, Uncle. Rohit is much more than just marks in an examination. In fact, I am actually inspired by him," said Om.

Rohit's father gave them both a polite smile.

"I have never seen such a big, personal library in my life," said Om.

172

"My grandfather started building it and I just carried it forward. It tends to get a little difficult at times because I have to relocate frequently because of my work, but you are right, this is my biggest treasure," said Rohit's father.

"Bigger than Rohit as well?" joked Om.

All of them shared a short laugh.

"All right, make way for me now. I need to send some emails," said Rohit's father.

In that moment, Om suggested that he should leave. His mother would be waiting for him, he told Rohit and bid him goodbye.

CHAPTER 19

RITU LOOKED UPSET that morning. She usually began the class with a smile on her face, but not that day. The classroom was noisier than usual. Perhaps it picked on Ritu's energy.

"Bro, last night dad came into my room to bid me goodnight. Just when he switched off the light and was about to close the door, he said, 'Rohit, you should learn how to delete history from the web browser'," Rohit murmured in Om's ear as Ritu had begun taking the class. "I buried myself in the blanket and was hoping for the bed to eat me up," he added.

Om looked at Rohit with his eyes wide open for a second and then sniggered. It caught Ritu's attention.

"You two! Om, in spite of being stripped of the class monitor role, you haven't learned a lesson," Ritu shouted at the two of them.

"Rohit, get up," continued Ritu.

Rohit did as he was instructed.

Ritu looked around for a second and then said, "Go and sit there." She pointed to the desk where Varsha and her friend, Neha, were sitting. "Varsha, get up and come sit here," added Ritu.

Om couldn't believe what was happening. Sure, the teacher intended the move to be a punishment, but for him, there wasn't anything else he could have asked for. Sitting close to Varsha was the dream he had nurtured for long.

Varsha and Neha seemed displeased, the latter in particular.

Rohit turned around to pick up his bag from the seat and winked at Om as he left. Om could barely control his simper. Ritu wasn't amused.

Varsha took her time to walk to her new desk, walking slowly in front of the whole class. Ritu noticed the attention she was getting and beckoned her to move fast.

She came next to Om's desk and suggested that she wanted to sit by the side of the window.

Om turned his legs ninety degrees to the right even as he sat, to make way for her to get in. She took a seat, and for a split second, his fingers touched her left thigh. It was like touching a feather. A current ran through his spine as if he was being tickled all over.

She seemed to have felt his touch because she looked at him for a second and then smiled back.

All that was on Om's mind throughout the day, was Varsha. He asked Rohit to take his school transport home and walked himself back home instead of taking the public bus. He felt like dancing; he wanted to dream about Varsha.

He imagined his hands touching Varsha's thighs and how he felt an electricity running through his body. He kept walking aimlessly, building a million air-castles.

Om was suddenly startled by a car that honked without barrage. His dream got a rude awakening. He didn't realize he had been leaning towards the center of the road. He sheepishly raised his hand to the driver, apologized for the mistake, and moved back to the side.

A few moments later, he started thinking about the dance steps for the song "Meri Mehbooba", a song from a recent hit film called 'Pardes' in which Bollywood superstar Shahrukh Khan urges the imaginary love of his life to break through the picture he had drawn while imagining how she might look like. Om imagined dancing solo to that song in front of the whole school in the amphitheater. He dreamed of everyone going gaga over his performance and Varsha watching, sitting right in the front row. By the looks of it, it didn't look like the dreams were going to stop anytime soon.

"Bro, it's something strange I want to discuss with you," Om said to Rohit, in a self-conscious way, as he met him outside the school the next day.

"It's just been one day that Varsha has been sitting with you and you're feeling strange already," taunted Rohit, with a wry smile on his face.

Om gave a sheepish grin.

"I got up this morning with my underwear sticking to my skin. I went to the bathroom and saw that there was a solidified white clump sticking to my underwear," said Om. "I was scared it might be some disease but was too embarrassed to tell anyone at home about it."

Rohit started laughing. "What were you dreaming about last night?" he asked, still laughing.

Om was embarrassed but felt that he was on to something. "Varsha," he said, embarrassed.

"Tell me more about it," Rohit said with a wink and a laughter he couldn't control.

"It was random. I was first by the side of a beach. A white-sand beach, same as the one on Desibaba.com where that gorgeous woman was naked. Varsha was sitting by the beach. Her breasts were fully exposed. I went and sat right next to her. I didn't look at her at first since I was shy, but she turned towards me and held my hand in hers. She then placed my hand gently on one of her breasts as she kept her eyes locked with mine. Her thick hair open, and sun shone brilliantly around the silhouette of her head. She then placed her hand on mine, which was on her breast and pressed it. All the while, looking at me in the eye. Right in that moment, I felt something rushing from the base of my penis, right out of my body. I woke up and felt something warm inside my underwear. I was sweating and had palpitations. I couldn't go back to sleep again, as much as I tried. I wanted to be in that dream again" said Om, seemingly embarrassed.

"You're quite creative, I must say" sneered Rohit.

"Stop laughing, bro, tell me if you know something about it," responded Om.

"Don't worry, it is normal. These are called wet dreams. It happened with me as well a few weeks ago. It was the night after Sara held my hand for the first time. I felt weird and scared, but let it go. Then it happened again when I watched Desibaba.com for the first time. I thought something was wrong with me. The next day, I couldn't concentrate at all in school, and immediately afterward, went to Yahoo.com and searched about it. You can search about such things on Yahoo and there are articles that come up. In one of the articles, I read that wet dreams happen when a boy becomes a man. You're a man now," said Rohit, and continued to laugh at Om.

"Anyway, we will discuss this in detail later. I have a surprise for you today," said Rohit as they walked into the class.

Om looked at him and thought what mischief he might be up to.

"I'm taking you to meet Sara today", said Rohit.

Om was excited, but a little nervous, as he was when meeting new people, especially girls.

The school had ended for the day. Rohit and Om walked through the district park in the suburb called Civil Lines, where Rohit and Sara lived. They reached a desolate bench in the corner of the park where they expected Sara to come. Though Sara studied in the same class as the both of them, she did so in 'Chandra World School', which was one of the poshest schools in the city. Some international students studied there as well.

Om and Rohit's school, 'Shah International', just had the word 'international' in it. There wasn't a single international student studying there.

Some distance away, a girl in gray school uniform walked towards them, wearing a cross-body bag.

"That's Sara," Rohit said with a gleam in his eyes.

As the figure got close, Om could see her clearly. She was tall; taller than Rohit with beautiful, light green eyes, brown hair, and a remarkable glow on her face. One could see why Rohit, or anyone else for that matter, would be smitten by her.

Rohit and Sara hugged, and then kissed each other on the cheeks.

Om extended his hand, but Sara leaned over to hug him. He stood rooted to the spot, clueless and feeling awkward.

"You must be Om," she said.

Om smiled, but from the corner of his eyes, he noticed his friend's wink.

"Rohit tells me you're so cool," she said.

Om had no idea that he was. He was simply wondering what to say next, which by any standard, wasn't cool.

"Which Chapter are you on in the Mathematics class these days? We're on co-ordinate geometry."

That was all he could say.

He noticed Rohit looking at him with a strange expression on his face.

There was an awkward silence before she replied, "I'm not sure. The last I paid attention, we were doing linear equations in two variables," replied Sara.

Both Rohit and Sara laughed as they held hands tightly.

"So, tell me about some of your hobbies," asked Sara.

If it was one question that baffled him, it was that. Sara had to throw him into the deep end. He couldn't answer that question, especially when these days fantasizing about Varsha seemed to be his favourite hobby.

"I like studying" was all he could manage to say after much thought.

Rohit and Sara broke into a hearty laugh.

"He's cooler than this, trust me. He's a great player of eight-ball Pool, as well," said Rohit as he wrapped his arms around Sara and held her hands.

Rohit signalled Om subtly to stay and wait as he walked ahead with Sara.

Om did as Rohit suggested. Sitting on the bench facing the two lovers, he saw Rohit walking as if he had all the time in the world, hand-in-hand with Sara. After a while, he saw Sara say something to Rohit. Om couldn't help but notice a certain reluctance on his friend's part. It was as if Rohit did not want Sara to leave at all. This sight confounded him and made him blush at the same time. He wondered whether he would feel such a thing with Varsha too someday.

After a while, Rohit and Sara gave each other a long and tight embrace. Sara looked around towards Om and waved at him. He waved back.

Rohit walked in reverse with his back towards Om and face towards Sara. He wanted to look at her every moment as she walked back home, which was a short walk from the park.

"I'm going to propose to her," said Rohit.

"Seriously? What are you going to say to her?" asked Om. He was both surprised and curious.

"I'm just going to tell her that I like her and will ask her to be my girlfriend," replied Rohit.

Om wanted to be this brave. What was stopping him? He thought to himself.

Mahesh was watching the news on the free-to-air national television network, Doordarshan, when Om entered home.

"Rabri Devi granted bail. Lalu Prasad Yadav's bail plea rejected. He will remain in judicial custody," announced the news reporter on live television.

"A few years ago, Lalu Yadav was the same man shaming the Congress for the Bofors Scam when he formed the government with VP Singh," said Mahesh with a sigh.

Om could not be less bothered about what happened with Lalu Yadav. He was much more interested in a place roughly two-thousand-and-three-hundred kilometres away from where that politician was – Goa.

He kept his school bag aside and took a seat on the sofa next to Mahesh. He deliberated on how he should ask his father permission to go to Goa. The last day to secure a spot on the trip was close.

"Do you want some water?" Om asked Mahesh.

Mahesh seemed a bit surprised at first and then nodded.

Om went to the kitchen and fetched him water.

"I got the highest marks in the class in the mathematics assignment," Om said to his father as the latter switched from watching television to reading the newspaper. The television at their house just had the free-to-air national channel, Doordarshan. For how long could one watch just one channel on the television? Mahesh hadn't subscribed to cable television because he thought it might conflict with Om's studies. Om wanted to mention getting cable television subscription, but he knew this wasn't the right time for that. There was something more important on his agenda.

"Will you eat pakoras with chai?" Om asked Mahesh.

Mahesh looked at him again, suspicion dancing in his eyes.

Om assumed that to be a yes.

"Mummy, please make pakoras and chai today for papa and myself," Om yelled from the living room, loud enough for Kiran to hear in the kitchen.

An awkward silence followed the next few minutes as Om sat on the sofa, waiting for an opportunity to start his conversation about Goa. His father, meanwhile, was engrossed in reading the newspaper.

"While Mummy gets pakoras, let me fetch some newspaper to spread on the table so that it doesn't get dirty," Om spoke loudly.

Mahesh's speculation increased.

Om kept a newspaper on the table. One of the headlines read: 'Best Gift for your Loved Ones - A Trip to Goa', an advertisement placed by a local travel agent in the newspaper. Om had strategically placed that clipping right in front of Mahesh.

Om opened one of his school books and started studying. He could feel the suspicious stares his father gave him, but he ignored it.

After a few minutes, Kiran came from the kitchen with two plates in her hand - one containing fresh pakoras and the other containing two cups of chai, one for herself and one for Mahesh.

Om would have preferred to drink as well, and his mother would have brought one for him. However, his father thought he was too young for tea and did not allow him. Not even a sip.

"So, this is what it is about!" exclaimed Mahesh as he leaned forward from the sofa to grab a pakora from the table. He didn't miss the headline in the newspaper placed on the table.

"That's why he is being so nice today - because he wants money for the school trip to Goa," said his father as he pointed Kiran towards the newspaper clipping in front of him on the table.

Kiran looked at Om, who didn't quite understand what that look was supposed to mean.

"I really want to go, Papa, please," begged Om.

"Om, he has told you many times earlier. We do not have the money for this. We are a normal, middle class family; we can afford your education but not your fancy wishes", said Kiran, firmly.

Om didn't understand why she was behaving like this. She was usually much gentler.

"Please, Mummy, please," Om begged again.

"No means no, Om," responded Mahesh.

"You always do this," said Om as he burst out crying and stormed out of the house.

———◆———

Om stopped for a few minutes by a tree near the community park to get over his crying. When he felt that he was ready, he wiped his tears, took a few deep breaths, and reached the nearest telephone booth. He rummaged through his back pocket to find his wallet, but soon realized that he had forgotten it at home. He didn't want to go back home and fizzle out the drama. He still had hope that he would somehow get the money for the trip. He searched his pockets again, and, to his surprise, he found a one-rupee coin in one of his change pockets. One rupee meant one minute of calling time.

"Hi, Aunty, this is Om. Can I please speak with Rohit?" asked Om as fast as he could.

Rohit's mother had answered the phone. "Ummm, okay," she said. She could feel the urgency. Om could hear her calling Rohit out. Time passed by. "Come on, Rohit, hurry up!" Om repeated to himself a few times as the clock in front of him read less than ten seconds. There was a voice at the other end.

"What happened, Om?" asked Rohit. He seemed a little short of breath.

"Bro, I had a huge drama at home. Meet me in thirty minutes outside the Pool Lounge. I don't have any money, so please get ..." Om spoke as fast as he could yet the phone disconnected in between. But fortunately, he was able to deliver the main chunk of his message.

He started making his way towards the Pool Lounge. It was a thirty-minute walk. The journey felt incredibly peaceful – the highlight of a rather forgettable day.

The lights were dim all around and he walked at his leisure. There was no rush. Rohit would take at least twenty minutes to reach. For Om, it was a short walk to the Pool Center, which made him reminisce the days at Jawahar Nagar with Naani and Babu.

CHAPTER 20

"WHAT HAPPENED, BRO? I was concerned about you. My father and mother were insisting they come along, but I had to force them to stay back," Rohit asked Om, with a look of concern.

"I just had this huge drama at home. I asked for the money to the trip, but Papa denied, again; and this time, Mummy joined him in the chorus as well," said Om. "I guess I will need to find a job and earn it for myself. But then there are only a few days left to the last date of depositing money. I don't think I can make it," said Om.

He was dejected. It felt like he was speaking to himself.

"I've told you so many times, just don't worry about it. I have some savings left over from my pocket money, and I will give that to you. Just forget about everything else," said Rohit.

"But why should you do this for me? Why not my parents?" exasperated Om.

"Bro, there must be some genuine concerns at their end. Your parents have done a lot for you -- to get you in the school you are, to get you the kind of education you are getting. You know it. Honestly, I am happy to give this money to you. If you're not feeling good about it, just think of it as a loan. Repay it back to me in easy instalments," explained Rohit as he tried to calm Om down.

Om just sat there silently. Somewhere within, he wondered what he had done in his life to find that kind of brotherhood.

"Leave all this. Have you eaten yet?" asked Rohit.

Om shook his head.

"Come, let's have some Kachori," said Rohit.

***

The next morning at school, Rohit got the money for Om, who returned his gesture with a kiss on Rohit's cheek.

"Bro, never again, or I am charging interest on this one," joked Rohit as Om let go of his cheesy display of brotherhood. They both shared a warm laugh before stepping into the class.

Sahil and Varsha stood at the door. Om looked downward and walked in, but not without wondering why Sahil had been fairly quiet after the fiasco at the Principal's office. What did he have to fear about? The Principal sucked up to his father who was one of the rumoured trustees to the school, Om was sure.

Ritu walked in, her hair tied up in a bow. It wasn't often that she would tie her hair up like that. But then, it was a hot day. Sweat dripped from the side of her neck on to her back.

Om walked up to her desk before she started her lecture and submitted the money for the school trip. Along with the money, a parents' approval form needed to be submitted. That was a formal permission given by the parents of the student, confirming their agreement to allow their child to attend the trip. Rohit had filled that form for Om and forged Mahesh's signature.

As he walked back to his desk, he looked at Varsha, who seemed impressed. Apparently, she hadn't expected a geek like him to be interested in a place like Goa.

"I didn't know you were a Goa kind of person," she said.

"There's a lot you don't know about me," Om replied immediately. He was starting to learn a bit of the ropes from Rohit. "I'm sure you are coming on the trip as well, but I haven't seen you depositing the money," Om said to Varsha.

"Yes, I'm just waiting for my father to come back from a business trip and give me the money. I'll deposit it before the last date," she answered.

A few other students had gathered around Ritu to deposit money for the trip.

"Do you like my henna?" asked Varsha as she showed Om her hands painted in henna. "I did it for my cousin's wedding this Saturday," she said.

Her hands looked like a piece of art with henna coming off in fine and exquisite lines, stark and dark brown, exactly as it was meant to be.

"Smell them, smell them." She moved her hands next to Om's nose.

His lips kissed her palms. He used to loathe the smell of henna so much that he would not eat food from his mother's hands around the annual 'Karva Chauth' festival when she would apply henna all over her hands and fast for the whole day to pray for his father's long life. But, in that moment, Om happily tolerated the smell. Perhaps he was only concerned about his lips kissing her hands.

Ritu started the lecture.

"Have you done that huge maths assignment meant to be submitted tomorrow?" whispered Varsha.

Om nodded.

"I've been having a really hard time doing it, and then I have my cousin's wedding this weekend as well," she whispered in his ears again, making a sad puppy face. "I don't know what's going to happen tomorrow," she added.

Her right thigh moved and touched Om's left hand.

He thought about moving his hand, but then he waited for her to move her thigh instead. Neither of them moved.

"I'll do your assignment. Just give your notebook to me at the end of the day." Om wrote on the back of her notebook, which was on the desk. He didn't want Ritu to change his seat again.

'Will you really do this for me?' she wrote back as she moved even closer to Om.

'Come and play Pool with me after school.' Om wrote back on the paper.

She paused for a moment and wrote, 'Next week. After I'm done with my cousin's wedding.'

The recess bell struck loud and clear. Om saw Rohit walk towards him. For the first time ever, Om saw his friend sporting an anxious look on his face and a beat of worry in his step. Rohit hadn't shown up outside the school gate that morning as well, so Om began to wonder.

"You look really worried, bro," said Om in a tone that said it was more of a question than a statement.

"I got a call this morning. It was Sara's brother. He said that Sara didn't want to speak with me anymore and then threatened me to stay away from Sara or else face dire consequences," said Rohit. There was a hint of helplessness in his voice.

"I politely said that if I heard this from Sara herself, I would happily go away, but not in any other circumstance," he continued.

"Then? What did he say?" asked Om, biting his finger nail.

"He said he wants to meet me at the Krishna temple today at 4 P.M," replied Rohit.

"For sure, we aren't going," Om responded immediately.

"We aren't. I am," Rohit corrected him.

"No way! You're not going there alone. Either none of us is going or we are going there together," said Om, assertively. Rohit didn't respond.

"Kachori on me today, after school; and then we'll go and meet that idiot," said Om and opened his lunch for both of them to eat. Roti breads with lemon pickle.

The two friends reached the Krishna temple – one of the oldest temples in the city. Krishna was one of the most unique gems this world had ever seen. He was a man for whom nothing was a boundary. The king of Dwarka and the king of his own self; as much a materialist as a spiritualist, as much a flirt as a lover, as much as philosopher as a knower. When Om was a child, Naani used to tell him stories about Krishna. If Krishna were to see the commotion performed in his name today, Om was sure that the first thing he would do was abandon these temples dedicated to him.

This has been one of the greatest flaws of humankind - to follow a person and not seek the path out for themselves. To believe someone and hold on to a said word rather than go where the word is pointing and experience it for themselves. To hold on to the finger pointing to the proverbial moon, but not looking at the proverbial moon itself.

"We will not start any fight," said Rohit. Perhaps he didn't want to make it difficult in any way for Sara, Om assumed.

"We will listen to what they have to say and I will politely explain my feelings for her. You don't say anything," Rohit added.

Om nodded in agreement.

It was ten minutes past four. They had been there for over fifteen minutes.

Suddenly, from their right-hand side, they heard a noise. As soon as they turned, they saw seven people marching towards them. Om patted Rohit's back, telling him that there's nothing to worry about, but his heartbeat was racing within.

One of those guys, who they both presumed was Sara's brother, asked, "Who is Rohit out of the two of you?" Rohit blinked his eyes slowly.

Before one could even take another breath, a full-blown punch landed on Rohit's stomach. He fell to the ground instantly.

191

Om immediately jumped in. He knew he was going to be battered, but it didn't matter. All this reminded him of that day years ago when five dogs chased him outside Naani's house. Only he was running from them, now he was running towards them. With all the power he had, he landed a punch straight on the nose of the guy who had punched Rohit.

Rohit was still in the ground, crunching in pain. The other goons jumped in. Within a second, Om felt a barrage of punches hitting him. Just like the episode with the dogs, the time seemed to freeze. Even the pain numbed out. He barely felt anything. Both of them were on the ground by now. Punches turned into kicks. The two curled themselves up to prevent as many as they could.

Sometime after, everyone heard the siren of a police van in the background. A good Samaritan, though not brave enough to jump in, might have alerted the police. The beating stopped.

"Don't you ever dare come near Sara again or this is just the beginning!" the boys heard a voice. Neither Rohit nor Om looked up.

Within a few minutes, the police arrived and immediately took them to the nearest public hospital.

"Why didn't you tell the police who they were?" asked Rohit's mother, holding her boy in her arms in a taxi.

The two boys had been discharged from the city hospital. Rohit had refused to identify the perpetrators and no case was registered with the police. The doctors at the hospital had bandaged the wounds. There were no serious or internal injuries to either of them.

"You know, your father wouldn't be happy about this. Fear and cowardice are not the values he has inspired you to adopt," continued Rohit's mother.

"It is not about fear or courage, Mummy. I could even have retaliated. I just understood, in a split-second, as I lay down there on the ground that this was just going to cause unnecessary trouble for a girl I really like. There's no end to this stupidity. We have our lives in front of us and many more enriching experiences to live. In that very instant, I decided to let go," responded Rohit.

Om looked at him. His friend never ceased to amaze him. A boy Om's age was saying something so mature which even a fully grown-up adult might not have said in that situation. At that moment, Om had a bizarre idea that Rohit could be a reincarnation of Naani but realized a moment later that it could not be possible as Rohit was the same age as he was.

Rohit's mother did not say anything. She trusted her child's words, it seemed.

"Please tell Papa it was a small fight at school and it was my fault," Rohit said to his mother.

The three reached Rohit's home. Rohit's father was busy speaking with someone over the telephone while sitting in front of the computer screen. Rohit and Om quickly sneaked into Rohit's room.

"Will you just let Sara go like this without even speaking with her? What if she wants to be with you and is ready to do anything for that?" asked Om.

He was curious. He felt like he was a part of Rohit and Sara's story. This just didn't feel like the right end for the story.

"I have to let her go, bro. Pursuing this will only create more trouble for her; and she has her whole life in front of her. So do I. It will be very selfish of me to try and hold on to her," said Rohit as he gently lay on the bed with a pillow under his head. He reminded Om of Naani again.

There was a knock on the door. Om went ahead and opened the door; it was Rohit's father. Om felt it was basic courtesy to go out of the room to allow the father and son some personal space. Om exited and closed the door.

A few minutes later, Rohit's father came out of the room and walked towards Om. He ran his fingers through his hair and ruffled through them. Om thanked himself for not sporting a mohawk that day. Om went inside Rohit's room. Rohit was sitting upright on the bed and gave Om the warmest smile anyone had given him in a very long time. He got up and hugged Om.

"Thank you!" said Rohit.

Om wasn't able to understand what had happened to Rohit all of a sudden

"Stay with me tonight," he said with such aplomb in his eyes.

Om couldn't say no to that look in Rohit's eyes. He also felt like Rohit really needed his company at that time.

"Let me go outside, call Mummy up and inform her," said Om, giving Rohit a warm smile.

⸺❖⸺

Ritu was a little late to the classroom the next day. So was Varsha.

Rohit was over at Om's seat. They were being frequently disturbed by the class mates – some concerned about their well-being and others just mongering their curiosity.

"Looks like someone got beaten up again," shouted Sahil from across the classroom with his side-kicks laughing at his crude jokes as usual.

Varsha walked in with Ritu right behind her. The class teacher, Ritu, kept her handbag on her table and started recording the morning attendance. She looked ravishing that day – Nude lips, a white sari, and a bite mark on her stomach right at the edge of her waist where she had tied her petticoat. It seemed fresh, just like Om's and Rohit's bruises.

"Today is the last day of depositing money for the Goa trip," announced Ritu. "Please come to my desk one by one, starting from the row next to the window," she added.

Varsha was the first to stand up. She walked up to Ritu with an envelope in her hand. Ritu counted the money and gave Varsha a receipt.

"What happened to you, poor boy?" Varsha asked Om, noticing his bruises and swelling when she came back.

"It's fine. It was just a fight Rohit ended up in and I was there with him," said Om.

"Why did you have to be there if it was his fight?" she asked back.

Om looked at her strangely for a second.

"He didn't want to fight; he was dragged into it," said Om, after a brief pause.

Ritu was collecting money from the last student for the trip to Goa.

"Yeah, but why did you get into the fight then?" Varsha asked again.

"His fight is my fight!" added Om, staring intensely into Varsha's eyes before looking away from her.

Ritu had started saying something. Varsha was taken aback, but at the same time, attracted to Om. There was an aggression and intensity in his eyes, something Varsha had not witnessed until then.

"So, the final list of students from Class -IX-A going to the trip is - Ashish, Piyush, Aman, Nikhil, Sahil, Rohit, Varsha, Swati, Mohit, Kiran, Om, Suraj, Nitin, Danny, Nimit, Jasmine, Payal, Tanya, and Shobhit. Get excited, all, and start preparing. The trip leaves on Friday," announced Ritu.

There was an excitement in her voice. She was going to be one of the supervisors on the trip as well – something most of the boys were looking forward to.

Varsha brushed her shoulders against Om's. Om turned to his left and looked at her. She wrapped her arms around Om's left hand for a brief moment, before raising her right hand. Om smiled and gave her a high-five.

"Let's go and play Pool after school today," Rohit said to Om, as recess struck.

Om looked at him for a second. His apprehension was clear. "I am feeling very tired, plus there's that Mathematics assignment to complete," responded Om. After all, Om had Varsha's mathematics assignment to complete – something he hadn't even told his best friend about. Om assumed Rohit wouldn't have been happy with that gesture by himself or maybe he feared that Rohit would have started giving him his own assignments as well.

Om's mind ran at full speed. Thoughts flew in his head – from Varsha's pink lips and lush hair to Rohit's contribution in his life to wondering where Farheen could be.

"I had a weird dream last night," Om said to Rohit as they walked, as if they had all the time in the world, through the school gate into the pathway leading to the main corridor.

"I ended up in the school naked. No clothes, none whatsoever, and I was the only one without clothes," began Om.

Rohit was listening with intent.

"Sahil was at the school entrance. I ran away as fast as I could to escape him, only to run into Viru Sir, who was appalled at finding me naked in school. He ordered me to do a hundred sit-ups, naked, and then escorted me to our class," added Om.

Rohit was attentive but amused.

"I was puffing and sweating profusely, as I woke up." Om took a sigh as he finished narrating his dream.

"I've dreamt about being naked in school as well." quipped Rohit. Om was surprised. He found dreams fascinating – how they were constructed; how seemingly random they looked yet perhaps they had a deeper meaning; how one would realize it was a dream, only after awakening.

Elsewhere in the classroom, there was a big commotion going on among the boys. One of them, Aman, had brought some magazine he had found in his father's bag. His father had just returned from a business trip to America, Om had heard someone in the class say.

Aman belonged to a rich family – that much was known. There was also a rumor that his father was among the school's trustees. Considering Aman was dropped off at and picked up from school in the morning by a chauffeur-driven car provided enough evidence of his privileges.

Rohit was on friendly terms with Aman as he sat right behind him in the class. He saw Rohit walk up to Aman, who, by now, had been surrounded by eight other boys. Rohit and Aman were engaged in a quick conversation, which Om longed to hear.

"Aman has got an issue of a magazine in America called the 'Playboy Magazine' with Pamela Anderson on its cover," said Rohit as he returned after his chat with Aman.

"Who is Pamela Anderson?" asked Om.

"Bro, I have seen clippings of her while surfing the internet. She has these humongous breasts! Think of her like all the girls we saw on Desibaba.com put together. She is fully nude in the magazine. The boys are queuing up to take the magazine and go to the toilet one-by-one to masturbate," replied Rohit.

"What's masturbation?" Om asked with great curiosity.

"You don't know what masturbation is? You are kidding me, right?" Rohit looked surprised.

"I don't know what it is," Om answered, sounding honest.

"So, you've never done it?" asked Rohit.

"I don't even know what that is," answered Om.

Rohit seemed to giggle a bit, yet, had a look on his face that bore suspicion.

"I'm going to ask Aman for the magazine. He's a good friend of mine and you're coming over to my house after school," said Rohit. Om was both, curious and bewildered. He nodded.

CHAPTER 21

ROHIT'S MOTHER GREETED them as they entered and served them a delicious lunch again. She was warm, gentle and had a rare grace about her demeanour. As always, Om called his mother up and let her know that he was going to be late. She did not sound happy with him. Given that he was spending most of his time outside home, that didn't come as a surprise. On top of that, she hadn't even met Rohit yet, which perhaps made Kiran worry about where Om spent most of his time after school.

Rohit, in the meanwhile, had an enigmatic look on his face throughout lunch as his mother was at the table with the boys.

Om felt both excited and nervous. However, more than anything else, he was just happy that his friend was enjoying himself, especially after what had happened with him over the last few hours.

As soon as they finished their lunch, Rohit's mother bid the boys goodbye and left for her room. The boys headed over to Rohit's bedroom.

Rohit locked the door from within, picked up his schoolbag, and took out the Playboy magazine he talked about in the school. He handed it over to Om.

Right on the front page was the woman everyone kept talking about – Pamela Anderson. Lying on her side over a red, satin sheet with her gorgeous face looking at Om. She wore a white, deep-neck corset with rose petals spread all over, hiding just enough of her immaculate breasts to make it tantalizing. White suspenders ran over her buttocks, holding her stockings in place. Om was turned on. He was growing inside his underwear.

Rohit understood what was happening. Even he felt the same way, standing right next to Om.

They opened the magazine and took a peek at the naked model. Her voluptuous breasts needed no support at all. Her buttocks rested against a rustic brick wall in a deserted compound.

At that point, Om understood why the magazine had become such a big rage in the classroom. Pamela Anderson was unlike anyone he had seen in his life.

"Let's do this," said Rohit after taking a deep breath. He opened the button of his trousers and took off his pants. He then took off his black underwear.

Om stood there staring at him. It was the first time Om was seeing someone else's genitals, other than his own. It felt weird.

"Take yours off," said Rohit.

Om was hesitant to say the least. He felt embarrassed and self-conscious.

"Come on! There's nobody here other than you and me," said Rohit.

Om took off his trousers and then paused for a moment. He was only wearing his underwear below the belt.

Rohit was in front of him, bare-naked below his waist.

Om looked away from Rohit and took off his underwear.

Both of them were bottom naked, standing in front of each other. Neither of them spoke or did anything for a few seconds.

Rohit grabbed both of them a chair and said, "Just look at me for a few seconds initially, see what I'm doing and then let yourself loose." Om didn't say anything. He was just looking intently at Rohit, with a look that bore immense curiosity and nervousness in equal measure.

Both of them sat on their respective chairs. The centrefold of Playboy magazine graced by Pamela Anderson was on a small table placed in between them, so that the both could look at it. Om was looking to his right, at Rohit. Rohit closed his eyes and slowly pulled the foreskin of his penis right to the top. He then rolled it back to the base, massaging the shaft.

Om started emulating Rohit. It felt grotesque to begin with, but as he continued stroking himself, he started feeling a strange sense of pleasure.

He was getting harder and Om was feeling more and more heat building up in the body.

"Now, forget everything else, and just think about being with Pamela Anderson, wrapped in that red satin sheet." began Rohit. His eyes were half-closed, and his head bent upwards.

"Imagine her asking you to come closer to her. So close that you can feel her breath, her touch" he continued as his hand movements became faster.

Om's heart was racing. Within a few seconds, he stopped looking at Rohit. The only thought on his mind was Pamela Anderson, right in front of him. His hand on her body, and hers on his.

Within seconds, an inexplicable current ran through Om's body. Suddenly, he felt this rush of energy running up from the base of his penis towards its head. Within a split-second, he felt the current leaving his body and something warm landed on his left arm. It was unlike anything he had ever experienced in his life. It was as if each cell in the body had been given an electric shock, as if every cell in the body was throbbing with incredible energy.

For a few moments, it was pure ecstasy. Not an iota of thought in the mind, not a hint of any deviation. He had never felt so total and complete in his life until that moment. He opened his eyes and saw some white, thick fluid on his arm.

He looked at Rohit who was vigorously stroking himself. His eyes were closed. Within seconds, Om saw Rohit's whole body moving as if he was having a seizure. A similar looking white fluid landed on Rohit's arm as well. After a few seconds and a few deep breaths, Rohit opened his eyes and saw Om looking at him.

"Go grab that newspaper, bro," said Rohit pointing towards his desk. Om still had that warm, sticky liquid all over his arm. He crouched in a half-sitting position, as if someone had forgotten to take toilet paper to the latrine and hopped over to grab the newspaper. He wiped himself up and threw some at Rohit, who wiped himself.

"Wasn't it the most incredible thing you've ever experienced?" asked Rohit, still reeling from the intensity of the experience.

"I haven't felt anything like this ever," responded Om. "Many years ago, I was chased furiously by five dogs. I almost lost my life. I ran hard. I felt like I was running for my life. During that incredibly intense run, I felt this strange kind of bliss. All thoughts disappeared and there was no disturbance in the mind. This experience was similar to that moment in my life," continued Om.

"How did you find out about this? And what is this fluid that came out of us?" asked Om.

"One of my elder cousins told me about it when he was here last month. I thought you would have known this," replied Rohit. "This white fluid is called semen. This is what creates life when it mixes with an egg inside a woman's vagina. That's how a child is born," added Rohit.

Om was intrigued beyond belief. He had always been told that the government or God puts children in a mother's womb.

"What are you saying? My father and mother told me that I was given to my mother by the government," retorted Om in disbelief. Both his parents had told him that since his childhood.

"Do you really not know how children are born? You've got to be kidding me," asked Rohit in a tone of amazement.

Om didn't say anything.

"I can't believe you don't know it by now. Those are just stories parents tell kids when they are small," said Rohit. "A girl gets pregnant when a boy's semen mixes with an egg inside her body. After nine months, a child is born," explained Rohit.

Om felt cheated and lied to, as he shook his head in disbelief.

Rohit didn't say anything further. Just pulled his pants up. Om did the same.

The boys quickly tidied things up. Rohit kept the magazine back in his school bag.

"I better get going now. We need to submit the maths assignment tomorrow" said Om.

"Don't even remind me of it. I haven't even started," said Rohit. Om tied his shoes, picked up his bag and began to leave the house. He had completed his own assignment but had Varsha's one to complete.

Another regular day at school followed the exciting afternoon of the day before. It would have continued to fare as usual except that the Mathematics teacher, Mrs. Mehra, came to the class in the first period instead of Ritu. Everyone was surprised.

"I've requested this first period from Ritu today and I will be conducting a surprise test, which will have a twenty percent credit towards the final examination at the end of the academic year. But, before that, please keep the assignment given to you for completion on your desk. I will come and collect it one by one," announced Mrs. Mehra to the horror of the students.

Many students hated surprise tests, especially when it had anything to do with Mathematics. Om, however, always had some sort of a fascination with mathematics. Numbers, equations, their relationships and their play somehow came naturally to him. In the superficial disorder of the world, lay hidden an extremely intricate order. Om found mathematics as a way to learn more about the underlying order in the universe.

Varsha was perhaps the most nervous. She looked at Om and he knew it was a cry for help. He opened his bag and took two assignments out. He kept hers on her side of the desk and kept his in front of him.

She gave him a flying kiss. Her lips were naked, raw pink.

Varsha gave a confident smile to Mrs. Mehra when the latter reached her desk to collect the assignment.

At the end of this exercise, there were four students who had not submitted the assignment. They were standing with their heads down. One of them was a girl, who had a few tears rolling down her cheeks.

"All four of you, out of the classroom! Now!" Mrs. Mehra reprimanded them with the humiliating punishment. They were also to get zero marks for the surprise test that was about to be conducted. There was a stunned silence in the class.

"Please keep your pens down. I shouldn't see a single pen in anyone's hands till the time I say 'Start'. You will have thirty minutes to complete this test. Be careful, there is negative marking as described in the instructions on the first page. Anybody caught cheating will be given a zero straight away," announced Mrs. Mehra.

She then went around distributing the question paper – an objective, multiple choice format.

"Start," she said.

Everybody had their pens in their hands. Most of the students, at least.

Om dug himself deep into the paper, hurriedly performing calculations on the last page of the answer sheet. After a few minutes, he felt Varsha's right leg rubbing against his left leg. He turned to his left and saw her making a puppy face. He understood what she wanted but was skeptical. He remembered that time in Alpha-Beta when Ratna Devi made him stand for a full day at the corner of the class when he had tried to help Gopal during a test.

On top of that, everyone had heard stories of how Mrs. Mehra had failed students in the past, even in final examinations, because of cheating. No one dared to cheat when she was the invigilator. But Varsha's puppy eyes were impossible to ignore.

He moved back a little, shifted his paper as left as he could without being obvious. He had already reached the second page of the test paper, but he flipped back to the first page and pretended to do some intense calculations while Varsha copied his answers.

Om was finished with the test paper inside twenty minutes and so had Varsha, but he decided to drag it further and continued pretending to work. He didn't want any suspicion regarding Varsha and him finishing at the same time. The bell rang. The period was over and so was the test.

Mrs. Mehra quickly went from desk to desk, collecting the answer sheets. From some students, she literally had to snatch the answer sheets as they had not finished the test.

Mrs. Mehra reached Om and Varsha's desk. Varsha smiled and handed over her answer sheet to Mrs. Mehra. So did Om.

"When are you asking Varsha out, bro? You seemed to have built a nice rapport with her these days. I see you guys sitting quite close together," asked Rohit as he winked at Om. The school had ended for the day.

"I'll do it soon, bro. I'm getting there. Maybe tomorrow," replied Om.

"Have you heard anything from Sara?" Om asked further.

Rohit shook his head and didn't seem very interested in discussing that topic any further.

"I forgot to ask you in the classroom. How did your test go?" Om asked Rohit, diverting the subject.

"It was fine. I'm not sure about two or three answers, though. Aman answered them differently from what I did," replied Rohit. "Now, before you start, I don't want to know which answers you marked for those questions. Forget about it. The test is done and I'll think about it when the results are out."

Om was curious to know which questions he was talking about. Nevertheless, he kept quiet.

"Are you going to shop for new clothes for the Goa trip?" asked Om. "Quite a few folks have been talking about it."

"I already have enough. I don't care," replied Rohit.

"Why do you ask? Are you planning to go shopping?" he asked Om.

"I might have to because I just have three or four pairs of clothes, that too old and daggy. I can't wear those in Goa," responded Om.

"I have enough clothes, bro. You can share mine. Just forget about it and don't waste any money on it," said Rohit.

"Are you sure?" Om wanted to confirm.

"Of course, bro. Just keep your stained underwear away from them," joked Rohit. Om rolled his eyes.

It was just a day prior to the Goa trip. There was a tremendous buzz in the air. Those who were going on the trip talked about what they would wear in Goa, what food they would bring along, who would be getting the camera and the film rolls, and all such questions that came to their mind. Those who weren't going, however, either burned with envy or felt happy. Well, the solace was that they were going to enjoy a lot of free periods over the next few days.

One more reason of excitement for Om was that he had got forty on forty in the surprise test. Varsha had got thirty-eight. That day he realized that even copying correctly was an art.

"You still haven't paid me back for the assignment and the surprise test," Om joked with Varsha as Mrs. Grover, the moral science teacher, delivered a lecture.

This was one period every week where no one paid any attention. Neither did Mrs. Grover mind the inattention. One of the things with actually teaching moral science is not to be a moral police officer yourself. Mrs. Grover embodied that well. She was relaxed and easy-going, which was why a lot of students respected her. The ones that were interested in what she had to say quietly went and sat in the front benches; the rest were free to go about their business -- study something else, play games, or talk softly.

"Would you like to come and play Pool with me after school today? There's a really cool lounge I go to in Sodala," he asked Varsha.

She looked away a little awkwardly and then replied, "Not today, my father gets home early these days, so I have to be home on time. Some other time. Definitely sometime after the Goa trip."

Om didn't say anything.

"Where will you be shopping from, for your trip?" asked Varsha.

Om got a bit conscious and replied, "I'll be going to this new mall which has opened up in Raja Park. It's called C-Square mall"

"Yes, I've heard about it. Neha went there the other day, but didn't like the brands there," said Varsha.

He felt embarrassed. He had heard a few boys in his locality praise the quality of brands at that new mall. He looked away and pretended to be interested in what Mrs. Grover was saying.

CHAPTER 22

ROHIT AND OM walked quietly towards the school gate. The school trip to Goa was leaving the next morning and Om had to select and pick up clothes from Rohit's house. Rohit had also printed some new images of Pamela Anderson from the Internet using his father's printer for Om.

"Meet me at the school gate at 4:50 A.M tomorrow morning," said Rohit as they walked outside the school to catch a bus for Rohit's house.

Rohit seemed emotional that day. Well, for the last few days, if Om's observation had been right. Perhaps it was because of Sara. Even though he had said he had moved on, perhaps he hadn't. But Om had no intention of rubbing salt on his wounds. He felt that it was best to avoid that topic.

"Thank you for everything, bro. I really mean it. I've had a great friendship with you. I think you're my first true friend," said Rohit.

"The things I have learned from you and the way you have inspired me with your courage have given me new wings in life. I, if truth be told, look up to you. I must be the one thanking you," Om replied.

They looked at each other briefly and walked around the by-lanes of the school in no hurry to reach anywhere.

"Did you ask Varsha out today?" asked Rohit.

Om nodded. "Yes, I did, but..," he began saying, as he heard Rohit shouting, "Watch out!" Rohit immediately pulled Om towards himself.

Sahil sped in his car with a girl next to him. It looked like Varsha.

"Was that Varsha next to Sahil?" asked Rohit.

Om looked at the car zip them by towards the national highway number eight.

Om entered the house and kept aside couple of big bags he had brought from Rohit's place. His father was home. He could see the newspaper open on the center table in the living room. The television played and as usual, Doordarshan on it.

A whistle from the pressure cooker sounded in the kitchen. The food was ready to be served.

His mother came out of the kitchen. She sensed that he was home. He wondered from where the mothers of the world inherited this remarkable talent. Despite the drama they had a few days ago, a mother could not be upset with her son for long.

"You barely spend any time these days at home, lalla. I'm worried for you," said his mother.

"Worried about what?" he asked in a stern voice, pretending to be upset at how she had shunned him in front of Mahesh.

"Worried about your future, your studies. I don't know who Rohit is. You haven't even made him meet me once, and you spend so much time at his house," she said. "See, beta, they might have money to ensure their child's future is safe and secure, but education is our only saviour. You have to study well and become an able man. We don't have any other option," she added.

"Oh Mummy, please! Not now. I know all that. I have a trip tomorrow, which I need to enjoy and I also have a life, which I need to live. I'll take care of it. Don't worry about it," Om said, frustrated.

"I've prepared your favourite soup today. I'll bring it to you now. Take your shoes off and relax on the sofa," said Kiran in a calm, reassuring way.

He obliged. No matter how much time he had spent at Rohit's place, this was still his home. It felt really relaxing to just lean back and wait for the food to arrive. Tranquil moments like these visited him every now and then and were his most treasured possessions. In one of those tranquil moments, he thought about Rohit, about mathematics, about Sahil, about his mother, and then about Varsha.

His mother came with a bowl of soup in her hands, kept it on the table in front of him and went back, only to return a minute later. She sat by his side, ran her fingers through his hair and extended her right hand forward. He looked up to her.

"I don't have much, but I know this trip to Goa is an experience of a lifetime for you. I have this money with me, which I would like to give you, to help you enjoy as much as you can in Goa," she said as she handed him two notes of five hundred rupees each.

He was taken aback and looked surprised. It took him a few seconds to process it. He saw her eyes wet with tears. He hugged and thanked her.

"I'll bring you some Goan cashews on my way back," he said.

"Let's go and pack your bag for the trip after you're done with dinner. You need to wake up quite early tomorrow, so let's hurry up." said Kiran as she moved back to the kitchen.

Everybody was supposed to report at the school reception at 5:00 A.M. The school buses were scheduled to depart the school at 5:30 A.M to reach the train station by 6:15A.M. Their train was scheduled to depart at 7:00 A.M for Goa.

Om could not sleep the whole night. What to wear to the beach in Goa, Sahil's car, Varsha sitting with him, Rohit and Sara, his parents, his future – all such thoughts ran amok in his mind.

At 4 A.M he arose from his bed. His mother had woken up as well to pack him some food. He picked up a green track pant with 'Area 51' written on his side. He had no idea what that meant, but it looked cool. Along with that, he wore a white vest, tucked out, and topped it off with a blue Nike wrist-band he got from Rohit. The Nike logo was at the front, clearly visible.

Despite not having slept the whole night, Om still managed to run late. His mother hustled with him as well and packed him his food. She asked whether he had kept the toothbrush, soap, and toothpaste in his bags. He had forgotten the toothpaste. He really pushed it to the last minute.

Eventually, he was set and called an auto-rickshaw. There was no time to catch any kind of public transport. The trip had begun with a big expense already.

Mahesh said a cold goodbye from his room. It was clear that he wasn't happy about Om borrowing money from someone and going on the trip.

Om didn't bother. He was running out of time and had to rush.

He reached the school gate fifteen minutes later to the time Rohit had initially requested. Rohit was there, waiting at the gate for him.

"I was about to go inside the school reception and call your home. What took you so long?" asked Rohit.

"Just last-minute packing and then Mummy wanted to pack me some food. Anyway, let's go inside now," said Om.

"You look great. The white vest and the green lowers – nice color combination. This wrist band looks cool as well. Where did you get it from?" Rohit asked as he winked at Om. "Thanks man, it's yours", replied Om, and winked back at him.

As they walked into the reception, Om saw Sahil who was wearing tall Woodland boots, blue denim, and a white t-shirt. He also had a cap. He was with his sidekicks – all dressed loud. They had Walkmans in their hands, headphones in their ears. They rolled their eye from side to side, checking everyone out, especially the girls.

Varsha looked stunning. She was accompanied by her sidekicks. She wore a pink skirt, shorter than the one she wore to school every day. A white tee adorned her upper half, which did not cover her midriff completely. Her hair was open. Ritu and Mrs. Mehra, who were both trip supervisors, were looking at Varsha and whispered something in each other's ears. Varsha saw Om from a distance and waved. He returned the gesture with one of his own.

He could see Sahil and his sidekicks look at him and Rohit. He saw them laugh their usual wry ones. He looked away, as usual.

❦

The train was coming from Delhi and would stop in Jaipur for only twenty minutes. Ninety-four students from the eight sections of Class-IX had chosen to go on the trip. They all waited where the coach was supposed to stop. Fifteen teachers and two strong male bodyguards accompanied them. Well, there were hundreds of others on the train platform as well, but they weren't from the school. At most other places, one never really had much of an inkling of India's magnanimous population; it was at the railway platforms that one really saw and understood the gravity of the problem.

As soon as the train arrived, there was a mad rush among all the students to get their bags on the train and to grab the best seats possible. Each compartment could accommodate eight people – three tiers on each end accommodating six people and two at the lateral end. Sahil, Varsha, and their friends were the first to nab the corner compartment. It was closest to the toilets and the doors. This also ensured that they were well-ventilated.

He and Rohit ended up in the next compartment with the nerds of their section. If not for Varsha and company, then they had hoped to be with Ruby and her friends from Class -IX-D. Luck did not seem to be on their side because they got neither.

There was a collective cheer once the train started moving. The teachers joined the commotion. It was finally happening – the ninety-four students from Class-IX of Shah International School were on their way.

Om couldn't believe that he was actually going to Goa. In spite of all that had happened at home because of the Goa trip, with all that drama and tears, he felt that all was worth it.. Om sat by the side of the window to savour the moment.

***

The train had left Jaipur behind and soon reached its full speed. Packets of chips and wafers were being passed around. Bottles of Pepsi, Walkmans, and tape cassettes accompanied the food. Om and Rohit had placed themselves on the lateral seats in the compartment, next to where Sahil and Varsha were. This enabled Om to look over every once in a while and see what was happening in the adjoining compartment. Sahil and Varsha sat together, laughing at each other from time to time and touching each other frequently. And here he was, playing cards with the nerds of Class -IX-A with the landscape of Mother India running in the background.

As the evening rolled on, boys and girls moved around compartments, playing games, sharing food and music. The morning wear had made way for new dresses. Om now understood why many of them had such huge bags for a five-day trip.

Rohit, during the course of the day, befriended Ruby and called Om along, later. As time passed, everything eased out. Rohit and Om started enjoying the company of Ruby and her friends. Om realized that he hadn't even thought about Varsha or Sahil for quite some time. It felt good that way. The singing, the dancing, and the eating continued well into the night in spite of their teachers trying their best to make the students go to sleep.

CHAPTER 23

THE TRAIN REACHED Goa at around seven in the morning. Most of the students, during those wee hours of the morning, repented at having stayed up all night. Somehow, they dragged each other out.

Buses waited at the station to receive and take them to the resort they were staying at. Everyone got off the train. The teachers asked the students to check whether they had grabbed all their belongings. The students were then asked to form a queue to board the bus that would take them to the resort. The students boarded the bus one by one. At the same time, one of the teachers counted the number to ensure that no one was missing.

More than half the students fell asleep on the bus from the train station to the resort. That included him and Rohit.

It was but a few moments later that Om felt something on his left shoulder. He turned and saw Sahil sitting behind him and laughing. He knew it was Sahil who had kicked him. Pretending that nothing had happened and thinking it wasn't worth it to disembowel his mood because of one bully, he closed his eyes again.

Rohit lay fast asleep on the seat right next to him.

Within a few seconds, he felt four – or was it five? – kicks at a time on his shoulder. A cacophony of laughter emanated behind him. But he kept his eyes closed, not wanting to get into a ruckus in the beginning of the trip. The kicks continued.

The bus came to a screeching halt. They had reached the resort. The teachers stood up and announced that they had arrived at their destination. He opened his eyes and then woke Rohit up.

"Shortly, we will be allocating rooms. Please form groups of four. There will be four students in each room; boys with boys, girls with girls. Any students left over at the end would be accommodated with us," announced Ritu.

A mad chaos ensued to form groups. No one wanted to be the least wanted person who ended up with the teachers. Both he and Rohit quickly teamed up with Piyush and Ashish, the front-benchers of Class-IX-A. Sahil already had his group; so did Varsha.

A few minutes later, all the students stood at the reception in groups of four. Two girls were left at the end, who were politely asked to stand aside by Ritu as she handed over the room keys to each group one by one. Soon, everyone knew what room numbers they were going to be accommodated in.

"Please assemble at 1 P.M at the restaurant, right next to the swimming pool. We will have lunch at 1:15, after which we will head straight over to Baga beach," announced Ritu as everyone started to disperse towards their respective rooms.

Om was simply excited to be in a resort for the first time in his life, and even more excited to check out the swimming pool, even though he did not know how to swim. Neither did he have a swimming costume.

Their room, 17-A, was on the ground floor. It was bigger than the living room of his house. It had one double bed and a sofa-cum-bed. The four of them threw their bags on the floor and jumped on the super-comfortable, bouncy beds. Before they realized it, it was 12:45 P.M. They had to reach the restaurant for lunch in fifteen minutes. Every one of them proceeded to what was perhaps the quickest shower of their lives and changed into new clothes. In ten minutes, they were out of their room, walking towards the restaurant, following the signs laid out on the pathways in the resort. He looked around to see where Varsha's and Sahil's rooms were. He didn't find them, however.

When they reached the swimming pool, they realized that most of the other students had already reached the restaurant and started eating. There were new dresses and skirts everywhere, new bandanas and hats. Ritu was a hot topic of discussion. She was wearing a sarong – a bold choice in the opinion of many. Mrs. Mehra was now alone with no one left to gossip about someone's exhibitionism.

There was a lot of talking and laughter all around. Rohit, Varsha, and their friends sat together at a large table.

At around 2 P.M, Ritu asked everyone to assemble at the reception from where they were supposed to board the buses that would take them to the Baga Beach. There was a lot of excitement in the air. Om assumed that many, like him, had never been to a beach.

———◆◆◆———

Turn by turn, everyone got off the bus at Baga Beach. The first glimpse of Arabian Sea from the parking lot was a sight to behold. Water upon water ran as far as the horizon. A cool sea breeze came floating over the waters and rustled through Om's hair. Beach shops at the seafront went on about their businesses. Small kids made sand-castles. There were a lot of foreigners from different parts of the world on the beach. And also, women in bikinis. Both he and Rohit exchanged glances with each other, excited at the delightful sight.

As they walked closer to the beach, the breeze became stronger. There they were – young, teenage boys from a city in North India, behaving like a bunch of aliens on earth for the first time. Some of them, like Sahil, had worn jeans and a full-sleeve shirt to the beach. For a change, Om found it was nice to see Sahil being the butt of all jokes by the foreigners on the beach.

He and Rohit stepped on the sand and then took their towels out and threw them. Some had already thrown away their slippers and were running towards the water.

Rohit tapped his shoulder and pointed at a blonde girl wearing a skimpy red bikini. They looked at each other and sighed. She spread her beach towel on the sand and lay down with her face facing the sand. She untied the straps of her bikini top after applying sunscreen all over her face and arms.

Om and Rohit had their eyes and mouths wide open when one of the bodyguards came from behind and tapped on their shoulders. They looked at him, embarrassed, and started to fix their beach towels before heading into the water.

Many of the teachers, including Mrs. Mehra, joined the students in the water. All of the students were having a gala time. They sang songs, danced and played in the water. Varsha and her sidekicks jumped into the wavy foams as well. Soon, Om and Varsha came close to each other. She wore a white tank top.

He realized that Varsha seemed to have an obsession with the color white. He threw some water on her, and then some more. He continued until her shirt was drenched and wrapped all around her beautiful chest.

All this while, from the corner of his eyes, he did see Sahil standing away from the water, lamenting about his choice of clothing.

Varsha started throwing water back at him, taking his glance away from Sahil. She complimented him about his looks on the morning they had boarded the train at Jaipur. However, she was visibly distracted throughout, though, looking at Sahil from time to time.

Ruby's friend, Shruti, called Om's name from behind. He gave Varsha a smile and turned around to join Shruti, Ruby, Rohit, and their group.

Rohit, it seemed, got along well with Ruby. They were getting close to each other. They played with each other and laughed at each other's jokes.

Om was just enjoying being in the water, flowing with the waves when they were on their way up and trying to float on the water on their way down.

In due course of time, most of the students and teachers had left the water and were drying themselves in the sand.

Om saw Varsha and Sahil at a distance, walking towards the far end of the beach amidst big rocks and boulders. He looked around for a few seconds, caught a wave, and then looked in that direction again. Both Sahil and Varsha had disappeared.

In the process, he also saw a few teachers look in the direction. One of them called one of the male bodyguards who were accompanying them on the tour.

Om went back to playing with water. Rohit got a volleyball from somewhere and they started playing.

A while later, Ritu got up and started clapping. She asked the students to come out of the water as it was time to go back to the resort. Om spotted Mrs. Mehra speaking with Varsha in the background. Sahil was being confronted by the bodyguard who had gone to lookout for them.

"We have the hall reserved to ourselves this evening. We'll have a performance competition beginning at 8 P.M. Everyone is welcome to sing, dance, act, or showcase anything they want. The winner will get a surprise gift and the competition will be followed by dinner and dance till midnight."

Om threw his arms around Rohit's shoulder in excitement while the latter looked at him, clueless as to what the fuss was all about.

CHAPTER 24

DANCE HAD ALWAYS been Om's hidden talent, his deep love. Whenever Naani told him stories about Meera, the first thought he had in his mind was dance. As soon as Ritu announced there was a competition, his first reaction was that of sheer excitement. But the next moment, fear and inhibition followed.

People would be watching. He would be judged. What if he forgot a step or missed a beat? Such thoughts, within a moment, overpowered the first instinctive reaction of excitement and celebration.

It is strange how there is a different rhythm to our breath, a certain dimension to our demeanour, when we are totally alone with no one watching. But suddenly when we feel eyes upon us, when we are being watched, our behaviour changes. This is quite akin to the double-slot experiment conducted in Germany in 1927 where a beam of electrons exhibiting a certain interference pattern immediately changed their behavior when a detector was placed to 'observe' them. The detector did nothing except watch the beam of electrons; and just that watching altered their behaviour.

"What are you thinking? You were so excited at the beach when the competition was announced," said Rohit after they had reached back to their hotel room. It was 5 P.M.

There were three hours left for the competition to start. He didn't know how and what to answer. Piyush and Ashish were on the bed, watching television in the room.

"Okay, let's look at all the tape cassettes we have and select a song," said Rohit as he went around and picked all the cassettes in the room.

"Okay, here we go... Pardes, Dil Toh Pagal Hai, Jazzy B, Jagjit Singh," he said while continuing, "Who got Jagjit Singh to bloody Goa?" Jagjit Singh was a masterful artist of slow, sad pieces of poetry coupled with music, called ghazals. Simply beautiful on a sombre and cold Sunday evening, but not something that belonged to a Saturday night in Goa.

"Anyway, moving on - Peter Andre, Backstreet Boys. Yes! That's the one. Backstreet Boys' 'Everybody'", or wait, there is Queen as well. So, 'Everybody' or 'We Will Rock You'?" asked Rohit.

Om wanted to pick ' We Will Rock You', but 'Everybody' was cooler. There was a line in the song where the singer asks - "Am I sexual?" and the answer comes 'Yeah!' Om used to love that.

"Everybody, by Backstreet Boys" he said.

"All right, guys, we need to make some room. Get off the bed and let's move it to the corner. Same with the sofa," said Rohit to Piyush and Ashish, who weren't pleased. They obliged nonetheless. Rohit connected his rather advanced Sony Walkman to the television to play the music.

The first step was the hardest to take. When Rohit hit play the first time, Om couldn't break into a step.

It was the same story second time round.

Rohit went up to him and said, "Just go for it. Forget all the opinions and the judgments that may come your way and let this be your dance. Come on now!"

The fourth time Rohit played, Om gave a spectacular performance. Within a few moments, the music took over and the rest flowed by itself, like a fallen branch of a tree flowing effortlessly with the current of a river. He did the entire song without any practice or rehearsal, completely impromptu.

"Wow bro! I never had an idea that you can dance so well," said Rohit, looking amazed.. Piyush and Ashish were suddenly interested and didn't mind being thrown off the sofa.

Om spent the next two and a half hours with Rohit, Piyush and Ashish. He needed to perfect the steps and get them right.

"It looks perfect," said Rohit.

Om felt nervous. It was 7:30 P.M. The time for the competition was very close. Seeing the look on Rohit's face, he thought that Rohit was more excited than him.

"Let's go and check out what others are doing," said Rohit.

"What do you mean?" he asked.

"Let's see what Varsha, Ruby, Sahil, and others are doing," said Rohit.

He looked at Piyush and Ashish. They could not contain their excitement.

Ruby's room was closest to theirs. They could hear the sound of the music from outside. The window curtains were slightly open in the middle and Rohit peeped in.

"Ruby and her group are rehearsing together. I think they are doing that step from 'Hit Me Baby One More Time'. Yes, that's it. They're dancing to Britney Spears," said Rohit. As an afterthought, he added, 'Damn, Ruby looks so hot in red!"

Everyone stared at Rohit, all amused and excited.

They then made their way up the stairs to Varsha's room. They could hear the music, but there was no way to look inside. Varsha knew well how to conceal and create a mystery around herself.

"Let's go and check out Sahil and his side-kicks," said Rohit.

Om could not help but feel apprehensive.

"Come on!" said Rohit. Piyush and Ashish followed him. He had no other choice but to follow.

"I can see Nimit and Suraj, topless and wearing jeans. They are doing Salman Khan's dance step from 'O O Jaane Jaana'," said Rohit. He couldn't control his laughter. 'O O Jaane Jaana' was one of the quintessential lover-boy songs in which the heartthrob of the nation, Bollywood actor Salman Khan, danced topless acting as a musician, playing out to a sea of females in the crowd.

"But, I don't see Sahil and Danny anywhere," said Rohit.

"Maybe they aren't performing," suggested Piyush.

Good for himself, Om thought.

Rohit wasn't too convinced with that idea. An alpha like Sahil not participating in a competition which was going to grab eyeballs of all the females – that was hard to believe.

"It's twenty minutes to eight. Come on, guys. We need to head back to our room and get ready quickly," Om said. The urgency had set in.

Everyone followed him.

On the way back to their room, the boys saw Sahil and Danny walking back to their room. Om avoided eye contact but could see both of them smile. It scared him whenever he saw them like that, but, that time, Om told himself to use it as a motivation.

The four of them entered their room to find suitcases thrown open on the bed. Each one of them started to rush since the time for the performances to begin were close. Ashish and Om had quick showers while Rohit and Piyush just wet their hair and applied gel on their heads.

Om took out a pair of washed denims and white body-fit tee-shirts. He thanked heavens for Rohit. He did not know what he would have done otherwise. As it is, he had not been given money for the trip to Goa. He doubted his father would have given him any money to shop.

"All right, guys, just five minutes to go. Come on," Om said, nervous. He took the support of a wall as he tied his shoe laces. "Rohit, pick the cassette," he said.

Rohit went over to the cassette player and opened the tray. Moments later, his friend passed him a stunned look.

Om got a feeling what he was about to say.

"The cassette is not in here," Rohit said.

Both of them looked at their roommates who told that the cassette was not with them either.

Rohit looked at Om and Om at him. They knew who had done it. Rohit ran outside, but Piyush, Ashish, and Om chased him down.

"What are you doing?" asked Om.

"I'm going to break the face of that fucker," said Rohit.

"Bro, there's no point. We have no evidence, and if another complaint reaches Mrs. Singh, both of us will be rusticated from the school," Om remarked.

"I don't care," Rohit said as he tried to break free from their clutches. They took him inside the room.

"It's almost eight. Let's just go and enjoy the evening. Forget that it ever happened," Om said with tears in his eyes. Rohit had tears in his eyes as well, though it was out of anger. Rohit just shook his head and didn't say a word. He was still fuming.

⋘⋙

The four boys reached the competition hall and took four vacant seats. There was a big stage in the hall in the middle. Chairs were laid all around it. Most of the students had taken a seat. Sahil and his sidekicks were across from where Om sat.

Om could see Rohit fuming and Sahil laughing.

He saw Rohit getting up from his seat. Fearing that he might confront Sahil and create a scene in front of everyone, he asked, 'Where are you going?". He held one of Rohit's hands, preventing him from leaving.

"I'm going to give your name for the competition," replied Rohit.

Om was shocked. "Are you mad? How can I perform? There is no music," he retorted.

Rohit paused for a moment and said, "I'm going to sing."

"WHAT!" was Om's first reaction. "No, no...," he said, trying to not be loud even as Rohit freed his arms from his grip and went ahead towards Ritu, who took entries for the competition.

A look of horror crossed Sahil's face for a moment. Perhaps he feared that Rohit might confront him or raise a complaint against him.

Rohit began saying something to their class teacher. He saw him make his puppy face. His friend sure knew how to work things and use his charm. The conversation ended and Rohit came back.

"Ritu has agreed to put your name last on the list. I told her that our cassette got lost last minute and that I will be singing for you. And you will perform," he said as he took his seat.

"All right, everyone. Silence!" exclaimed Ritu. "The competition is about to begin. Are you ready?" she asked, prompting the students to shout a loud 'yes'. There was a feeble collective shout of 'yes' at first, but she asked again, prompting the students to go louder. Most of them did.

"The first performance is going to be by Ruby, Nisha, Prerna, Komal, and Simran. Give it up for them," announced Ritu.

Ruby and her friends came to the stage amidst a loud cheer, wearing red ghaghra-choli -- a traditional dress with a long, fairy skirt and a blouse to go with it. They danced to a medley of Sridevi songs, getting multiple cheers during their performance. Ruby was the highlight of the performance. Om saw the teachers make some notes while the performance was going on, presumably scoring each performance.

The next to follow were three boys from Class -IX-E, dancing to 'O O Jaane Jaana', the same song Suraj and Nimit from Sahil's group were practicing to earlier in the evening. Om could see Sahil and his friends whinging and rolling their eyes as they saw those three boys dancing to the same song.

Rohit and Om shared a hearty laugh, the first they had had in the last one hour.

After a few performances, the announcement Om was waiting for rang in his ears.

"Varsha Sen from Class IX-A is going to be perform next," Ritu announced.

Everybody knew Varsha. There was no need of an introduction from Ritu, albeit she was just running through the routine. There were a few quiet moments in the hall. Some took a deep breath. The envious girls bitched among each other as to how loudly dressed she was and the boys geared up for a show.

Varsha was going to perform solo. She was wearing a white skirt, short enough for Mrs. Mehra to shake her head, and a white shirt with two buttons at the top, undone.

"Hit Me Baby One More Time". The music started playing. Britney Spears was like an icon for all of them. Being young, bold, sexy and uninhibited, she represented everything most of the students wanted to be. No one in the motley group of students embodied that spirit though, except for Varsha. Right from the start and to the finish, her performance elicited cheers and whistles from the boys, much to the dismay of Mrs. Mehra and the other girls on the trip. By the end of her performance, most of the students had an inkling who the winner of the competition would be.

Next came Sahil and his quartet. This was surprising since Rohit had only seen Suraj and Nimit practicing, not others. But as Om thought more about it, everything made sense.

The performance by Sahil and his three friends began with the four of them taking their shirts off. This sent some section of the crowd into a sardonic laughter and the other into a loud cheer.

The music started to the tune of 'O O Jaane Jaana, dhoonde tujhe deewana", which meant, 'Oh, my beloved, your lover is looking for you.' Sahil danced in the front while the other three were placed behind him. Danny was almost invisible. The performance started off well with the crowd getting behind them before Danny forgot one of the steps. They played catch-up after that. To top it off, there was a moment when Sahil attempted a back flip and landed straight on his knees. The performance ended and the four of them didn't even look at one another.

"The final performance is going to be by Om Vats from Class -IX-A. Om lost his music cassette minutes before the performance, so his friend, Rohit Sahu, will be singing the songs to which Om will dance," announced Ritu.

Om was highly strung and anxious. It was palpable. He was looking at Rohit.

Rohit got up in a second and looked back at him, asking him to get up.

Om got up, nervously, and started walking behind him. His heart was racing and pulsating. His eyes glanced upon Sahil for a second.

He stood right in the center of the stage and Rohit at the corner near the teachers. He looked at Rohit for a second and blinked his eyes to indicate that he was good to go. He took a deep breath at which Rohit started to sing.

He opened the sequence with a whirlpool, something he had not shown anyone during the practice. There was a deafening cheer in the hall, which got him pepped up. Rohit's voice grew louder as the crowd's cheer got louder. Om flowed from one step to another, engaging the audience and the teachers. In one of the sequences, he grabbed a rose from where the teachers sat and moon-walked up to Varsha to present it to her. He finished off with a one-hand stand before he jumped back on his feet. All he could hear were the claps that thunders in the hall. He looked at Rohit, who punched his fists into the air.

It was a remarkably profound moment for Om. He had confronted so many latent fears and apprehensions leading up to that performance. He looked at Rohit for a moment and saw the look of wonder and happiness on his face.. There was so much of noise and chaos around, yet that moment felt deeply peaceful.

"So, we had some great performances tonight. Some were group-dance sequences, the others were solos. There were a few singing performances, apart from Rohit's unintentional singing performance, which we loved", said Ritu, sending everyone into a laughter. "However, the performance that wins the award tonight was a performance of sheer grit, skill and entertainment," she continued as the crowd got silent. The winner was about to be announced.

"The award for the best performance goes to…," said Ritu. She took a long pause. "Om Vats from Class -IX-A."

A thunderous applause followed. There were cheers from all over the hall. Om stood with Rohit who patted him on the back. He looked at his friend with moist eyes and wondered what he had done to deserve a friend like him.

Om walked up to Ritu, who stood on the stage, where she handed him a bouquet, a trophy and an envelope. He took them in his hands and asked Rohit to join him in the middle.

Rohit, however, felt apprehensive, but Om went up to his friend and dragged him to the center-stage. This belonged to Rohit as much as it belonged to him. Of that he was sure. Both of them displayed the trophy to the entire batch. A round of applause reverberated at the display.

The teachers came and congratulated him one by one. Ruby and her friends arrived next. Varsha seemed disappointed at her own loss but thanked him for the rose he had given her during his performance. Before she left, she kissed him softly on his cheeks. Sahil and his friends were the only silent ones, sitting in a corner.

Om and Sahil locked eyes. For the first time ever, Om stared into Sahil's eyes until the latter looked away.

CHAPTER 25

A DINNER AND a dance party followed the competition. The DJ had begun setting up his equipment after the results were announced. Most of the students grabbed a quick snack. Some took soft drinks to hydrate themselves.

In about fifteen minutes, the DJ played the first song – 'Brazil' by Vengaboys.

Om had always wondered if that song was as popular in Brazil as it was in India.

Within seconds, everyone rushed to the dance floor and formed dance trains. Om had suddenly become hot property. People wanted to dance with him, especially a few girls. He tried to act cool and stuck to some basic moves with a can of Coca-Cola in his hands. At the same time, he looked out for Varsha.

Varsha was dancing really close to Sahil. Nimit, Suraj and Danny stood behind them, not dancing much. It looked like they were trying to act cool like Om was.

A few minutes later, Danny and Suraj went somewhere and came back with two glasses of soft drinks – one for Varsha and the other for Sahil. The dancing continued as more people joined in.

Ruby and her friends had formed a group with Om, Rohit, Ashish and Piyush.

Varsha was getting even closer to Sahil; at times she was turning away from Sahil to grind her hips on his body. Sometimes Sahil was holding her by her waist to pull her close, with her breasts pushing hard against his chest.

The teachers did not fail to notice this. Mrs. Mehra was quick to walk up to Varsha and Sahil and seemed to speak with them in a harsh tone. After that, Varsha was taken away by Mrs. Mehra. Sahil, clearly disturbed, looked in the direction Varsha was being taken.

"There's a rumor that Sahil and his friends have arranged alcohol from somewhere, which they have mixed in the drinks," Rohit whispered into Om's ear.

Om looked at his friend, amazed.

A few moments later, Varsha returned and started dancing near Om. Perhaps Mrs. Mehra had warned her about dancing so close to Sahil. Both Om and Varsha exchanged looks. He tried to get closer to her.

Varsha came really close to Om. The tip of her plum breasts pushed against Om's chest. Om felt embarrassed and instinctively pulled himself away. There was a strange smell emanating from Varsha's mouth and she stuttered a bit as she spoke. He wanted to get closer and pull her close to himself like Sahil had done, but he just didn't feel right about it.

Varsha wasn't impressed. She turned around and started dancing with Rohit, who was busy jiving with Ruby. Ruby wasn't amused by this unwarranted intervention. Rohit ignored Varsha's advances.

Varsha soon made her way towards Sahil again, only to be taken away by Mrs. Mehra once again. Sahil was displeased and left the dance floor.

———◆———

"This one's for all you beautiful boys and girls tonight. The last song goes out to the rock-stars of Shah Internationallllll!" announced the DJ in a typical DJ fashion. The last song to be played was 'Everybody' by Backstreet Boys. There was a huge roar as everyone looked at Om. By this time, almost everyone was on the dance floor, including the teachers. Ritu looked at Om, asked everyone to make some space in the middle and asked him to showcase some of his dance steps.

Om jumped in and performed a whirlpool followed by a handstand before everyone joined in and danced and jumped till the last beat of the song was played.

The party and the day...both had come to an end. There were chants of "one more song..." across the hall, but the DJ just smiled and began to pack up. Disappointment of the evening coming to an end was in as much measure as the hugs being passed around and the photographs being taken.

———◆———

"It has been the greatest night of my life," Om said to Rohit as they gave each other a fist bump. "Only if I could have danced really close to Varsha," he joked as he started walking towards the bathroom.

He had lost count of the cans of Coca-Cola he had consumed that evening. Rohit followed him.

Rohit suggested that they go to the bathroom at the opposite end of the resort since that was closest to the beach. Rohit wanted to take a quick stroll on the beach before the teachers ordered everyone to get back into the rooms. Om didn't mind.

Most of the students were still in the hall, talking and taking pictures with each other.

Rohit put his arms around his shoulders and said, "I'm proud of you, bro. If ever you think you can't do it, just remember this moment. You killed it tonight. If there's one memory with me that you always keep with you, let it be this evening".

"Don't kiss me now," Om joked as he pushed him away. The two of them broke into a laughter that filled the silent pathways of the resort.

As the two friends reached the men's room, Om heard some noise coming from the narrow pathway near the side of the restroom. He knew it led to the beach. However, he moved sideways, to look where the noise was coming from.

Sahil and Varsha were kissing each other. Varsha's skirt was on the floor and Sahil's shirt was open. Sahil had one of his hands on Varsha's breasts. Varsha's left hand was inside Sahil's pants. Just then, Sahil looked sideways and spotted both Rohit and Om looking. Varsha was oblivious to what was happening and didn't seem like she was in her senses.

Sahil kept looking at them as he turned Varsha around. Her back was now facing Rohit and Om. He then grabbed her buttocks with both his hands. His eyes were wide open, staring at Om the whole time he engaged Varsha.

Om turned around. He couldn't take it anymore and rushed into the toilet. Rohit followed him.

Om opened the tap to wash his hands after he had taken a leak in the bathroom. He couldn't get the images of what he had seen out of his head. Thoughts of jealousy, envy, possessiveness, et cetera were running amok in his mind. So was the water running from the tap. Rohit turned it off.

He stared at his reflection in the mirror for what seemed like ages. A few moments passed. He didn't want to go out; rather, he wished he could bury himself in that restroom. Rohit left the room and returned after a few moments.

"There's no one outside now. I'll wait for you at the beach," said Rohit as he moved out.

Om splashed water on his face a few times and exited the door. He walked the same pathway where he saw Varsha almost naked, but with another boy. He turned his gaze away from the spot as he walked towards the beach.

The night was serene. The moon was almost full. Tides reached way further than they did during the day.

Rohit lay down on the sand, staring at the stars. Om went and laid himself down, next to him.

"How do you feel?" Rohit asked as he turned towards his right and acknowledged Om's presence.

Om kept looking at the sky. The silence after all that had happened was enrapturing.

"Many years ago, when I was a child, I was in love with this girl called Farheen. Every day, we would travel back home together in a cycle rickshaw. I would rush out of the school to catch a glimpse of her as she walked out of the gate, share my lunch with her, watch her when she would offer namaaz with her parents. One day, she suddenly stopped talking to me. I reached home badly hurt and upset. That day I had taken a flower from the community garden for Farheen. I thought it was an expression of my feelings for her. By the time I came home, the petals of the rose flower were almost dead. They didn't have any life. That day my Naani gave me a lesson - how love needed to be free, how love needs to empower and not enslave. The moment love tries to possess, that very moment it dies," Om said softly, after a long pause.

"Of course, I wanted me to be in Sahil's place. Of course, I was livid when I saw her with him. But then I remembered Naani's lesson. Our consciousness must transcend our instincts if intelligence has to flourish," he added, softly.

Rohit turned around and ran his arm around his chest. Just like a lover would.

CHAPTER 26

THE NEXT MORNING, Rohit woke all of his roommates at 7:30 A.M. The breakfast was scheduled at 8 A.M. Thereafter, everyone was supposed to head out to visit the famous churches of Goa. Rohit was ready with his hair neatly gelled in place. He looked sharp in a beige-colored denim and white shirt.

"How come you're up and ready so early?" Piyush asked Rohit. He was perplexed. So were Om and Ashish.

"That's what the most handsome boy in the batch does," joked Rohit. The others weren't convinced. They got ready as quick as they could.

On their way to the restaurant, Rohit was unusually quiet. He put his arms around Om's shoulder and said, "Last night was the best night of my life."

Om didn't say anything. Something just didn't feel right to him. They kept walking towards the restaurant.

As they entered the restaurant, Sahil looked at them, a tad grim. Varsha sat at the opposite end with her friends, laughing about something.

The four of them took a plate each and served themselves some breakfast.

"Everyone assemble here, please," announced Ritu when everyone was done with the breakfast.

"Today, we are going to bid Rohit Sahu of Class -IX-A goodbye", she said. Everybody was stunned, no one more so than Om.

Rohit walked forward to stand beside Ritu.

"Rohit's father has been transferred to Mumbai for work. He is outside the hotel right now to pick Rohit up and take him to Mumbai. Rohit will be starting a new life in a new school. We all at Shah International had a great time with Rohit and wish him the best going forward. Please wish Rohit the best from your end as well. Please assemble outside the reception in exactly fifteen minutes for our excursion of the day," added Ritu.

Om couldn't believe his ears. All of a sudden, his world was shaken. He already had tears roll down his cheeks. He couldn't process what had just happened. Rohit was leaving!

A lot of students and teachers approached Rohit. He responded to everyone who wished him well with a simple smile. After exchanging pleasantries for a few minutes, he walked up to Om and threw his right arm over his shoulder.

"Let's go outside," said Rohit.

Om heard Ritu in the background, asking the students to leave the two friends alone.

"Why didn't you tell me?" Om asked. He tried controlling himself but started sobbing.

"I wanted to keep you away from this for as long as possible," Rohit replied, mellow.

Om kept crying and shook his head. None of them spoke anything for a few seconds.

"When did you find out?" asked Om, trying hard to control his tears.

"It was something that was building up. My father was working towards it. He always wanted to move to Mumbai where the headquarters of Air India are. Sooner or later, I knew, it was bound to happen. But, it officially happened the day you and I were beaten by Sara's brother. My father told me when he came into the room and you left the two of us alone. Remember?" he answered.

Om started walking towards the beach. Rohit followed him.

"Go away!" Om shouted and started running.

"Not before you give me a last hug," Rohit shouted back and ran towards him.

Om started running and tried to get away from him. Rohit caught up and grabbed hold of him.

"I can't go away without letting you know how much I love you and what you've given me," said Rohit.

Om pushed him away. Tears left his eyes again. Rohit didn't move. He stood there.

Om again started to walk in the other direction, away from everything – Rohit, the resort, the whole situation. He turned around after a few moments. Rohit still stood there, looking at him.

Om shook his head and ran with as much speed as he could, as if all the dogs in the world were chasing him. He jumped right on Rohit. They both had tears flowing like a river from their eyes as they hugged each other.

"Keep this with you," said Rohit as he handed Om a chit of paper.

It had a number written on it.

"This is my phone number when I will be in Mumbai. If ever there's anything or at any time you feel like reaching out to me, I'm always there," said Rohit.

"I won't," Om said.

Rohit smiled back at him and shook his head.

Om saw Rohit looking over his shoulder and getting a little uncomfortable. Om turned around and saw who it was. It was Sahil and his friends. They were mocking them both.

Om turned to Rohit, who smiled again. Rohit knew it didn't matter. But in that moment, it mattered to Om more than anything else.

He turned around. Sahil was still mocking both of them. Om paused for a moment before he started running up to Sahil with all the energy that he had. Om was so fast and his action so unexpected that Sahil couldn't react. Within seconds, Om was right in front of Sahil. Sahil was frozen and hadn't moved an inch. Om lifted his arm and punched Sahil straight in the face with all his energy. There was no one else around.

"Go run towards the reception. I'll take care of him," shouted Rohit from where he was standing.

Om landed another punch on Sahil, who lay writhing on the ground. He turned around, smiled back at Rohit, and ran straight towards the reception.

PART 3

CHAPTER 27

"JUST TEXT NATASHA we'll be in college for the next lecture. I've already asked Mohit to put an attendance proxy for us in the lecture today," said Om to Arun.

Om and Arun had studied together a long time ago. Alpha-Beta school to be precise. Arun was the class teacher Ms. Ratna Devi's favourite student, and Om, the least favourite.

However, much had changed since those days. Arun was no longer the front-bencher and Om no longer lived in Jaipur. As fate were to have it, both were studying in the prestigious University of Technology in Delhi, and in less than one year, they were going to call it their alma mater.

University of Technology, Delhi, brought together the brightest engineering minds in the country and was also the largest source of what was commonly referred to as 'brain drain'. More than sixty per cent of the students would get placements abroad and leave in hope of a better life, not to mention the pursuit of a stronger currency.

The 'Algorithm Analysis and Design' lecture was going on. Om and Arun had their attendance levels dropped to below fifty per cent, which could cause them some trouble during the final year placements. But, apparently, checking out girls at Lady Shri Ram College, or LSR as it was commonly called, was an equal priority.

LSR was about nine kilometres from their university or thirty minutes in the usual traffic. Om, however, on his second-hand 180cc Pulsar motorcycle, had mastered the art of manoeuvring the Delhi traffic.

"Look at that girl, bro," said Om. "That serenity in her eyes, the way her hair is clutched all the way up, with just a loose strand running over her eyes. That's the kind of girl I want to love."

Arun stood right next to Om, staring at him. "You just keep on standing here, among the hordes of other desperate wannabe boys on their bikes, but never manage to actually go up to a girl and woo her," joked Arun.

"Just because you are with Natasha, it doesn't mean you go about taking everyone's case," responded Om. "I want to love; I want to feel it deep within me. I want it to move mountains, for it to come and mutate every cell in me."

"You also want to lose your virginity," joked Arun.

Both of them laughed. LSR and many other colleges in the south campus of the Delhi University attracted some of the most beautiful girls in the country. For engineering college boys, where the sex ratio was heavily skewed in favor of the males, a motorcycle ride to the south campus colleges provided a regular dose of entertainment.

South Delhi was also home to some of the richest people in the country. It was fascinating to see how material richness and physical beauty often went hand-in-hand. Sometimes, the former led to the latter. At other times, it was the opposite.

"She's right there alone. Go and ask for her number," Arun murmured in Om's ear.

"No way. This is so creepy. What if she has a boyfriend?" asked Om.

Arun shook his head, turned away from Om's face to light up a cigarette, and turned back around. The girl was off on someone's Royal Enfield motorcycle.

Mobile phones had made their way into the market in a huge way. They had revolutionized how people connected with each other. Recently, Vodafone had just launched a Two-to-Talk scheme, which offered fifteen-hundred free text messages a month. This, of course, meant that the inboxes on the girls' phones were inundated with jokes and friendship requests.

———◆◆◆———

Om and Arun soon realized that they were late for another lecture and took off on their motorcycle. Despite Om's antics with his motorcycle, they failed to reach in time for the lecture because of a major truck breakdown on the Savitri flyover.

Professor Sonali Joshi was giving a lecture on 'Database Management Systems', the course in which Om was dangerously low on attendance. Sonali, however, had been kind on him. Even though short on attendance, he was well-known as one of the brightest students in the class. Being that, most professors, especially Sonali, excused the lack of attendance on his part. Add to that, he was the teacher's favourite, which had been a rare occurrence in Om's life as a student.

250

Arun, however, was more adept where attendance was concerned. He was seeing Natasha, an outgoing girl in the class, which was somewhat of an unheard combination at engineering colleges in India. Being a good lover, she ensured Arun received his regular share of attendance proxies, assignment completions, and important reminders.

Sonali had begun the lecture. Om and Arun were outside the class. Om tried to find Natasha through the small opening in the entrance of the class room.

A phone vibrated and Natasha picked up her cell. The message read: 'See outside, stupid.' It was from Om.

Natasha looked at Om for a second and then turned around to concentrate on the lecture.

Another ping made her squirm. This time the message read: 'Please, please, please.'

She paused for a while and picked up the phone in her hand.

This time, Om received a text back from her. Her message said, 'I texted you guys about an hour ago. Go to hell. This is the last time I'm doing your proxy attendance call. You both will get me suspended one day.'

Om smiled and gave her a flying hug.

"Companies have begun registrations for campus placements. Sonali Ma'am announced in the class today," said Natasha as the lecture finished.

Om and Arun were finally able to enter the classroom.

"We all know where Om is going," quipped Arun as he ran his arms around Natasha.

She kissed him on the cheeks.

Om's dream company was Softzone Corporation, a multinational software giant that had its headquarters in San Francisco, California. Well, it wasn't just Om's dream; it was almost every other engineer's. The company was at the forefront of an internet revolution in the world, transforming the way information was stored and shared in the world. Also, it was his dream to build a better life, to experience the American ways that he had so often familiarized himself with, through their television shows, movies, music, art and literature. But getting into the company wasn't easy. About one in a thousand made the cut.

The college's placement cell had one thumb rule. A student was allowed to have only one placement in hand. As soon as one was placed with a company, the college barred that student from applying for another. This was done in a bid to ensure equal distribution of placement opportunities among students rather than a few top students bagging placements at multiple companies.

"Are you sure you are going to hold out for Softzone?" asked Natasha as she ran her hand over Arun's shirt, caressing his chest.

Arun and Natasha were particularly notorious for their public displays of affection.

"It's one of the last companies to hit the campus, so if you miss out, then it's big trouble," she added.

Om nodded. Safety and security had never been Om's motivations. He was either all in or all out. Lukewarmth and insipidity were not his ways of life.

Monali Mehrotra, the lecturer who took Software Systems, entered the class. Natasha's hand slipped away from Arun's shirt immediately.

CHAPTER 28

IT HAD BEEN a busy weekday evening at 'Pizza Corner', the local pizza joint in Paschim Vihar, a western suburb in the sprawling metropolis of Delhi. Western Suburbs were to South Delhi what New Jersey was to New York. Trying to get there, but not quite. Om worked three to four evenings a week. That covered his living expenses.

Om was doing his final chores before closing shop when his mobile rang. He answered the call.

"Namaste, Mummy, how are you?" asked Om.

It was his mother at the other end. "I'm fine. Just missing you a lot today," she replied, her voice breaking up a little.

She had suffered a stroke a couple of years ago. It had left her body paralysed and bed-ridden. How painful it must have been for a mother to miss a child, with every cell of her body wanting to be with him! But then, she wasn't able to move even an inch. The agony between desire and outcome, between dreams and reality – she had to suffer through it.

She was not that old. Not more than fifty. Her treatment was going on in the public hospital, but the family had lost all hopes of recovery. She had lost it a long time ago.

"I miss you too, Mummy. I want to send you a lot of love. I will visit you soon. The companies are now beginning to visit the campus for placements. Once the placement season is over, I will come running to you," said Om as he held the phone between his right shoulder and left ear while cleaning the kitchen with the other two hands.

"All the best, lalla," she wished. *Some things never changed.*

"I asked your father to make a visit next week to Delhi to give you some Kachoris from Shankar and the lemon pickle I had asked him to prepare," she said.

Mahesh had to leave his job and look after Kiran full-time when she got sick. Fortunately, Babu had left them some money. Mahesh himself had saved a bit to last the family some time, at least until Om started earning.

"Mummy, there's no need. Let it be. I will have the kachoris and pickle when I come to Jaipur," said Om with a sigh.

"But you haven't spoken with you father in over six months now. He never calls you, you never call him. I'm worried for him. Where will he go when I die?" asked his mother as she broke down over the phone.

"Mummy, it doesn't matter whether we speak or not. I promise you that I will do my duty as a son, irrespective..." responded Om.

There was a pause on both sides.

"I have to hang up, Mummy, and head back home," said Om. He bid his mother goodbye.

The clock had touched midnight with the moon at it apex. Distant barking of dogs replaced the chatter of dinner-time guests. Most of the restaurants and shops had wrapped up, but Pizza Corner was running for a long time even after that. The last-minute, night-time munchers, those people who were hungry even after dinner or the average Delhi alcoholics, were all regular customers of the joint. But that night, Om was greeted by a new customer.

"Hey!" Om heard a female voice in the background and turned around.

The girl was petite but well-endowed. By the tone of her skin, she could be construed as though she was an Afghani or Kashmiri. The complexion of her skin suggested so. Her hair was lush and let loose, collected on one side and placed in front of her right shoulder. Her light-green eyes reflected the light bulb behind Om's head in the background. She was dressed in a blue kurta with exquisite chikankari on it. A small bracelet adorned her right wrist while her left hand held a white wallet.

Whenever such moments, few as they were, unfold in front of us, time seems to often freeze. Whether it is magic or shock, none can tell.

Time had frozen when the dogs chased Om outside Naani's house; time had frozen when Naani passed away; time had frozen when Om saw Farheen for the last time near that tree; time had frozen when Om ran away from Rohit; and time froze that fateful evening when Om saw that girl in the blue kurta.

"Can I get a Spinach and Corn Pizza?" the girl asked.

Om heard it, but remained still, aware of the feelings he experienced. He could not immediately respond.

"Hello!" he heard the voice again.

"Sorry, we're ... closed," uttered Om in a mellow voice with a duster in his hands.

"Not even a packed one? The last one left over?" the girl asked.

Om just shook his head without saying anything.

She heaved a deep sigh, rolled her eyes, and took out a Blackberry cell phone from her wallet. She did something on her phone and placed it on her ears as she turned around to leave.

Om didn't move an inch; he was still enamored by her presence. The moon had been full for many an age; but the allure in the moonlight was quite extraordinary that night.

———◈———

"Do you want to go to Miranda College today?" asked Arun as he and Om lay on the lush green grass under the shade of a tree in the Lodhi Gardens.

"Why doesn't Natasha kill you?" asked Om, sarcastically. "Does she know what we get up to most of the times when we bunk classes?"

"Dude, she will, if she finds out we go bird watching. She just thinks we go out and play Snooker or Cricket somewhere. Plus, to be fair, I'm just watching, not really doing anything," remarked Arun.

"What's your problem, why are you being judgmental?" retorted Arun, defensively, moments later.

"I'm not being judgmental, I was just asking," said Om with a smirk.

Arun shook his head.

"I met an incredible girl last night," said Om after a long pause.

"And?" questioned Arun after another long pause.

"And it was pure magic. Never before did the breeze feel so cool when someone opened the gate and entered the restaurant. Never before did anyone speak with such tenderness in her voice. Never before did someone's eyes look so innocent," said Om softly.

Arun started laughing, which he just ignored.

"She asked a couple of questions. I just stood there as if time had frozen. I don't even know how I responded," continued Om. "I just wanted to keep looking at her."

Arun kept laughing, even after Om sent a water bottle flying at him.

"Did you ask for her number, at least her name?" asked Arun, after a little pause.

He shook his head.

"Forget about it then. Go home and find a hair loss remedy that works," joked Arun, hitting him right where it hurt.

It seemed like Arun wasn't happy about Om making him conscious about his bird-watching escapades in Natasha's absence. But a retort about hair loss did not seem fair either. For Om, it was a sensitive issue. He was barely twenty, just out of his teenage years. And his hairline was receding already around the temples. Faster than the reputation of the Indian Prime Minister, Manmohan Singh, even.

Baldness was supposed to be genetic. His father had a full head of hair even at fifty-five. Considering that his father's side did not suffer from the malady either, the only way he could be bald was for his genes to pick the X-chromosome from his mother, who in turn, would have inherited it from Babu.

"At least I don't have a small dick," retorted Om, clearly offended.

Arun kept laughing, rubbing it in to Om even further.

⬦

Om lived as a paying guest with an old couple in Naraina, a suburb half-way between his college and the Pizza Corner where he worked. The nights he didn't have to go on the job, he spent them in engineering research, completing assignments, and of late, his final year project. He had been developing a text-to-speech engine, which was a software program designed to convert a piece of written text into spoken word. Many of Om's nights were spent writing code for it. Of course, he never stopped his random internet surfing.

Many times, he would end up searching for hair loss remedies and cures on related blogs or forums. He was an active member of the forum, ' Big Life, Thin Hair'.

An advertisement popped up on Om's screen as he was browsing the internet, claiming to be the newest revolutionary product for those who suffered from hair loss. He was amazed at how businesses chased people down on the internet with advertisement, knowing exactly what they wanted. That was a technology Softzone Corporation was at the forefront of.

The 'Before' and 'After' pictures using the revolutionary hair loss product were unbelievable. A man with less than half a head of hair in the 'before' picture had a full head of hair in the 'after' one. All with the help of 'Putit Hair-Building Fibers', which one needed to sprinkle on their head like seasoning on food. Within a short time, the hair micro-fibers would give one a full head of thick hair.

The product page listed a thousand rupees for a ten-milligram bottle. But would it be useful for him? Om asked himself. His hair was receding near the temple and not at the top of his head, which was called 'Bodhi' by the Hindus. But, it might work if he did a combover to cover his temples and then used those fibers to give his hair a fuller look. The product would work, he convinced himself, and searched for the shipping terms. The product, it said, would be shipped from America and would take up to twenty-one days to reach Delhi. Too long, he thought. What if that girl came to the Pizza joint again? He needed to be ready for a date with destiny that might show up anytime.

There was another option. Another five hundred rupees would ensure that the courier delivered it to him within a week. That's perfect, he said to himself.

It was an expensive affair – almost half his monthly wage at the pizza place. But a full head of hair – priceless indeed.

CHAPTER 29

ALONG WITH OM'S, Arun's final year project was one of the most anticipated ones at the University of Technology in Delhi. Students and professors alike looked forward to it. He was building a language translation engine, specifically for India. It was a project of remarkable ambition, considering that India had over one-hundred-and-fifty languages spoken. The project was garnering attention from other colleges across the country and even a few companies in the market. This was also one of the reasons why both Arun and Om had it easy with their attendance situation. Their academic achievements made up for their lapses in formal requirements.

"Bro, let's go to the Kulcha Corner. Come on," said Om to Arun as the latter was writing his code sitting in the college library.

"Come on!" Om poked his friend again.

"Just two more minutes," said Arun.

Om tried to get close to Arun's laptop.

His friend, though, smiled and tapped him to get away.

He tried again, determined not to let go.

'Fine, fine, let's go!' Arun remarked as he got up with his hands raised, frustrated after Om's repeated attempts to take a peek at his project.

A few moments later, they were speeding away on Om's motorcycle.

'Chole Bhature' was a famous North Indian dish that had achieved a God-like status in the country, especially in the states of Delhi, Punjab, Haryana, and Uttar Pradesh. It was a combination of spicy chickpeas called 'chole' served with fried bread made from white flour called 'bhature'.

Kulcha Corner, situated in a suburb called Karol Bagh, was one of the most famous joints for Chole Bhature. People from all over the city converged at that joint for a delicious meal. The portions were so generous that whenever he and Arun had a serving each for lunch, they did not feel the need to eat again for the rest of the day.

On the way back, Arun asked him to let him ride the motorcycle. He agreed, though hesitant. His friend wasn't as bad as Babu was, but only marginally better.

It was a pleasant winter afternoon in Delhi. The city's winters were famous across India as Rajasthan's summers or Meghalaya's monsoons. The sun shone bright. The parks were full of people bathing in the sun during the daytime and the evenings were a perfect time for a cup of tea with a dose of television.

Arun drove through the bustling streets of Delhi as if he had a lot of time on his hand. Usually, they would take a more direct route to the college from Karol Bagh. This meant passing through Moti Bagh straight into RK Puram. Once there, the college wasn't too far.

But Arun took a detour that day through a suburb called Vasant Kunj. This area, as most of the southern Delhi suburbs, was one of the focal points of the young college crowd. Om didn't mind the detour, although he did check on the fuel indicator from time to time.

Arun stopped at a tea stall right outside PVR Priya, one of the oldest movie theatres in Delhi and a favourite of the youngsters. It was a perfect day for it -- bright and sunny. There was no class to rush back to.

Arun ordered two cups of ginger tea and led Om to a seat on the bench right next to the stall.

"Natasha has been acting a bit weird, bro," said Arun. "She's been talking about which company I plan to secure a job placement with, whether I would ask for a job location in Delhi itself. I mean I haven't even started my career and she wants to control it already," said Arun in a way that sounded more like a complaint. "I mean, I love her, but..." Arun, at that moment, noticed that Om wasn't paying attention to him and was focused on something in front of him.

Arun turned around and saw a girl who looked as if she had come out of a painter's dream. The sight was so enchanting that he stopped whatever he was complaining about and looked at the miracle in front of him. Her aura had a brilliant resplendence. The girl was standing next to a Levi's jeans showroom, wearing a black maxi dress, her hair tied up in a pony tail, and a light blue canvas tote bag rested on one of her shoulders. She seemed fashionable yet seemed to have a depth than went way beyond the external appearance.

"This is the girl I saw the other night at Pizza Corner," said Om after a long pause.

Arun looked at Om and said, "She is way out of your league bro. Forget about it."

Om didn't seem to care a bit about what Arun had said. He got up from his seat and started walking towards the girl who stood across the busy main road. For a brief moment, their eyes locked. She looked at him for a moment and then at something to her right. A bus honked at Om, startling him. He stepped back to let it pass.

"Are you blind or what? Bloody idiot," shouted the driver from the window as the bus drew closer to him.

Om wasn't bothered. The bus sped away, but when Om looked in the direction of the girl, she had vanished. Om shook his head in disbelief and turned towards the bus in dismay.

"As expected, Librasoft is the first company to hit the campus," said Natasha.

The last lecture of the day had come to an end. Most of the students headed towards the exit gate.

"Arun and I are registering our candidature. We just want to play safe and get a placement rather than holding out till the end. Are you sure you don't want to sit for Librasoft?" Natasha asked Om.

Om didn't say anything for a few seconds, but then nodded. He was sure he wanted to be a part of Softzone more than any other company.

Arun, Natasha and Om walked for a while before reaching the latter's motorcycle.

"Natasha and I are planning to go to Hauz Khas Village this evening. There's a techno night happening at Social. You should come along as well," Arun said to Om.

"I will think about it," Om said.

"Two of Natasha's hottest friends are also coming," joked Arun.

For that, Natasha slapped him on the back of his head.

The trio shared a warm laugh. "See you at eight outside Social at HKV," Natasha said to Om before she walked away, arms-in-arms with his friend.

Om arrived early at Social. The traffic had been lighter than usual. Strange, he had thought.

Hauz Khas Village, or the 'Village' as it was called, was beginning to be seen as one of the most happening spots in Delhi. It was an artsy neighborhood that comprised of a number of lanes criss-crossing each other, only meant to be navigated by pedestrians and not vehicles. The bustling by-lanes had cafes, art galleries, funky shops, independent fashion boutiques, massage parlors, trendy restaurants, and hip bars. All of this was housed by the side of the ruins of a fort, said to have been built around the 13th Century. To top it all, was a lake.

Om saw Arun and Natasha, along with two other girls, walk up the only street that led up to the village. The other two girls were drop-dead gorgeous. One wore a little black dress and black heels. The other was dressed in a skirt with a halter top.

"This is Simi," said Natasha, pointing to the girl in the black dress. "And, this is Monica," she pointed towards the girl in the skirt and halter top.

Om shook hands with Simi and extended one towards Monica. The latter came forward and gave him a hug. He turned his hand around her back to reciprocate. He was surprised at the gesture but felt welcomed towards it.

The niceties done, all five of them headed into Social and were greeted by a staff member who provided them with a table. They ordered a bottled drink to begin with, which arrived at the table in no time.

Arun and Natasha headed to the dance floor, which was already buzzing with people and the latest techno music. In no time, Arun's and Natasha's arms were around each other.

"Natasha was telling me great things about you. She said you're a great dancer," said Monica as she bent in towards Om's ear. The music was getting louder.

"I'm okay, I guess. Nothing special, really," said Om, in a rather cold tone. A stunning girl, all dressed up, expected a warmer response to her conversation starter.

"Are you going to show me some of your dance moves?" Monica replied, trying to take the conversation forward. Perhaps, she expected him to lead her towards the dance floor.

"After a drink, maybe," replied Om.

Simi, in the meanwhile, had been picked up by a boy who struck up a conversation with her outside the girls' toilet.

Om and Monica sat there, feeling awkward, watching Arun and Natasha kiss the daylights out of each other on the dance floor.

Where's Simi?" asked Natasha as she and Arun returned to the table.

"She's with that guy there," answered Monica, pointing towards Simi and the black-haired boy having a conversation by the corner of the dance floor.

Natasha and Monica started talking about something. Arun and Om managed to do the same. A few minutes later, Arun and Natasha signalled to each other that they should hit the floor again and this time, they took Om and Monica with them.

Natasha started to grind with Arun when the DJ played, 'U Can't Touch This' by Tetrixx. Monica watched on, standing right next to Om, who had a drink in his hand and made some customary moves on the floor just to show he was enjoying the music.

Monica started showing her moves, flicking her hair on one side, throwing her arms up in the air and swaying her body even as Om watched. She came closer to Om, took his hands, and put them around her waist.

Om grooved for a while before excusing himself to the restroom. A while later, he returned to the table and resumed his drink. Monica was alone on the dance floor.

—◆◆◆—

"What's wrong with you today? Why are you so cold?" Arun asked Om as he returned to the table.

"Nothing's wrong, why do you think so?" Om questioned back.

"Monica has been all over you from what I can see and you're being so cold," said Arun as Natasha and Monica looked at the table a couple of times from the dance floor.

"Nothing bro, I just can't get that girl out of my head. That's all on my mind right now," said Om. Arun was at a loss of words. Om didn't seem interested in anything happening around him.

"Sorry bro, I think I need to head out now. There's a lot of work to be done on my project, yet, and time's running out," added Om as he got up and gave Arun a hug. He went to the dance floor and hugged Natasha and Monica. He whispered in the latter's ears, "Sorry, it's not you; it's just that I have something going on in my mind."

CHAPTER 30

THE NEXT DAY, Om set himself on the bench of the tea stall opposite PVR Priya in Vasant Kunj. He hoped to catch a glimpse of the girl who had captivated and taken over his senses. The tea vendor didn't mind at all. He would rather have ten roadside Romeos than nobody as long as they had cups of tea in their hands.

The sun descended steadily, and so did the day. Buses, cars, two-wheelers, auto rickshaws, all passed one by one. So did a line of people that included children, men, women, animals and the elderly. But there was no sign of that girl. Om waited nonetheless. There was a strange allure in the wait. Om felt sure that he was going to meet that girl one day or the other, sooner or later. From where that conviction arose, even he didn't know.

'Natasha and I have registered our candidature for Librasoft. Just letting you know. Didn't see you the whole day. I think I can guess where you are :P' read a text on Om's phone. It was from Arun.

"Sir, it is time for me to close the shop now," said the tea vendor.

Om stood up without complaint and helped the gentleman pack up. "If you don't mind, can I ask you a question?" the tea vendor asked Om.

Om nodded, aware of what the question was going to be.

"What is it that you keep staring at, on the other side of the road?" asked the tea vendor.

Om smiled and paused for a bit.

"There's a long-lost friend I'm searching for," answered Om.

"Can I help you find that friend?" asked the tea vendor again.

"No," replied Om calmly. "If you find her for me, then my search was futile. It's as much about the journey as it is about the destination," added Om.

The tea vendor listened patiently.

"What's your name?" asked Om.

"Charan Singh," replied the tea vendor.

"The times have really changed. Five professors and the Chancellor of the college are waiting for a student to bestow the honour of their arrival," taunted Ashok Dayal, the Chancellor of the college, as Om walked into a lecture hall to deliver a presentation on his final year project – the 'Text-to-Speech' engine he was building.

Om was ten minutes late for a presentation. He had had a long night the previous day, partly because of giving final touches to the project before the presentation and partly because of trying out the new hair fibres that had arrived in the mail.

"I'm really sorry, sir," said Om as he jostled to take out his mammoth Dell laptop that was heavy enough to be used for body-building. He connected the laptop to the projector and began the presentation. As the presentation went along, the professors and the Chancellor were mighty impressed with the way the software worked. It offered a remarkable breakthrough to make knowledge on computer more accessible to the visually challenged population. It proposed a new way to consume books, novel, or any form of textual material on a computer screen.

"And each spoken word by the bot in the engine is recorded into a relational database, which can later be used for breakthrough insights into how language is used across the world. This data, later on, can be more valuable than the application itself. The only thing now left for me in this engine is to iron out some bugs, which should take another week or so," said Om as he finished his presentation.

The professors and the Chancellor congratulated him on the progress before dismissing the meeting. They were amazed at the finesse of the project.

Om was ready to get on his motorcycle again and do what he had been waiting to do since the day began.

⊰⊱

"Welcome again, Sir," said Charan Singh as he saw Om approaching his tea stall.

Om raised his hand and smiled in acknowledgment before taking a seat on the bench near Charan's tea stall.

Om placed his legs, one on either side of the bench and rested his back against a wall. In spite of not having been successful in finding the girl, he was enjoying his time. It reminded him of the time he had spent alone as a child in Naani's house when both his grandparents would be fast asleep. He would sit by the window next to the cooler and watch the world pass by. There was a profound peace in that solitude, one that was entrenched deep in his psyche.

The tea vendor handed him his first cup of tea for the day. He, on the other hand, took out a CD player, connected the head phones, and put them on his ear. Song after song passed and so did the world. However, the girl Om was searching for, did not.

Charan Singh handed Om what seemed like the last cup of tea for the day. Om played his last song for the evening. '*Yoon shabnami, pehli nahi thi chaandni*', it was titled. The words were in Urdu, which when literally translated would mean, 'the moonlight was never as resplendent as it is tonight.'

<hr>

"Come, Sir, please have a seat," said Charan Singh as Om reached the tea stall again. Third day in a row.

There was a cooler box placed at the end of the bench where Om used to sit.

"I had placed this here so that no one could take your place," said Charan as he lifted it up and placed it on the ground behind him.

Following the ritual, Om crossed his legs across the bench, with one leg hanging on either side of the bench, took a CD player out, and plugged the headphones in. Charan handed over the first cup of the day to Om.

Many songs had passed, but there was no hint of the girl Om was pursuing. Yet, Om was persistent, without a crease on his forehead.

The lovers must have been made of different flesh and bones, with each cell trying to be crazier than the rest. They must be able to see something beyond the anxieties, the insecurities and the uncertainties that love comes with. They must be able to see something that gives them a kind of patience that doesn't belong to the realm of rationality, but to the realm of devotion.

The sun was setting again, indicating the end of the day. Charan handed over the last cup of the day to Om, who by now had developed enough credibility with the tea vendor so as to have a credit with him. He sipped the last tea from the cup, got up from the bench, and threw it in the dustbin.

'Where have you been? Haven't seen you since Thursday. It's almost the end of the weekend' read a text from Arun as Om started walking towards his motorcycle after another unsuccessful day.

'Will see you next week in the college. Just busy with some stuff', Om sent a text message back to Arun.

Just as he had pressed the *Send* button, the sound of a bus's engine reached his ears.

'Tired of searching? Be Found by your soulmate. Register at ArrangedLove.com', read an advertisement on the bus. He found it amusing.

The bus passed and he saw a girl walking towards the corner of the Levi's showroom. He rubbed his eyes and then kept staring. He couldn't believe it. It was the same girl who had come to the pizza shop.

Om couldn't believe it. He had found her again.

There was a subway built to cross the road to the other side. It was a short walk but he was afraid that the girl would disappear by then as she had done the last time. He ran across the road as soon as he saw an opening. A few angry drivers honked and hurled abuses at him. He was now on the divider in the middle of the road. She was still there, but the traffic was high-speed and non-stop.

She saw him from across the road and stared strangely at him. Anyone would, if they saw someone standing on a narrow divider trying to cross a road when a whole subway had been built for that same purpose.

Om managed to get a dash in and cross the road. He came to a stop right in front of the girl, huffing and panting. He gained his balance and smiled at her. "Hi, I am Om," he said.

She pulled her head back a little, a tad startled, but returned his smile with one of her own. "Hi, I'm Ayesha," she introduced herself.

Both of them smiled at each other and didn't say anything.

"I've seen you around, but can't quite remember," said Ayesha.

Om smiled but didn't say anything.

"Would you like to come with me for a cup of tea sometime?" asked Om.

Ayesha was shocked at his direct approach but smiled nonetheless. .

"What makes you think I'm going to go out with someone I don't know?" she asked.

"I've had too many cups of tea alone, waiting for you. What took you so long?" joked Om, pointing at the tea stall on the opposite side of the road.

Ayesha couldn't stop smiling.

"You're weird, aren't you?" she said.

Om shrugged his shoulders.

"Meet me tomorrow outside 'Mocha', the one at the Village. 5 P.M. Now go, my car is here," she said as she stopped looking at Om and moved aside.

A chauffeur-driven Mercedes Benz S-Class stopped by the kerbside to pick her up.

Om didn't work that night at the Pizza Corner. He opened his laptop and started researching on hair loss again. The hair fibers he ordered were good, but could not be used daily, especially when he rode a motorcycle and had to wear a helmet. It was a good concealment solution for a party or an evening out in dry weather but did not offer a lasting and permanent solution.

Arun's comments about his hairline the other day still triggered him. He felt bullied. Connecting with people over the Internet facing similar issues gave him some sort of a temporary solace. People on hair loss forums had been talking about this revolutionary new hair transplant technique that involved no grafts and had minimal scarring. Om knew about the traditional hair transplant technique, but it produced a big scar at the location on the head from where a strip of skin was removed to extract the hair follicular units and also had a long healing period.

The new method involved removing follicular units directly. Skin strips were spared, so there was minimal scarring and less healing time. It was also expensive. Om checked many forums, websites, and blogs. The cost came up to around INR 150,000 for the whole procedure at a reputed clinic.

He would have to secure a job at Softzone and save for a considerable amount of time to be able to afford that kind of treatment.

◆◄►◆

"Congratulations, man. Well done," said Om to Arun at the college canteen the next day.

Both Arun and Natasha had cleared the first round of the selection process at Librasoft.

"What are the next steps?" asked Om.

"Well, there's a technical round next and then a round with the HR department after that," replied Arun.

Natasha walked in the canteen and slapped Arun's bum before taking a seat.

Om congratulated Natasha.

"Why are you looking to so happy today?" Arun asked Om.

Om started smiling.

Arun poked him a couple of times as Natasha looked on.

"I finally saw her," said Om.

"No way!" exclaimed Arun as they all started laughing and gave each other hi-fives.

"I hope you weren't a sissy and went ahead and got her number at least," added Arun.

276

"She has asked me to meet her at Mocha today at five," said Om. "I've called up the boss at Pizza Corner requesting him to allow me to start a little later today."

"What are you going to wear?" asked Natasha.

Om had thought about wearing his favourite sky-blue denim with white shirt and Woodland boots. But, Natasha's question made him question his own choice. Confusion was apparent on his face.

"Come home with me. My brother and you should exactly be the same size. He has a great collection of jackets," said Natasha.

Arun looked at Natasha weirdly.

"I know where you're going. You're bigger than my brother. So shut up," she said to Arun.

All three of them got up and started walking. Natasha's house was a fifteen minute walk from the college. She didn't have to pay any rent since she lived with her parents. Some just have it easier, Om used to think many times.

As the three were walking towards Natasha's house, a bucketful of water fell straight on Om's head. He was drenched in water. Startled and shocked, he looked up. It was a middle-aged man, clearing out water from his balcony.

"Can't you look down before throwing?" shouted Om from the street.

"Can't you look up while walking?" shouted that man back.

Arun and Natasha cracked up.

Om shook his head and moved on. Thankfully, it was not when he was on the way to his date.

CHAPTER 31

OM HAD REACHED the Village earlier than the said time. He wasn't sure how much time he would have with Ayesha, so he didn't want to waste even a single moment.

It was a quiet and peaceful evening at the village. The crowd hadn't arrived yet and the music wasn't loud. Om stood outside Mocha, one of the most famous cafes in the Village. It overlooked the lake.

"Idiot!" Om heard a voice from behind him.

It was Ayesha. He smiled back at her.

"How long have you been here?" she asked.

"Not long," answered Om.

She smiled back. "Let's go inside," she said.

The café was a dimly lit joint that exuded a rustic ambience. Shisha and coffee adorned every table. There was a small seating space outside as well where it was difficult to get a table if one came later in the evening. Since they were one of the first entrants for the evening, they were able to nab a space outside. They ordered a shisha, which was a rage among the youth those days, and a couple of drinks to go with it.

278

"Do you know that there were two lovers during the reign of Allauddin Khilji. The boy was a Hindu and the girl was Muslim. They were madly in love with each other, but the boy was captured and imprisoned by Khilji. On the night of the full moon, the girl committed suicide by drowning herself and cursed Khilji that he would never be able to find love himself. And legend has it that many years later, Khilji was inexplicably enamored by a Rajput queen called Padmaavati, for whom Khilji waged many wars. When Khilji won the war and was about to enslave Rajput women, Queen Padmaavati burned herself with thousands of other Rajput women before Khilji could capture them. This, in turn, led Khilji into isolation and an untimely death." Ayesha narrated a story.

Om looked at her, amazed at the story as much as he was captivated by the presence of Ayesha. He turned his gaze towards the lake and imagined the story Ayesha had just narrated. It looked so serene and peaceful despite having seen lovers upon lovers and agonies over agonies. Perhaps it did understand how love and agony complimented each other.

Om and Ayesha didn't say anything for the next few minutes, just kept looking at each other. When they had had enough of looking at each other, they would turn to the lake. There was an enchanting vibe and peace in the air.

The opposite sex, many times, is able to instigate emotions within a person. Pulse starts rising; goose bumps race across one's skin. The heart beats faster. There is either excitement or anxiety. Rarely, only rarely, is someone able to soothe the nerves and make the heartbeat lighter. That is when there is a rhythm to the heartbeat, a music in the heart.

Om felt a pleasing symphony playing inside his heart.

"Would you like something to eat?" Om asked as a waiter brought the drinks they had ordered.

Om and Ayesha looked at each other at the same time. He handed over the menu to Ayesha.

"Al verdure risotto with bread and cheese," requested Ayesha.

The waiter acknowledged the order with a smile and took the menu away.

Om was about to say something when a cluster of bees started flying around both of them. Om raised his hands to deter them away, but Ayesha held his hand.

"What do you do at the Pizza Corner?" asked Ayesha.

"I work there about twenty hours a week to be able to pay off my college fees and have some money to go out on dates," said Om.

Ayesha smiled.

"What about you?" asked Om.

"I'm studying to go to medical school. Just next to the Village is the institute where I study," said Ayesha.

"What were you doing at the Pizza Corner in Paschim Vihar then, the other night?" asked Om.

"Just getting pizza for my boyfriend," joked Ayesha.

Om looked amused.

The risotto arrived, hot and fresh. The rest of time at Mocha was very little talk, a lot of silence, a lot of smiles, and a lot of holding hands.

"Let's go to the lake," said Ayesha as she paid the bill.

Om insisted that he pay it, especially since it was the first date, but Ayesha asked him to save up and buy his mother a gift.

"Khilji might still have his soldiers on the prowl," joked Om as they walked hand-in-hand around the Hauz Khas lake.

The way to the lake went through the ruins of the Hauz Khas Complex. The ruins, at one time, hosted a mosque, an Islamic seminary, and a tomb. It was one of the most picturesque spots in Delhi.

Many couples would grace the ruins, find desolate corners, and engage in lovely affections. Ayesha took him to the ruins of what looked like an old window overlooking the lake.

Om and Ayesha sat down on the stones by the side of the window.

Ayesha took out a pack of cigarettes and offered one to Om.

"I don't smoke", said Om.

"I don't either. This is just menthol, a mint flavoured cigarette. Come on, try it," said Ayesha.

Om looked at her for a second and said, "I'll share with you."

Ayesha smiled and lit one of the cigarettes.

"Can you drop me to the same location? Near the Levi's showroom in Vasant Kunj?" asked Ayesha.

Om would have accompanied her even to the gallows of hell if she had asked. Dropping her off wasn't a favour; it was a privilege. It also meant that Om would have some more time with her.

Ayesha ran one of her legs over his motorcycle and sat behind him. She wrapped her arms around his shoulders. For a moment, he felt a subtle current flowing through his body. Om drove as slowly as he could until she intervened and asked him to ride faster. It was beginning to drizzle.

Om stopped by the side of a tree, some distance away from the spot where Ayesha's driver was going to come and pick her up. It was a dark and secluded spot – perfect for some shelter from the drizzle and also for some intimacy.

"It was incredible to see you," said Om, looking deep into Ayesha's eyes.

His lips quivered a bit. It was getting cold.

Ayesha kept looking at Om and smiled back.

Suddenly, the moment was disrupted when Ayesha's mobile rang.

"Shhhh, don't speak anything. It's my mother," said Ayesha as she answered the call. "Okay, Mummy. All right. Thank you. Yes, I'll wait there," said Ayesha and hung up. "The driver is going to be ten minutes late," informed Ayesha.

Om gave a virtual hi-five to the gods up there.

Ayesha laughed.

"Sing me a song," said Om as he placed his arms around Ayesha's waist.

"Which one?" she asked, placing her hands on his face.

"Anything," whispered Om. It was not the song he was interested in, anyway.

"Love I get so lost, sometimes…

Days pass and this emptiness fills my heart…

When I want to run away,

I drive off in my car...

But whichever way I go,

I come back to the place you are..." sang Ayesha, facing Om but her eyes lowered and arms in embrace.

"Peter Gabriel?" whispered Om in her ear.

Ayesha nodded, closed her eyes and bit her lower lip. "All my instincts, they return; and the grand facade, so soon will b...", she continued humming the song, getting closer and closer to Om's face. "Burn... without a noise, without my pride..."

"...I reach out from the inside," Om completed the lines from the song, taking over from Ayesha.

Ayesha opened her eyes.

He was right in front of her, his eyes closed and his body quivering.

"In your eyes, the light the h...," Om continued humming the song.

Ayesha held him by his neck and pulled him closer to her lips. She placed his mouth on hers. Her lips were thick and plum, smooth as silk. His stubble tickled her lips.

They caressed each other as gently as they could. She took his right hand and placed it on her waist. He pulled her in as their mouths danced inside each other.

Ayesha bit Om's lower lip before pulling away. Her hair was messed up, but not more than her lipstick. "I need to leave now," she said, slowly opening her eyes.

"Just one more minute," said Om and pulled her in again. Her hands started going inside his shirt. He ran his hands over her back.

Suddenly, a light flashed from across the tree behind which Om and Ayesha were. Their intimacy broken, he looked around and saw a man on a motorcycle some distance away. He shook his head.

"I really have to leave now." Ayesha turned Om's face towards herself.

Om nodded, breathing deep. She took a brush out of her bag and combed her hair. She then took a compact mirror and lipstick out and handed over the mirror for Om to hold. Om's domestication had already started as she applied lipstick back to her wonderfully smothered lips.

"This is my number, but don't ever message me," she said to Om as she saved her number on his phone and gave him one last hug.

"Will you at least message me when you reach home?" asked Om.

She nodded.

Ayesha started walking towards the Levi's showroom. Om stood there and waited. He observed a car pull over and saw her getting inside.

The car left.

Om looked up, waved a kiss at the stars, and got on his motorcycle.

There were no lectures scheduled for the class the next day because Librasoft was conducting their interviews. The technical round came first. The ones who cleared it would then proceed to the final one with the Human Resources department of the company. Om lingered in the Microprocessor lab since the morning, working on his final year project. He itched to write Ayesha a message, but he couldn't. That made him feel really restless and anxious.

"Use this energy to build your dreams. Use this energy to build your dreams," Om kept telling himself.

Om made good progress during the day on his project. It was a really silent day in the classroom. He was one of the only two students who had opted out of placement for Librasoft. Well, technically, only he had opted out. The other was a boy named Mohan, who had a backlog in seven courses and wasn't eligible to sit for placements.

'I've cleared both the rounds, so has Natasha! Yayyyy! Where are you?' Arun had sent him a text message.

'Mlab,' replied Om.

A few minutes later, Arun and Natasha reached the microprocessor lab and jumped on Om.

"Congratulations, guys," said Om and hugged both of them. Their happiness didn't seem to know any boundaries.

"You finally got what you wanted," said Om.

"Well, we have submitted Delhi as our preference," said Natasha.

Om and Arun both looked at each other but didn't say anything.

"Thirty-two students from our batch got placed today. That's a record number for the first company to recruit," said Arun, giving the conversation a detour. Om looked on.

It was another regular evening at Pizza Corner for Om. The neighbourhood was buzzing. The wall behind the oven was sullen, in spite of being covered with a wallpaper, which had a pattern of printed bricks. There was a Lebanese joint on one side of Pizza Corner and a Chinese take-away on the other. Om was amused at the irony of Pizza 'Corner' not actually being in a corner.

The atmosphere was relaxed; the evening was yet to get busy. Om's heart was beating with a peaceful rhythm. Life was looking up; everything seemed brighter than it actually was.

"Can I have a Spinach and Corn Pizza?" Om heard a voice from behind him as he was stacking the cardboard boxes for packing pizzas.

"Which base would you like, Ma'am?" asked Om with a smirk.

It was Ayesha. She was wearing a black off-shoulder top with a skinny fit blue denim and black boots. It looked like she wanted to redefine ravishing.

"You," she said.

"I'm afraid, that's not on the menu," he said from behind the counter.

"I don't care. I want it, right now," she said.

Om looked at Sumit, his colleague, who was watching this strange banter with the customer. Om signalled something to him and went out with Ayesha. There was a parking lot some five minutes' walk from Pizza Corner. Om and Ayesha stood between the two tall SUVs and passionately started kissing each other. Om's hand went inside her top.

"Not so soon," she said as she pulled back and slapped his hand.

Om took his hands out, visibly disappointed.

"I've missed you so much. I couldn't stop looking at my phone. Was dying to receive a message from you," said Om and gave Ayesha a peck on her nude lips.

"I missed you too, sugarball," she said, kissing him back.

"Sugarball!" he exclaimed.

Both had a raucous laugh.

"Isn't there a way we can communicate when you are home? What if I give you a phone with a new number?" asked Om, running his hands through Ayesha's silky-smooth straight hair.

"I'll be dead if I get caught. So will you," she said, massaging the back of his neck.

"We'll have to meet like this till the time I get admission into a medical college," she said.

Om kept looking at her. Whatever she said wouldn't have made a difference. He just wanted to be with her at any cost, come what may.

"Do you want to meet tomorrow? I can bunk classes. My parents are going to Chandigarh and will be back late in the evening. Hence, I don't need to rush back home," she said.

Om thought about it for a moment. He was rostered in to work at Pizza Corner the next evening; he needed money. His final year project wasn't complete yet and Softzone was on the cusp of arriving at the college for placements.

"Of course," he said, the next moment, pulling her closer to him.

"Pick me up tomorrow at 6 from our spot – that tree," she said.

Om nodded.

"You should head back to work now," she said and gave him a final kiss.

"I should," he said, trying to kiss her again.

"Go now," she pushed him away. He walked backwards, facing Ayesha. He looked at her for a few seconds, and then turned around.

❧

Om worked on his project the whole night. He could barely sleep. He was alive and bursting with energy, like a newly wedded wife who had not taken off her veil yet, like a freshly mature flower waiting to be pollinated. Ayesha was at the back of his mind, no matter what he did.

He had applied for a leave from Pizza Corner, citing a critical presentation at his college for his final year project, which the management had approved without much chagrin.

For his next date with Ayesha, Om had rented a car – a Suzuki Swift. One of his peers, Sumit, had referred him to his father, who ran a vehicle renting company. Even after a bargain on the list price, the rent of the car was a week's worth of his wages.

Om arrived at that tree half an hour before time. He wore a pair of Levi's jeans, which he had borrowed from Natasha's brother, along with a brand new white tee and a faux leather jacket he had purchased in the morning. The straps of his black seamless jockey hung outside the denim on his waist. It was the latest fashion trend during those days.

The wait for Ayesha didn't seem like a wait at all. True, the heart raced a little too much, the breath was a little too short; but every cell in his body pulsated with an intense energy. Love had always been a conundrum for the philosophers. Was it meant to soothe the essence inside or excite the core being?

From a distance, he saw Ayesha walk towards their spot. She wore a floral jumpsuit and had her hair untied. She stood by the corner of the Levi's showroom and looked every bit the magic she was when he had seen her the first time. He took a moment to relish the view from a distance.

He blew the horn on the car.

Ayesha looked at the car for a second and then looked away. It was understandable given the number of roadside Romeos in Delhi. He honked again. Perhaps two or three times. She didn't look, but when he honked for the last time, she looked at the car once again. He waved from inside the car. She recognized him and walked towards the car with a look of surprise on her face.

"Whose car is this?" asked Ayesha as she got in and gave Om a peck on the lips.

"I got it on rent," said Om, winking at Ayesha.

"That's so cute," she said and hugged him. "Where are you taking me?" she asked, holding his hand.

"We'll drive around and see where we go. It's a beautiful day, almost as beautiful as you are," he said.

She smiled back at him. Om started driving.

"This hotel was built by my father's company," said Ayesha as Om drove around the Continental Hotel near Connaught Place.

"And... what does your mother do?" asked Om.

"She is an interior designer working with my father's firm. She doesn't need to work outside," she said.

"What do your father and mother do?" she asked Om after a while.

"My mother was a homemaker for most of her life. She worked for a bit, when I was a child, to help me get admission in a private school, but never again. She suffered a paralytic attack a couple of years ago and has since been bed-ridden," replied Om.

"My father..." Om paused, hesitating, but then continued, "is retired now. He worked as a salesman most of his life. As you can see, my background is humble compared to yours." She held his hands and kissed them.

Om stopped at 'Lodi - The Garden Restaurant', one of the most famous restaurants near the sprawling Lodi Gardens.

"I don't want to go to a fancy restaurant. You've already spent enough money on the car and the new clothes that you're wearing," joked Ayesha with a simper.

Om turned a shade of red, embarrassed.

"I want to walk through the Lodi Gardens with you. It's a gorgeous, sunny day," said Ayesha.

Om smiled and nodded.

"Would you mind if I kissed another guy right now?" asked Ayesha as she and Om entered the Lodi Gardens.

Om threw a strange smile, rather taken aback.

"Why do you ask?" asked Om.

"Just answer me," demanded Ayesha.

"It would hurt, but I would let you go. To feel hurt is an instinct; to let-go with love is intelligence. I would choose intelligence over instinct," answered Om.

Ayesha seemed impressed.

"What about you?" asked Om.

"I think I would rip the bitch's head apart," said Ayesha, "before throwing you in a barrel of burning oil, of course."

Om laughed.

Ayesha didn't.

"Many years ago, my Naani taught me a lesson, which has stayed with me ever since. It has been repeated many times by many people, which makes it a cliché on one hand, but also universally true on the other," Om began saying as Ayesha held his hand and dragged him on the pathway that led to the small lake in the middle of Lodi Gardens.

"Love gives freedom. It nurtures and nourishes. If I say that I love you, then my love for you must be based in your growth, your evolution, in the expansion of your intelligence and perception. For that, one of the key ingredients is freedom. I want you to be with me, not out of compulsion, but out of your own freedom; and I want to help you grow, evolve and reach the pinnacle of your potential. Whether that happens with or without me is immaterial. That devotion is love," continued Om as they reached the lake.

There were a few ducks, maybe twenty, by the side of the river. Not a lot of people though, perhaps ten.

"You must be a philosopher. How did you end up in computer engineering?" taunted Ayesha.

"Well, that's exactly what I would have done if my father was a rich man and I had a chauffeur driven car to drive me to tuitions," said Om with a wink.

Ayesha slapped his shoulder before hugging it tight.

"What does your father exactly do?" asked Om.

"He owns a construction company. Tirupati Developers," she answered.

"I have heard about them. There are advertisements all over the city and even on the radio," responded Om.

Ayesha didn't seem to care.

"What if your parents find out that their daughter loves a boy who works at Pizza Corner?" asked Om, a while later.

"Shut up!" said Ayesha. "There's nothing wrong with working at Pizza Corner. Plus, that's not your end goal in life. You are so intelligent, well-educated, and studying in the topmost engineering school of the country. They will understand your capability and respect it," added Ayesha.

"Why are you scared of telling them about me, then?" asked Om again.

"I'm not afraid. I'm just waiting for the right time. As soon as I get into medical school, I will tell them about us," she said and rested her head on his shoulders.

Om turned around and planted a peck on her forehead. They sat there in silence, a leaf or two brushing against their bodies every now and then. The sunlight shone on them through the gaps between the trees. No branch or leaf could stop the golden fireball in the sky from bestowing its grace upon the two lovers.

Ayesha and Om had parked the car in somebody's empty garage near Ayesha's house. She, on the other hand, had told the chauffeur that there was an emergency with one of her classmates and she needed to be with her. A bribe of five thousand rupees had ensured that the chauffeur would keep silent.

"You know... How you... my love... Taste like sugar...," hummed Om as he held Ayesha's hands and kissed her fingertips one by one. He wrapped his lips around her fingers.

"Let's go to the back seat," said Ayesha.

Om blinked his eyes.

Ayesha hopped from the front passenger seat to the back seat and lay down. By the time Om had done the same, she had undone the buttons on her floral jumpsuit. Her breasts fell to the side under their own weight.

He placed one leg on the floor and the other across her legs. His chest was against hers and her lips right in front of his mouth.

She held Om's neck and pulled him, place his mouth on hers. What began as a sombre play on the lips turned into a sloppy exchange in no time.

'Caress me,' said Ayesha as she took his right hand and placed it on her left breast. He slid his hand underneath her dress and took her breast out. He pulled away from her mouth and started to kiss her nipples tenderly until she asked him to bite them.

He had grown hard, as his abdomen rubbed against hers. Both of them moved their bodies in a rhythm.

"Go inside me," whispered Ayesha in Om's ear before licking it softly with her tongue.

Om took his mouth off Ayesha's breast and paused.

"I wouldn't like to do it with you for the first time in such a rushed way," said Om. "It's my first time, and I want it to be memorable," said Om. He felt sweaty and breathed with heavy gasps.

"Do you realize that, under normal circumstances, I should be the one saying those lines?" said Ayesha as she squeezed his butt with her hands. Both of them stared at each other for a moment and then broke into a laughter. And when they stopped, they resumed their kisses again.

"I think I should leave now," said Ayesha, breaking a long kiss.

"Just five more minutes," murmured Om.

"No, I have to leave." Ayesha pushed him away. "We can't get carried away. It's already beyond 9 P.M right now. I can't believe we got this late," she added as a bit of worry set in.

Om looked displeased but hopped back on to the driver's seat. She got up, adjusted her breasts properly in her bra, buttoned up her jumpsuit, carefully brushed her hair, and cleaned her lips as if nothing had happened.

"Don't apply that lipstick or I'm going to devour those lips again," said Om as Ayesha took out a lipstick from her bag.

Ayesha shook her head and applied the red matte lipstick.

Within an instant, he jumped from the driver's seat, right onto Ayesha. Within seconds, the color red was smothered all over her lips. She bit him a few times and pulled his hair. Their pretty faces were doused by each other's passion.

She pulled his hair again and bit him hard on his neck. He slid his hands inside her dress and before abruptly pulling himself away.

"Do your hair and lips again, and leave now. Quick, lest I do it to you all over again," warned Om and jumped back to the driver's seat.

She adjusted her dress, brushed her hair, and wiped her face. She did not apply the lipstick again.

Taking one last look at Om, she opened the car's back door and left.

"Message me when you get home," said Om as he rolled the windows down and heaved a big sigh.

'The answer my friend, is blowin' in the wind. The answer is blowin' in the wind,' said the song playing on the radio in the car. Om drove around the city, passing each spot he had visited with Ayesha during the day. There was a zen saying that you don't step in the same river twice. Om must have understood it deeply that evening; his traces were there in those trees and branches and leaves; so were Ayesha's; and so were those of a hundred different lovers and of those not yet born. Each moment, every space in the universe, was having fresh traces imprinted upon itself. Even though the space might look the same from the outside, something new was getting added to it each moment.

A couple of hours had gone by since Ayesha had left the car. There was no message from her. Om checked his phone, one traffic signal after another.

However, it was time to return the rental car and walk back home.

CHAPTER 32

"SOFTZONE IS FINALLY coming to the campus. The registrations have begun," announced Sonali as she dismissed the class after her lecture had ended.

Arun and Natasha looked at Om, who sat on the last bench, looking dull and dry. He hadn't received any message from Ayesha after she left last night.

"Why do you look so off?" asked Arun after Sonali had left the classroom.

Om didn't answer.

"Tell us, what's wrong?" asked Natasha.

Om didn't say anything.

"Go and register for Softzone now," ordered Natasha, pulling him from the bench.

Om went to the auditorium where the registrations were happening and filled out the forms and completed the formalities. The first round of interview was going to be conducted in three days.

He then exited the auditorium and saw his friends waiting outside.

"How far are you with the documentation of your project?" asked Arun.

"I'm in the final stages now. Just finished compiling the entity-relationship diagrams for the relational databases used," said Om as if he wasn't even bothered.

"Why aren't you telling us what's wrong with you? Your hair looks fine today," joked Arun.

His pun got him a tight slap on his back from Natasha.

"Come on, tell me what's wrong?" requested Natasha as she placed her arms around Om's shoulders.

"I was with Ayesha yesterday," began Om and paused.

"So, that's the problem?" hesitated Natasha.

"I asked her to message me when she got back home, but I haven't heard from her since the last evening," added Om.

"So, just text her," said Arun.

"I can't. She specifically asked me not to. Her phone is regularly checked by her parents; and if they find out, we're both in great trouble", responded Om.

"Is it really the 21ˢᵗ century?" questioned Arun.

Om had no answer to that.

"I need to leave now," said Om. "Softzone is on the campus in three days and I still haven't finished my project documentation." He got up and started walking. All of a sudden, an urgency had settled onto the nerves on his body.

The sun was already high up in the sky, its light blazing through the space between the blinds, right on the blanket Om had curled into. Some mornings, it was really hard to get out of the blanket, putting on a mask on, and carrying on being a functional part of the society. It was one of those mornings.

With not one message from Ayesha the whole day yesterday, Om had a shallow sleep because of the anxiety. As soon as he opened his eyes, he grabbed his phone and checked for any message or call from Ayesha. There was none. His anxiety hit the roof.

It was almost noon now. He had skipped college. By the next day, he was supposed to have his final project report compiled and hardbound.

A lowly grunt escaped his mouth, and lazily, he pulled the blanket off his head. The sunlight blinded him for a second. Breathing became problematic too; it was if someone had tied his lungs into a knot.

He pushed the blanket off his body, swung his legs, and stood up. Looking at the window, he felt the sunlight again; although, this time, its rays were therapeutic. It soothed his cold body after a long, sleepless night.

The phone rang. Om shook, startled. He ran and picked up the phone. One look at the dialer told him that it was his mother calling. Taking a long, deep breath, he clicked on the green button to answer his phone.

"Namaste, Mummy," greeted Om.

"Namaste, lalla. How have you been?" asked his mother from the other end.

"I've been fine, Mummy," said Om with a sigh. "Just a lot of work at college and then job. You know how it is."

"How are you, Mummy? How is the pain in your back you were telling me about?" asked Om after a brief pause.

"It's been fine, beta," his mother replied, this time with a sigh. "Your father is coming to Delhi tomorrow to collect my medicine from the All India Institute of Medical Science. I've sent your favorite lemon pickle packed in a jar for you," she said.

"Why do you do this, Mummy? I told you I will come and see you soon," he complained. There was a little gap of silence in between.

"Where do you want me to meet him?" asked Om, breaking the silence.

"New Delhi Railway Station at five tomorrow. He is in Coach S1, seat number 12," his mother answered.

Om confirmed his acceptance.

"Be nice to him. You both are seeing each other after almost six months," said Kiran.

Om did not say anything, though he drew a long deep breath, which his mother heard. "I need to hang up now, Mummy. Have lots of work to do before I start work in the evening," said Om. "I love you," he added.

"I miss you," said Kiran from the other end.

Om hung up the phone and heaved deep once more.

Om spent the afternoon giving the final touches to his project report. It was hard to concentrate given the recent events, but he pushed himself to do it. It needed to be done. One could say this was one of his greatest strengths – to be able to dig and persevere through the difficult times. Even if it was bit by bit, breath by breath.

On his way to work at the Pizza Corner, he handed over a soft copy of the project report to the printer for publishing. The latter told him that the hardbound cover would be handed over to him the next day.

The evening of work at Pizza Corner started quiet as usual, but bustled with activity later on. He kept going through his routine – smiling and greeting the customers, asking them what they would like to order with a wide smile, recommending something based on their vague explanations. His heart, though, skipped a beat every time a girl entered the door. His heart, somewhere, expected Ayesha to show up.

The evening ended. He and Sumit cleaned up the kitchen and placed the chairs upside down on the tables. He then went out and looked around one last time. Perhaps Ayesha lurked somewhere around, about to surprise him and say that it was all a prank.

New Delhi Railway Station dotted the center of Delhi on a map. It was one the most fascinating melting pots of culture in the world. On one side, it neighboured the posh 'Connaught Place' where the richest in the world shopped and dined. On the other side, was a suburb called Paharganj – home to the budget hostels for backpackers from across the world.

He made his way through the barrage of porters and other people who had come there to see someone else off. In India, one could see the extent of population explosion at two places: railways stations and public hospitals.

Platform Six for the Kalka Mail, read the notification board at the railway station. He took the stairs and the crossover bridge that connected all the platforms and walked down to Platform 6.

The Kalka mail hadn't arrived yet. Regardless, he walked towards the section which indicated the Coach S1 in red dotted lines. He knew that was where the coach would be parked when the train came. There or somewhere around.

The trains were long in India. They had to be, given that the trains carried over six-hundred-million unique passengers in a calendar year. The walk to where the Coach S1 was supposed to land was a long one. It felt even longer since he was going to meet his father. All the while, he kept checking his phone. There was nothing from Ayesha yet.

When the train finally arrived, he saw his father from a distance. The latter saw him too. Wearing a blue kurta with a plain, beige-colored trouser, he had a duffel bag hanging on one of his shoulders and a polythene bag containing something on the other.

He stood in front of his father. Both looked at each other for a while and then looked away. Om then took a deep breath.

"Your mother has sent this for you," said Mahesh, handing over the polythene bag to Om.

He took it and looked inside. There was a jar full of lemon pickle, another steel container which had something in it, and a recent picture of his mother. He took the picture in his hands and looked at it for a while. He hadn't seen her for more than six months.

"How are your studies going?" asked Mahesh, after a period of awkward silence.

"They're fine. Getting the final project report printed," answered Om.

"Make sure you focus on your studies and not waste time at a restaurant or roaming around on your motorcycle," said Mahesh, a few moments later.

Om didn't say anything.

"How is mother's back doing now? She called me yesterday," asked Om.

"You should come and see for yourself," said Mahesh.

Both looked elsewhere but not at each other. The silence was awkward.

"I have to go now. Need to collect my printed project reports from the publisher." said Om.

He and his father looked at each other again for a while before he turned and started walking.

"Thank you for the laddoos, Mummy. You really didn't have to do it," said Om as he ate a laddoo his mother had sent him in the steel container.

Laddoos – a round-shaped sweet dish – were made from chickpeas flour. They were quite famous among the kids, adults and the elephant God alike.

His parents were great devotees of the elephant God, Ganesha. As the name suggested, he had the head of an elephant and the body of an American burger worshipper. Given his inconspicuous size, he wondered if Ganesha had been inconsiderate to choose a mouse as his official vehicle.

"Did you taste the pickle? I added a little extra asafoetida," asked his mother.

"Not yet, Mummy," he replied, still gorging on the laddoos. An anxious mind loved a dose of sugar.

"What did you and your father talk about?" she asked.

"Nothing much, Mummy. I had to leave and collect my project reports from the publisher. There was barely any time," he responded after a pause.

"For how long will the two of you behave like this? I'm on my death bed and...," His mother began to cry midway through her sentence.

"Mummy, come on!" Om said after a few seconds had passed.

"It's almost four years now since you left home. You are on the verge of graduating and have a bright career in front of you. Leave all your grudges behind. Your father has always done his best for you," his mother started saying.

He noted that she was still crying.

"Mummy, I really don't want to talk about this, please. I already have a lot going on. I will speak with you later. Love you. Bye," said Om. There were a few moments of silence at the other end before his mother said, "Bye".

Om paused for a few moments and hung up.

CHAPTER 33

IT HAD BEEN a while since Om had an evening off. He needed one desperately. The last few hours had been full of anxiety, pent-up emotions, and drama. He picked up one of the hardbound paperback project reports he had gotten printed and flipped its pages around. He smelled them again and again – the fragrance of fresh paper, not yet marred by someone's fingerprints.

He sat next to the window and looked out, just as he used to do when he was a child in his Naani's house. The sun had set, yet he could still feel its lingering presence. The sky had turned a shade of pink – somber and quiet.

The birds and insects flapped their wings around, some bearing the messages of lovers and others with messages of the Gods. Perhaps those two were the same, he thought.

His phone buzzed. He picked it up. Ayesha had texted him. Finally! His eyes opened wide and his heart started racing. He opened the message.

'Sorry, sugarball, I've been away and lost. It's been a really hard couple of days. My parents found out about us. If you are available to talk at midnight, send a message within the next five minutes, else don't reply' read the message.

An incredible energy flooded his body. There was an answer, at least. It meant that she was alive and still with him. He had finally found some closure to his worries.

It was what he had always thought. She had landed in a soup. He took a deep breath and texted back within a minute. 'Yes, sweetheart, midnight tonight. I can't wait to talk to you. I've been dying.'

⚜

The clock struck midnight. He was on his bed, constantly staring at his phone's screen. The battery was fully charged; he had decided not to leave anything to chance.

He had to attend college the next morning, but that had taken a back seat.

"Hey, sugarball," whispered Ayesha on the phone.

A moment later, all of his anxieties and fears evaporated as he melted into her voice. All the trauma he had endured the last few hours seemed to have been worth it. Anything to be able to listen to her whisper like that!

"Hey, baby," he whispered back in return, tucked up inside the blanket in his room. "I was so scared and anxious about you," he added.

"I know, baby. These last few hours have been the worst of my life," Ayesha responded. "I don't know how they found out about us, but they fired the driver and snatched my phone away from me. Today was the first time I was able to catch hold of the phone for a few minutes after convincing them that I would never speak with you again," she added.

"Just tell them that we love each other. Tell them that I am a well-educated boy and from an educated family. If you want, I can come and meet your parents," said Om, his voice strained and stressed. The last sentence she spoke had sent shivers through his spine.

"I have told them all that. They just wouldn't listen. I can't even tell you the ridiculous things they accused me of," responded Ayesha.

"Like what?" Om asked.

Ayesha paused for a few moments. "They suggested that you might have made sex-tapes of me like the girl from Delhi Public School, RK Puram and that you might blackmail me later using them," she said in a reticent manner.

There was a stunned silence for a few moments.

"Unbelievable," he murmured.

"They also said that I can find a much better guy somewhere else," said Ayesha.

Om didn't respond. He was frozen.

"Do you want to be with me?" he asked, softly, however, the worry in his voice was palpable.

"Of course, I do, baby. Which is why I am talking to you right now, after what happened. I want to be with you. I love you," she answered.

"Then what do we do? How do we go about this?" he asked, anxiously.

"We need to really keep it under the wraps till the time I get admission into a medical school. It is my parents' dream to see their daughter become a doctor. Once that happens, I am sure I will be able to come out with the truth and stand behind my decision," she said. A few moments of silence followed.

"Are you with me?" she asked.

"Of course, I am with you," he said. "I love you."

"I love you too, sugarball," she said.

"What happened at your end over the last few days?" she asked.

"I met my father after about six months, which brought up a lot of emotions. I finished and finally got my final project report published," he replied.

"Congratulations! I'm so proud of you. What about Softzone? When is the company coming for placements?" she asked further.

"In a couple of days," Om answered.

"Will you take a placement in America now after what has happened over the last few hours?" asked Ayesha in a tender yet subtly suggestive voice.

"Of course not," answered Om. "I want to be with you. Though once you become a doctor, we can both look to move to America and build a life there together," he whispered on the phone, curling up inside the blanket.

"And have three babies together," she whispered back.

"Only one. Kids are so much trouble," he murmured. The breathing was becoming heavier at both ends.

"Okay, two," she said. "Please... Please...," she begged.

"The names will be Rahul and Sonya," he said.

"Rahul and Amber," she replied. He agreed, as he curled up inside his blanket.

"I need to hang up now," she said.

"Give me a kiss first," he demanded.

"Dry one or a super sloppy one?" she teased him.

"Super sloppy," he said.

'Muuuuaaaahhhhh' He heard her kiss from the other end of the phone.

"I really love you," he said.

"I love you, too," she said and hung up.

"It's been a while since you and I hung out, bro," Arun said to Om as they sat in the college canteen. "It's like suddenly so many things have been happening -- placements, decisions about the future... and, your love affair," continued Arun. "Let's go to my place today. We'll have a beer and watch some porn. Just some guy time together."

Om looked at him strangely but didn't respond.

"Come on, bro!" Arun egged Om.

Arun lived as a paying guest in a suburb called New Friends Colony, a relatively posh locale in South Delhi, largely populated by affluent families from the state of Punjab. Arun took the keys from Om insisting that he ride the motorcycle and sat on the rider seat before even Om could speak.

The road to Arun's place passed through Lodi Gardens, which caught Om's attention. There were those same ice-cream and flower vendors, snacks and cold drink stalls. All of them were going about their usual business. They would have reached faster had they not encountered a big traffic snarl around Nehru Place. There was a big event happening at the now defunct Paras Cinema in Nehru Place.

The latter was named after India's first Prime Minister, Jawaharlal Nehru, who Babu always chided to Om as his Naani's first crush.

'Project Commencement Ceremony of the largest Hotel in Delhi - 'Anilid Suites'. Proudly brought to you by Tirupati Developers', read the banners all around.

Om kept looking at the event proceedings and the banners even as Arun swerved through the lanes on the motorcycle.

Arun went to get beers for the both of them.

"Fosters or Kingfisher?" shouted the shopkeeper

"Fosters, mate," replied Arun. Everyone in India thought that everyone in Australia drank Fosters. The liquor store was right opposite where Arun lived.

Om, in the meanwhile, had grabbed his friend's laptop.

"What's this website - Orkut.com?" asked Om as Arun came back with a six pack of Fosters. Arun opened a can each for both of them.

"It's this new website which has become quite a rage, bro. I've only just signed up for it after Natasha asked me to. Apparently, it's a social network, meaning you can use it to add people to your network on the internet, send them messages free of cost, share images and engage in discussions," responded Arun.

Om browsed through Orkut.com with a strange intrigue.

"Does it mean that people from all over the world can register here and you can find them and add them to your network?" asked Om with a great deal of curiosity.

"That's essentially what it's supposed to do. Stories are going around that the founder, Orkut Büyükkökten, a Turkish engineer, actually built this to find his long-lost lover in Brazil," replied Arun.

"How do I search for someone here?" asked Om.

Arun sat beside Om and pointed to the small search bar at the top right of the screen.

Om immediately had a gleam in his eyes. Arun wasn't sure why Om was so excited.

Om started typing letters one by one, 'F', 'A', 'R', 'H', 'E', 'E', 'N'.

"Who's Farheen?" asked Arun as he kept looking at the screen.

A huge list of girls named Farheen popped up on the screen.

"Just the first name is not going to help. You need to at least enter the last name as well to be able to have some sort of a list of people you can practically go through," explained Arun.

"She's a friend from Alpha-Beta. Do you remember that girl I used to sit with at the back of the rickshaw after school?" asked Om, still trying to understand how Orkut's user interface worked. Arun shook his head.

"We barely spoke with each other during Alpha-Beta days", said Arun, taking a large sip of the beer.

"Do you know some other information like school or city, maybe?" asked Arun, further.

"No, just her first name – Farheen. And her parents, Uncle Tariq and Aunt Nargis," replied Om.

"That's not going to help," said Arun.

Om started typing another set of letters in the search bar one by one: 'R', 'O', 'H', 'T', 'T', space, 'S', 'A', 'H', 'U'.

Quite a few search results turned up on the screen, spreading across three pages. That number, though, was still feasible enough to scan through.

"Who's Rohit Sahu?" asked Arun again.

"He is a friend from secondary school when I was in the ninth grade. He was an incredible guy, who I owe a lot to. He had to leave Jaipur because his father got posted in Mumbai. He gave me a landline number before leaving, but that number never worked," said Om as he carefully scanned all profiles by the name of 'Rohit Sahu'.

"I tried searching for his father too, who I knew worked at Air India, but didn't know his first name and could never get through," mentioned Om as he continued scanning through the profiles.

"None of those are him," said Om, a little dejected, but finally took a sip of his beer.

"Leave it. Let's go outside in the balcony and chill," said Om after a while and closed the lid of the laptop.

Om's phone buzzed at the same time. It was Ayesha calling. Smiling, he answered the phone.

"Hey, baby!" said Om.

"Hey, sugarball! Very quickly, are you available to meet at Khan Chacha tomorrow at 6 P.M?" she asked

"Ummm, sure love," said Om, with a little reluctance.

"All right, see you there. I'm going to hang up now. Love you," said Ayesha before hanging up.

"What was she saying?" asked Arun.

"She wants to meet tomorrow at 6 P.M outside Khan Chacha," said Om, biting his phone between his teeth.

"Do you have work tomorrow?" asked Arun.

"Yes, 6 P.M at Pizza Corner," replied Om.

"Idiot," Ayesha shouted as Om zipped past her on his motorcycle, in the parking lot near Khan Chacha. Khan Chacha was a famous restaurant and an equally famous landmark in the upscale Khan Market of South Delhi.

Om stopped and turned around. She stood behind, her hair tied up in a bun. Before he could even let the majestic view sink in, an angry honk startled him.

"Jump on the motorcycle," he shouted.

Ayesha was surprised for a second, but quickly ran over, crossed her legs, and jumped on his motorcycle.

"How much time do we have?" asked Om.

"Around an hour and a half. There was an official function at the coaching institute, so I could manage to sneak out after marking my attendance," said Ayesha.

"Let's go to Café 91 then," said Om. Ayesha nodded.

Om parked his motorcycle and they walked into 'Café 91' at the Khan Market.

Cafe 91 had become one of the most famous cafes over the years. It was largely frequented by the young, college-going crowd. The bustling ground floor had a big dance area and the first floor was dimly lit, suited for couples. The partners, who managed this café, had ended up in a disagreement, which they had been unable to resolve, rendering the partnership untenable. This was the last month this café was going to be operational. The building was being sold to John Jacobs, a leading luxury eyewear brand to open their flagship store in what was the Champ Elysees of Delhi.

Om and Ayesha walked straight up to the first floor and took a corner seat.

"I missed you so, sooo bad, baby," said Om softly, holding Ayesha's face in her hands.

"Me too, sugarball. Only I know how I have survived the last few days without you," said Ayesha and began to shower his lips with pecks.

A waiter came from behind and placed the menu cards at the table. Revenue generation and meeting sales targets usually took precedence over courtesy.

"Diet coke on ice and an apple juice please. Thank you," said Ayesha.

The waiter smiled and left. Too small an order for occupying a table, he must have thought.

"How is everything at home now?" asked Om, tucked into a corner with Ayesha, holding her hands.

"It's fine, I guess," she said in a pondering manner. "I've told them that I will never see you again. I've been very quiet at home too, just pretending to study all day long," she continued.

"I'm glad you still chose to be with me," said Om.

"I cannot live without you," said Ayesha and began kissing Om again. "I'll always be with you," she murmured, in between the kisses.

"Even if I lose all the hair on my head?" asked Om, his lips still on Ayesha's.

Ayesha broke into a laughter.

"I think you'll look great being bald," said Ayesha, laughing.

"Now I know why you always push my hand away whenever I try playing with your hair," she added and winked at Om.

"No, you don't," said Om, and ran his fingers through her hair, his head leaned against the wall behind and eyes on Ayesha. She grabbed his hand and kissed his fingers one by one, with her supple, lush lips.

CHAPTER 34

SOFTZONE WAS FINALLY on the campus.

Om felt a bit drowsy. He had slept less last night. In part, it was because he had to prepare for Softzone. Another reason was because he was dreaming of Ayesha all night long.

The first round was an aptitude test for each of the candidates registered for the selection process. The test began at 10 A.M sharp in the campus auditorium and finished an hour later. They were all objective-type questions, though the examiner had stressed on negative marking. The results were to be announced at 1 P.M. To pass the time in between, Om strolled around the campus and checked his phone from time to time.

'Hope the test went well. Keep me posted xoxo' read a message from Ayesha.

'It went all right, I guess. Results at 1. Xoxo,' Om replied straight-away.

'All the best. I love you. Don't message now,' arrived Ayesha's text.

Om walked to the campus garden and lay down on the grass, in the sun.

He thought about his journey thus far, almost twenty years of toil and effort to be able to be in a position where some American company would come and give him a chance to apply for a job with them. Like Om, it was the dream of millions of other youngsters across the country and hundreds of others within the same campus. Out of this, only a select few would get the opportunity to live that dream.

⊰❖⊱

Om had fallen asleep in the warm sun, a cap on his eyes and music in his ears. It was 12:50 P.M when he woke up. Just in time, he told himself. He jumped on his feet and rushed towards the auditorium.

The names and identification number of the students who had cleared the Aptitude Test were going to be announced by one of the recruiters from Softzone. Thereafter, the results were also going to be published on the college's notice board.

The clock struck one. Someone from Softzone began to list the names of the short-listed candidates. "Ayush Kumar number 121, Romil Jain number 320...," began the recruiter. With each pause, the heartbeats of the students whose name hadn't been called out jumped a pace. With each name called out, the list became smaller.

Two minutes into the announcement, the recruiter announced his name. "Om Vats number 198." A slight cheer erupted in the crowd.

The Chancellor of the University and other professors were also in the auditorium, seated in the front. They looked at Om, who in return bowed his head in acknowledgement and smiled.

He quietly navigated his way through the students in the auditorium and exited. As soon as he was out in the open, he pumped his fist into the air and ran towards the campus garden.

Arun and Natasha were there. They saw Om and understood what had transpired.

"Congratulations, bro. First step, done and dusted," said Arun and gave Om a hug.

"Congrats, dude. You can be proud. Historically, not even twenty percent of the applicants are short-listed by Softzone after the first round. Well done and all the best for the next rounds," said Natasha and hugged Om.

Om started walking towards the college canteen, elated and jubilant. His phone was in his hands the whole time.

'How did it go?' read a message on Om's phone. It was Ayesha.

'Can you call me? Just five minutes.' Om replied immediately.

Ayesha called back.

"I made it!" Om exclaimed on the phone.

"Congratulations, sugarball. I knew you would do it. But I have to hang up soon; Mom could be here any moment," Ayesha whispered from the other end.

"Please meet me today. Please, please. Just five minutes," begged Om.

"Today's not possible, baby. I don't even have classes today," said Ayesha.

Om made sad puppy sounds.

"Tomorrow, I can meet you for fifteen minutes. The biology teacher usually ends the lecture ten minutes early and takes questions from students. Don't meet me at the tree though. Meet me behind the bakery shop near the tree at 7:45 P.M tom..." Ayesha hadn't even finished when she hung up.

It was 7:45 P.M the next evening. Om rested against a brick wall behind the famous Wenger's bakery in Vasant Kunj. Flies hovered around him, courtesy of an open garbage bin nearby. Thankfully, he wasn't on the work roster that evening, given that the owner of Pizza Corner had already expressed his displeasure with Om a few times. One more misdeed, and Om may have been fired.

Ayesha walked up to Om and hugged him, suffocating a few flies in between. "Let's walk to that corner," said Ayesha, pointing towards a space that seemed cleaner and free of the flies.

"Congratulations, sugarball," said Ayesha as Om kissed her hands.

"Thank you, baby," responded Om. "I just want to do it for you. Be a well-settled, well-earning man, so that I can walk up to your dad and ask for your hand with confidence."

Ayesha held Om's hand tightly and got a little overpowered by emotions. "I just can't thank you enough for being with me through this. You are the only one I can count on," said Ayesha, her eyes moist.

Om took her in his arms.

"I really want to spend a night with you," said Ayesha.

Om's eyes lit up.

"It's my cousin Neeta's birthday this Saturday night. I have taken her in confidence. In the pretext of spending a night with her on her birthday, I'm going to spend it with you," said Ayesha.

Om couldn't believe what he was hearing.

"Let's go camping," Om said impulsively.

Ayesha looked a little confused. "I've never camped in my life," hesitated Ayesha.

"Neither have I. We will figure it out. It's going to be so much fun. I'll hire the same car," beamed Om.

Ayesha's eyes lit up as well.

"Gosh, I am so excited!" exclaimed Ayesha. "Pick me up Saturday evening 5 P.M. near the tree," said Ayesha.

Om kissed her ring finger and nodded.

"I have to leave now. Do well at the interview tomorrow," she said and placed her lips on his for a moment before walking away.

Those were the moments that felt like magic - the flickering light from the halogen lamp in the background, the earthen buildings smelling of love and patience, pathways made of stones being walked upon by gods in flesh and bones.

Om's technical interview with the Softzone team was scheduled for 10 A.M on a Friday morning. He had looked up to this moment and company for years, yet when the actual moment arrived, something else occupied his mind. Or, rather someone else who had entered into his life just a few weeks ago.

This was the most crucial round. Five executives from Softzone were to interview and grill the thirty-eight short-listed candidates based on technical parameters. Historically, each interview lasted well over half an hour. Sometimes longer, sometimes shorter.

His interview was scheduled for 10 A.M. He arrived at the campus at 9:45 A.M, dressed in a plain blue shirt, black trousers, and a blue dotted neck-tie. A satchel containing his resume and final year project report rested on his shoulders. He had taken the public bus rather than his motorcycle as he believed that the helmet ruined the hair and the motorcycle ride disturbed the dress-up game.

The Chancellor and other professors, especially Sonali, wished him well for the interview either in person or through the phone. The Chancellor specifically asked to see him after the interview.

A 9:55 A.M, a candidate named Ankit Dubey came out after his interview. Stress was written all over his face.

Om was next. He stood up, adjusted his neck-tie, pulled his pants up a little, and waited to be called inside. The placement committee volunteer, who managed the influx and the outflow of the candidates, had gone inside immediately after Ankit had come out. When he would come out, it would mean it was time for Om to go in.

The door opened at 9:59 P.M. The volunteer came out with a paper in his hand and looked at him. His heart was racing faster than the bulls facing a matador. He took a long deep breath and stepped in.

Fifty-five minutes had passed since his interview had started. It usually didn't take that long.

Just when the interview was about to cross an hour, Om stepped out of the room and saw the next student waiting outside on a row of chairs next to the entrance. The volunteer also sat on a chair right next to the entrance door.

"What was happening inside?" joked the volunteer, who was his junior.

Om smiled back and said, "They were just having a bit of fun with me."

"I have a feeling you will pass through to the final round. The interviews that don't go well, generally, end earlier than usual," said the volunteer.

"I'm pretty sure I will," said Om with aplomb, unusual to his generally reserved demeanour.

CHAPTER 35

OM WAITED NEXT to the tree Ayesha had asked him to wait at. He had rented the car once again and pulled out of the work roster at the Pizza Corner. The owner had given him a "last warning" – perfectly legitimate given how he had skipped work multiple times over the last few days. However, he felt more relaxed now. He could sense that Softzone was well within his reach now. He felt he was almost there.

Ayesha arrived, wearing a pair of denim and a white figure-hugging top.

"It was so hard to leave the house. She insisted on speaking with my aunt. I had to tell her that Anita, my cousin, was throwing a party at a restaurant. On top of that, I then had to make Anita call my mother and take her into confidence. So annoying," Ayesha said as she entered the car, the last part of her tirade ending with a sigh. She put her bag on the back seat of the car.

"Forget everything else and let it be. The next twelve hours are just yours and mine -- just you, me, the road and the music, the sky and the stars, the meanderer and the lover," said Om and planted a kiss on Ayesha's lips.

"Where are we going?" asked Ayesha, slowly opening her eyes. Deep, passionate kisses were like spells of magic, transporting the kisser and the kissed into their own heavens – exactly what a great story did.

"We're the meanderers, going from here to there, like a river going through its windy course; with the figs and the branches, with the leaves and the ashes, with the lovers and the dead, with the sinkable ships and the unsinkable paper boats," said Om, leaning back into his seat, looking into Ayesha's eyes. The sun had set and it was dark outside. Albeit, feeble rays of light from a lamppost reached Ayesha's face.

"You could make a decent poet, if not a software engineer," said Ayesha.

Om looked at her for a few seconds, then adjusted his seat upright and started driving.

<hr />

Om was taking her to Neemrana. About a couple of hours' drive from Delhi, it was an ancient historic town in the state of Rajasthan and housed a 16th Century hill fort.

He had found a quiet and private campground in Neemrana using Softzone's search engine on the internet.

Within half an hour, both of them were beyond the clutches of the city traffic, cruising along the highway. It was dark outside. The dulcet ambient lights within the car had set the mood for the evening. He drove mostly on the left-most lane, the slowest one. He wasn't in a hurry to reach their destination. Soft, country music played on the radio. None of them knew most of the songs, which were being played. It did not matter.

Om held Ayesha's hand and did not let go even when he had to change the gear. Ayesha, on the other hand, leaned over and rested her head on his shoulders.

Om turned his head and planted a kiss on her forehead.

Ayesha kissed his cheek in return before leaning all the way back to the other end. She opened the window, stuck her head out and let her hair fly wild with the wind. She lifted her legs and placed them on his thighs.

Om looked at his lover, who stared at the sky without any aim. Her toes moved around his body from his thighs to his arms, from his shoulders to his neck.

Every now and then he would turn around and gaze at her. The moonlight shone off her face. Her hands held each other and rested on her belly.

It was cold outside, yet she let the winds gust in and dance with her hair.

There was no rush. One moment flowed into another without any conflict or turmoil. Or, even ambition. Their breathing was full of rhythm. One long breath in and another long breath out. It repeated itself on its own, accompanied by the background music.

They reached the campground at nine in the evening. The last few hours on the road were as surreal as anything either of them had experienced.

Om checked in at the reception and asked them to allot him a space as secluded as possible.

"The campground is barely occupied during winter. Drive around and set up your tent wherever you like," the attendant at the reception said, handing over the map of the campground to Om.

He drove the car to the farthest end of the campground. There were some tents set up on the way, but they were few and far in between.

It was getting colder. Ayesha put on her turquoise-colored beanie and slipped one on Om's head as well.

He parked the car at the corner of the campground.

They got out and saw a vast uninhabited land on either end of the barbed wire fencing that separated the campground from it. He then took out the tent from the boot of the car.

"Do you know how to do this?" asked Ayesha.

"No, but we have this," said Om pointing towards a booklet – a manual on how to assemble the tent. Ayesha and Om smiled for a second or two.

"Let me play some music," said Ayesha, taking the phone out of her pocket. She clicked on 'I Want You' by Bob Dylan.

Meanwhile, Om started following the steps laid down in the manual. A few minutes later, the tent was up. Ayesha looked animated and excited, seeing the tent set up. She took a picture with her Nokia-6600 cell phone. It was the most expensive and feature-rich phone in the market at that time. The first of its kind to have a

1.3 mega-pixel back camera and one of the only few in the market that could play MP3 songs.

"It's going to get really cold in the night," remarked Ayesha.

Om looked at her for a second and winked before walking back to the boot of the car. He took out an inflatable air mattress along with two pillows and a quilt.

Ayesha shook her head in disbelief with a smirk on her face. She was impressed. Om had done his homework and was prepared.

Om blew the air in the inflatable mattress using a pump and placed it inside the tent. He went inside and covered it with a bed sheet before neatly arranging the two pillows and the quilt. His lover looked on and sometimes volunteered, which Om resisted. He wanted her to allow him to build the moment. He wanted to be entirely responsible for creating golden moments for her to savour.

Om returned to the boot again. He took out two foldable camp chairs along with a small battery-powered lamp. He placed it right next to the tent and looked at Ayesha, whose charm knew no bounds. She stepped towards him and embraced him in a tight hug.

Ayesha sat on one of the chairs. He, however, proceeded to walk up towards the boot, again.

"Now what?" she asked, wondering what he was upto this time.

Om looked at her and smiled. He took out a bottle of red wine along with two glasses and returned to Ayesha. She looked floored, which brought a smile onto his face. He had succeeded in his intentions.

"Would you like olives with your wine, Ma'am, or cheese?" asked Om with the bottle of wine in one hand and two glasses in the other.

Ayesha raised her eyebrows, tittered a bit, and said, "Cheese."

Om poured the two of them a glass of red wine from the Sula vineyards in southern India before taking out a packet of finely cut cheese.

"Looks like you're pretty experienced," said Ayesha, a tone of sarcasm in her voice and a wry smile on her face.

Om pulled his chair in front of her and started running his fingers on her thigh. He bent over and kissed her left hand, which rested peacefully on her right knee. Her legs were crossed.

Ayesha got up from her chair, kept it aside, and sat on Om's lap with her back on his chest. Om wrapped her with his arms around her stomach, a glass of wine in his right hand resting gently on her right thigh. She let herself loose in his arms and lay all the way back, her weight on his chest and her eyes on the stars. They sipped their wine, bit by bit, without saying anything to each other. The silence in between them was the love letter, too profound to be carried in the weight of words.

"Do you think we were destined to be together?" she asked, gazing at the stars on that clear winter night.

"I don't know. I don't think there is destiny, at least the way we understand it. There is free will, there is liberty. You are with me and I am with you, out of our own free will," said Om softly into her ears.

"Will you ever leave me out of your free will then?" asked Ayesha and looked at Om.

Om turned her face towards her and asked, "Will you?"

She shook her head and leaned a little closer. He too repeated the gesture. This sequence repeated until he leaned right in to kiss her on her lips, which were stained with the Shiraz. She wrapped his head in her arms, the glass of wine still in her hands. The music still played on her phone. The stars still shimmered bright in the sky. The breeze was still cool and the night was still young.

"Let's go inside," she whispered as she broke the sweet, deep kiss, that tasted of good wine.

Om kept looking at her eyes. She kept their wine glasses on the ground and got up. She held his hand, slowly pulled him up from his chair, and took him inside the tent.

She got in the quilt first, placed her head on the pillow, and turned towards Om. He closed the tent from inside and looked at Ayesha. He slowly got into the quilt. The air inside the tent was getting warmer. Both were inside the quilt now, looking at each other. She placed her arms around him and tucked in close.

He wrapped his arms around her back and pulled her even closer. Her breasts pressed against his chest, their legs crossed with each other, their lips right next to each other.

"Make love to me tonight," she said.

Om gazed into her eyes. He said nothing. The only sound that escaped him was that of his deep breath. Ayesha took her left hand and slipped it inside Om's t-shirt and pulled it upward.

Om slipped his right hand inside Ayesha's top and pulled it upwards. He sat up; so did she.

Ayesha took off Om's shirt and ran her hands over his chest.

Om took off Ayesha's top and pulled her closer, looking into her eyes.

She got up slowly, crossed her legs around Om's waist and sat on his lap, facing him. A mellow light from the lamp lying outside the tent, conjoined with the moon light, radiated across the two bodies.

⊰⊱

Om woke up first the next morning, by the chirping of the birds. Ayesha was still fast asleep. Those big beautiful eyes seemed peaceful, closed as they were; those soft, silken pink lips, kissing each other; her right arm carelessly rested around her neck, covering a part of her stunning face. The previous night was the stuff of dreams. Om had lost his virginity, so had Ayesha. It was magical – the set-up, the moment, the experience, and the culmination.

He put his shirt, as quietly as he could, and left the tent. The lamp outside had switched itself off by then. The empty glasses of wine still lay on the floor, stained with their lips. He started cleaning up and put all the things back in the car.

Ayesha stepped out of the tent with messy hair and cute, fluffy eyes that were still not ready to take the full might of the morning sun. Om walked up to her and kissed her forehead. She embraced him in return.

"Is it time to go?" she asked.

Om nodded. "You know your parents better than I do," he said.

Ayesha rolled her eyes.

"I'll go and freshen up," she said, picking up a bottle of water and her toiletry bag from the back seat of the car.

"I have some snacks for you in the car to eat on the way back," said Om.

❦

"It was the greatest night of my life. Thank you," said Om, touching her face. He had parked the car beside the tree near Ayesha's house. The sojourn had finally come to an end.

Ayesha gave Om a tight hug. "I can't thank you enough for what you did last night. I never felt so special in my life," she said. Her eyes had turned moist.

She picked up her handbag, which was on the rear seat of the car, and searched for something in the bag. After a few seconds, she took out a piece of stone..

"I love stones," she said. "They remind me of love, and most importantly, patience. Many of the stones that we see around us have seen billions of years pass them by. They carry within themselves, countless stories," she continued, looking into Om's eyes.

Om extended his arm and took the stone in his hand. He kissed it.

"Do you really have to go?" he asked, making a puppy face.

She looked at him and gave him a kiss. It was time to leave.

Picking up her bag from the back seat of the car, she adjusted the rear-view mirror towards her face. She took out a hair brush and then combed her hair.

She gave him a final kiss, looked at him for the last time, and exited the car.

"Message me when you can," shouted Om.

Ayesha didn't look back.

Om looked at her leave. Every step she took, heavier his heart became. He rubbed his upper lip against his lower one and took it to his nose. He smelled of her. He wondered if she smelled of him.

Ayesha was no longer in sight. Om started the car and drove away.

CHAPTER 36

OM RETURNED THE rental car soon after and called Arun.

"What are you doing?" asked Om.

"I'm with Natasha at the Janak Puri District Center. What are you up to?" responded Arun.

"Bro, I just had the greatest night of my life. I was wondering where you are. I thought maybe we could hang out," said Om.

"Come over here. The chickpeas salad stall," replied Arun.

"Yeah, come over here. We are waiting," said Natasha from the background.

"All right, I'll be there in half an hour," said Om.

Om parked his motorcycle right next to the chickpeas salad stall at the Janak Puri District Centre. People from all over Delhi came to this vendor. His specialty was the chickpeas that he mixed with onion, tomato, capsicum, and topped with his own special dressing. There was also an option to serve this with a special bread called 'kulcha' and a pickle made of carrot.

Arun and Natasha sat right next to the stall on a large piece of stone placed under a tarpaulin shed. It was meant for the customers of the salad stall.

"Why are you smiling from ear to ear?" Natasha asked Om.

He ordered himself a portion of the chickpeas salad with the kulcha and took a seat next to Arun and Natasha.

"I took Ayesha to camping last night. In Neemrana," said Om with a coy smile on his face.

Natasha's jaws dropped. She looked at Arun, who was equally interested in knowing more about the story.

"I took a car on rent from Sumit's father," started Om.

"Yeah, yeah, we know who Sumit is. Get to the main part," Arun interrupted Om.

"Well, if you are not going to be patient about it, I'm stopping right here," warned Om as he got up and walked towards the stall to see if his food was ready.

"Sorry, baba. Come here. I will make him shut up," said Natasha.

Om came back to his seat again.

"I took the car and picked up Ayesha from near her house," Om resumed. "The drive all the way to Neemrana, after the sun had set, was pure magic. Her hair dancing in the wind, her legs massaging my thighs as I drove, was surreal," added Om.

The vendor called his name out; his food was ready. Om picked it up and returned to his seat.

"We set up the tent. We were so excited. It was our first time camping. I then took the chairs, lamp and the bottle of wine out," Om continued.

"I like where the story is going," joked Arun.

Natasha slapped him on the back, which made Arun shut up.

"She got up and sat on my lap after a while. I wrapped her in my arms as she gazed at the stars. A few loose strands of her open hair danced with the halo formed with the light of the lamp on the ground. We kissed, with lips and tongues smeared with red wine," said Om.

Arun and Natasha listened. Such a focus they had not shown any time before in the time he knew them. .

Om took the first bite out of his salad.

"She then asked me to go inside the tent with her," said Om, a sheepish look on his face.

"And?" said Natasha, suggestively.

"I went inside with her as she asked me to," said Om and laughed, his eyebrows drawn together.

"Did you guys... umm... Do it?" asked Arun.

Om smiled back and winked.

Arun looked at Natasha, who immediately looked away from him.

"Make sure you don't lose focus of your career and goals. Your final round at Softzone is day after tomorrow. You've dreamt of it for years," said Natasha, changing the topic.

"I'm going to apply to some Delhi based companies as well. Softzone mostly gives placements in Bangalore or at its headquarters in California. Fresher openings in Delhi are very limited," responded Om.

"Are you mad?" exclaimed Natasha. "People here would give an arm to go to America and work for Softzone; and you are now looking to find other companies to stay in this crowded and polluted rat house that is Delhi?" she continued, getting really annoyed at Om.

Om didn't respond. He was busy finishing his food.

"All right. I'll go now. I have work this evening. I thought of catching up with you guys and sharing the story with you," said Om. He quickly finished his food, got up and threw the plastic disposable containers in the dustbin near the stall before getting on his motorcycle.

Om returned to his room once he had completed the evening shift at the Pizza Corner. It was half past midnight. He hung his cap on a nail on the wall, took his clothes off, and grabbed a towel. A hot shower at the end of a long weekend was as magnificent as sipping wine with Ayesha. Well, not quite.

Om stood in the stream of running hot water below the metallic shower head. Calcium deposits clogged the holes in it.

Anxiety had taken root in him since late afternoon. Ayesha hadn't messaged since she left the car in the morning. Worry about her well-being replaced the enrapturing thoughts of the night gone past.

Om arrived at the college the next day, well before the first lecture. It was Monday and Professor Sonali was supposed to be handling the first lecture. A bare fifty-percent of the class marked their attendance. Most of the ones who had been placed didn't bother any more about the attendance and the ones who hadn't, they were busy preparing for the ones in the line-up.

Sonali was surprised to see Om in the classroom.

"How come you are here? You have your final round of interview tomorrow," she said.

Om wasn't able to figure out how to answer that question. The actual reason was that his anxiety had grown over the course of the night. He had kept on checking his phone at every toss and turn, but to no communication from Ayesha's end. The college and the classroom provided a change of environment.

"I'm fully prepared for it." It was all that Om could manage, with a smile and a big sigh.

He might have been ready intellectually, but not mentally. His breathing had become shallow and forced. Every now and then, he had to rock his chest and suck air into his lungs with a lot of energy, yet he felt as if he needed more. He tried to yawn but failed. It seemed like his body was in want of more oxygen, yet it kept sabotaging his attempts at obtaining it.

<hr />

More than thirty hours had passed since Om had dropped Ayesha off. There was still no trace of her. The last lecture of the day was over. He started walking back to his motorcycle that he had parked outside the college. In a few months from now, those by-lanes in the campus, those classes, and those corridors were going to be just memories. Mostly fun memories, some challenging, but all of them fond. He moved through the campus with earphones in his ears, his CD player playing some of his favorite music.

He reached his motorcycle in the parking lot. It was pretty desolate. Most of the students parked their vehicles inside the college.

Om, however, preferred to park outside, even if it was a little walk. It was cheaper too. He inserted the key into the keyhole and lifted his right leg to cross over and take a seat. He had just done so when someone grabbed him by the scruff of his neck. A moment later, a powerful punch landed on his face. Om saw that there were four people; though by their strong and muscular build, they could be counted as eight. Two had baseball bats in their hands. Before Om could process anything more, they began to deliver punches and kicks. One of the men with a baseball bat hit Om on the head. Om immediately fell to the ground. The others continued showering him with kicks. There was no response from Om. He lay motionless on the barren ground, unconscious.

A few minutes later the goons saw a police van approaching the scene and fled with quick feet while Om bled profusely. A small crowd had gathered around the parking lot where Om was being beaten mercilessly. Perhaps some good Samaritan, who wasn't brave enough to jump into the fight, had alerted the Police station nearby.

CHAPTER 37

THE SOFTZONE RECRUITMENT team was in the campus for the final round. The interview panel consisted of the head of the Human Resources Department, the Senior Vice President of Technology, and the Chief Operations Officer. The brightest minds were going to be recruited for one of the greatest companies in the world. It had one of the most handsome salary packages for freshers anywhere.

It was Tuesday morning and perhaps the most important day of their lives for those who had made it this far. Om was one of them. However, that day, he was nowhere to be seen. His name was second on the list of candidates to be interviewed. The candidates who had their interview were meant to wait outside the interview hall, seated on the chairs placed in the corridor for that purpose. Everyone had already taken their positions except for Om. The volunteer rushed to inform Professor Mehta and the Chancellor about Om's absence, who were on a quick round of the proceedings. The Chancellor himself called Om's phone, but there was no answer. He dropped a text message, asking Om to reach the campus immediately and call him when he arrived.

The first candidate was called in for the interview. The Chancellor suggested that the volunteer, one of the third-year students named Rahul, inform the interview panel that Om had been summoned by the Chancellor for urgent work on the college's database server and that the Chancellor had requested that his interview be shifted to a little later in the day. The Chancellor then shook his head and walked away with Professor Mehta.

The first candidate came out of the interview after half an hour. The volunteer, Rahul, stepped inside the interview hall. The volunteer informed the panel that Om had an emergency work that needed to be on the college servers and asked if his interview could be moved to the last slot in the day. The interview panel was fine with it.

Rahul then came out and sent the next candidate in. As soon as the next interview began, he dashed towards the Chancellor's office.

"Sir, Om is still not here. I have informed the interview panel exactly as you asked me to. Luckily, they have moved Om's interview to the last slot in the day," said Rahul.

The Chancellor was in his office with Professor Mehta. The latter was a professor who excelled in Microprocessor Systems. Having mentored him on his project, he was quite close to Om. "We should call Arun, his best friend, and ask him to find out what's wrong. This is the day Om had been looking forward to ever since he started college. He wouldn't miss it for anything. There's definitely something wrong," the Professor said.

The Chancellor opened the college database using the computer on his desk and looked up the phone number of Arun.

"Hello, Arun, this is Mr. Dayal," said the Chancellor after Arun answered the phone.

Arun was still half-asleep when he answered the phone from an unknown number, but as soon as he found out that it was the Chancellor on the phone, he jumped and sat up.

"Yes, Sir. Good morning, Sir," said Arun, trying to not sound as if he'd just woken up.

"Arun, Om was supposed to be here for his final interview with Softzone, but he still hasn't reached. Do you have an idea where he is?" asked the Chancellor.

"Sorry, Sir. I have no idea. Even I sent him a text message last night wishing him good luck, but he didn't reply," said Arun, after a brief pause. "Om lives about thirty minutes away from where I am. Please give me some time. I will find out and bring him to the college."

The Chancellor thanked him and asked Arun to give him a call as soon as he has any news.

Only nine students had made it to the final round of the interview. Seven of them had already completed their interviews. The eighth candidate, who was waiting outside patiently, was now slated to be called.

Rahul came out of the interview hall and requested the last candidate to go inside. Time seemed to be running out for Om.

<hr />

Arun came running into the corridor and saw Rahul standing at the entrance of the interview chamber. "Where's Mr. Dayal? I can't find him in his office and I don't have his mobile number," asked Arun, panting and short of breath.

"He must be in his office," said Rahul. "What happened? Do you have any news about Om?" Rahul asked, concerned.

Arun started running again. "He has met with an accident and is in the hospital," shouted Arun as he caught the stairs to go to the first floor.

Arun ran frantically across corridors, peeping into classrooms to find Mr. Dayal. He finally found him on the third floor with Professor Sonali.

"Sir, Om has met with an accident. He is at the public hospital across the road. He has gained consciousness but is still in the intensive care unit. I tried calling you, but your phone went unanswered," informed Arun, still trying to catch his breath.

A look of concern showed on their faces.

"Let me go and speak with the Softzone team first," said the Chancellor. "You go and tend to Om. I'll be there soon," said the Chancellor.

The Chancellor walked downstairs and took a seat outside the interview hall, waiting for the final candidate to come out after his interview.

As soon as the candidate walked out, the Chancellor wasted no time in walking in.

"Hello, Mr. Dayal. We were actually about to send a message across to you through Rahul. This one candidate, Mr. Om Vats, hasn't appeared for the interview," said one of the gentlemen, Mr Iyer, who was the Indian representative on the interview panel.

"This is exactly why I'm here. He is our brightest student. Unfortunately, he has met with an accident and is in the hospital across the road right now. Is there a chance we can schedule his interview for later?" asked the Chancellor, reluctantly.

"Well, it's unfortunate. We are concerned for the boy; however, we are afraid that the interview cannot be rescheduled. Mr. James Slaven and Mr. Ebiyadi Konzra have flown down from San Francisco, especially for today, and they leave tonight," informed Iyer with regret.

"We are really sorry because he looked to be the brightest candidate as well. Based on the previous rounds, he had the highest score by quite a margin. We were really looking forward to meeting him in the interview," said Iyer after a brief pause and an exchange of looks with the other panelists.

The Chancellor looked helpless. The interview panel could feel it.

"Please allow us to have an internal discussion for a few minutes and we'll see what can be done," said Mr. James Slaven, the Head of Technology at Softzone, looking at his peers.

The Chancellor suddenly had a glimmer of hope in his eyes. "Sure," he said.. "I'll wait outside." He then exited the interview hall.

❖

"I think we need to meet this guy. He has the highest score I've ever seen after two rounds, and I was specifically given a call by Anand Bansal, who took his technical round, to watch out for this guy. He has apparently built a world class text-to-speech engine, which will add tremendous value to the operating system we are building for the next generation of mobile devices," said James to his peers, Konzra and Iyer.

"I think I agree," said Konzra, the head of human resources department.

"But he's in the hospital," responded Iyer.

"We'll go there and meet him," said James, after a brief pause.

"I'm not sure if the doctors will allow that," said Iyer.

"We'll see as we go and make a decision about the boy, there at the hospital," suggested Konzra.

Once their thoughts resonated, they collected their paperwork in their briefcases and exited the interview hall to find the Chancellor still waiting outside.

"Mr. Dayal, we have decided that we will go and meet Om at the hospital if the doctors allow," said Mr. James.

The Chancellor couldn't believe his ears.

"That's so wonderful and kind of you. I am sure Om will be forever indebted to you. I just received a call from his best friend, Arun, who is at the hospital with him. He informed me that he is fully conscious now and in a stable condition. However, he is still in the intensive care unit," said the Chancellor.

"Let's go and meet the boy," said Iyer.

"But I can't allow anyone to meet him right now. That's against the protocol. I haven't even allowed the police to record his statement yet. Although he is stable, we are still closely monitoring his condition," said the Doctor in-charge at the Balaji Hospital where Om was in the intensive care unit.

Arun, the three-member team from Softzone, the Chancellor and the doctor were outside the glass-walled ICU Om was admitted to. Om had his face towards the six people outside, watching the proceedings. He saw the Chancellor taking the doctor into a corner for a while and explaining something to him, animatedly. The doctor shook his head and glanced towards Om.

Om nodded as much as he could. His plea was obvious to the doctor. The doctor started walking towards the ICU and entered the room.

"How do you feel?" asked the doctor as he looked at a few readings on the screens of the machines placed inside the ICU. He took a syringe, a bottle of medicine, and injected it in Om's veins.

"Totally... Fine...," muttered Om with as much energy as he could.

The doctor looked at him, shook his head and smiled. Om tried to smile as well, but it hurt because of the injuries on his head.

"Those three people from Softzone are outside. Do you want to meet one of them?" asked the doctor, sitting next to Om.

"Yes... Please...," said Om, nodding with as much speed and force as he could.

"I'm going to send one person in," said the doctor.

Om smiled at the doctor.

The doctor exited the ICU while he looked at the team outside.

"All right. I'm going to allow this. But only one of you and for only ten minutes," said the doctor.

James, Iyer and Konzra discussed with one another for a few moments. "I will go in," said Mr. James, the Head of Technology at Softzone.

"Please follow me now," said the doctor.

James took a seat next to Om. The doctor exited the room.

"How do you feel now?" asked James, in a soft, reassuring voice.

"I'm alive and kicking, Sir," said Om with a little stutter but an inexplicable enthusiasm. It was taking a lot of energy for Om to speak out loud. But then, this was one of the moments he had waited for his entire life.

"Forget about technology and the job. We're going to talk as friends, heart to heart. Tell me, how did this happen?" asked James.

"I think the parents of a girl who I love, sent goons to beat me up," responded Om as he mouthed each word slowly.

James was a little taken aback. Perhaps he didn't expect such an honest answer.

"Do you still love her?" asked James, after a brief pause.

"She has just disappeared. I don't even know where and how she is," said Om. "Of course, I do love her. Love doesn't just disappear into thin air. My love for her is not dependent on her. It is my own expression, an over-flow of the feelings arising from within me," continued Om as he winced with pain.

"Don't speak so much. Give your body some rest," said James, watching Om grimace.

"I'll tell you a Zen story my grandmother told me when I was small," said James. He sounded like a raconteur, a poet; a rare talent for a person with a background in technology.

"Once upon a time there were two monks crossing a river together. They came across a woman at a point where the currents were very strong. The woman didn't know how to swim and looked helpless. She asked for their help to cross the river. The young monk hesitated. The older monk picked her up on her shoulders and dropped her on the other side of the river. The woman thanked the monk profusely before the two monks continued with their journey. However, the young monk was restless. He waited for a while, but when he couldn't bear the restlessness anymore, he asked the older monk, 'We aren't supposed to touch women, so why did you carry that woman on your shoulders?' The older monk looked at him for a moment before replying, "I set her down on the other side of the river. Why are you still carrying her?'"

Om looked at James, amazed. It was a profoundly poignant parable. It seemed like grandmothers across the world were great story-tellers.

"Let it go. You have an entire life in front of you and you are one of the most talented engineers in the world right now. I have seen your text-to-speech engine and it is revolutionary. It's unbelievable that it has been built by just one person," continued James.

Om smiled and blinked his eyes, as a gesture of gratitude and acknowledgment.

"We will offer you a job," Om heard these words from James' mouth. Om's eyes lit up.

"Come to California after your college ends," said James and patted Om's shoulder.

"But...," began Om. "Can I request for a position in Delhi?" he asked politely.

James looked at Om for a moment before responding, "We will hire you, no matter what. I will leave this decision with you. I'll leave my contact details with Mr. Dayal, the Chancellor. When you get fully fit, write me an email and I will accommodate you in a team at whichever location you prefer; though, this will be the first time a fresher denies a posting at the company headquarters in California."

"Get well soon," said James as he got up to leave the room.

Om gave him a big smile and thanked him from all his heart.

Dayal, the Chancellor of the college, looked at Om from outside the ICU and gave him a smile. So did Arun.

Mr. Dayal said goodbye to Arun and thanked him for his help before escorting the Softzone executives back to the college where a chauffeur driven car was waiting to take them to the airport.

Arun requested the doctor's permission to enter the ICU. The doctor denied. Arun begged, but the doctor was persistent. The doctor was preparing a sedative to be injected into Om. Arun kept begging. The doctor said that Arun could only accompany him for a couple of minutes when he went inside to sedate Om. Om needs a long rest after that, explained the doctor.

"When are his parents coming over?" asked the doctor.

"His father should be here, later tonight. His mother can't move. She is paralysed," replied Arun.

The doctor made his way into the ICU and so did Arun.

"Can you give me my phone, please? It was in my bag," Om asked Arun.

"It is with the police. They will hand it over to your father. He is on his way," replied Arun.

The doctor was about to inject the sedative into Om's veins. "You informed my father," said Om in an irritated tone. "Aahh!" he exclaimed as the doctor inserted the needle.

"I didn't. The police informed your parents. Your father had to arrange someone quickly to take care of your mother while he comes and visits here," explained Arun.

"Anything from Ayesha?" asked Om.

"All right, out now. He needs rest," doctor said, looking at Arun.

"Are you mad? Forget her," said Arun as he exited the door while the doctor waited behind him.

Om's father reached the hospital and found that Om was asleep. He had been so for the last eight hours. His friend, Arun, had been waiting outside along with Natasha.

Mahesh thanked Arun for his help and went up to the glass walls of the intensive care unit. He looked at his son who had bandages on his head, arms, and legs. Seeing his son in that condition made him remember the first time Om had injured himself as a child. He had been three or four years old. He had fallen to the ground while playing cricket and had come running to his father in tears. Mahesh had then placed him on the dining table, cleaned his wounds with Dettol as Om cried in pain, before he bandaged him. It had been a sunny Sunday afternoon in the winter of Jaipur. He had just bought his motorcycle, Yezdi. Kiran had been out grocery shopping and also to buy a beanie for her son. Vivid images of those moments played out in Mahesh's mind as he gazed at his battered and bruised son.

Seeing Om showing signs of waking up, Mahesh went to the doctor to inform him of the progress. The latter asked the nurse to go and check on Om, informing her that he would follow soon.

"Mr. Mahesh, your son was attacked. The police have filed a FIR and some of Om's belongings are at the Saket Police Station. Om has been responding well to the treatment, and hopefully, we will be in a position to transfer him to the general ward tomorrow morning. I'm going to call the police here tomorrow to record a statement," the doctor said to Mahesh.

Mahesh politely thanked the doctor and followed him as he made his way to the ICU.

The doctor went inside the ICU, asking Mahesh to wait outside. The latter kept gazing at his son. Om looked outside for a moment with his eyes half-open. Om's head still felt heavy with the sedatives. He stared into the eyes of his father before he closed his eyes again.

The doctor and the nurse came out. "Om is totally stable now, but really weak. It's just a matter of time now until he recovers fully. We will transfer him to the general ward in the morning, and hopefully, in four days, he will be discharged," the doctor informed and bid Mahesh a good night. Mahesh folded his hands and thanked the doctor.

CHAPTER 38

AT 7 A.M IN the morning, the nurse arrived to conduct a regular check-up on Om. Mahesh sat on one of the benches he had slept on over the night. He got up and stood outside the ICU while the nurse performed her usual protocol. Om was awake and noticed his father waiting outside.

The nurse came out after a few minutes. "He seems to be responding very well to the treatment. You can go inside and meet him. We will start the process of moving him to the general ward in a few minutes," she said.

Mahesh thanked her for her help. She acknowledged the gratitude and left.

He then opened the ICU door slowly and entered the room.

Om looked weak.

They looked at each other. Mahesh walked up to Om and sat next to him.

"Who did this to you?" asked Mahesh.

Om shook his head, indicating he didn't have an answer.

"The doctors say you are recovering very well and will now be moved to the general ward," added Mahesh.

Om nodded.

"How is Mummy?" asked Om after a brief pause.

"She is very tense. It was hard to find someone to take care of her while I am away, hence I was late in coming here," replied his father. "I told her that I will make her speak with you at the earliest opportunity."

Two nurses entered the room with the doctor and three compounders. It was time to move Om to the general. They asked his father to wait outside.

"Thank you for coming," said Om. Mahesh looked at Om and put a finger on his lips.

It took about an hour to move Om to the general ward. Mahesh was asked to sign some papers on Om's behalf. The doctor informed him that he had notified the police on the status of his son's health and they would be coming in the afternoon to record a statement and also bring Om's belongings with them. In all probability, Mahesh would not need to go to the police station.

One of the nurses adjusted Om's bed to help him sit upright and served him breakfast. They had served him vegetable soup.

Mahesh helped put a napkin around his son's neck and sat beside him. He fed Om, spoon by spoon, without speaking to each other.

"Do you want to sit upright for a while before I make you lie down?" asked Mahesh.

Om nodded in agreement.

"I'll return this to the kitchen and be back in a minute," said Mahesh as he picked up the empty bowl and spoon.

Mahesh returned and sat right next to Om with his back resting on the wall. Both of them faced the same direction.

"Congratulations on your placement with Softzone," said Mahesh.

"Thank you," responded Om.

"So, will you be going to America now?" asked Mahesh.

"Don't know yet," replied Om after a pause.

None of them said anything for a while.

"Did Mummy send you here?" asked Om after a long period of silence.

"I have cradled you in my lap, Om. I don't need your mother to tell me to go and take care of you," replied Mahesh.

Both of them looked outside the window in front of them. A newly inaugurated Delhi metro line, connecting South Delhi with Central Delhi, saw one train run after another.

"And you also left me to rot when you were tired of cradling me in your lap," said Om.

Mahesh didn't respond.

"All you ever wanted was for me to stand first in the class, secure the highest marks; be the best student, the best sportsman, and the best at everything. My life was all but a burden of your failed aspirations," said Om. "I still remember how you didn't speak with me for a week when I scored ninety-seven out of one hundred in mathematics in Class-X board exams, instead of hundred out of hundred you were expecting."

"And how I had to earn my own way to the school trip; to buy myself a pair of school shoes when my shoes were torn, to get myself a job and pay off one loan after another," continued Om as he continued staring outside the window at the trains passing by.

There was a long silence in between.

"He is still sitting upright. What are you doing, baba?" the nurse remarked, looking towards Mahesh. She adjusted the bed flat again to let Om lie down and rest.

Mahesh pulled the blanket up towards Om's neck and tapped his chest.

Over the next three days, Mahesh took great care of Om. They did not speak a word to each other except functional matters but interacted often with their eyes. Om's mother would speak with her son every few hours. That was her only solace – hearing her son's voice. Mahesh could not imagine the agony his wife felt. Her son was on the hospital bed and she couldn't even see him because she was paralysed.

Sometimes, Arun would fill in and ask Mahesh to rest. Natasha would visit a few times.

The police did too. They had recorded Om's statement, which was basically a polite 'I don't know anything. Please forget about it.' Clearly, Om didn't want any trouble for Ayesha, who hadn't replied yet. Om still had no idea where and how she was.

Om had got his phone back. Mahesh did not allow him to keep it but would hand it over every now and then for a few minutes.

A week had passed since Om had dropped Ayesha off that fateful morning. They had made love the previous night and the next day she had vanished. He had asked Arun to give her a call from a public telephone booth; the number had been rendered inactive. He would have had some closure if he knew what had happened. Had she left out of her own will? Or was it forced? Did she still want to be with him? Was she even alive? Om's mind kept circulating such thoughts like clockwork.

"The hospital is going to discharge you tomorrow morning," said his father as he came back from a meeting with the doctor.

Om blinked his eye in acknowledgment.

"I have spoken with Arun and his parents. You will be living with them for a few days until you are completely all right. I wish I could have stayed longer, but your mother needs me as well now," said Mahesh.

Om nodded.

"Thank you," Om said to his father, who looked at him for a few seconds before walking to the opposite end of the wall to draw the curtains. It was time to go to sleep.

Om was discharged the next morning. Arun and his parents arrived with a car to take him back to their place. His father greeted them; they reciprocated with an equal kindness. Om, though, still had his arms and head wrapped in a bandage. He could walk in comfort, though not for long.

"Take care of yourself and don't be too adventurous," his father said, bidding him goodbye.

Om looked at his father and smiled, a moment that would have melted his mother's heart had she been able to see it.

He opened his arms and reached out to hug his father, who took a second to realize what was happening. He slowly lifted him arms and wrapped them around Om.

"Take care of Mummy," said Om before sitting on the backseat of the car. He rolled his window down and looked back at his father as Arun's father drove the car away.

The very next day, the moment everyone left for the day and there was no one at Arun's home, Om quickly went out and caught bus 479 to Vasant Kunj.

Charan Singh, the tea vendor, was thrilled to see Om. He immediately made space for him even though Om's usual spot was occupied by someone else. Perhaps a new lover was in town.

He took the seat, a cup of tea and rested his back on the wall of stone behind him. It all seemed familiar, yet nothing was quite the same. The buses were the same, so was the rush of the crowd; the buildings were the same, so was the warmth of the sun; the air was the same, so was the fragrance of the tea. Yet, something felt different. It wasn't the same place, it wasn't the same moment, and it wasn't the same river he was stepping into, twice. The river was new; each drop was new; so was its meandering.

He sat there for the whole afternoon. Perhaps Ayesha might come out again and visit the same shop. Perhaps he could go and introduce himself to her again. Maybe even ask her out a second time. The river kept flowing and the sun set, but the lover didn't show up.

It was time for Charan Singh to close the shop and it was time for Om to go back to Arun's house.

———◆———

The next day, Om followed the same routine. As soon as Arun was off to college and his parents to their work, Om would leave the house, catch bus number 479, and reach Charan Singh's tea stall.

There was a theory going on in his mind. Perhaps he didn't want to find Ayesha anymore. Perhaps he was going there to save himself from the pangs of regret he would feel for not doing enough to find her again. The deep anxiety in him was slowly making way for peace, even though there was still a void in the heart. The breathing was becoming deeper and deeper, with fewer and fewer violent gasps of air.

Charan Singh had saved Om's spot for him today. Perhaps he was aware that Om's mission was still incomplete, or perhaps, he understood that the search for a lover was a process that took time and was not going to be fulfilled so soon.

Om didn't take his regular spot today, much to Charan's dismay. He sat on the other side of Charan this time. Perhaps a change of spot would mean a change in destiny. But the wind blew in the same direction, the sun lit up the atmosphere as usual, the honking vehicle drivers hurled the same abuses, the passers-by smoked the same cigarettes, and the lovers wrapped themselves in the same arms. But, the tea tasted a little different, a tad less sweet; the stone at the back was colder than usual, the sand was a little lighter, and the rush of the crowd was a little more maddening. It was quite unusual for a Saturday.

Om, as usual, sat with his back to the stone and stared away into oblivion, sipping the tea bit by bit. Suddenly, his heartbeat started rising. He had to gasp for a dose of oxygen. He kept the cup on the side and sat upright, trying to suck air into his lungs, but it went straight to his chest. He tried a few times, but just couldn't get enough air to gratify his body.

Across, on the other side of the road, was Ayesha. She didn't lean against the walls of the Levi's store. She just walked past it and kept walking. Her hair was open. There was a certain sadness in her steps. Her eyes were a little swollen and her face naked. She kept walking and he kept looking.

She paused on her way in front of the gas station, took out her mobile, and made a call to someone. She stood there, right there in front of the gas station, sometimes looking at the ground and sometimes looking at the sky. Her demeanour was mellow.

Om kept sitting; he didn't move an inch. His body was suddenly breathing in a rhythm – peaceful and content. She was alive; she was breathing. A car soon stopped in front of Ayesha, she stepped in to the car and left.

CHAPTER 39

OM REACHED ARUN'S home just in time before anyone else in the house did. Thankfully, Om had memorized the number lock to get into the house when Arun keyed it in front of Om after they had come home from the hospital.

He took a seat on the sofa, leaned all the way back, and kept staring at the ceiling. He took out his mobile phone after a while and texted Dayal, the Chancellor of the college.

'Dear Sir, Mr. James Slaven from Softzone must have shared his contact details with you. Could you please forward me his email address?' he texted to the Chancellor of his University.

The Chancellor replied within five minutes, giving Om the email address and asking about his well-being.

Om thanked the Chancellor and assured him that he was well.

He logged into his email account using Arun's laptop and typed an email for Mr. James Slaven.

'Dear Sir, hope you are well and my email finds you in good health. First of all, I want to thank you from the core of my heart for the generosity and kindness you exhibited by interviewing me in the intensive care unit of a hospital. I am forever indebted to you and the profound Zen story of love, loss and letting-go you shared with me. You asked me to choose between Delhi and California. I have made the decision, Sir. I will start work with Softzone in California.

Kind regards,

Om Vats'

———◆———

Six months flew by. It was the last day at college. All the students had gathered for an official farewell party. The four years at the University of Technology, Delhi, had come to an end. The results for the final semester had been declared. Om, Arun and Natasha had all passed with first division.

Om was slated to join Softzone in California, the next week. James had wanted him to join even earlier since the new operating system for mobile devices that Softzone was building was one of the company's top priorities. The text-to-speech engine was going to be an important component of the next generation of operating systems. However, given the rules of the organization, it wasn't possible to hire him until the final results had been declared.

His friend, Arun, was slated to join Librasoft in a month's time and so was Natasha, who had been placed in Mubi Technologies. Both were in Gurgaon, a bustling town flooded with multinational corporations, particularly in technology. India had established itself as a leader in IT services and outsourcing.

Om had dressed himself in a gray suit, which he had borrowed from his peer at Pizza Corner, Sumit. He wore a white shirt and a black bow-tie. He had left the job at the Pizza Corner after he had secured a job with Softzone Corporation. He apologised to the owner about not being able to serve a notice because of his hospitalisation. He also thanked him for his support during the college days.

The police had never found the people who attacked Om in the parking lot that fateful day; Om never even thought they would. Rich people always got away with crimes, he thought to himself. He didn't chase the police. He never intended to ever since he had seen Ayesha's sombre and subdued eyes. It had been six months, but the image of that scene was as vivid in his mind as it was when it happened. Perhaps even more.

Memory is a strange thing. Sometimes, one is able to recollect a memory far more vividly than the time when the said event actually took place.

The boys were generally dressed in suits. Some of the fancy ones had come in tuxedos. The girls had opted for a sari.

The afternoon was flagged off by the juniors who staged a few performances for the graduating students. That was followed by an awards ceremony in which Om was awarded the 'Best Project of the Year' for his work on the text-to-speech engine. Finally, the Chancellor of the university, Ashok Dayal, was invited on stage to address the graduating class.

The students bid their final goodbyes to each other. Some of them would keep in touch while the others would not. There were a few smiles, a few tears, and a lot of nostalgia. It was strange how in hindsight, all those moments of pressures, stress and tension at the university seemed trifle, but when they were actually happening, they were all encompassing and consuming. Soon, even that particular moment would be reduced to hindsight, to make way for something else. Hindsight and nostalgia – they are truly strange concepts; sometimes misleading, sometimes offering a perspective.

"I'm going to miss you, bro," said Arun and hugged Om. "I've heard America has some great hair transplant surgeons."

Om shook his head while Natasha stood behind Arun and laughed.

"So, you two have just decided to simply hang by each other's neck," said Om, looking at Arun and Natasha.

"I'm even thinking of buying a leash and tying Arun to one," joked Natasha.

All three of them laughed.

A few other students, Nikhil, Ronny, Mohit, and Sara came along and called in the three of them to come together for a picture. Apple had launched a new phone – the iPhone. It had been the latest rage among students. Never in the past could a phone do as much as the iPhone did.

While the iPhone clicked the picture, Arun raised a victory sigh. Natasha pouted, showing her left profile.

"Do you mind if I took the window seat, please?" Om asked the gentleman sitting on the seat 17C by the side of the window. Om had boarded the Shatabdi Express from Delhi to Jaipur to pay his parents a final visit before he boarded the flight to San Francisco. The gentleman looked at Om for a second and pulled his eyebrows together. He then shifted to the aisle seat.

Om thanked the gentleman and proceeded to the window seat. Two suitcases were all Om owned, which he had packed neatly and kept them safely at Sumit's house. He had sold his motorcycle and used that money to buy a one-way ticket to San Francisco.

It was his last journey to Jaipur in perhaps a long time. He didn't know when he would visit Jaipur next. He didn't intend to either. He had seen those lanes many times. The once brilliant clouds had gone pale, having rained on the same trees many times. The same stories repeated themselves in the same nooks and corners. There was a voice from within him to broaden horizons, branch out, see new lanes, stand under new clouds, and form new stories.

The station master sounded the alarm and the train started moving. Om pushed his seat as further back as it could go and rested his head on the headrest. He plugged his earphones. A live montage of Incredible India ran itself before his eyes, faster as the train picked up speed.

Om reached his parents' house. The wooden door was unlocked. He opened it and knocked on the door a couple of times. No one showed up.

It was a small one-bedroom house in the south-eastern suburb of Jaipur called Model Town. He placed his backpack on the floor next to the door and took his shoes off.

The wall on the right had pictures of Naani and Babu, right below the poster of Lord Krishna. It was the same poster that hung on the wall at Naani's house in Jawahar Nagar. A defunct cash-counting machine was kept in one corner, which doubled up as a table for a vase that held artificial flowers. The rightmost corner of the wall in the living room was damp, the ceiling was stained, and water slippage had caused the plaster to bubble. The family living upstairs hadn't yet sorted out their water leakage issues.

Om quietly started walking towards his mother, who lay on her bed in the bedroom. He tried to be as discreet as possible. She sometimes took tranquilizers so that she could sleep longer, which had become an extremely rare occurrence for her.

"Om...lalla...," said a voice from the bedroom.

In spite of her health issues, she had not lost the talent of knowing when her son was around. Perhaps that innate talent of a mother never fades away.

Om took a couple more steps and stood at the bedroom door, looking at his mother. She lay there on her bed motionless, but the immeasurable joy in her being at the sight of her son was palpable.

Om walked up to her, pulled a stool, and sat right next to her.

"I didn't want to disturb you from your sleep," he said, caressing his mother's forehead.

"Don't be silly. I've been waiting for you," she said with tears in her eyes. "It's been so long since I saw you, lalla." She was unable to stop her tears.

"Have you taken your afternoon medicine yet?" asked Om.

"I haven't," she said.

Om opened the drawer next to her bed, opened the box containing pills, and took out the medicines marked 'afternoon'. His father had picked up one thing from Babu -- a meticulous and pedantic habit of labelling and organizing things.

Om poured some water into a glass from a flask, both placed next to her bed on an old bamboo table she had purchased on one of the afternoons from Johri Bazaar, on the way to consult Doctor Jolly because the ten-year-old Om had a severe fever that just wouldn't come down.

Om placed the medicines next to the glass of water on the table by the side of her bed. He inserted his left hand between her back and the bed and used his right hand to support her neck as he lifted her up. Once his mother's body was upright, he placed his left arm vertically, supporting her neck and the back at the same time. He used the right hand to put the tablet in her mouth one-by-one, followed by water. He lay her back down on the bed carefully, afterwards.

"Hold my hand," she said to Om as she lay back on the bed again.

He did as he was bidden.

"Life for me over the last two and a half years has been nothing but living for you and living through you. I prayed every day for your well-being and that you get whatever you want in life," she began, tears flowing through her eyes.

Om kept caressing her hands.

"Now that you have graduated and have found the job of your dreams, I can now die peacefully," she continued, as did the tears from her eyes. "Allow me to go now."

"And don't come back here," she said after a long pause.

Om didn't interrupt her anywhere in between. He wanted her to release everything that had built up inside her.

"I love you, ma." That's all Om said and kissed her hands. Maybe he could feel her pain, agony, and depression.

For two and a half years, she had been living a life completely dependent on others even for the most basic of things like cleaning herself and attending nature's calls.

"Whenever you need me, I will come flying," he said, smiling at her. "I'll also go and consult doctors in America. I will be taking your reports with me. Perhaps there is treatment available for you, in America."

"There is nothing anywhere, lalla. Just let me go peacefully now," she said.

Om kept caressing her hands and let her sob for a few minutes.

"There is something I want to give you while your father is still away," she said as her sobbing receded. He looked at her.

"Please open the almirah there and unlock the safe in it with the code 0786," she said to Om, pointing towards an almirah at the other end of the room.

Om got up and did as she asked.

"There will be a small white box with your name on it," his mother instructed him. "Bring that to me," she added.

Om held the box in his hands and came back to sit next to her. She asked him to open it. There was a watch and an envelope inside it.

"Your father kept this watch aside for you when you were thirteen. And this envelope has the details of the recurring deposit account in your name in which your father deposited money every month since you were seven till the time he had a job. The money will be useful to you as you start a new life in America," she said. "He thought about giving it to you many times, but never did because he feared you will reject it and break his heart."

"I have one request for you. Please accept it," she added. "He has truly loved you. When you were born, he went running and distributed sweets to all the people in the Aatam Nursing Home; when you first started walking, I saw tears in his eyes; and I saw tears in his eyes when you left Jaipur for Delhi to pursue higher studies. He was never expressive, but he has always loved you and me; and he did whatever he could for us. He did his best."

Om had his head lowered. He kept the watch and the envelope back into the box, held her hand and smiled. "You take rest now, Mummy. I'll go and do the dishes in the kitchen," said Om, as he left his mother's bedside.

❖

Om finished doing the dishes in the kitchen and sat on the sofa in the living room. It was the same sofa that Naani had at her house. The sofa was perhaps older than everything else in the house, even Mahesh. No one knew for sure and there was no way the sofa could tell.

He sat on the sofa, leaned back, and looked at the pictures of Naani and Babu. It had been fifteen years since Naani passed away, yet some of the memories were more vivid than what they were when they happened. He got up and went to the showcase that was adorned with pictures in old photo frames and a few show pieces thrown in between.

There was a picture from the time when Naani and Babu moved to the Sapra House in Jawahar Nagar and Om was just two and a half years old. Naani was holding Om, who was wearing a white underwear and nothing else. She held him up above her head. The two-year-old Om was ecstatic with this thrilling ride, smiling from ear to ear.

The twenty-year-old Om also smiled from ear to ear.

Om heard the sound of footsteps outside the main entrance door. He turned to see who it was. His father had returned home, holding two bags of grocery in his hands.

Om walked up to Mahesh, grabbed the bags from him, and placed them on the slab in the kitchen. He saw his father walking towards his mother's bed.

"I have given her the afternoon dose already," said Om.

His father stopped mid-way and turned around.

"Would you like a cup of tea?" asked Om.

Mahesh was perplexed. He nodded, timorously.

Om went inside the kitchen. A while later, he came out with two cups of tea placed in an off-white bone china tray. "This is the one with low sugar," Om said, pointing out to a cup he held in front of his father.

His father nodded and picked it up. Om picked up his too and returned the tray to the kitchen.

"Would you like to come out for a walk with me while Mummy is asleep?" asked Om.

Mahesh was bewildered but agreed, anyway. Om led the way out of the house into the street outside.

❖

"Do you know where your Yezdi is?" asked Om as they both saw a Yezdi parked by the side of the road. That company had shut down operations in 1996.

"I don't know. I sold it to Ram Narayan, the milkman, and I have no idea where and how it is. I have no idea where even Ram Narayan is," said his father, looking at the Yezdi on the road with a tinge of nostalgia in his eyes.

"I remember when it was my last birthday celebration at Alpha-Beta. I was holding two bags of Natkhat, one in each hand, seated behind you on your Yezdi," said Om and smiled.

Mahesh smiled as well. Both of them continued walking leisurely with a cup of tea in their hands.

"Mummy shared with me the watch and the recurring deposit that you had saved for me," said Om after a long period of silence.

They continued walking without another word being said. Om turned around to look at his father, who stared ahead at the walls of the Goddess Bhawani's temple at the end of the road. He turned his head again and kept walking. When his father turned towards him, he was looking at the community garden behind Lord Hanuman's temple.

"I want to tell you that I have loved you always and acknowledge the sacrifices you always made for me and Mummy," said Om, staring at his father, whose eyes had turned moist. A tear dropped down his cheek into the cup of tea. Om looked away.

They both kept walking. There was no one else on the road. Not a single vehicle passed by. Under the shades of the trees on both sides, the breeze felt good – cool and salubrious.

❦

Om had spent the previous day by his parents' side. His father had prepared his special mint chutney and bread pakoras. He, on the other hand, ordered south Indian food from the famous restaurant 'Sagar Ratna' in the evening.

The next day, he requested his father for his scooter's key, which his father readily gave. He grabbed the helmet and rode off.

Jaipur had changed. Many of the bullock carts and camel-laden by-lanes had made way for modern flyovers, but Om could navigate the streets with ease. Being in Delhi for a long time had made him adapt quickly to the modernization. Despite all the changes, the city still retained the shades of pink and carried the vibe it always had.

The first stop Om rode to, was the Alpha-Beta school. It was now defunct. It had been taken over by a consortium of schools called 'Birla International School'. They had built a big building right next to the old school building and had moved all the classes there. But the old building which belonged to Alpha-Beta was still intact, just as it was fifteen years ago. He remembered Ratna Devi taking classes and reprimanding him for staring out of the windows. He remembered the old man who used to sit by the side of the window every morning, watching the world go by.

The walls had grown darker. The gates had a thick lock on it. The energy of the young lives was missing. He gazed through those same windows he used to look out of and saw into the empty room, which used to be filled with students – with Arun, with Ratna Devi, with her punishments, and his antics.

He stood right opposite the school gate. He remembered how Farheen used to walk out of it with a bag on her shoulders and a bottle around her neck, how she would climb to the back seat of the rickshaw, how she would take his lunch and tell him what her Ammi and Abbu had fought about the night before.

Tears of joy welled up in his eyes as he looked at the building for one last time before kick-starting his scooter and riding away.

He then went to 3/38, Jawahar Nagar. Sapra House, as it was called, named after the surname of the owners. Jyoti, the landlady, had passed away. The park was still there. It had that metallic fencing which Om jumped to save himself from the five dogs that chased him when he was five years old. The grass was a brilliant shade of green and the roads were much cleaner. The alley at the end of the road was still there, but the convenience store had made way for a dairy booth. A few clothes hung in the balcony of Sapra House, but there wasn't anyone outside.

He started to ride towards the alley to park the scooter. Once the scooter was parked, he walked towards the dairy booth. As soon as he turned right, he paused and slowed down. He took a step further and looked to his right. There was no one there. Perhaps he expected his five canine friends there waiting for him.

He walked up to the dairy booth. Surprisingly, they still sold his favourite snack - Natkhat. He bought five packets and opened the first one. It was as crisp as they used to be. He gnawed at them like a rabbit, just as he used to when he was a child.

He then glanced at the tree where he had last seen Farheen, the day Naani had passed away. He turned to his right and stared at what used to be Farheen's house, right next to Naani's. There was a young girl sitting in the sun on a chair. Her mother was behind her, giving her daughter an oil massage.

He stood there and took it all in until he finished his packet of Natkhat.

He then rode the scooter all the way to Shyam Nagar and Sodala. Shah International School had become more glorious, courtesy of a few students like Om getting admission to the topmost universities of the country. Sahil had become a sought-after model and actor. He had no idea where Rohit was.

The Pool lounge had closed down. There was a new bowling alley in its place. Shankar's Kachori joint still flourished, though. He parked his scooter, ordered a fresh plate of Kachori and sat by the side of the stall, on one of the rocks. He remembered the time he had a fallout with his father over the money for his Goa trip, after which he had called Rohit there. Once he had finished with the Kachori, he left for his home, his heart heavy with all the nostalgia.

Om sat by his mother's side. It was time for him to go back to Delhi. His flight to San Francisco was scheduled for day after tomorrow. He held her hands with his father right behind him.

"Make sure you eat well and healthy. Don't neglect your health," she said. "Even during college, all you ate was junk food."

Om kept smiling and kissed her hands.

"Take care of yourself," she said again with tears flowing down her face. "I will, Mummy, and I'm always there. Whenever you need me, just ask Papa to give me a call," Om reassured her as he got up and kissed her forehead.

His mother smiled. Tears streamed down her cheeks.

"Try and find a good Indian girl there," she said as Om turned around and started walking out. He turned around and laughed. The other two followed.

Om put his backpack on his shoulders and stood near the door.

"I will come and drop you to the railway station," said his father as he picked up the keys to his scooter.

"It's not needed, Papa. Mummy needs you. You stay here, please," responded Om, immediately.

"It's just an hour. Kiran has already eaten and taken her medicine."

His father hugged him and did not look as if he would be released soon. He felt a dampness on his shoulders. He pulled himself back and stared at his father, who was in tears. As soon as his father looked at him, the former began sobbing. Within seconds, Om too was in tears. Both embraced each other once again.

His father finally pulled himself back and said, "I'm proud of you, son. I'm proud of you."

Om had never heard his father say this. The tears just wouldn't stop flowing down his face.

"All right, I need to go now," said Om as he wiped his tears and looked away. His father patted his face and opened the door for him, unable to stop the flow of his tears.

—◆◆◆—

Om reached Arun's house at four in the evening and quickly asked him for the keys to the new car Arun had bought. He had to travel to Gurgaon back-and-forth each day, so his parents had finally gifted him a car. Arun wasn't excited about this prospect but given the number of times Om had lent him his motorcycle, it was time for payback.

Om's flight to San Francisco was at 1 A.M the following morning from Indira Gandhi International airport. He had to be at the airport by 10 P.M.

Om quickly jumped into the car and the first place he drove to was Charan Singh's tea stall. He parked the car right next to the tea vendor's stall. The soft hues of the stone welcomed him once again. So did Charan Singh, who had no idea that he was going to see his favourite customer for the last time.

Om took his spot and rested his head against the stone. The stone was cool, resting in the disloyal shade, which moved around as per the whims and fancy of the sun. There was a girl leaning against the wall of the Levi's store at the corner on the opposite side of the road. Within a few minutes, a boy came near her. They hugged and then started walking hand-in-hand. The wall was lonely again until a few minutes later a boy took refuge by its side, only to ditch it a few minutes later. The commotion, even though it looked usual, felt peaceful. In spite of the maddening exterior, there was stillness at its core. All noise was on the outside, the interior was silent.

Om hugged Charan Singh after finishing his cup of tea. He told him he was going away for a job and won't be back for a while. Charan didn't take money from Om for the tea. Om thanked him again and wished him well.

Om took a drive around the Lodi Gardens. The snacks and ice-cream vendors outside catered to families and the stags, lovers and business people. The same clamor with similar characters in different outfits. The trees and the branches and the leaves and the grass had seen it all, too many times to even be bothered. They remained there, silent and peaceful. if a storm came, they swayed with the storm. When the storm left, they stood there still.

Om drove all the way to Naraina, driving the car right up to Pizza Corner. Sumit was there. His peer at the shop had helped him on so many occasions. . Whether it was filling in for him when he couldn't make it to work or lying to the owner if need be. Om hugged him and bid him goodbye. Sumit gave him a portion of garlic bread before he left. There was no evening a garlic bread could not make better.

Om then drove all the way to the Hauz Khas Village. The lake in which the lovers drowned, the ruins amidst which Goddesses in flesh and stones danced, and the pubs in which young lovers gathered, still lay rooted to their spots.

Finally, Om drove all the way to the tree near Ayesha's house. That was their Mecca. Om never knew where Ayesha lived. That Banyan tree was Ayesha's home for him.

It was dusk. The sun had set, but it was not dark yet. The twilight shone off Om's face and a glass of wine by his side. He had parked the car next to the tree as he used to do with Ayesha. Six months had passed since he had last seen her. It was time to say goodbye. He took out a folded envelope from the back pocket of his jeans and a stone from the front pocket.

It was the same stone Ayesha had given him on the night they first made love. He crouched on his knees and began digging the ground near the tree with his bare hands. He placed the envelope and the stone on the ground and covered it back. He stomped on the ground a few times before looking at it one last time. He turned around and left.

EPILOGUE

OM REACHED ARUN'S home around 8 P.M. As soon as he parked the car outside, he remembered he had forgotten something. He drove the car to the nearest convenience store and bought a razor and a shaving cream.

"Bro, you are running late. What are you doing with this razor and shaving cream? You don't even have a beard. Shave when you get to San Francisco," said Arun as Om walked into the house.

Om threw the car keys at Arun and headed straight to the bathroom. Arun's parents were there and so was Natasha, all of whom were confounded at his strange behavior.

He went inside the bathroom, collected the shaving foam on his fingers, and applied it all over his head. He then took the seal of the razor off and placed it by the edge of his right temple. He stared at the mirror for a second, took a deep breath, and ran the razor in one stroke from his temple to the back of his head.

Forty-five minutes later, he came out. All of them had knocked on the bathroom door a couple of times to ask what he was up to. Now, they had their answer. He had shaved his head. Arun and his parents kept staring at him. Natasha raised her brows and her jaws had dropped.

"You actually look kind of sexy," quipped Natasha.

Arun looked at her, amazed.

"All right, it is time to leave now," announced Om emphatically, reaching out for his bags. Om had two bags packed, which were supposed to be checked-in, and one backpack, which he would carry on.

Om hugged Arun goodbye, who had been rendered speechless.

Arun's parents wished Om good luck. Natasha held Om's bald head down and kissed it.

He picked up his bags and called the taxi.

Om reached on time for the check-in. Flights and passengers travelling to America were checked rigorously, which was why it was advised to reach the airport at least three hours prior to departure. He reached two and a half hours prior.

He called up his parents as soon as he got the boarding pass, who wished him a safe flight. It was his first time at an airport. And his first ever flight was to San Francisco, the technology capital of the world.

There was a whole gamut of retail stores – from well-known international brands to exclusive designers, from shops selling top-end headphones to neck pillows. But the thing that caught his fancy the most were the duty-free liquor shops.

Air India called out the passengers to board flight AI-173, which he had booked his tickets on. He walked to the departure gates and then on to the plane. His seat – 24F, was by the window. He placed his carry-on backpack in the overhead bin after taking out his CD player with earphones. He did not carry any food since Arun had told him that he would be served food and liquor on the flight, free of cost. In fact, he hadn't eaten his lunch to save his appetite for his first in-flight meal with drinks. Little did he know that that's one gourmet experience one could safely miss out on.

The in-flight safety announcements were demonstrated by the cabin crew. Om felt pity for the air-hostess, who looked completely dispassionate while acting out the safety instructs played out from the speakers in the airplane. Maybe there was a better way of doing this using virtual reality technology, he thought.

Within a few minutes, the captain of the flight introduced himself and announced that the take-off was about to commence. The airplane started moving, although it did so at a snail's pace for a long time. Om thought perhaps Boeing had developed a technology he hadn't heard about, which allowed the planes to take off at snail's pace. But that was not the case.

The airplane suddenly began accelerating, and within seconds, Om felt a tickle in his gut. The plane was off the ground. Om looked outside the window. The millions upon millions of lights that illuminated the city of Delhi became smaller and smaller. The sky flaunted a lavish display of its concubine, the moon. It was full, almost, but kept becoming bigger and bigger as the airplane kept gaining altitude.

Delhi, on the other hand, became smaller and smaller, and not long after, it was no longer visible. All that was then visible was a vast, empty sky and the glorious veneer of moonlight across its infinite fabric.

Om kept looking outside the window at the evocative moon and remembered the words buried under the Banyan Tree.

Fire in the village!
Flame yours,
Fuel mine...
Raw,
Organic,
Burn, I might...

How was my weather?

Fear of opinions,
Of voices of minions...
Missing angels,
Assembly of demons...

Sleep, I might...

Where do you come from?
How did you find me?

Lucid conversation,
Cool breeze...

Al-verdure Risotto,
With bread and cheese...
You're you.
I'm me.
Suddenly the angels,
Are flying around like bees...

Dream, I might...

Do you know how magic feels like?

Battle again, that eyelash,
Kiss again, that wineglass...
Sing again, that first song,
Smoke again, that menthol...
Sit again, in those stones,
Like a goddess in skin and bones...

Talk again to your mom,
In masculine gender form...
Tell her you'll be late,
You're on a date with fate...

Adore, I might.

That magic in you.
Not yours,
Not mine...
Not under control,
Non-monopolized...

That twinkle in your eyes,
Belongs like the stars to the skies...
That fire in your heart,
Must reach out far and wide...

Inspire, I might...

Travel, wander, get lost,
Hitchhike through the December frost...
Fall in love, fall out of love,
Fall in love, fall out of love...
Make love to men around the world,
With your lush hair, open, uncurled...

Wish, I might...

Before you go...

Ignite me,
For the first time once again...
To shreds and pieces,
Burn me,
For the first time once again...
Let nothing of me remain in me,
Before you meet me,
For the first time once again...